AF430366

WHERE THE LIGHT SHINES

For all of you who choose not to veer out of your lane, but instead to add another.

This is me.
Hello, Women's Fiction.

PROLOGUE

was warned about the river. They said if I listened just right, I would be able to hear it speak. Whispers would float up to the glassy clear surface when least expected, sometimes with words for the heart, other times with secrets stolen from the soul. It's always giving and taking, and just like the ebb and flow of the current, it's always changing.

The one constant, however, is that it's there, winding its way through the town, making its presence known, while time becomes irrelevant as days, months, and years fall in sync and just drift by. It's a connection to the past and a foreshadowing of the future, and as much as it's a source of healing and inspiration, there's that part of us deep down that knows, not only can it absolve the essence of life, it can capture it too.

Fortunately for me, I was open to any possibility and welcomed the outcome.

I came to the river trapped inside my life with nothing left but a stack of fictional memories, a shattered heart, and regret—regret for a life I felt I'd lost, regret for a life I felt I should have had. It called to me, this place, this place I didn't know, and as I found myself at the edge, leaning toward the unknown, it was with the crystal blue-green silky waters drifting through my fingers and the steady lapping sounds reverberating against the shoreline that I implored the river to take my sorrows, drown them beneath swaying grass and empty scallop shells, and set me free.

1

———

The streets are dark and there is a single yellow-tinted light hovering over the three-way intersection where I've come to a stop. Large, winged bugs are circling the bulb as it illuminates the road, and I look left and right. Exhaustion weighs me down as I've just driven almost seventeen hours from Chicago to an old fishing town on the west coast of Florida. There's no one in sight anywhere, but then again, it is the middle of the night.

Not bothering with my blinker, I ease out and turn left onto East Pines Drive. The GPS directions tell me this will lead me to my new house, which I bought sight unseen. Well, that is aside from the photos the realtor provided and the virtual tour. I'll admit and agree with my sister, who was absolutely appalled that I was considering doing this and called me irrational and unsensible, that it's not much to look at now, but by the time I'm finished with it, it will be.

I flip on the brights, my eyes narrowing with strain as I look at the numbers on the mailboxes. The boxes aren't close together like you would find in a standard neighborhood, and my chest tightens as the road winds around and reaches the end, a dead-end cul-de-sac where the last one stands with dull gold numbers stuck on the side—my dull gold numbers.

Directly behind the mailbox, peeking out from the darkness, is an old wrought-iron gate that's open to the driveway. There's no telling if it's functioning and was left open by the realtor or stuck that way, but entwined within the metal on each gate is a large letter E, and I find I don't mind that it doesn't match my surname. Behind the gate, there are tall trees etched in the night, looming over, and if I wasn't so struck by the thought that I've never owned trees before, I would call the scene before me eerie.

A rush of emotions hits, overwhelming me, and a sensation of relief, fatigue, and anxiety has my eyes burning with an all-too-familiar feeling. "I made it, I finally made it," I whisper to myself, and then I squeeze my eyes shut tight, pressing my fists into them to will it away. I refuse to shed one more tear. I've cried more in the last six months than I have in my entire life, and I will not dwell in that place any longer. Instead, I turn off the satellite radio, pick up my phone, raise my chin a little higher, and call the most important person in my life: my sister. There isn't even a ring as the call immediately connects.

"Rylie," Ivy says, sleep and anxiousness heavy in her tone.

"I made it," I tell her as I stare down the long dark driveway. I can't see the house, although I knew I wouldn't be able to. The over-one-hundred-year-old home sits almost two-tenths of a mile off the road.

"How does it look?" she asks.

"I don't know yet. I'm calling you from the driveway, because I don't know what the cell service will be like when I get to it. It's already been kind of spotty," I say, looking around and still seeing nothing but darkness.

"You're not going to have cell service?" she asks, her voice now becoming animated and echoing throughout the car's speakers. The blankets on her bed rustle as it sounds like she sits up.

"I didn't say that. I just said I didn't know and wanted to call you just in case."

The trees are still; there isn't even a breeze, which just adds another level to the expression the dead of night.

"This whole scenario just keeps getting worse and worse."

She's made it known since I began talking about coming here that she is not a fan. She thought I should just continue to lie low at home—a home that didn't feel like a home anymore.

I laugh. "No, it doesn't."

She lets out a long sigh that drips with disapproval.

"I'm excited to be here," I remind her. I've thought about nothing but this house since the moment I found it.

There's a long pause, and I know she is conceding in defeat. Over the last two weeks, we've talked ad nauseam about my move to the south. There's no argument she will win with me.

"Fine. I just worry," she says. I feel guilty at the unease behind her words.

"I know, and you don't need to. Seriously, what could go wrong?" I ask with forced enthusiasm. After all, I might be nervous, as change is hard and pushes us out of our comfort zone, but I'm ready and open to it.

"Snakes. Alligators. Killer spiders. People who hunt single women who live on the river and kill them."

I laugh at her overeager imagination.

"What if you get hurt?" she asks.

"I won't. It's fine." I try not to think about that, because at this moment I don't have an answer. But I'll figure it out. "You didn't tell anyone I was coming here, right?"

"Of course not. You know your secret is safe with me." Her voice is muffled a bit, as if she's lain back down and is snuggling into her pillow.

"Thank you," I tell her.

"Ry, I understand, I do ... I just wish you were closer." She lets out a deep sigh.

"I know," I whisper, my eyes stinging again as a lump climbs its way up into my throat.

"I'm going back to sleep. Call me later to check in and send me pictures," she says through a yawn.

"I will."

My heart aches. As much as I need to do this by myself, it would be nice if she were here with me.

"Be careful," she mumbles.

"Of course."

"Love you." And with that she hangs up.

Silence takes over as I slowly pull onto the driveway and pass through the entrance of the gates. The car dips and bounces over roots, holes, and rocks. Large, aged oak trees and tall Florida pines canopy the property and block out the sky. I knew it was going to be dark by the time I finally pulled in, but I didn't expect it to be this dark. When I dreamt of this moment, the moment I finally crossed the boundary from my old life and into the next, the moon would be shining bright and everything about this place and this home would welcome me with open arms.

Then again, I should have known. Reality is never quite like we imagine it, and this home was sold to me as is.

The hairs on the back of my neck rise just before panic streaks through my chest as something not so small scurries across the path in front of the car and I slam on the brakes. Fight-or-flight instincts try to take over, but as I grip the glossy steering wheel of my Mercedes SUV and force air through my lungs, I slow my breaths to calm myself.

What was that?

Looking around, I struggle to see past the dust-particle-filled path of the headlights, but there is nothing but a black void.

"It was nothing," I tell myself, grasping the steering wheel a little tighter. "Just a rabbit or something like that."

A rabbit.

A laugh bursts out of me, and I shake my head. Pieces of my blonde hair slip free from the messy bun on top of my head, and I swipe them out of the way. I've lived in downtown Chicago most of my life, and the only furry scurrying things we had to worry about were rats. If I can do rats, I can definitely do rabbits.

I think.

But what if it was a bobcat and it's here to eat my face? My thoughts drift back to Ivy and her alligators.

"Rylie, pull it together," I mumble, still slowly breathing in and out while staring down the driveway.

A few more moments pass and nothing else makes an appearance, so I ease off the brake and continue until I pass the turnoff for the circular drive that leads to the entrance of the home and reach a small parking pad at the end.

Here the trees have cleared, letting in the silvery glow of moonlight, and when I look to the left, I can finally see the outline of the monstrosity that is now my home.

Under the moonlight, its white exterior stands out sharply against the dark trees. It's large, two stories with massive pillars, a covered wraparound porch, and an upper balcony. Excitement bubbles inside of me, because at this moment, all I can see is six thousand square feet of blank canvas, six thousand square feet that is all mine. Maybe Ivy was wrong and coming here wasn't the craziest idea after all.

Then I look forward and find what it is I really drove over 1100 miles for. Yes, the home is practically ancient, run-down as it's sat abandoned for decades, but it wasn't just the house that interested me. What sold me on the property was the small wooden two-story boathouse sitting at the end of the dock over-looking the Chuluota River. Chuluota means beautiful view in the Seminole Indian language.

The pictures the realtor provided of the boathouse, with the transparent blue-green waters of the inlet surrounding it and the river just beyond, called to me like no other property, and I knew, regardless of the shape of the house, it was meant to be mine. I saw myself standing on the dock, breathing in the salty, humid air of this southern coastal place so different and distant from my own, and I felt with a certainty I hadn't felt in so long that this was where I was meant to be.

Turning off the car, I grab my large Louis Vuitton bag, climb out, sling it over my shoulder, and just breathe. The air is unpol-luted and damp with a hint of nature, unlike the city, and any nervousness I felt vanishes as the calm atmosphere of the mild May night wraps around me with that welcome home I so desperately needed. Surprisingly, just like that, the feeling I've been longing for upon arrival settles. I do feel welcomed, and I do feel at home.

Reaching into the back seat, I grab an overstuffed laundry basket of things I knew I was going to need and glance over at the one and only box I brought from my old life. My heart lets off a forceful ache, but I tear my eyes away to not ruin this moment. I didn't intend to keep any of those things, but the nostalgic part of me said one day I would wish I had, so there it is.

Bumping the door with my hip, I close it along with my eyes as I allow the pain of the memories of that box to wash through me. The sting is only there for a second, but that second is long enough to remind me that I will never again be the person I once was. Ever. Shaking it off, I begin heading for the dock. When I'm halfway across the yard, the headlights shut off and the world around me goes still.

Stars ... so many stars shine above me that I'm momentarily awed. Tiny pinpricks of light that twinkle and, along with the moon, reflect across the inlet, which stretches before me. I don't think I've ever seen so many in one place. They are beautiful, and together it's just bright enough for me to see.

Continuing on, I carefully make my way to the water's edge and the dock. The old wooden slats creak and groan as I step onto them and make my way toward the end to the small house. Nearly calm waters gently lap against the posts and the shore-line, and as I reach the door of the boathouse, which is just past a screened enclosure with an outside picnic table, I'm not surprised to find it unlocked.

Prior to arriving, the real estate agent, Natalie, arranged to have the boathouse cleaned, the light bulbs and the toilet changed, and she made sure the utilities were working across the property. She had a ceiling fan with lights installed, and it drops down from the vaulted roof. She told me I was absolutely crazy for wanting to stay out here. Maybe I am crazy, but I'm past caring about what others think at this point. I've already spent too many years worrying about that, and well, no more.

Inside it's just a little larger than the size of my bathroom back in Chicago, but I don't care. The downstairs is one room with a mini kitchen, the sink in the corner, and a single toilet-only bathroom, with the upstairs being more of a large loft that stretches over where one parks the boat outside underneath. It's so cute and compact it reminds me of one of those "tiny houses" that are the trend right now, and given the life I used to live, I'm surprised to find I like it so much.

Dropping the laundry hamper, I pull my brand-new air mattress out of the box and plug it in. As it inflates, right in the middle of the room, I open the new package of sheets and fluff out my pillow. Pushing the blow-up against the wall, I make the bed, toss on a blanket, turn on the fan, and open the large windows facing the inlet and the river beyond to let the air circulate. Again, I'm surprised by how it smells fresh and different, or maybe it's just me that's different. Either way, I more than welcome this. I need it.

"C'est la vie with the old me, and in with the new," I say to myself while staring out at the silver streak the moon has cast upon the river. The water sparkles underneath it as it basks in the attention. It's a beautiful sight and one I'm certain I'll remember for the rest of my life. My new life.

The Dalai Lama says the purpose of our lives is to be happy, and I just know deep down, with this river and my new home, I'll finally find that happiness here. I have to. Because if not here, then where?

It's been a little over six months since the beginning of the end, and I know things will get easier—they already have. I know this deep ache in my chest will one day be gone, but today was not that day. I had hoped it would ease seeing how it's day one of my new life, but today feels just like yesterday, and this ache ... unfortunately, it still feels permanent.

2

When I was a little girl, my sister Ivy and I would daydream about what it would be like to marry a prince. We would lie under a shimmering fabric that became a castle in our playroom, stare up at construction paper hearts we'd cut out, colored, and hung, and talk about how kind, doting and good-looking he would be. After all, it's the illusion of the perfect tall, dark, and handsome guy corporations like Disney have created to make billions of dollars that plants this fantasy in the minds and hearts of little girls everywhere. What no one actually discusses is that Prince Charming—he doesn't really exist. Instead, they've sold a false reality that leads to many broken hearts and much disappointment, and unfortunately it also sets an expectation on guys that isn't fair either. The truth is, no one is that perfect, no matter how much we might want them to be.

Okay, so I suppose my father is pretty close to holding the title, but then again, what do I really know about my parents' marriage? Not much, just what they choose to share with us. As for my own personal experience, it turns out Carter was far from it.

Carter.

Even now, after everything that's happened, everything he's put me through, when I think of him, I see different snapshots of our years together play out like a montage video. In all of them, he's smiling, happy, mine. From his blond hair blowing across his forehead from the downtown winds of Chicago as he would laugh and reach for my hand on the sidewalk outside our condo building, his perfect smile that would find its way to me first thing after he woke up in the morning, to when standing in a crowded room, he would whisper the sweetest things to me to make me feel like the most beautiful girl he'd ever seen. It was moments like that that make me miss what I thought my life was —the lie, not the reality.

To know someone for years then realize you didn't really know them at all ... it changes you on a fundamental level. It makes you question your judgment of character, makes you question the sincerity of others, and well, it makes you question everything. What is true, and what is not? I've never been a skeptical person, but after all this, I don't know how not to be.

Keeping my eyes shut, I exhale slowly and focus on the sounds around me.

"Time," they said. "Just give it time." Well, I've given it time, and the hours—no, minutes of each day seem to move slower and slower, suspending me in this state of forlorn mourning, and I hate it. I hate that it consumes me and confuses me. I hate that I ask this question, but seriously, what did I ever do to deserve this?

I didn't sleep hardly at all last night. Instead, I fell into that state of in between that left me just conscious enough to know I was going to be worn out and dragging today. I'm not sure why I thought I would sleep peacefully, maybe because of the long drive, or maybe because I've been telling myself things will be better here, believing once I arrived, I would finally be free, but I couldn't fully relax. Although the setting is different, I am not different; I am still the same.

Then around 4:30 in the morning, the loud piercing cry of a bird made itself known, and it didn't stop. At one point, I dragged myself out of the little bed and went outside to look for it, but amongst the blending shadows of the trees, there was no way of finding it. Part of me enjoyed the sound, but the larger part that was feeling the effects of a sleepless night wished I had a long-range shotgun, even though I've never fired a gun.

Eventually, I gave up on sleep, wandered back up to the car to grab a fold-up beach chair I bought along with the air mattress, and set it up at the end of the dock. The realtor, Natalie, lightly stocked the refrigerator, and I was quite delighted to find jars of iced coffee. Without even looking for one, I already know this isn't the kind of town to have a gourmet coffee shop. I'm not sure what I expected my first morning to be like, but it wasn't this.

However, truth is, this isn't so bad either.

Sitting in the chair, the minutes slowly tick by as an orange glow lazily grows over the trees on the far side of the river and subtly begins to give light to my new world. The color is warm, and just watching it brighten thaws a piece inside of me that felt locked, hard, and frozen. This feeling gives me hope that maybe I will heal here, maybe I will find that happiness I'm searching for.

I've thought a lot about the word "happiness" over the last couple of months, what it might mean for me, and how I'll find it. How will I know if I'm truly happy? How does anyone know? After all, I thought I was before, but what does it mean to be happy? Is that definition different for everyone, or is there a universal answer I've not yet been privy to? I just don't know, but coming here, chasing it, I do believe I might find it. I have to believe that; it's currently what's keeping me going.

Cool air drifts across the water, and as the sky has shifted from an orange glow to yellow, more birds awaken and make themselves known. It's a symphony of sounds as they talk and call to each other, and I find it absolutely lovely.

"Good morning, good morning, good morning," I hear from behind me, and I can't help the grin that splits across my face. Getting up, I go inside the little boathouse to grab Coco's travel cage, and I bring her outside to sit next to me. After I set up the bed, I made a quick second trip to the car to grab her.

"Good morning," I say back, and she dips her light gray head up and down. "I think you're going to like it here," I tell her as she's taken a curiosity to the new environment and the bird calls surrounding us.

Coco, named after Coco Chanel, was a wedding gift from Carter. While most brides get pieces of jewelry or something timeless, Carter delighted me in buying us a Timneh African Grey parrot. He had heard me mention that I wanted a pet, and as he is allergic to cats and had zero interest in walking a dog in the winter, he thought of this beautiful exotic bird. Coco and I quickly bonded, and she is the best thing to come out of my time with Carter.

Carter. Again, at just the thought of him, my heart dips and then aches.

He would have hated it here, but then again maybe that's another reason it called so strongly to me. This is such a different life from the one we had together. He believed the only place to live is in a city. Cities represented the epicenter of society, and beyond that were people not worth his time. Did it bother me that he felt this way? Not really. After all, we are the product of our environment, and he was raised to believe that in order to be someone and remain someone, you have to make yourself known. And that he did. Everyone knows Carter Crest, heir to the world's largest luxury hotel chain.

Higher and higher the sun climbs into the sky, and as the world around us shows itself for the first time, it's just as I pictured it. Blue-green, crystal-clear water fills the inlet in front of and around my dock, fading off into a darker shade of blue and to the most beautiful river. There's a small beach off to the left of the dock, but past that the water's edge is lined with overhanging trees that provide privacy from one home to the next. Then again, I'm the only house on the inlet. There's a home to the right, more on the river than in the inlet, but there's no one to the left. My entire life I've lived practically wall to wall with other people, and it's a strange feeling to be so alone, so isolated. Surprisingly, I like it.

Six feet away from the dock, I spot two hairy nostrils as they make their way to the surface just before a gray head pops up. Gasping with delight, I jump from my seat and lie face down on the dock to dangle my arm over the edge so my fingers can brush the water's surface. Coco fluffs her wings at my sudden movement. I didn't mean to startle her.

"Well, hello there," I say to the large manatee who happens to be floating up from underneath my dock and moving closer to my fingers. Once in school, we studied marine animals, and I know manatees are herbivores and gentle giants. "Were you down there all night, or did you just show up?" It's crazy to think this giant sea animal could have been sleeping just a few feet below me. Although I didn't know it last night, now I do, and it excites me to think I have some company.

It drops back down, and as the water is so transparent, I marvel at all the algae growing across its back. Underneath, the tall river grass sways, and I find it hypnotic.

My lawyer asked me why the town of Chuluota Springs, and I didn't really have an answer for him that would make sense to his cynical mind, so I shrugged my shoulders and told him, "Why not?"

The truth is, when I was a child, I was in love with mermaids. Some little girls love horses, others dolls or cats; for me it was mermaids. I was convinced they were real and I could somehow become one. As a surprise, my parents booked us a vacation to Florida, and along with a trip to Disney World, they took us to a place called Weeki Wachee Springs where they have live mermaid shows. It was the highlight of my childhood, and of all the places I've traveled over the years, that's the place I've remembered and cherished the most.

What do I know about being a Floridian? Nothing. What do I know about humidity and bugs, coastal storms, owning an old home, and fishing towns? Not a single thing. But I've never been one to shy away from a challenge, and when I began searching the area near Weeki Wachee for a house for sale, this one popped up almost immediately, and I was sold.

Speaking of sold, a car door slams behind me, and I look up to find Natalie walking my way. I would recognize her anywhere after seeing her realtor picture on her website.

"You made it!" she calls down as she waves, her smile so big.

"We did." I stand to greet her, brushing my hands across the black designer workout pants I slept in.

"We?" Her brows pull down as she steps onto the dock, making her way toward me and looking around.

I can't help but laugh at her confusion and point to Coco's cage.

"This is Coco Chanel, but I just call her Coco." The bird is watching her approach, and she shifts back and forth across her perch.

"Wow! She's beautiful," Natalie says as she comes to a stop next to me and bends down to get a better look.

Old habits die hard as I take in her outfit. She's wearing a white button-down shirt, a stretchy navy skirt, and gold ballerina flats. Her brown hair is pulled into a ponytail, and she wears gold starfish earrings and minimal makeup on her sweetheart-shaped face. She's very petite, she's giving me serious bubbly vibes, and from what I can gather, she's roughly my age. Although she doesn't know it yet, she's going to be my friend. I can feel it already.

"Hello there," she says to Coco.

"Hello," Coco answers, and Natalie's face lights up as she stands back up and looks at me.

"I love that she talks." Her eyes are bright, not a trace of bags under her eyes—clearly she got a full night's sleep.

"You say that now, but sometimes she doesn't stop talking." I laugh. "Hi, I'm Ryla. It's nice to finally meet you." I extend my hand to shake hers, and she takes it immediately.

"Natalie, and you too."

We're both smiling at each other as the manatee behind me again breaks the surface to see what the noise is all about. Natalie steps to the edge of the dock and peers down into the translucent waters.

"Hey there, Jessie," she calls out. The manatee doesn't acknowledge her, just paddles its tail, glides by and then disappears again.

"Jessie?" I ask in confusion.

"Yep, he has lived here under your dock for years. At least I was told they think it's a he—there's never been a calf along with him."

"Wow, so this place hasn't been completely vacant then," I tease, and she laughs.

"I guess not, that is between him and bugs." She scrunches up her nose. "River house and all," she says, as if that explains everything, and it does. When we were kids, every summer our parents used to rent a lake house in Minocqua, Wisconsin, and it always had little spiders and such.

"Thanks for the food you stocked. I didn't think ahead

enough to figure out coffee, so I was beyond delighted, and I'm super appreciative." I glance toward the picnic table. It's covered with coffee jars, a banana peel, and a muffin wrapper.

"Of course! I wasn't sure what you would like, but I've seen enough shows on TV to know city girls love their fancy coffee, and those are my favorite." She points to an empty jar she's discovered next to my chair. "There's a diner in town called Dockside where you can grab coffee and a pastry to-go. It's not Starbucks, but to me it's better."

I nod my head. "Sounds perfect. I can't wait to try it. And now that I'm here, I'm thinking let's change that from city girl to small-town girl."

"If you say so." She grins. "So, are you ready to tour your new home?" she asks, all excited, rubbing her hands together. She looks briefly back toward the house and then at me.

"I am. I've looked at it a few times this morning, tempted to walk up there, but I waited for you, just like I promised."

I slip on a pair of flip-flops I left by the boathouse door, and together we make our way up the dock and through the yard toward the large, white, definitely-going-to-need-a-lot-of-work house, leaving Coco behind.

"Well, I'm glad. There are some beautiful features of the home, and I can't wait to show them to you." She smiles at me.

Most of the features I did see on the virtual tour, so I'm not sure what's new, but I'm not going to burst her bubble. After all, she showed up here at eight in the morning.

"As mentioned in the description, the home is antebellum style, antebellum meaning 'before the war', the war being the Civil War between the North and the South in the 1860s. This home, like those, has all the architectural characteristics one would expect from a Greek Revival, Neoclassical style: multi-level porches, a sweeping staircase, large foyers, incredibly elaborate woodwork, enormous pillars, and grand front and rear entrances to the home. But, we say antebellum style because it was actually built in the late 1800s. It isn't a true antebellum, not that homes are really called that anymore.

"One of the unique features of this particular house is that the front and the back are identical, from the six large columns —three on each side of the door—to the second-level balcony. Whereas for most homes, guests would arrive through the front entrance, here on the river, quite a few, if not more, entered from the back."

That explains why the dock is so elaborate. It's wide and long, on each post there are rusted hurricane lanterns to light it up, and while the boathouse is on the left, the dock makes a hard right and extends out so several boats can be tied up at once. There's even a wooden bench.

"In older homes, the front was one of the most important features, and in the time before air conditioning, large porticos or porches were the first impression. It was an invitation, a place to greet your guests with open arms, and also the place to hug goodbye. A covering was needed as a protection from the elements, and it was also a place to socialize. If the home is where the heart is, it must start at the front door, right?" She grins at me. "And in the case of your home, the back too."

That makes sense given how the house perfectly sits on the little inlet next to the river's edge.

As we approach the double back doors, which are inlaid with beveled glass, the three things I notice right away are: the wraparound porch is severely damaged with missing or cracked boards; the base of every column needs to be replaced as some spots look rotted and pretty beat up; and from a distance, the house looks white, but up close, the paint is badly peeling.

We both pause to look at the outside, and out of the corner of my eye, I see Natalie pinch her lips together, exhale through her nose, and slouch her shoulders just a little.

"Hey," I say to her, placing my hand lightly on her arm. She's frowning, and I can understand why. "I knew this was going to be a big project. I knew what I was getting into."

"I know." She frowns. "We discussed this before the purchase. I've just been so worried that up close you would be disappointed, and I was so excited to show you the home." She glances at the door and toward a piece of beveled glass that's broken in the corner of the design.

"I'm not disappointed. I promise." Turning around, I look at the river and smile. Even from here it's blue-green, crystal clear, and just beautiful. "How could I be? Just look at the view," I say, trying to reassure her.

Her smile is wary, but she follows along. "All right, then let's go in."

Together we move up the creaky back steps, and she hands me the keys. I unlock the door, and we step inside.

Unlike the boathouse, which is small, this house is not. Just like the outside, the inside is in similar shape, but my designer's eyes don't see curling old wallpaper or water damage on the ceiling. They see a fleeting view of the beauty it once was and the splendor of what the finished project will be.

Natalie begins listing off some of the details of the home that were relevant to the time it was built, but as we walk into the foyer, I'm transfixed by the grandeur and the faint smell of lemon-scented polished wood and stale dust lingering in the air. Do all old homes have this smell, or just mine?

Looking up, I see there's a very large multi-tier candle chandelier. It must be at least five feet long. There are a few glass pieces missing, but I'm in awe at the thought of the old antique and what the value of it might be.

"I thought the house was empty." I cut her off and point to the light fixture. "Does it work?"

She follows my gaze, and a moment of silence falls between us.

"There are a few pieces left behind. This is just one of the few features of the house I was talking about." She grins. "I specifically didn't post them on the listing because ... well, I wanted them to be like finding a hidden treasure for the new owner, and I also didn't want to invite thieves, as the house does not have an alarm. If you don't want any of the items, just let me know, and I'll have them removed. At present, it doesn't work, but I'm certain that has to do with wiring, which we can have replaced. There are stories about this chandelier through old maritime records—for starters, it's crystal, not glass. Inside the home, when it was lit, it cast a spectrum of colors against the walls, and it's brighter than an average chandelier. It's also perfectly positioned so the light shines out the second-level window to act as a beacon for those on the river." Her skin tinges pink. I'm not sure if she's embarrassed or excited for me to find these treasures left behind, but I have to admit, I am intrigued.

"That's really interesting. Are there a lot of stories out there about this house? I can't imagine what this chandelier must have cost, then and now. It must be worth a fortune. Do you know who the designer was?"

She shakes her head. "No, but I'm certain we can send some photos off to have that explored."

"It's like a long-distance porch light," I say, more to myself than her as my head tips backward and I stare up at the heirloom bronze finish, at least 30 bulbed candles, and decorative ceiling medallion. "But, shouldn't this have increased the price of the home?" I look at her, confused.

"The price was set when the listing was given to me," she answers. "There's a smaller version of this one in the front foyer as well." Then her gaze shifts toward a large old mahogany grandfather clock in the adjacent room—another "feature" for me to find.

Huh. Not for the first time, I can't help but wonder about the identity of the anonymous trustee who sold me the house. After all this time, why sell the property now? And wouldn't you want to keep exquisite pieces like this?

Leaving the foyer, Natalie moves us into what I assume would have been a parlor room where the old clock is and resumes pointing out the different aspects of the house. The wallpaper is two-toned where large framed pictures or paintings once hung and have been removed, the ceiling paint is chipped, and the wood floors show where the center was once preserved by a rug and now the perimeter is scratched and stained from condensation by the windows.

As Natalie talks, I remain silent, but I move with her, completing 360 degree turns in every room to take in each and every detail. I'm so inspired I can barely contain myself.

Mentally, I begin making a list of things I would like to do. For starters, I know I need to have the electrical and plumbing looked at. After that, a new roof, patch and paint the outside, repair the columns, and replace the porch. On the inside I want to start with refinishing the floors, repairing the cracked plaster of the walls, and installing new baseboards. Then I can tackle the kitchen and the bathrooms. Decorative tile has recently become the trend, and I know the perfect one for the kitchen backsplash. Oh, and light fixtures flash through my mind, large and bright to match the double chandeliers.

Carter hated bright colors and old things. He preferred a cool palette with a sleek modern vibe, but as this is my home, it's going to be exactly what I want it to be, what I've always dreamed my home would be.

I know it looks and feels like a lot, and essentially I'll have a brand-new home at the end, but this is the most excited I've been in a really long time. Would it have been easier to tear down and rebuild? Probably, but there's something very therapeutic about taking something that is damaged, forgotten about, and in desperate need of some love and making it beautiful again. I'm not naive to the fact that this is how I feel about myself and what I need. I just hope through this process, I'll be able to dust off and polish the beautiful parts of me too.

3

---

t 4:30 in the morning, the obnoxious bird returned. My eyes flew open at the still unfamiliar sound, Coco became restless and curious, and instead of being able to fall back asleep, I stared at the ceiling until I decided to just get up. With the new Keurig I picked up at the grocery store yesterday, I make myself a cup of coffee and pull out my laptop.

I've decided to create a website and a social media page documenting this journey from beginning to end. It'll keep me grounded with a little more purpose than just the house, and I know my family will get a kick out of it. I've talked about this before with past projects; I just didn't have the time, and now I do. Hopefully it will help ease their worries for me too. After all, construction, refurbishing, and design run in the family. Granted, my father now has people who do these things for him, but the craft for it I inherited from him, and it runs through my veins.

My father is an architect, and right after he obtained his degree and his license, he started a commercial construction company. With grand visions, he hired the best architects, engineers, and crew and bid on the largest jobs the city had to offer, and within a couple of years, his company was contracted to build most of the new high-rise condominium buildings in the West Loop and south of State Street. One building after another went up, and soon enough he added hotels and standard business high-rises to his portfolio.

By the time he was thirty, he had gone from middle class to the upper one percent and become what people called "new money". He's humble enough that he just laughed off the attention, but that didn't stop it from coming. He became very well known, as did my mother. People always approached them, wanting to meet them, and once my sister and I were born, it seemed the world went even crazier. There wasn't any one thing that made them or us famous, other than the money and being the idyllic Chicago family. People know recognizable names like Walton, Mars, Campbell, Duncan, Goldman, and well, ours—Kent—became a household name too.

Of course, they could have lived anywhere they wanted and most of the elite had moved to the North Shore, but they wanted to remain in the city they grew up in and loved. My father renovated a three-story brick walkup in the Gold Coast neighborhood and turned it into a grand single-family home. They stayed true to their roots. This in turn made them even more endearing and more accessible to people. My whole life has basically been documented in some form of media, the good and the bad.

As for college, I bounced from the third largest city in the country to the first, New York City, where I attended Parsons School of Design. My name moved with me, and periodically I graced Page Six with the other elite socialites.

It was there, in New York, that I received a degree in interior design and met Carter Crest, heir to the world's largest luxury hotel chain. I should have known things weren't going to be as perfect as they seemed. After all, I grew up in the lifestyle. Character, morality, lack of loyalty, entitlement—I saw it all, but in my mind (well, in my heart), Carter was just like me: unpretentious and a little free-spirited. Boy was I wrong.

After I graduated from college, we moved back to Chicago where I started my own interior design business. Granted, I had advantages and was favorably given jobs by my father, his clients, and Carter's hotels, but it didn't change the fact that I loved being my own boss. As long as the projects were completed ahead of time and exceeded the client's expectations, I had the freedom to do what I wanted when I wanted.

For years, I've wanted to blog about the different projects I've worked on, to keep a catalog of them, but with being in the spotlight and inadvertently putting Carter and our families in the spotlight, it was just better not to. People love to be keyboard bullies and doing something that would draw negative attention —I just didn't want that for any of us. Considering how things went down over the last couple of months, I'm glad I didn't. There's no way to undo internet damage. Once it's there, it's there forever, and people would have delighted in ruining something I loved. But being here, with this house, I can't imagine not documenting the restoration of the home. It's going to be amazing, plus it'll be a personal website, more lifestyle and less business.

With a block tile format on the home page, visitors will be able to select different projects to view, as well as other fun things I choose to include, like the blog, favorite vendors, and a section on Coco. For four hours I work on this, and I've just laid down on the edge of the dock to look for my underwater neighbor when the unexpected deep timbre of a man's voice comes from behind me.

"I wouldn't do that if I were you."

A scream rips from my lungs, echoing throughout the inlet, which in turn causes Coco to squawk loudly as I jump up and whip around to see a guy and his boat coming into view from the other end of the dock. The sun has just risen over the trees on the east side of the river, and the orange glare reflecting off of the water and him is bright.

"You scared me half to death!" I yell. "What are you doing here sneaking up on me so early in the morning?" I firmly press one hand to my chest, the other holding half a head of lettuce.

I take the guy in. He's wearing a long-sleeved white sun shirt with some branded logo on it, athletic shorts, flip-flops, and a pair of Wayfarer sunglasses. His hair is windblown, and he appears to be in his late twenties or early thirties, but with the tightness of the muscles in his face and the angry scowl he's directing my way, I could be wrong.

"I didn't sneak up on you. This is a no wake zone. I just glided in and found you. You were the one who wasn't paying attention, and you shouldn't be here—this is private property," he says, his jaw hardening as he takes in all of my things spread along the dock: the beach chair, a small cooler, my laptop, a camera. He lingers on Coco, who is watching him with interest.

"Is that so?" I raise my hand to my forehead to block out the sun and glower down at him, half annoyed because he's being presumptuous, but also half grateful because this tells me he looks out for people and their places.

He brings the boat to an idle stop in front of me. It's a nice boat, looks new, but then again what do I know about boats? Very broad shoulders and long tanned legs tell me he's not a small guy, and I wonder if I should feel fearful of him, but strangely I don't. An uncomfortable silence hangs between us for a moment, and I can feel him drag his eyes up my body, even though he's wearing shades. Goose bumps strangely race across my skin. Glancing down at myself, I see that I'm adequately dressed in cutoff jean shorts and an old tank top with *Be Kind* stamped on the front in typewriter font.

"We understand that Jessie is pretty much a sure thing for

people like you," he says, annoyance clear in his tone, "but you can't be here." He then tears his eyes off of me and looks around to see if there is anyone else.

"Jessie? People like me? Excuse me?" My free hand falls to my hip. That gratefulness dissolves, ire taking over in its place. Just who does this guy think he is?

He turns his head away from me for a second as if this will help him gain some composure, and I see him glance up toward the house. The eastern sun bounces off the side of his face, making his skin golden. A breeze whips through his dark brown hair, and unconsciously he runs his hand through it and over the top of his head. Then he looks back at me. If I saw him on the street, I would think he was incredibly handsome, but his personality is quickly ruining it.

"You heard me. Jessie." He points to the manatee who is floating near the surface to see what all the noise is about, as if I should have known that and am an idiot.

"I know who Jessie is," I reply sharply, and I swear, even though he's wearing those sunglasses, I can see him roll his eyes. Coco flaps her wings at my tone. She's picked up on the fact that this guy is making me upset.

"It's illegal to feed manatees," he states as if I should have already known this.

I glance at the lettuce in my hands and suddenly feel a little awkward. I didn't know it was illegal; I just remembered seeing the people at the zoo feed them with heads of lettuce when I was a kid. When I bought it yesterday, I was thinking it would be a nice treat. I didn't mean anything malicious by it.

"Go on, pack your stuff up and head out." He waves a hand in the direction of my things. "Or I'll have to call it in that you're out here, trespassing."

The boat sways a little and his body just moves with the flow, natural like the water.

"What did you say your name is?" I ask. This exchange will be worth mentioning to Natalie—maybe she can give me a little insight into his abrasive intrusion—and I'll most definitely be telling Ivy.

"I didn't," he replies.

"Humor me." I move to the cooler to set the lettuce down. It will still make for a great salad, and I'll just share it with Coco; she'll enjoy it.

"Jake," he declares, as if having to give me just this tiny bit of information about himself is adding to his distaste for the situation.

"Well, Jake with no last name"—I place both my hands on my hips—"this private property just happens to be mine." I pause so that little tidbit can register. "So while I'm appreciative that you're the leader of the neighborhood watch club, this isn't necessary."

Instead of responding, his lips pinch into a thin line. He's nonplussed, but he tilts his head slightly as this sinks in. Did the people of this town not realize the home was for sale, or that it had sold?

"You're the new owner?" His voice is laced with disbelief and, well, displeasure.

Why does he sound so surprised? And what's it to him? I get it—it's a big home, and I'm younger than most probably expect, but the price was really good for what I feel like I'm getting.

"Yes." I glare at him.

"What did you say your name is?" he asks, sarcasm echoed back at me between his words.

"I didn't," I reply, repeating his rude behavior. There's another long moment of silence as we stare at each other. In my peripheral, I notice Jessie has gone back under the dock and Coco has settled down. I decide to end this conversation and the tension between us. "But thanks for stopping by." I wave my hand at him, letting him know he can go.

"Bye now. Bye now. Bye now," Coco tells him, and internally I fist-pump at my backup.

Turning around, I walk away, filled with an anger at the audacity of this guy radiating through me. Who does he think he is? And what business is it of his who I am or who the owner of this house is?

When I reach the end of the dock, I startle as I realize just a few feet away, with nervous lines etched around her face and in her posture, is a girl of about ten years old. I'm not sure when she got here or where she came from, and I look around for an adult, but no one is here. Except for Jake who is still watching me, but at least he's pulled away from the dock and is leaving.

"Well, hello there," I say warmly, brushing my hands off on my shorts and propping them on my hips. Her eyes are large, curious, and she has the most gorgeous coffee-colored skin with freckles across the bridge of her nose. As her eyes land on me, I see they are a light caramel color. Stunning, just stunning.

"Hello," she responds shyly. She's wearing the cutest navy with white polka dots romper, and I think Ivy needs to make something like this for adults.

"What's your name?" I ask, taking a few steps toward her. Sweat rolls down my back, the heat surrounding us has shown up early today.

"Juniper," she answers. "But everyone calls me June."

"Well, that's a pretty name. It's nice to meet you, June. Are you here by yourself, or did someone bring you?" I again scan the yard for other visitors and find none.

"Yes, ma'am, I'm by myself. My mama sent me over to say hello. We live over there."

She turns around and nods toward the only other house I can see on this side of the river. At the entrance to the small inlet of my home sits another dock. It's long, big enough to tie up multiple boats at once, and there look to be two large wooden signs facing opposite directions. They're painted red, and I can see the white letters on one read, *You catch it, we'll clean it. You find it, we'll shuck it.*

"What's the sign for?" I ask her.

"It's for the tourists. My mama sits out in the shack, and as people return from their day on the water, they stop and see us. She's famous around here, because she's the fastest person I know when it comes to skinnin' a fish, and she's shucked so many scallops I bet there are a million shells down there in the water." She's so proud.

"Is that so?" It never occurred to me that people would come here to go scalloping. Fishing and shrimping, yes, but scalloping sounds fun.

"Yes, ma'am." She sways from side to side.

"How does someone go scalloping?" I ask.

Her face lights up. "You boat out to where the sandbars are, then you snorkel down and find them buried in the seagrass. I like it better than Easter egg hunting—I always find the most."

"Sounds fun. I think I'll have to give it a try soon." More sweat rolls down my face, and I wipe it off with the back of my hand.

"You should, and when you go, don't forget to bring them over so Mama can shuck them for you."

"Of course. I wouldn't go anywhere else, and I happen to love fish and scallops, so maybe you and your mama can both come over for dinner sometime soon." I glance back into the house. "Well, maybe after I get the kitchen fixed up a bit more and buy a table."

She looks at the house, frowns, and, after a few moments, looks back at me. "You know this house is haunted, right? My mama says you are crazy for buying it, although she told me not to say that to you, so please don't tell her I said it, but everyone wants to know why you would buy this place."

I would be lying if I said it hadn't crossed my mind a time or two to wonder why no one had bought this house before me. It's on a beautiful piece of property here on the river, and quite frankly, it would have been easy enough to bulldoze the house and rebuild. But as I look at her and think about her statement about it being haunted, if she didn't look so forlorn and concerned, I would laugh.

"How can that be? Just look at it—it's beautiful." I swing my hand up toward the dilapidated house and cringe at the sight. "Besides, there's no such thing as haunted."

"You're not from around here, are you? My mama said that had to be the case. You do know no one has lived there for over seventy years, right?"

Seventy years. My heart sinks.

Maybe I should have done a little more research on the house before I decided to buy it. Natalie and I never discussed the previous owner, just that it belonged to a trust, the owner wished to remain anonymous, and, after all this time, they were finally ready to sell it. From the images online, I knew it was severely outdated on the inside and would need a lot of work, but the bones looked strong and sturdy.

"Well, that is a long time." My hands fall to my sides as I again take in the back of the house, a structure that surprisingly pulls on my heart strings. I feel like I understand how it feels and what it needs, and because of that it feels like it's always been mine, even though I've technically only owned it for two weeks and have only been here for two days. "I look forward to fixing it up and decorating it—maybe you can help me."

Her eyes widen. "I don't know. My mama's always told me to stay away from the house, and to never, ever go in it."

"Oh, come on. I'll have a chat with her and invite you both

over. She'll see it's just fine, and then you can drop by whenever you want." I do like the idea of having a couple of neighbors. She seems sweet, and if her mother sent her over here to say hello, she must be nice as well, and possibly near my age.

She looks at me skeptically then glances down at the dish in her hands. She shoves it in my direction, and I step forward to take it. "My mama wanted me to give you this. She says it's to be neighborly."

I take the plate and see it's covered with cornbread muffins. I've always seen things like this happen in the movies, where new neighbors are welcomed with goodies, but it's never occurred to me that this would happen to me. I'm touched and smile at the girl.

"June, you tell your mama thank you and this means more to me than she knows. I look forward to eating these muffins and meeting her soon." The plate is warm, and my stomach growls.

Chewing on her lip, she glances toward the dock then back at me. "Have you seen it yet?" she asks, her eyes widening with fear.

"Seen what?" I tilt my head a smidge, curious as to what she's about to say next.

"The light at the boathouse." She answers like I should have known.

"Well, I'm staying in the boathouse until the house is a little more inhabitable, so if you see a light, it's probably mine."

She inhales sharply and takes a step away from me.

"But that's where Mrs. Easler lives."

"Who's Mrs. Easler?" I ask, a little taken aback by her reaction.

"Your ghost," she replies as she runs off and into the trees.

4

____

I've never been one to believe in ghosts or spirits. I know there are a lot of people who do, but I guess I've just figured people are crazy, like they'll believe anything, even if there's scientific proof to falsify the claims.

"Haunted"—what does that even mean? And telling me "someone" lives in the boathouse...umm, that's not creepy at all, especially since I'm living there too. I contemplate this as I get into my car, turn the air conditioning on high, and begin to make my way down the driveway.

Sure, as a kid, I was certain there were monsters under the bed and in the closet, but I outgrew that pretty quickly. My parents taught us that there were no such things as ghosts, and that's what I've always believed. Horror stories and movies don't scare me—in fact, I love them. I'm not a superstitious person, I don't spook easily, and that's just how I've always been, no matter how many black cats cross my path.

My father, who I take after the most, has for years eschewed the notion of skipping the 13th floor. Sure, he's always understood that his stance on this will lead to problems with the tenants, occupants, or customers, but I agree with him—having a fear of a number being unlucky is irrational. The 13th floor isn't haunted, it's no more likely that a fire will break out there than any other floor, and quite frankly, should there be a problem, it's irresponsible to skip the numerical order because it could lead to mistakes for first responders.

Now, all that being said, I would be lying if I said I was unaffected by the girl's words, and last night my mind launched into overdrive every time I heard a noise outside. Don't get me started on if I thought the noise was inside the boathouse. The blanket remained firmly clenched in my fists and pulled up over my nose, just leaving my eyes out, and even though I started sweating, there was no way even one toe was coming out. I knew I was being completely ridiculous, but by the time the sun finally started lighting up the sky, I felt such relief that only then did I fall into a short, deep sleep.

Does everyone in this town think the house is haunted? Is that why it sat here so long uninhabited? I guess I just don't understand what the little girl and her mother think they saw on the dock; I haven't seen anything out of the ordinary. But here I am now, another day later, still tired, and even that's not going to stop me. I am excited to get going with the house.

Most people think because I was born into a life of high society, I wouldn't understand what it takes or what it means to get my hands dirty, but they are wrong. I grew up visiting the construction sites with my dad. He was a very hands-on kind of guy, and he taught me to be handy too.

"Never rely on someone to do something for you that you can do yourself," he used to say. While I fall in line with this philosophy with most things, some things I've always just chosen to not do myself, like my nails.

Nails that have seen better days, I think as I glance down at them draped over my steering wheel and let out a sigh.

Yesterday, as I stood in the middle of the kitchen of my new home, I realized it was time. I gave myself two days to settle in, get my bearings around the house, and become acquainted with it, but I knew before I even arrived that I wouldn't be able to do a lot of the heavy lifting, like the masonry around the porch and the roof. I am in need of a contractor, and soon, even if for the sole purpose of getting the permits pulled.

This house is well over one hundred years old, and since it hasn't been lived in for so long, I'm not naive enough to think the electrical wiring has been replaced or the water pipes aren't corroded. While I believe the structure of the home is sound, it's the other components I'm worried about. So, after texting Natalie to get a referral for a general contractor in town, I gave them a call and was invited in to discuss the project.

I left the house giving myself plenty of time as this was my first trip to my new downtown, which is on the other side of the river. Directions on my phone told me I could go back inland and circle around or head farther west and take a drawbridge that crosses the river. I chose the bridge, which gave me a perfect view of the Gulf of Mexico, miles and miles of open water with no end in sight except for the deep line of the horizon.

Crossing the bridge, I turned left along the river and took in the dozens of docks that line its edge. As I pull into downtown, to my right there's a large grassy park, to my left there are boat-up restaurants and a large inn, and directly in front of me is the marina.

A few blocks down, I make a right onto Main Street. The brick buildings are mostly old-looking, one or two stories, and the businesses are what you would expect to see in the center of town: a law office, a doctor's office, a fishing supply store, a fabric store, and an antique store, things of that nature. As I'm winding through the streets, I find a bookstore, the town hall, art galleries, a brewery, a few more restaurants, a movie theater, and four churches, each with an accompanying cemetery. What I thought was supposed to be a sleepy little fishing town is actually bustling with people, and the more I see, the more I realize it's quaint and charming.

Eventually, I make my way to the contractor's office just off Main Street. I park on the road out front and stare up at a home. It's also brick with a portico in the front, the lawn is manicured perfectly, and it sits just behind a small gate on the sidewalk. On the front door it says to enter, so I do, hearing a bell ring to alert whoever is inside. Immediately I'm struck by gorgeous teak floors, detailed wainscoting across the lower half of the walls, a brick fireplace with what looks like an old farmhouse mantel, classic crown molding, and a combination of the three types of lighting: general, task, and accent.

"Hello," calls a cheerful voice from the back of the house.

"Hello. Mrs. Hawthorne?" I respond, stepping farther inside. It smells like vanilla, and I love it.

"Back here, dear."

I follow the sound to find her in the kitchen. I know manners dictate that I should be greeting her, but if I thought the front room took my breath away, this kitchen is like a dream come true. *Hello Viking appliances and hello marble.*

"Your home is lovely," I tell her, in awe as I look around at all of the details.

She chuckles. "Not my home—it's my nephew's. Garrett owns the company. He's always believed his work should speak louder than him, and I can tell by the look on your face it has." She beams with pride.

"Well, he's talking to me from every angle. This place is beautiful." My eyes catch on the built-in wine cellar, which covers the entire wall leading into the dining room.

"Thank you," comes a voice from beside me.

Turning, I find a tall, fit guy with short brown hair and hazel eyes smiling down at me. He's wearing a dark gray polo that has

Hawthorne Construction embroidered in white on the left side, a well-worn pair of jeans, and a pair of construction boots.

"You're welcome," I stutter, pulling the baseball cap I'm wearing farther down on my head. I may not be in the market to meet a guy, but that doesn't mean I'm not rendered awkward when in close proximity to a good looking one. Plus, I know the hat isn't much of a disguise, but I really don't need to be recognized.

"You're in luck, Mrs. Corcell," he says as he moves past me to a large round wooden table.

"Oh, it's just Ms., or better yet, call me Ryla." I follow him to the table. While Rylie is legally my first name, and although it isn't that common, when put together with my married name, Crest, or my maiden, Kent, it is recognizable to many. While I'm not ashamed of the names, that period of my life is over. It's funny—I was a Kent for most of my life, and after only a few short years being a Crest, both now feel foreign, somehow wrong, which is why I've chosen my mother's maiden name. Coco calls me Ryla, so I searched the internet for a Ryla Corcell and nothing came up. For now, that's who I'll be.

"Apologies, Ryla." He smiles at me warmly. "Garrett Hawthorne." He holds out his hand, and as if on autopilot, mine slips into his. We shake, warm and friendly.

"Nice to meet you, and no worries. Tell me, how am I in luck?" I ask, dropping his hand, curious to hear what he has to say.

Together, the three of us sit at the table. There in the center is a pitcher of lemonade and sliced pound cake, and his aunt pours us each a glass. I take it and sip the drink. Delicious.

"I did a little research on your house after you called and found a few very important details. First off, as I'm sure you know, since your home is over fifty years old, it's considered historic. Sometimes we can run into complications with this label, but since the property has been vacant for so long, we are in the clear, and since it is not an actual true antebellum home, it's not registered as one. Also, historians, architectural historians, and archeologists have already studied the property. Other than it being relevant to the town, no one has tried to landmark it, therefore we shouldn't get pushbacks when we begin the renovations. Are you planning to keep the original integrity of the home?"

"If you mean do I plan on tearing down walls and changing the layout, no. But I do plan on repairing the outside, resurfacing the floors, and updating things to code, as well as cosmetically changing the kitchen and the bathrooms."

He grins. "Then I don't see us having any problems with what you're wanting to do."

"How soon do you think we can get started?" I'm eager. I mean who wouldn't be?

He leans back in his chair and eyes me curiously. "Once we get the permits filed, for residential it usually takes about two weeks. But that doesn't mean you can't start on your own side projects in the meantime. Are you planning on doing anything yourself, or are you wanting to outsource the majority of it?"

"Oh, I plan to be knee-deep. It's why I bought the home. I'm an interior decorator and designer. Most of the projects I've worked on over the past couple of years have been from the new construction phase, but I couldn't resist this home when I saw it. I've already started stripping the wallpaper, and so far there doesn't appear to be any mold on or in the walls."

His brows pop up; he's surprised. "Well that's good, but we'll take a better look once we get our hands on your house. Mold is common here, especially if a home sits at over eighty degrees."

My eyes widen. "Maybe we should work on installing the air conditioner first then." I glance over at his aunt, who smiles at me but is just sitting there observing us.

"That would make working inside more enjoyable for you." He grins again. "Have you thought about a budget for the project?"

"No. I was aware when I bought the home that the repairs would be pricey, and I'm willing to do what needs to be done. As long as the work is good and the price is reasonable, there won't be a problem."

"I think we can manage that." He nods, pleased.

You know how, right off the bat, some people give you a vibe? Well I'm getting one from him, and it's friendly, welcoming. Something tells me deep down that having him around the property will be nice.

"How did you hear about us?" he asks as Mrs. Hawthorne stands to grab a folder that's lying on the counter. She hands it to me, and I flip it open. It's a packet with an introductory letter, a copy of his license and services offered, the contract between us, and a few testimonials.

"Natalie Wood, my realtor, told me I should call you, said you're the best."

He doesn't say anything right away, but his eyes flare for just a second before he presses his lips together for a closed-mouth smile and nods his head. *Interesting.*

"How about I swing by tomorrow and begin working on an estimate for you?" he asks.

"I would like that a lot." Reaching into my bag, I pull out my iPad, swipe open a few pages, and then hand it to him. My hand is shaking a little, because I know things like this aren't normal, but I have to protect my anonymity as much as possible.

"What's this?" he asks, sitting up and pulling it a little closer to inspect it.

Trying to act as if this is no big deal, in a steady tone, I tell him, "A nondisclosure and a photo release."

Wrinkles form between his eyes as he scans the document. "What for?"

I want to say, *Because I'm trying to start my life over, and I don't need any more drama or people camping out around my house trying to get pictures of me*, but instead I explain, "I'm blogging about the house, and I imagine you'll be in the photos eventually. I don't mind you using your own photos as this is going to be a big project, but I prefer not to be mentioned or photographed at all. If you are asked about me as the new owner of the house, this just prevents there from being a gray area. Where I come from, it's best to have these things in place, just in case. You understand, right?"

His brows rise, and he looks across the table at me. His hazel eyes lock onto mine, and we stare at each other, having an unspoken conversation. "And where do you come from?" he asks.

"Chicago." I leave it at that.

I wait to see if there is any flicker of recognition, but there isn't, and relief sweeps over me. After another beat, he nods, swipes his finger across the screen for his signature, and hands it back to me.

"You're probably smart to do this. Your home has been here a long time, and it's bound to garner some attention eventually. No worries, though. Chuluota Springs is a small town, and we look after each other. My men will keep quiet."

"Thank you." I tuck the iPad back into my bag.

As we finish the drinks, he and I talk more about the vision I have. He pulls up some photos of other projects he's worked on, and I just know he and I are going to do great things. Should I interview other contractors? Probably, but with the referral and from what I've seen, I know this is the right choice.

As I walk out of the house, seagulls call to each other and soar overhead. The skies are clear and blue, and I decide to walk the block back to Main Street while I'm here. I can't help but smile at my new little downtown.

My eyes catch on a young couple strolling down the sidewalk toward the marina. They look as if they are headed out on the water with their bag of towels and cooler. He says something to her, and she throws her head back and laughs. I can't remember the last time I laughed like that.

This summer would have been mine and Carter's four-year wedding anniversary. He wanted to get married in July. That was the month we met, and well, I just wanted to marry him, so I didn't care when. Maybe I should have considered this a little more. It's true what they say about love being blind.

At the end of Main Street, I spot Dockside Diner, and my mouth waters at the thought of a latte. As I approach, I spot a walkup window on the sidewalk, and I'm thrilled.

A woman about my age comes scrambling over. Her dark hair is all twisted up on top of her head, and she's wearing a blue gingham apron around her waist and bright red lipstick. She's frazzled, and I smile at her.

"Good morning." She smiles back with a pen and a small pad of paper in hand. Then her smile drops a little as she looks at me, and small wrinkles form between her brows. "Wait a minute—do you know who you look like?"

My heart rate instantly rises, and I cut her off before she can go any further.

"I do, and unfortunately I get that all the time." I smile back at her but self-consciously pull the hat lower. I just want anonymity for a little bit longer.

It's easier for people to believe they are seeing a resemblance than an actual "celebrity". I mean given what the tabloids have said about me for years, my socialite status, and what's happened over the last couple of months, why would Rylie Crest be in Chuluota Springs?

Moving right past the moment, I change the subject. "I was told I had to stop by and try a hummingbird muffin, heard they're the best." Natalie texted me this tidbit when she sent over the contact information for Hawthorne Construction.

She smiles proudly. "They really are. It was my grandmother's recipe, and although people have tried for years to get it out of my mother and me, it's never going to happen," she says while shaking her head.

"Now I'm even more excited." My stomach agrees, loudly announcing my hunger.

She leans a little closer to speak quietly to me. "But I will tell you, if you try to make them on your own, make sure you brown the butter and candy the pecans. Makes all the difference, you'll see. My name is Corrie, by the way."

Browned butter—interesting. "Sounds scrumptious."

She turns around, moves to a large glass case, and grabs the muffin. Putting it in a white paper bag, she rolls the top down and places it in front of me. "Can I get you anything else?"

"By chance do you make lattes?"

She laughs. "Nope. Plain old diner here. Although I tried to talk my mother into buying an espresso machine, she refused. How about an iced cafe con leche instead? It's shaken with sweetened condensed milk. I like to add a little cinnamon, and voila, it's delicious."

"How can I refuse after that?" Plus, she's onto something—it's way too hot for a hot coffee.

"You won't be sorry." She grins.

While she goes to make the drink, I think about Natalie, my neighbor with her welcome goodies, Garrett and his aunt, and now this girl. Everyone in this town has been nice, and technically here, I'm no one. Even though I'm now a resident, I'm still a stranger, but that doesn't matter to them. It's almost a heady feeling, one I'm definitely welcoming. I don't think I realized how lonely I've been over the last couple of months.

After paying and saying goodbye, I stroll down the board-walk along the riverfront drinking the coffee, which definitely hits the spot. The river looks different here, not as translucent as it is by my house, but it's still beautiful all the same. Houses dot the shoreline across the way, there are many boats tied up to short docks that look like public boat parking, and there are more businesses. There's a boutique, a place to rent boats, kayaks, and paddleboards, a seafood market, and even a hardware store, which catches my eye.

Wandering into it, I think there's no time like the present to go about buying a few things I'll need.

"Welcome. Let me know if I can help you find anything," comes from a gentleman behind the counter. I smile to acknowledge his words then grab a cart. I know with the renovations on the house, it's not going to be easy, but if I can survive the last couple of months, I can do this too.

Slowly, I stroll down each aisle looking at everything from doormats to grills to paint colors. I start taking an inventory of the things I think I'll need and finally stop when I spot the portable air conditioning units. I imagine the temperature is just going to get warmer at night, and I'm already no stranger to the humidity, so this will be perfect for the boathouse. Well, the boathouse and the main house until the central air is installed. Grabbing it, I place it in the cart then move on to ladders. Eventually, my cart is full, and with a giddiness I haven't felt in a while, I head to check out.

Giddiness, that is, until I spot my face on the cover of a magazine with the word thief in large yellow letters stamped next to my head. It's stacked next to the home improvement and gardening magazines and the books for sale. There, right in the middle, is a trendy tabloid. It's at least a month old, but it's there and a solid reminder that it doesn't matter where I go or what I do—I can't escape my past.

Fear slices through me as anxiety tightens my chest. I quickly look around to see if anyone is looking at me, but they aren't. I'm certain if they see me and the magazine together, they'll know we are one and the same. It's not that I thought I could stay hidden forever, but it hasn't even been a week, and I'm just not ready.

5

———————

It never fails. You always think your life is going to go one way, and inevitably it goes another.

Why is that?

We work so hard on goals and how we can achieve them, relationships, life, work, and well, when things go upside down, it's disappointing and sad—sad because lately I seem to be wondering if it's all worth it.

Granted, I know I'm not in the right headspace. I haven't been for months, but my heart was broken in more ways than it should be, and seeing that magazine yesterday, so many feelings came rushing back. I don't know why I thought I would be able to escape that life if I moved here, but I did, and now my bubble feels like it's been popped. I've spent these last few days floating by in what I guess can loosely be described as vacation mode, and now it feels over. I feel like any euphoria I was experiencing is gone, and I'm back to this: sad, embarrassed, smothered, and above all, heartbroken.

I know it's only a matter of time before the people here realize who I am. What am I saying? It's only a matter of time before the world knows I'm here and my freedom from judgment is over. It makes me feel one hundred percent defeated. Just the thought of sneaky cameras and being followed was enough to have me buying a month's worth of groceries and spending the remainder of the day hiding in my big house. I wandered the rooms and then soaked in the new clawfoot tub I found in the en-suite to the master bedroom.

I don't know why this tub is here; it's one of those completely random things Natalie mentioned I would find in the home, and I'm grateful for it. When I turned on the faucet, I expected the water to be orange considering this house runs on well water, but it ran clear, and I said why not. I stared at the water as it dripped out, and I couldn't help but wonder if it will always be like this—me trying to escape from my past just to feel a sense of normalcy—or if one day this too shall pass. I tried to clog it with my toe, but the water kept coming, just like my memories with Carter, the treasured ones and the hated ones too.

I can still hear his laugh, and it causes my chest to tighten and ache. I loved his laugh. He was always so happy, and his personality was infectious too. The thought forced me to realize I can't remember the last time I was that happy, truly happy, and the sorrow of this had me slipping below the water to hide. I'm not sure who I was hiding from—after all, it was just me—but for some reason that water felt safer than the air.

Eventually, the water cooled enough that goose bumps rose, and I shivered and decided it was time to go to bed. Wrapped in a thick, soft, fluffy towel from my laundry hamper, I made my way back down the dock to my little boathouse.

Coco was happy to see me, but as she said hello, I barely mustered a smile and found myself staring out the window at the river. It called to me. It has several times since I've arrived, and always when my heart has felt the most shattered.

Why is that?

The waters were smooth and mimicked obsidian—black,

glassy, and somewhat mysterious—and there was something calming and hypnotic about the way it endlessly moved. I continually find myself transfixed as I stare beyond the surface. It's as if it feels what I need and magically soothes my soul. Then of course come morning, it's back to cool shades of aqua, clear and peaceful, a reminder that something beautiful is always around the corner. It's as if the river understands that at night, no matter how hard we try, the darkness settles in, but when the sun rises a few hours later, it's a new day to start all over.

So that's what I'm doing.

Today, I'm starting all over.

Again.

Sweat rolls down my face as I stretch on my toes to pull down the loose wallpaper in the breakfast room where a casual kitchen table will sit and look out over to the side of the inlet and the river beyond. I can tell it was once beautiful with its cream color and antique blush roses with greenery, but today it's browned with age, the roses faded and discolored. The breakfast room is connected to the kitchen on one side and on the other to the parlor room, which sits across the foyer from the back entrance to the library. It's also the most casual room on the back side of the house. I figure the kitchen is where I'll be spending most of my time, so this space is as good as any to start in.

All the windows downstairs on this half of the house are open as the home doesn't have central air and no one has lived in it since it was invented in the 1970s. At some point, someone began to install the duct work, but it was never completed. At this point, any kind of draft I can get, even a warm one, is welcome.

I would be lying if I said I wasn't feeling slightly overwhelmed by the enormity of this project. As the days have passed and I've started working, my unease has begun to grow, and I could have sworn the size of the rooms did too. This is a big house, like really big, but I know I can do it, one room at a time. It's not like I have anywhere else I need to be, so I'm doing my best to not let the anxiety creep in and take over.

Besides, I've never been one to back down from a challenge.

In my back pocket, my phone vibrates. Pulling it out, I see it's Ivy and can't help but smile.

"So, tell me! How's it going? I've been waiting for you to send me more pictures," my sister states. I should have called her yesterday to reinforce that I am fine, but I just wanted to continue settling in, wander around the house, and hide. She may be two years younger than me, but she fusses like an old mother hen.

"It's beautiful, quiet. Well, not really—the birds here are insane." I drop another strip of loose paper I've pulled from the wall and kick it over to the pile I started earlier today.

"Really? Like how so?" she asks. People's voices are muffled in the background; she's walking outside, and I can just see her now: hair pulled tight into a high ponytail, couture outfit complete with a cute top, long flowing skirt, and designer flip-flops. It's summer in Chicago, and whereas my design love turned to rooms and spaces, hers turned to fashion. Just by taking a stroll, she is her own best marketing for her line. Cameras can't help but follow her like she's royalty, and between social media and the paparazzi, she gets ridiculously incredible coverage.

Then again, so did I.

"They are loud. Just you wait, I'm going to record them and send it to you." I glance out the window toward the trees. Of course I can't see them, but my eyes narrow because I know they are there.

"If you insist." She laughs. "How's Coco adjusting?"

"Ha! Well, I can't tell. She's really into the birds and keeps calling out, 'Who's there? Show your face.' It's what I used to say when Carter came home from work and closed the front door, and she picked up those phrases quickly. It was funny then," I tell her, frowning. "I guess it is now too…it's just different. Poor thing, she's looking all over, but only a few have flown by."

"I remember her saying that! And of course it's funny. I can hear her now. *Show your face! Show your face!* She's the best. But really, tell me, how are you? How's the house?" The pinging of the crosswalk timer counting down echoes in the background, and I find I'm not even the slightest bit sad to not be in the city.

"I'm okay, and you'll be happy to know it's just as bad as we thought it would be." I chuckle, turning around to stare at the severely outdated white appliances in the kitchen.

"Oh no, Ryla." Her tone is laced with pity, but it's more than that; she's made it clear she thinks moving here was a terrible decision.

"Don't worry, I've already got a vision, and it's going to be superb. Just think: a huge inviting white marble breakfast bar, gorgeous patterned wallpapers, a swing on the back porch to overlook the river," I say, trying to soothe her. "When you come here, it'll be like visiting a swanky bed and breakfast."

"Well, I do worry. We all do. Mom is still beside herself that you moved somewhere so remote where we know no one. You're, like, all alone there, and we hate it." And I hate causing them distress. We've always been very close-knit as a family. Me going to college was one thing because they knew I would return, but this is completely different. I've broken up our unit of four.

"It's not that remote. I mean, come on—it's Florida, not some small island off the coast of Indonesia. You know this. Look, we're talking, so cell service is good to go, and besides, we've gone round and round about it, and all of you have got to let it go. I need this. I need to be here and away from there. Feel free to come visit whenever."

"We understand, we do, but that doesn't mean we like it." I can picture the pout on her face perfectly, the scrunched brows and downward smile.

"Good thing this is my life and I get to make my own choices." Choices that, up until recently, felt as if they had been taken away from me.

She groans, and I hear her let out a deep sigh. "Well, you must send pictures," she declares as I move through the rooms to sit outside on the back steps and hope for an arctic breeze to magically come by. It's warmer today than it was yesterday, or maybe the reality of the heat is just catching up to me. There are very few clouds in the sky, and the mugginess seems to follow me no matter where I go. I smack my leg as a mosquito lands on it and mentally add four bottles of bug spray to my grocery list.

"I'll do you one better—I started a website. Of course I've left my name off of it, just in case, but this way all of you will be able to follow along and never wonder what I'm up to. I've already put up a few photos of the house, the inlet, and the river."

Knowing in advance there wouldn't be Wi-Fi at the house right away, I purchased a hotspot and brought it with me. It's a good thing too, because last night I browsed image after image of design ideas and began a folder of colors, furniture, and custom designs.

"Are you sure that's a good idea? I know you've talked about blogging your projects before, and as much as I think it's great, I'm still going to worry."

"Stop it. Don't worry. There's no trace of me on it, except for my feet, hands, and thoughts. They can't recognize me. No one will know it's mine."

"What's the name of it? I'm going to look it up right now," she says.

"Something Old, Something New," I tell her proudly while leaning forward to pull on a piece of wood that is covered in dry rot. These poor stairs. Who am I kidding? This poor house.

"Fitting." She snickers.

I think so. This way, no matter what kind of project I take on, whether it's refurbishing or new construction, the name fits.

"Well, you didn't think I was going to call it Rylie's Renovations, did you?" Although that does have a nice ring to it.

"No. It's perfect—perfect for you. And don't forget, if you need any help with it, my friend Molly owns her own web design company, and she can help you."

My heart swells at her sincerity, and I do remember. I met her once when we went to the Kentucky Derby, as she lives in Louisville. Maybe I'll give her a call.

"It is perfect for me, and it's a great name for design and transformation projects."

"It really is." I can hear the smile, and I know some of her worries have lessened.

"Listen, I'm going to go. I need to finish what I'm working on before the contractor gets here."

"At least you won't be the only one there," she nags.

"Nope. Soon enough there will be teams of people here working."

"You take care of yourself, and seriously, Rylie, I know you're determined to be some kind of recluse right now, but don't be a stranger. If you need anything, you know I'll be there in a heartbeat." A car honks in the background.

"I'm not being a recluse. I'm just lying low for a bit and working on a new project. You do know this, and I love you for caring, but I'm okay. Trust me."

"You know I do, or I would be dragging you back kicking and screaming."

"You could try."

"Love you," she says just before she hangs up.

A few hours later, a truck door slams, and I head outside to find Garrett parked next to my car and standing there looking around the property. I find I'm curious to know what he's thinking as he looks at my home. It's then I catch a glimpse of a familiar boat in the inlet. Garrett sees him too and lifts his hand for a wave, presumably to wave at Jake-with-no-last-name on the water, and I grit my teeth. How many times has he come by and I've not known it?

"I take it you know that guy?" I ask as I approach, not bothering to turn around and acknowledge the dark-haired boat driver. Garrett's wearing another Hawthorne Construction polo, this one forest green, a pair of jeans, and his work boots. This must be his standard work uniform. He shoves his hands into his pockets.

"Yep, since diapers. He's my older brother," he says, almost reverently.

Brothers. Of course they are. This is small-town life at its finest. I didn't notice a resemblance, but then again, I was too busy seeing red.

Garrett gives me a tentative smile, not even bothering to ask why I'm frowning, so I decide to keep my feelings about our tense encounter to myself.

A long time ago, I learned to never speak my mind when it comes to other people. Gossip among socialites can kill your image, and you never know who that person might be to the person you're talking to. It's bad taste, bad manners, and best avoided.

"Huh," I respond, leaving it at that. "Thanks for coming over so quickly. Just because I'm excited about the project doesn't mean others are too." I smile, hope wrapped around each word.

"Are you kidding? I'm just as excited—I barely slept last night. I've been wanting to get my hands on this renovation for years … this is like a contractor's dream." He grins, his hazel eyes wide with elation.

"Did you look at the pictures of the inside? They were posted with the sale listing."

He glances at me strangely and then says, "I did, but nothing beats seeing the real thing." Squinting, he looks up, scans the outside of the house, and then pulls his phone out to take a picture. "I think you're right that the roof needs to be replaced first. It doesn't look that bad from here, but I have no idea when it was last replaced, and I have to believe the wind damage of summer storms has taken a toll."

"Are those bad around here?" I ask, looking at the roof to see if I can spot missing shingles, and then at the sky: no clouds in sight.

"They can be. It's about to be hurricane season, and although Chuluota Springs has never been hit directly, at least one or two come by this way a year, and the outer bands can be fierce."

"I've never experienced a hurricane." I know they happen, but the thought of being in one terrifies me. I've watched enough movies to know nothing good is ever left behind.

"Well if you're lucky, you won't this year either." He smiles down at me. "Also, as lovely as these oak trees are"—he points at the two identical live oak trees on either side of the house—"the branches need to be cut back away from the house too."

It's clear they were planted at the same time, and they shade large pieces of the property.

"Okay, you know best." I just agree with him. Call it a hunch, but I don't think he's going to steer me wrong. The eager energy pouring off of him as he looks over the outside of the house makes it apparent this project is love at first sight for him as well.

Moving up to the front entrance, I pull my phone from my back pocket and snap a few pictures of him for the meet-and-greet blog post on the contractor and the house while he pauses to look over the porch, take another picture, and then write something in a small notebook. Once we pass through the entrance, I try to follow his gaze to see what he sees: the tall ornamental ceilings, the dusty old front-of-the-house crystal chandelier that still hangs in the foyer, and the sad way the buckling wallpaper is drooping off the walls.

"It's beautiful," he mumbles, his eyes trailing over the worn, run-down staircase.

"You say that now, but you haven't seen the whole house yet."

"Doesn't matter. It's easy to see how much work went into this home so long ago, and I can appreciate the detail." He takes another picture, this time of the ceiling.

"Do you know much about this place?" I ask him, genuinely curious to know more about the previous owner.

"A little, mostly that it's haunted." He grins at me as we move to the kitchen.

Haunted. There's that word again, which leads me to believe everyone in this town must think that. I almost laugh at the absurdity but decide against it.

"When would you like to move in?" he asks, glancing at me before he strains to look in another room.

"I haven't really thought about it. I guess we'll know when the time is right. I'm using a bathtub upstairs, and at some point it would be nice to cook a regular meal."

He looks at me skeptically.

I can't help but laugh. "Yes. Surprisingly, there were several new things left behind. The house wasn't completely empty, and fortunately for me, the tub appears to be brand new."

"I was more concerned about the water, but what else?" he asks, brows raised.

"Like the painting back here." Together we make our way to

the library. I know this from the built-in shelves and the bar that once held a ladder.

The painting is at least four feet by four feet, and it's a replica of the house at night from the viewpoint of the river. The rear chandelier is shining brightly, and the light from it runs straight down the dock and onto the river. It's a gorgeous piece wrapped in an ornate wooden frame, and on both sides are long tall windows with faded-looking navy drapes.

"It is beautiful." He leans closer to it to get a better look but doesn't touch it.

"The initials CB are in the corner, but other than that, Natalie doesn't know who the artist is."

He stills at the mention of her name but then resumes inspecting the details. I watch his eyes trail over it from corner to corner, and then he takes a step back, placing his hands on his hips.

"Have you done any research on the home?" He looks at me with an open curiosity.

"Not yet. I'm sure there have to be records located in town somewhere. I'll get to it eventually."

I know I should. I've bought this gorgeous, mysterious home where tiny pieces of its history show themselves to me, and I don't know how to fully appreciate it. Plus, it'll be good for blog posts. I just need to get up the courage to go back into town.

"You should try the library. My mother mentioned that there was a lot of interest in this place when she was a girl, so I imagine something would be there. The man who built it—his last name was Easler, and he was a founding member of this town. It was a gift for his wife."

I finger the edge of the navy curtain that hangs to the left of the painting. There's a design swirled into the fabric, and I trace the pattern as I think of the E in the gate at the entrance and let the word Easler roll through my mind. June said the name too, and I realize I like it. Now knowing what it stands for surprisingly makes this home feel even more like it's mine, and the people who built it too.

"Then surely if he was a founding member, there must be plenty of records of him and of his family." I feel another layer of purpose to the project slide into place and turn to look at Garrett. He's moved to the entrance of the room and is looking at the arched doorways. He runs his hand over the curve, appreciating the craftsmanship.

"You would think," he replies as silence falls over us.

Leaving the library, we walk from room to room and then back to the kitchen. He looks around the space, his gaze pausing on an interior decorating magazine I bought at the hardware store.

"You mentioned doing a lot of the inside work yourself, so I'll take the lead from you as we go. If you start something and then decide it's not for you, my team will take over. How does that sound?" He turns to face me.

"That sounds great." I'm not so naive as to think I'll be able to do it all on my own. Some of the work will be difficult with just one person.

Moving to the large windows that look out toward the boathouse, he examines the window and the wood frame around it. "We'll get started on the outside while you work on the inside. I'll have electrical, plumbing, and air conditioning come by in the next couple of days, and I'm going to recommend you call in a restorer to look at the windows. I know there are a lot of them, and although these appear fine, who knows. I don't want to remove them for the sake of updating—these old wood windows are part of the character of the home. I don't know what your long-term goals are, but if we replace them, it will lower the historic value." He takes a picture of the window.

"Okay. I agree with you." And I do. Like I mentioned to him

at our meeting yesterday, I don't want to change the integrity of the home, and hearing him say this reaffirms that I'm hiring the right guy to do the job.

"Good." He turns to face me. "I'll text you the name of a company we've used before so you can give him a call when you're ready. Be thinking about this sooner rather than later as we wouldn't want any of them to leak once we've refurbished the inside, as well as for when we're ready to paint the outside."

"Perfect. I'll call him as soon as you send it over. I appreciate you supporting me and this home, and for not giving me a hard time about the things I want to do myself."

"Of course. You're the boss." He grins.

6

———

*S*tripping wallpaper is not as easy as I thought it would be. I was certain most would just peel off because it's so old, but boy was I wrong. With whatever adhesive they used back then, this paper may as well be cemented to the plaster wall behind it.

Of course, I found myself back at the hardware store to buy supplies, and I've spent the last several days scuffing over all of the walls with coarse sandpaper, so when I spray the paper with a liquid stripper, it can soak in. In a normal-sized house, this probably wouldn't be too much work, but here, it's been daunting. I would also be lying if I said I wasn't sore from the process. This morning, my arms protested greatly as I lifted the putty knife and got back to work.

That's okay, though; I don't mind the repetitive work. It's tedious, and it's good for me to keep moving, to keep myself occupied. It prevents my mind from having down time and wandering to places I just don't want to go anymore. I find it therapeutic.

Every day when I wake, I remind myself that today will be better than yesterday, and eventually all my days will be great again. They have to be. These feelings can't last forever; I just need more time—time I'm taking here in this house, by myself, in this faraway town.

Well, not really by myself.

Garrett's men have started too. In two and a half days, they removed the old roof and replaced it with a new one of the same color, and a few have been working inside to try to figure out the best way to continue installing the central air duct system. I'm most excited about that, and as much as I love my boathouse, once it's installed, I might move my air mattress inside earlier than planned.

"Hello? Ryla, are you in here?" I hear called from the front of the house. Along with the windows, I left the front and back doors open to help push a draft through the rooms.

"In the back," I yell in response, and soft footsteps make their way toward me.

"Well look at you," says Natalie, eyes wide with delight, taking in my mess, the room, and me. At the same time, I can't help but take in her Lilly Pulitzer dress, gold sandals, bright pink lipstick, and picnic basket. If the south needed an advertisement, it could be her. My sister would be proud.

"Yeah, it wasn't coming off like I thought it would, but that's okay. I figured it out and I'm moving right along." I drag my hand over the smooth section of the wall I've been working on. For the last couple of days, I've been in the dining room and the parlor room stripping, and there are piles scattered across the drop cloths on the floor of each room.

"Well, it's looking great. Have you come across any mold?" she asks, looking around.

I grin. That is such a realtor question to ask.

"Not yet, thank goodness. At least nothing that needs replacing."

Climbing down the ladder, I brush the dust off my shorts,

swipe a hand over my forehead to push my hair off my face, and move into the kitchen. Setting the scraping tools down on the counter, I take a long drink of water. It's so cold my insides rejoice. Garrett told me the air conditioning should be installed by the end of next week, and once the electrical wiring is figured out, we can talk about ceiling fans too. Can't come fast enough.

"Hello, Coco." She walks over to the nook where a small table would normally sit.

"Hello," Coco replies, bobbing her head and fanning her tail.

There are two large windows that give a perfect view of the inlet, and since it's just her and me, I don't need a table there. I'll sit at the breakfast bar or in the breakfast room once I order a table.

Natalie peers up and smiles at Coco sitting on a perch that rises just above the top of the cage. "That's a mighty fine home you have here."

"Yeah, it was too hard to transport hers from Chicago, and since I was getting a new home, I thought she should too. It was delivered yesterday, and two of the men put it together. I love this one because it's more aesthetically appealing than just the wire cages with the glass wall and open top, and if I have some help, because of the wheels, it can be moved outside. Or I'll buy her another one, who knows. She's loved sitting on the dock in her travel cage in the mornings, and I figure in the months it's not so hot, moving her to the porch will be perfect."

"Sounds like a lucky bird to me." She grins at Coco again.

I can't help but think I'm the lucky one.

Last night, while the sun was setting, Coco and I were sitting on the dock, and out of nowhere, she snored. She snored! It was the cutest sound, if you can really even call it a snore, but just her presence makes me so happy.

Turning to face me, Natalie walks back toward me and holds up her picnic basket. "I brought some lunch if you're hungry."

She wiggles it. "I thought it might be nice to eat outside in the shade under one of the oak trees. It's not too hot outside yet," she says, hopeful.

Not too hot...

Is she crazy? If it gets much hotter, it's possible I will melt.

But just her mentioning food has my stomach growling, and I would eat on the surface of the sun if I had to. I'm starving. "That sounds great."

I did stock the little refrigerator in the boathouse, but mostly it's premade salads, yogurt, and containers of things that can be microwaved.

I've tried to stick to the house as much as possible. There really isn't a reason for me to go anywhere, and after seeing the magazine, I think my fears win out over rationality. I know the gossip storm that awaits me when I'm discovered, and it's so disheartening. I knew when I married Carter that I would indefinitely stand in the spotlight, but it's been so bright lately I've burned more than I've shined. Can anyone blame me for wanting to slip into the shadows? Oh, wait—they do blame me.

Moving outside, I follow Natalie as she returns to her car and pulls out a large blanket for us to sit on along with a few bags from the grocery store.

"I picked you up a shrimp salad sandwich," she says as we walk to the far side of the house away from the construction trucks. "I wasn't sure if you would like it or not, or if you have a shellfish allergy, but if you're going to live here, you may as well get used to the seafood." She smiles.

"It just so happens I love shrimp." I smile back.

Now, I know we have oak trees back in Illinois, but there's something about them here, on this property, that makes me feel like I've stepped into the Deep South. Yes, I know Florida is in the south, but this is different. Maybe old Florida is the best way to describe it: a slower way of life, nature that's a bit more wild, and humidity that just begs for sweet iced tea. That's how I feel when I see these timeless, massive trees.

Flipping the blanket open, I spread out the patchwork of colors while she unpacks the food. Taking a seat, I stare up through the thick, large branches to the midday sky and marvel at all the Spanish moss hanging down. *If these leaves could talk*, I think. And she's right—it's pleasant in the shade, and we fall into easy and comfortable conversation. Natalie knows my story. She never asked for it, but I freely gave it during the purchase of the home, and in return, I've opened up to her becoming a friend, one who has no expectations, no judgments. She just seems to enjoy my company as I enjoy hers.

"So, I have a question for you," I say between bites of the best shrimp salad I've ever eaten. She knows it's a loaded question, and her brows pop up in curiosity. Along with the sandwich, she packed us a small charcuterie platter of cheeses, crackers, and fruit. "What do you know about my house supposedly being haunted?"

She bursts out laughing. "I was wondering when you were going to ask me about this. Not much, just that it supposedly is." She stretches her legs out in front of her, crosses them at the ankle, and leans back on her elbows.

The inlet is super turquoise today, and just the sight of it in front of us gives me a nice level of contentment. They say colors can affect your mood, and this one sure does. It's very tranquil.

"I haven't seen any signs of it being haunted, but you're the third person now to know about this. Does everyone in town think it's haunted?" I pick up the cold can of tangerine sparkling water she brought for me and take a sip.

The smile that was on her face slips off, and she looks at me strangely. She's pulled her brown hair up into a messy bun on top of her head, and this makes her almond-shaped eyes appear bigger. "Did you do any research on this town before you moved here?"

"I did a little bit. I searched for top places to eat and things to do nearby, but I didn't go researching the history. I was looking for a house to buy on the river, and once I found this one, the rest seemed irrelevant. I mean never ever would I have thought about a house being haunted and have that play into my consideration for purchasing. It's just absurd and, honestly, not something I really believe in."

She studies me for a moment before she grabs a grape and pops it into her mouth. "Absurd it might be, but if you had done some research, very quickly you would have discovered it's not just this house that's haunted—it's the whole town."

"What?" I don't know whether to laugh or be shocked. That's not what I was expecting her to say.

"Yep. Chuluota Springs is one of the most haunted towns in the south." She rolls to her side and props her head up on her hand.

"How is that possible?" I sit up a little straighter. She must be mocking me, and I would be lying if I didn't admit it's kind of funny.

She sees my skepticism and laughs. "I'm serious! It started with the native American Indians. Just up the river is an old archeological site where there's evidence that it was once a ceremonial and burial site. Records show thousands of Indians a year would travel here with their loved ones. They say the spirits watch over the river."

This triggers my memory of seeing a brown state park sign when I was on my way in that first night that was directing visitors to the burial grounds. I don't know whether to think this fact is fascinating or creepy. I mean just how many people died in this area and are buried all under the ground?

"Next is the springs. This river we live on has more than

seventy natural springs. In the early half of the 1900s, people would visit from all over to enjoy the consistent year-round cool waters. Like their counterparts in the Midwest, travelers were told of their healing powers through the minerals in the water. Inevitably people would die from illnesses, or even by accident, and supposedly some of their ghosts remain behind."

Midwest counterpart—she must be talking about Alton, Illinois. It's famous in the Midwest for its ghost sightings and hauntings. They have hot springs, though, not cold ones, but I can see how people who didn't have modern medicine like we do now would seek out alternative healing measures as a last resort.

"Also, as you know, this is a fishing town. Many ships have gone missing over the years, and people say the loved ones are still lingering, hoping they return home. There's even a captain who's seen boating up and down the river at night with his lantern, searching for lost crew members."

"You're joking, right? And why would it be the loved ones waiting and not the other way around, the fallen fishermen looking for their way home?"

She's packed brownies too, and I grab one from the plastic container. Ooey-gooey chocolate is just about one of my most favorite things.

She scrunches up her shoulders as if to say, *Who knows?* "I'm not sure, this is just what they say."

"What they say is senseless. Ghosts aren't real."

"You can think that all you want, but there are plenty of others who say they are. Some things can't be explained. I was told when I moved here that if you live here long enough, you'll just come to accept this."

Like myself, Natalie is a transplant to Chuluota Springs. She's only been here for about a year.

"So all of this is just folklore? Like these supposed sightings,"

I say with air quotes, "they don't actually happen on the regu-lar?" I take a bite of the brownie, and it's so good I want to moan out loud.

"Other than me, because I'm relatively new here, everyone I've met has talked about some ghost here or there that they've once seen." She picks up a brownie too and takes a bite.

My face falls. "But what about my house? What does it have to do with Indians or mineral springs?" Sunlight and shadows move back and forth across her face as the branches of the tree sway in the breeze. Sometimes when she looks at me, her eyes, which are green, look almost translucent.

"Nothing that I know of. Supposedly, the man who built this house served in the Spanish-American war at the end of the 1800s. Even though the war was short, like most of the men back then, he was changed. He was from Tampa, and as the city was growing with cigar production, he didn't like the noise or the crowds of the factories. So, he promised his wife this large Greek Revival home if she would move north to Chuluota Springs. It wasn't much of a town then, so he's considered one of the founders. He did contract out for some of the construction, but as money was tight, most of the house he built himself, and all for her. If she wanted it, she got it. He wanted her to be happy here."

I glance over at the house and think about how hard it would be to build it. And where did they live while he was building it? "Wow, that's so romantic. But how does that make it haunted?"

"The stories say his plan was to come here and solitarily fish, and fishing is exactly what he did. Hours and hours he spent out on the water by himself catching fish, and then word spread that he was here. Several of his fellow soldiers followed, as well as some of the immigrants who came in through New Orleans. Over the years, he built a kind of fishing empire down the west coast of Florida and through the Caribbean, selling the fish commercially. He was fair on his prices, and people and restaurateurs respected that more than anything. While others struggled, he thrived."

"A fishing company ... that isn't what I was expecting, but it makes sense." I've seen plenty of fish in the inlet while I've spent time on the dock.

"Yep, and they ended up having three children: two boys and a girl. It should come as no surprise that the oldest boy headed off to World War I and never returned."

"That's sad." An ant crawls onto the blanket to inspect what we're doing, and I swipe it off.

"Rumor has it the wife went a little crazy from losing her son, and shortly after that, her husband left to go fishing with two crew members, and they never came back. Supposedly, she would sit on the dock and watch for her son to come home, and then once her husband went missing, him too. She refused to leave the dock. The middle son had the boathouse built, and that's where she stayed until she died."

I glance down at it. While it looks dated, it doesn't look that dated, and it certainly doesn't look like it's been worn down from years of harsh weather. Someone must have put in a new one at some point.

"What happened to the other two children?"

"I'm not sure about the son, but it's been said the daughter couldn't leave her mother in the state she was in, so she moved just a ways down the river, closer to the gulf, where the town popped up. Eventually the mother died, and no one has lived in the house since. People claim to still see her on the end of the dock holding a lantern to guide them home. That's your ghost."

A lantern. I quickly flip through the last couple of nights in my head to see if anything like this registers. The answer is no. There haven't been any mysterious floating lights on my dock.

"What year did she die?"

"I'm not sure. 1940 something?"

I glance back at the boathouse. Yeah, there is no way that dock and house have been here that long. No one might have lived in the house, but someone was taking care of it. People have still been here over the years, and recently too, as evidenced by the bathtub.

"Wow. Well if she is there, I wonder if there is a way to get rid of her."

Natalie laughs. "Why would you want to do that?"

My eyes get large as I look at her. "Because I live in the boathouse. This isn't creepy or anything."

"But I thought you didn't believe in ghosts," she teases, sitting back up to take a sip of her drink.

"I mean, I know they say seeing is believing, but one can only be told so many times. It's not like I think there's this massive joke being played on me. Everyone says this is a real thing, and just because I don't believe, that doesn't mean it doesn't exist. I just have to wrap my head around this and figure out what's next."

"Well, if you want to stage a coup on your dock, just let me know when, and I'm there." She grins.

7

I can't stop thinking about the ghost.

Several days have gone by since Natalie was here, and every day I feel a little edgier than the last. I've never believed in ghosts, but all of a sudden, I'm now wondering if I was wrong. Which on one hand feels completely preposterous to me, but then on the other I can't help but wonder what if?

It's not that I'm afraid of the ghost; it's more an anxiety about where and what I'll be doing if and when she finally does decide to show herself. Add that to wondering why she hasn't shown herself already, and I'm kind of going crazy. I moved here to be alone, but I don't feel alone anymore. I feel as if there's an invisible person hovering around watching everything I do, which I know is irrational, but I can't help it. Then again, all this worrying over my ghost has helped me keep my mind off of what brought me here, so I guess that's a good thing.

The restorer was here yesterday looking at the windows. He's on the upper-middle-aged side, and he kept looking at me as if I had two heads. Several times he asked me what I was doing here and why, as if it's any of his business. He kept going on and on about how he was shocked that someone would choose to live here. He is someone who grew up in this town, and apparently my house was the one teenagers would try to sneak into to wait for the ghost. He claimed he's seen the ghost of Mrs. Easler more times than he can count, and that was when he started eyeing me even more suspiciously. If Garrett hadn't given him such high praise on quick, efficient work, I would have considered firing him. After that, I decided it would just be best to stay in the boathouse until he finished, and I asked Garrett to follow up with him so I didn't have to. He didn't question me, just said, "No problem."

I get it—I do. People are curious about me as the new owner, but it doesn't matter what I tell them; they'll never understand. I didn't know how legendary this house was, and even if I had known, I don't think it would have mattered. I needed to be free, I loved this home the moment I saw it, and quite frankly, it isn't anyone's business what I'm doing here or why I bought the house. I needed to come here, I need this house, and despite the stories floating around about the home, it needed me too.

"Ryla?" I hear called out. It's Garrett. He mentioned he would be stopping by. The restorer is scheduled to finish today, and I'm so glad. I've been down here hiding for days, and I'm ready to get back into the house.

"On the dock," I yell back.

To get into the boathouse, you have to walk through a screen door, which is open to a small screened-in covered section just next to the boathouse. The only thing enclosed is a picnic table, but it's made a great place for me to work and keep Coco outside, and it's covered, so I'm shaded.

The heavy tread that is so distinctly male makes its way toward me.

"Hi," I say, smiling at him as he comes closer.

"Hey." He smiles back.

Coco shifts so she's standing on the table next to me. She doesn't say hello but bobs her head.

Garrett's wearing his standard work uniform of a Hawthorne polo and construction boots, but today he's wearing khaki shorts. His brown hair looks like he's attempted to style it, but it still stands up all over the place. I would be lying if I said I didn't notice how well the shirtsleeves hug his biceps and the cute dimples that grace his face when he smiles. He really is an attractive guy.

"Still hiding I see," he teases. He doesn't enter the little screened-in area, just stands outside it on the dock.

"Do you blame me? That guy is straight-up obnoxious." I glance up toward the house to see if his truck is gone. It's not.

"Yeah, I'm sorry about that." He rubs the back of his neck. "I didn't expect him to be unprofessional toward you. He may be obnoxious, but on the bright side, your windows are going to look great." He gives me a warm smile, and I raise my hand to block the light and see him better.

The sun is bright today. I saw a sign in the hardware store that said, *Red sky at night, sailor's delight. Red sky in the morning, sailors take warning.* Every morning now, when I wake up, I check the color of the sky. This morning it was glowing yellow.

"He's almost finished?" I ask, more hopeful about him leaving than the windows being completed.

"Not quite. He's going to need one more day."

I let out a groan of disappointment, and he chuckles.

"He's gone for today, but he'll be back in the morning with the rest of the supplies he needs. He says there isn't much wood rot, just a few spots where he'll use an epoxy filler, and a couple need new rails and mutons. For now, he's stripped the paint and the putty and filled in the cracks. With his team, I really think he'll be done after one more day."

"I hope so," I say, deflating and frowning. I'm certain the

pout stretched across my face is a little dramatic, but I'm ready for that guy to go.

"He and I are both in agreement that you should replace the doors. We could repair them, but it's more cost-effective and more weatherproof to just replace and make sure we get a good seal."

"That's good, because I've been looking at doors online, and I found a few that I think would look great." I love the beveled glass, so I found some similar ones that will be perfect.

"Excellent. Send them to me so I can make sure they'll work or see if they can be modified."

"I will." I smile at him.

"You sure you're good down here?" he asks, tilting his head a little. His hands are now resting on his hips.

"I am. I'm working on my website and lining up furniture I want to order, and he hasn't stayed too late. He usually leaves just after lunch, so I have all afternoon to work in the house." I run my hand down Coco's back; she's pleased with the attention.

"Seen anything out of the ordinary worth mentioning to me?" he asks as he looks from her to around the dock and toward the direction where people claim to have seen the light.

"Nope," I reply, popping the P.

"Okay," he draws out, still looking around. He doesn't say anything, but I can see the skepticism layered within the wrinkles between his eyes and in the way his jaw has hardened. "You have my cell phone number if you need anything," he says, probably more for his sake than mine.

"I do. Thanks."

He says goodbye, and I watch as he makes his way back up the dock but then turns to look back at me. I wouldn't necessarily say he's worried about me being down here, more like he doesn't understand why I want to be. Thing is, people not really understanding me—it's been that way my whole life.

I am an individualist. I know this. I always have been. I've never felt the need to apologize for who I am, but at the same time, I've always felt like I've walked through life with people who just don't grasp me. They accept instead of appreciate all that I have to offer, and I've struggled with not feeling insignificant. I know I'm creative, sensitive, emotionally honest, and self-aware, but I'm also very intuitive with others. Whereas it's easy for me to recognize parts of my personality when others may not, I often feel like I'm standing in a crowded room and either not being seen or being judged because of who my family is or who I'm married to. How hard is it to look at someone and acknowledge that they aren't cookie cutter, that they are unique?

Carter used to joke and tell me I would go into hyper mode, not in the physical sense, but in my mind where I worried about how I was perceived. As much as I tried not to, when you're in the spotlight as much as we were, it's hard to not worry about what others think. For years, I've worked on not withholding my true self from others, but over the last couple of months, I just couldn't do it any longer. All of these people who don't know me have never taken the time to see me, not the real me, or they wouldn't have said the things they said or behaved the way they did. My self-conscious spirit had all it could handle and went into overdrive; I just couldn't take it anymore.

I know I've been floating by on survival mode, but I had to escape, had to remove myself from the circulating negativity, if only for my sanity. The thing is, I had finally understood who I was with Carter, and now, I find I'm having to discover who I am all over again. It's harder than I thought it was going to be, because that me was me just about my entire adult life. If I'm not Carter Crest's wife, Chicago socialite, recognized upscale interior designer, who am I?

Should I be doing this alone? Probably not. My family most definitely had something to say about that, but I needed the noise to stop. Has it completely? No, but with each passing day, it is dulling, enough where I can hear my own thoughts and feel myself breathing again, which tells me I am healing. It may be slow, but it's happening.

Maybe it's the sweating from the heat, the steady lapping of the river's water, or the birds singing instead of voices, but it's been a little over two weeks, and the tightness that has been squeezing me has started to loosen. It isn't gone completely, but I don't feel as if I'm going to suffocate under it either.

Now, if only I can get these townsfolk to forget I'm here or have them say to themselves, "Hey, that's cool that someone bought the old Easler house. It's going to be nice to see it restored to its former glory." At least that's what I tell myself as my arms are still shaking from the days and days of pulling wallpaper.

Sand, soak, strip, repeat.

The rooms are coming along nicely, and in a few more days I should be done with stripping all the wallpaper. Even Garrett said he was impressed, and although it was such a small compliment, those words were like life to my soul. But as the days and hours have passed and as I've been lost in my thoughts, I can't help but wonder a little bit more about the family who lived here and why Mrs. Easler felt the need to stay. I also can't help but wonder if I will ever see her, or this supposed floating light so many others have seen. I'm not sure how I will react to seeing a ghost, and the absurdity of me even thinking about this eventually has me calling it a day, finishing a little earlier than I planned.

Cleaning myself up, I decide there's no time like the present to take the neighbor's plate back to her. Earlier, laughter floated across the inlet and through the windows of the house, so as far as I can tell, they are home.

The sun has already moved behind the western tree line, so

although it's not as bright out, the sky is still touched with the warm golden light it started the day with as I walk into the trees that separate our two homes. There's a small path. It's obvious it was once well traveled by the width of it, but now it's overgrown with an excessive amount of foliage. Some I recognize, but most I don't: palmetto bushes, ferns, rhododendrons, and tons of trees, large and small. The path hugs the inlet and leads directly to the house on the point. I find this interesting and can't help but wonder why. Overhead, the buzz of the cicadas rubbing their wings together gets louder, but as annoying as it is, I know soon they will stop.

The house looks nothing like my own. In fact, it reminds me more of what one would expect to find on a river's edge. It's bungalow style, lifted off the ground in case of flooding. It's painted light blue with a wraparound porch, and it has two black rocking chairs facing the water. It's quaint and well kept, and there just past the house is her dock. On the side toward town, she's had an addition built on that looks like a covered gazebo. This must be where she shucks the scallops.

Walking up the steps, I take notice of the little details that show this house is lived in and loved. There are seashells lining the porch banister, there's a wind chime with sea glass hanging in the corner, and there are pots of well-maintained herbs and flowers scattered about and shoes strewn everywhere. The scent of something cooking inside wafts by, and I smile even though nerves have settled into the pit of my stomach. Meeting new people is hard. Throw in the fact that I'm not sure if I'll be recognized or not, and it adds to my level of anxiety.

But I'm here, and I can do this.

Taking in a deep breath, I knock on the door, calling out "Hello" at the same time I exhale. The pounding of little feet gets louder as someone approaches the door, and from behind it I hear June's sweet little voice: "Who is it?"

I love that she knows to not open the door right away. If tourists or people wander up this way seeking out help with the fish or scallops, anyone could be out here.

"It's me, Ryla."

The door swings open, and I grin from ear to ear as I take in the mess she's covered in.

"Hi, Ms. Ryla!" She beams up at me from behind a screen door.

"Well hi there, June. Looks like you're making some magic somewhere." I point to the flour all over her bright pink T-shirt.

She looks down and tries to brush it off. The flour falls to the floor and makes even more of a mess.

"Oh, yeah. Mama and I are making chicken and dumplings. It's my favorite. Did you want to come in?" She opens the door wider, and more of the delicious scent floats my way.

"Sure, if you think your mama won't mind." I peek around her to see if I can spot her.

"Ryla, come on in. I'm back here in the kitchen," she calls out.

Following June through the house, I do my best to not let my decorator's eyes come out and soak up the details. As much as I'd love to take in all the unique particulars, my gaze stays straight ahead until, out of the corner of my eye, I spot a worn and gorgeous quilt.

It's draped over the side of a large, comfortable-looking chair in their family room. It looks hand sewn, and it looks old. Where some of the fabrics might have once been bright and rich with color, they're now dull and probably filled with generations of memories. I love that quilt, and I love that she's kept it all these years. It makes me want to make one of my own.

In the kitchen, I find a woman maybe a few years older than me clinging to the counter and standing on one foot with a medical crutch lying on the floor.

"Mama, let me get that for you." June rushes over and picks it up. Her mother takes it graciously from her and pats her head, and the resemblance between them is so striking I'm momentarily awed. June is the exact mini of her mama, from her skin color and the pale honey of her eyes to the shape of their frames.

"Thanks, my love," she says to her daughter and then turns to me. "You must be Ryla." She gives me the biggest, most welcoming smile. "I'm Willow, and I'm so sorry—I've been meaning to come over and say hello, but as you can tell, I'm a little slower than normal these days." She points toward her foot with the bandage wrapped around it.

"Oh my goodness, no worries. It's so nice to meet you. I just dropped by to say hello and give you the plate back." I move to set it next to the sink. "Thank you for the cornbread—it was incredible and hit the spot," I tell her and then openly stare at the gorgeous hand-painted backsplash tile she has.

"Great! I'm glad you liked it. I've discovered over the years, either you like cornbread or you don't. And if you don't, well, I'm not sure we can be friends." She grins.

"Well, I loved it and would really like a copy of the recipe to make it for my family sometime, so I guess that makes us friends."

We smile at each other, and it's true and genuine. My heart recognizes that I've just found another friend, and it's a wonderful feeling.

"Stay for dinner?" she asks, waving her hand over the mess on the small block kitchen island.

"Only if I can help," I say, feeling excited to be included.

"Yay!" June chimes in. "You're going to love these. They're the best."

We fall into a rhythm of conversation and watching June roll out the dough, slice it up, and toss the dumplings into the pot of chicken, vegetables, and broth. She asks me why Chuluota Springs, and I give her the simple answer of needing a change then ask if she's ever been to Chicago. She knows there's more to my story, but she lets it go for another day. Meanwhile, she tells me her life story and how she's never lived anywhere else, never even thought about it, says this house has been in her family for generations and here almost as long as the Easler house.

"So what happened to your foot?" I ask after dinner is done and June has cleaned up our plates.

"You cannot laugh," she says, shaking her head. "Skin infection from stepping on a scallop shell."

My lips twitch. Oh the irony.

"Seems like it must have been a bad infection."

"You're tellin' me. I got the bright idea to get out there and rake down the shells some since the season is about to start, I step on one the wrong way, and then the next thing I know, I'm waking up with gawd-awful pain shooting up into my leg. It all happened so fast. I should have known better. Shells and skin infections are a common thing."

I glance down at the bandages wrapped tight around her foot and ankle. How inconvenient it must be for her.

"Well, I wouldn't have known any better, so now I do," I tell her.

"Yes, make sure you always wear shoes near the water's edge." She shakes her head as we make our way into the living room. I sit on her navy blue couch, and she takes the adjacent chair to prop her foot up on an ottoman.

"So, I hear my house is haunted," I say, giving June side-eye.

Willow gasps and looks disapprovingly at June. "Tell me you did not say this to her."

"Why not? You talk about it all the time!" she cries out as she sits on the opposite end of the couch next to me with an iPad.

"Maybe so, but that didn't need to be the first thing out of your mouth," Willow scolds.

"It wasn't," she whines.

"It's fine. I've heard it a few other places as well, but I'm still on the fence. I definitely haven't seen anything out of the ordinary." I laugh, but they don't laugh with me. Instead, they both just stare at me. "Oh, come on. Do you really believe there's such a thing as ghosts?"

"Some people see things that aren't supposed to be there, or are they?" Willow shrugs her shoulders.

"Have you seen my ghost?" I ask, almost afraid of her answer.

"Many times," she says confidently.

Silence falls over the living room as I absorb what she's just said. She truly believes she's seen a ghost at my house.

"That just seems so preposterous to me. I mean, in a way I understand. After all, the stories, legends, psychics, and things —well there's a huge market for it, but I guess I've always been one of those who has to see it to believe it, and I never have."

"With individuals like yourself," she says, drawing out her thick Southern accent, thinking about how to best word her statement, "the spirits will only show themselves for one of two reasons: one, they desperately feel the need to tell you something, or two, they like you."

"They will like me." I state this more than form it as a question. My brows pull down in confusion. "What would make a spirit decide all of a sudden that it likes me?"

"Most likely the ghost will feel a connection to you. Can't say what that connection is, but if you see her, I'm sure you'll figure it out."

"Do a lot of ghosts like you? Do you see more than just mine?" I'm curious but still disbelieving.

"I do." She gives me a slow, knowing smile while looking over my shoulder.

8

The average African Grey parrot starts talking anywhere between twelve and eighteen months, but Coco—she's always been above average and said hello for the first time at ten months. Carter had just gotten home from work, I called out hello, and she responded hello as well. Carter came running into the living room where we kept her and we both just stared, delighted and awed. Of course we encouraged her to say it over and over again, which she did, and we rewarded her with treats. That should have been our first indicator that she was going to be a very vocal bird, but we loved it all the same. She talked so much it was like having a third person in our home, and on the nights Carter traveled, she kept me company, just like now.

Which is why last night, after staring at her for an extensive period of time, I had a sinking feeling something was wrong with her. She hadn't uttered a word in hours, and she just sat on the bottom of her cage and stared back at me. So, when we moved to the boathouse, I let her out of her cage and let her sit on the floor next to me. Several times I asked her questions like

"Are you my pretty bird?" and "Is Coco okay?" and all she would answer me was "No."

So, first thing this morning, I called the town vet at the top of the list on the internet search and made an appointment. Their website says they see all kinds of animals from domestic pets to marine rescue, and front and center was a large pelican. If this doctor sees pelicans, he should be able to see Coco too, right?

Pulling up to the veterinarian's office, I find it's an old two-story bungalow-style home that also sits on the river just a few blocks from the main street of town. It's a simple building, painted light gray, and it has the options of a ramp or stairs to get to the main door. Outside it is a white plaque that reads *Chuluota Springs Veterinary Clinic* along with *Dr. Hawthorne*, the office phone number, and the hours they're open. I can't help but wonder if this Hawthorne is also related to Garrett.

A bell rings over the door as we enter. Once inside, I find a nice large waiting room with an older woman sitting behind a desk. It's clear this was once a home and the downstairs has been converted, and my stomach rolls over at why we are here.

"Good morning, dearie," says the smiling woman. "Who might we have here?" She stands to glance at the cage, and I have to fight the lump in my throat and the burning in my nose so I can respond to her.

"This is Coco Chanel. I called earlier to make an appointment."

I called in a full panic with my heart racing out of my chest and tears in my eyes. After everything that's happened over the last couple of months, the thought of no Coco is just not an option.

"Oh, yes. You're new in town and new to us, so I'll need you to fill out this new patient paperwork." She moves to grab a few papers, and the distinct smell of Chanel No. 5 wafts my way. My heart constricts, and I take it as a sign that this was the right veterinarian's office to call.

"Certainly."

With shaky hands, I grab the clipboard, set Coco in the chair next to me instead of on the tile floor that looks like hardwood, and answer all the questions in the packet: her breed, how old she is, what brought us in today, her past veterinarian to obtain Coco's records, etc. My stomach lets off another dull ache as I glance over and again think something might be wrong with her, something that's not fixable. I've lost so much recently, and the thought of losing her too makes me almost seize up with fear.

After I hand the clipboard back and take a seat, I look around the office. It has the typical things one would normally find in a veterinary office: a large fish tank, certificates and news articles framed on one wall, and large canvas pictures of animals I am assuming are patients, but the variety is large. There's a pelican, a dolphin, a manatee, a monkey, a dog, a cat, and a sea turtle.

How amazing would it be to be swimming in the ocean and a giant sea turtle slides up next to you?

"Ms. Corcell," the woman calls, moving out from behind her desk and breaking me from my thoughts. "If you'll follow me this way." She smiles warmly, and right next to her stands a German Shepherd with a prosthetic foot. The shock of seeing the artificial limb momentarily pulls me from my anxiety as I think how amazing it is that they can help animals this way too.

I pick up Coco's cage, and together we make our way down the hall to the farther of two rooms. My guess is that this was previously a bedroom or an office as it's rather large and next to the back door of the home.

We settle in, and I set her cage on top of the exam table.

"He'll be right in to see you two." She smiles again, both her and the dog giving off encouraging vibes. I smile back, but it's one hundred percent fake.

The door closes, and I wrap my arms around the cage as if to feel like I'm hugging her. I lose myself a little as an unwanted tear falls down my face.

Emotions are a strange thing. I know life moves on, and I have been. Just like one foot in front of the other, it's been one day after the other, but this feels like five steps back. Having Coco keeps me from feeling so alone, so deserted, and the idea of not having her ... well, I just can't go there.

Staring out the window, I see the river is darker in color than by my house, but it's still just as beautiful. It's not as smooth as there are endless ripples racing but seeming to go nowhere, and I find it calming as it is a presence I've found to be reassuring and unexpected. The waters are rougher here; it matches my mood, and I like that. Glancing to the left, I notice we're close enough for me to see the openness of the gulf. I knew my new home was close, but I forgot we were that close.

Behind the house, across the riverfront street, there's a short dock. On the last post there's a large pelican standing so still he could be a statue. I wonder if he was once a patient too or if he's just passing by. Tied up beneath the large bird is a nice white and navy boat.

The door opens behind me, and I turn to find the doctor coming into the room instead of a technician. His head is down, he's looking at Coco's chart, and all I can see is dark brown hair and black scrubs. They look like they were cut and sewn just for this guy's tall and very athletic build.

"Good morning," he says.

My jaw drops open, and pinpricks of awareness float across my skin as I recognize his deep voice and then his face as he lifts it to look at me. He's not wearing sunglasses, but that doesn't matter, because with the shape of his jaw, the bridge of his nose, the broad width of his shoulders, and the way his hair looks windblown even though he's in an office, I'd know it was him anywhere.

"You," I say quietly, shocked and somewhat flustered as to how to proceed.

"You," he says, his face dropping into a scowl as his spine straightens, taking him to his full height. He towers over me by at least ten inches, his size more appropriate for the NFL, and whereas before when I was standing on the dock, I felt like I had the upper hand, now I feel small and awkward.

Never in a million years would I have thought the rude guy at my home was a veterinarian, but here he is, unexpected piercing blue eyes burning me up with unfamiliarity and disdain. Have I thought of him over the last couple of weeks? Yes, but more along the lines of wondering if I would run into him in town or if he planned on coming back to my house to yell at me more. Blinking, I try to clear the lingering tears to hide my vulnerability, but I know the moment he sees them, because the scowl disappears, smoothing out the muscles around his face, leaving behind just the frown.

Clearing his throat, he breaks eye contact, lays Coco's chart down on the counter next to the sink, moves to wash his hands, and then stands next to the examination table. Ignoring me, he goes into professional mode and bends down to take a look at Coco, who's sitting not on her perch but on the bottom of her travel cage. It makes sense to me now why he stared at her longer than normal that day on my dock—all animals are patients to him, and he was assessing her.

"Tell me what's going on," he says calmly, ignoring the elephant in the room while his eyes scan every bit of her.

"Something's wrong with her." My voice has a rough edge to it. I'm trying so hard to not show how much anxiety I have in front of this guy, but I'm on the verge, and I'm certain he can hear it. "She won't talk to me, and yesterday she kept falling off her perch, so she sat at the bottom of the cage. She fell so bad this morning—in her larger cage, not this travel one—and I'm worried she bruised her breast bone." I can still hear the sound of her feathers and the thud. It sounded so awful, and all I can compare it to is that it would be similar to me falling from a one-story roof.

His eyes flit to mine briefly—they're the color of the sky on a cloudless winter day—and my insides tighten in a twisty way, then they move back to her. He doesn't move while he and Coco stare at each other.

"Hello, Coco." His voice is soothing, and although it's meant for her, I feel it melt down into my bones, loosening the tension in my muscles.

"Hello," she says back.

The corner of his mouth twitches with a smile as he moves to open her cage. Sticking his hand in flat, he brushes it against her belly, and she steps up onto him. As he pulls her out, she wobbles, I gasp, and he gently wraps his other hand across her back to steady her.

He raises her so they look at each other eye to eye, and he says, "You're a very pretty bird, Coco."

"Pretty bird. Pretty bird," she repeats, and my heart flips with joy to see her talking to him and not saying just the word no. "You also seem to have a nice vocabulary." He grins, and I'm momentarily awestruck by this other side of him. The angry man who was attempting to order me off my own property is gone, and in his place is one who appears so gentle and kind I'm having whiplash.

"Do you know what's wrong with her?" I ask, voice just barely over a whisper.

His smile drops, and his eyes come back to mine. Well, never mind. Of the two of us in the room with him, it's easy to see who he prefers and who he doesn't. Maybe that's why he's a veterinarian—his social skills just aren't there.

"I might have an idea, but I'm going to ask you a few questions and then run some blood work."

Keeping her on his hand, he moves over the table, just in case she falls, and begins examining her one spot at a time, starting with one of her wings. He pulls it out and spreads the feathers. I'm not sure what he's looking for, but I'm glad he is looking, and I feel better already. Next he runs his hand across her chest, both sides, and down the middle, locating something as his head tilts, and then he shifts around to her back.

"She does have a bump on her chest. It's essentially the same thing as when a child knocks their head on something and they get a bump. It'll go down soon enough. How long has her imbalance been going on?" He lifts her tail feathers and looks at her backside then moves to her beak.

"I thought I noticed it two days ago, definitely yesterday, and then this morning when she fell." Guilt that I should have recognized it sooner washes through me. She was getting sick, and I was oblivious.

I start breathing harder. Whether or not he notices, he doesn't say anything, just keeps on going.

"How old is she?" He rubs under her neck then behind her head, where he gives her a massage. Coco dangles her head and half closes her eyes; I can only imagine how good that feels.

"She's four."

Flashes of my wedding night with Carter run through my mind. Baby Coco was just the sweetest, and honestly Carter was too. He was so proud to give her to me. He'd had someone sneak into our hotel suite with her giant cage and her inside. He'd bought a ton of toys, and instead of having this grand romantic night, we ate delivery pizza because we were starving, drank a bottle of champagne, and played with her on the floor. African

Grey parrots live forty to sixty years, and he said he couldn't think of anything more perfect than her to start our life together with.

"Any eggs recently?" he asks while looking at her feet, breaking me from my thoughts.

"No, but I read that can happen due to climate changes, so I wouldn't be surprised if we had one soon."

He thinks about this for a moment.

"Do you think she had a seizure this morning?" he asks, stroking her feathers.

"A seizure?" I ask back, alarmed, and his hand stops moving as he again looks over at me.

My chin quivers as I try to fight the fear that something is terribly wrong with her, and he stands up straight, pulling Coco against his chest.

He and I stare at each other, me wordlessly begging him to fix her and make her better, and him...well, who knows what he is thinking. Silence fills the room until Coco decides she's had enough.

"Ryla. Ryla. Ryla." *Squawk.*

My gaze instantly drops to her, and I step closer and rub my hand over her head. "It's okay," I say to soothe her, and she pushes her body in my direction.

She's staring at me, almost at eye level as she's up against his chest, and that's when I realize how close I'm standing to him as well. Salt water, sandalwood, and a hint of coconut drift my way from his skin. It smells so different from Carter's cologne; I'd forgotten how unique someone else can be. Taking a step back, I keep my eyes on her, hoping he doesn't see the flush of heat hitting my cheeks from my embarrassment.

"So, Ryla is your name?" he asks, raising Coco again to get a better look at her chest. He's looking to see if she's plucking her feathers, which is common when birds are bored or need more exercise or time with their owners. It's something I watch for too, but so far she's never plucked her feathers.

"Yes." Suddenly, I feel childish for not giving it to him before.

Gently flipping Coco around, he pets her head and her back again then returns her to her cage. She immediately turns and stares at him.

"How long have you been in town?" he asks, picking the chart back up and making notes. I watch as his large hand scratches illegible words on the paper. I'm struck by his hands and how gentle and tender he was with her, and I realize how long it's been since someone was tender like that with me.

"A couple of weeks now, almost three." I slide her cage closer to me, and he pauses, noticing the movement, but doesn't look up at me.

"What are you feeding her?"

"Food I brought with us. It's what she's always eaten."

"From where? Brand?" He keeps his head down, waiting for my answer.

"Not sure, and a pet store in Chicago. They keep large coolers in the back and you just scoop it out. You pay by weight."

"That's where you're from?" He glances up at me again. I'm certain this question really doesn't have to do with Coco, more with his curiosity about me owning the house, but I don't care—I'd tell him anything if it meant he would tell me what's wrong with her.

"Yes."

"Hmm," he mumbles as he thinks, breaking eye contact. "Is the food seed or pellets? Have you given her any vegetables recently?"

"Seed-pellet blend with some dried fruits. Millet seed balls for treats, and just some extra lettuce I had lying around." His blue eyes flash to mine. He knows what lettuce I'm talking about even though he doesn't acknowledge it. "She used to get a premade vegetable blend from the pet store too, but we haven't had any here."

He drops his gaze back to the chart. "How about her activity level or weight—any changes?"

"Not that I've noticed."

Tucking the chart under his arm, he looks at the cage then back at me. "Okay. I'm going to take her in the back and draw some blood—"

"How do you do that?" I squeeze the cage tighter.

"Through a vein under her wing," he answers directly, his eyes wandering over my face.

"Will it hurt her?" Distress clearly radiates off of me.

His expression softens. "No, she'll be fine." He gives me a small, closed-mouth, reassuring smile. A smile.

"Okay," I tell him, looking at Coco and feeling an almost unbearable ache in my chest.

"Ryla." My eyes jump to his as my insides again do that tighten twisty thing. "She's going to be fine."

I know I'm probably overreacting and should listen to what he says, but I just can't calm down. I can't. "Do you know what's wrong with her?" My eyes burn as they try to fill with tears. I'm almost begging for him to tell me something.

"Not just yet, but I have a hunch," he says, shifting his weight so his hip is leaning against the counter away from me.

"Tell me."

"After I saw her on your dock, I refreshed myself on her breed, just in case, as I haven't seen an African Grey in several years. Twenty to twenty-five percent of their diet needs to be vegetables and berries. They can quickly and easily get a calcium deficiency."

My stomach drops.

"Oh. I should have known that. Carter always got her food." Guilt swamps me as I realize I wasn't properly taking care of her.

"Carter?" he asks.

Not really sure what to say about Carter or what to call him, I just shake my head, and he seems to understand. I also hope he's not the kind of guy to stay current on celebrity gossip—the names Rylie and Carter are recognizable to many. And Ryla isn't that far from the truth.

"Got it. Well, I'm going to finish her exam in the back. We'll return in just a bit."

"Thank you," I reply softly, and with his lips pinched, he moves from the sink, gently picks up the cage, nods his head, and leaves.

The door closes behind him, and silence settles around me. Just like that, the little love of my life disappears with enemy number one. Well, maybe after today he won't be our enemy. After all, he admitted to thinking about us after the dock incident and took the time to educate himself on African Greys. An enemy wouldn't do that, only someone thoughtful and intelligent. He took a proactive stance just in case, and for that I will be forever grateful.

9

Walking into Dockside Diner, I would be lying if I said I wasn't salivating at the idea of getting another one of those iced coffees and a muffin. When Natalie texted earlier and asked if I wanted to meet, I answered yes without hesitation. It took a few days, but I am happy and confident that Coco is now back to her normal chatty social self, and with the new air conditioners—upstairs and down—finally being installed today, there is no need for me to be around and in the way.

A bell rings over the door as I walk into the cafe. The smell of baked goods assaults my senses, and my stomach squeals with delight. I find Natalie sitting in a booth that overlooks the river walk. She beat me here, and she's laughing at whatever she sees on my face. I'm certain it's a combination of longing and utter bliss. Given that the morning rush has come and gone, the diner is fairly empty, and I'm glad. I wonder if she picked this time purposefully for me. Leaning against the booth and talking to her is the girl who served me last time.

"I know what that face means." Natalie grins at me.

"That I hope this place serves their coffee through an IV

drip?" I say to both of them as I slip into the booth across from her.

She laughs again, but if that was such a thing, I'd be the first to try it. Every night in the early morning hours, that noisy bird is still making itself known. I thought for sure by now it would have found a mate and flown off into the sunset, but nope, like clockwork it shows up, leaving me exhausted the next day. I'm hopeful this is a seasonal thing and not a year-round issue.

"Ryla, did you meet Corrie last time you were here?" Natalie waves her hand toward the waitress. Just like last time, her brown hair is pulled back, but instead of a blue gingham apron, today's is lime green, and her lipstick is bright pink.

"Ryla." She whispers my name, her eyes landing on me and growing as large as the cups behind the counter. She was suspicious before, but now that she's heard my name, well the similar one, it just confirms what she already knows.

"Sort of, but not really." I hold my hand out to her, and with clear words, I say, "I'm *Ryla Corcell*. It's nice to meet you." My brows rise just a bit in a knowing gesture that silently implies to keep it on the down-low. It's not that I think I can stay anonymous forever, but for right now, to me, it's still important to not have my cover blown.

"Corcell," she whispers again, nodding with me, understanding, and then she snaps out of it and shakes my hand in return. "Corrie. So nice to meet you too."

The awed expression on her face continues to grow as her smile slowly stretches all the way to her eyes and she hunches up her shoulders in excitement. She looks down at her hand that was just in mine then reaches for the outside edges of her waitress apron, where she squeezes. Bless her, she's trying so hard to act normal, and I can't help but smile along with her. Natalie watches us. She's always known who I am, but she's getting a front-row seat to what happens when I'm recognized.

"Cor, knock it off," Natalie says to her.

"I can't help it. This is so exciting," she whispers. "I've never met a celebrity before."

"And you aren't right now either," she says, protective of me. "Ryla is just a woman who's moved to a new town to start over. Got it?"

"Got it," she says, nodding aggressively, but the happiness pouring off of her could fill this entire place.

"I mean it, Corrie," Natalie says.

"I hear you loud and clear, and I'm sorry I'm doing such a poor job at containing my excitement, but Rylie Crest—"

"Corcell," I remind her as the bell over the door rings again and another customer enters.

"Right, Ryla Corcell is sitting in my diner. Gah. Don't worry." She leans over and puts her hand on my arm. Then, as if realizing what she's done, she rips it off. "I won't tell anyone."

"Thank you," I tell her. "I look forward to being friends with you."

Her smile at my words is so large and infectious I can't help but smile back.

"Iced con leche and hummingbird muffin?" she asks, remembering my order from a few weeks ago.

"Sounds perfect."

Quietly squealing one more time, she heads off behind the counter, the extra pep in her step noticeable. I smile on the inside, a twinge of hope following her. Even though she knows who I am, maybe that's all right. After all, two people now do, and I guess it's just a matter of time before everyone does.

"Sorry about that. Corrie's sweet, and I've known her since I moved here. She won't say anything."

"I'm not worried. It is what it is and I am who I am, right?"

"Yes, but still."

Today, Natalie's hair is pulled up into a messy bun. She has on just a tiny bit of makeup and large gold hoop earrings. Every time I see her, she looks beautiful, and she's so kind I can't help but wonder what her story is. I know she moved here not too long ago, but that's about it. As far as I know, she isn't married or dating anyone.

"This place is super cute," I tell her as I look around.

Large windows line the wall that faces the river. The light shining into the cafe is warm but not stifling. The floors are terrazzo, speckled with black and gold, and the booth seats and stools that run around the diner counter are emerald green. Behind it, the wall is a chalkboard where you can find the menu, and all around the cafe are black and white pictures of the town and its people.

"It really is. I know I'm biased because I live here, but there really isn't a cuter place around. They do a great job decorating for each holiday, and once a month, they have live music."

"That's great."

"Yeah. Dockside Diner is a staple in this town. I can't imagine it not being here." She smiles as she looks around.

"So, how's work been?" I ask. "Sell any houses lately?"

"Actually, yes. Summer is always busy since kids are out of school and big moves usually happen then. But, I don't want to talk about me—I want to talk about you."

"Me?" I point to myself. "Why?"

"Word on the street is you met Jake," Natalie says slyly.

Heat creeps up into my cheeks, and my gaze narrows at her sitting across the booth from me. She looks like the cat who got the cream. "How do you know that?"

"Mr. Frier saw you leaving his office with Coco. He was on his way to his lunchtime euchre card game in the park. Chuluota Springs is a small town. Not much stays private around here, believe me, and as you are all anyone can talk about, that was prime gossip."

"Me? Why?" I ask again, alarmed.

"Because you bought the old Easler house. That's like the most exciting thing to happen around here since … well, forever."

Natalie laughs at the horrified look on my face. I mean I kind of figured people would be curious, but to call it the most exciting makes me wonder if hordes of people are going to start showing up to say hello. Maybe I should have Garrett work on the driveway gate. It probably wouldn't hurt to have that functioning; then again, any outsider can just walk through the trees or pull up from the river.

"Natalie," I quietly groan.

"You did buy the town founder's home." She giggles. "Should have thought twice about that one."

It just never even occurred to me that this home would be more than it is. An abandoned old run-down river house. And I didn't know it was previously owned by someone named Easler, I wouldn't have been able to look it up anyway. I look out the window to see if anyone is spying on us. There isn't, of course, just people randomly walking by the window, but I can't suppress the urge to want to sink down in the booth to hide. Back in Chicago, I got used to the feeling of being followed and watched. Here, I haven't given it much thought, but maybe I should.

"Yeah, maybe I should've thought more about that. In my mind, a small town means not a lot of people. I think I thought I was moving to more of a solitary-type situation. My sister keeps telling me I'm being a recluse. I tell her I'm not, but maybe she's right."

She laughs. "Small towns are anything but solitary. Think boring, so the only way people entertain themselves is to be all up in each other's business. And you're too young to be a recluse —I won't let you be."

I groan again and drop my head into my hands on the table.

"How's the house coming along?" she asks.

I pick my head back up and smile at her. I could talk about this house all day long. "Great. Garrett has so many men doing so many different things, and I think it will all come together much sooner than I anticipated. The new doors are being installed today, and they're working on the outside, repairing the columns, pressure washing, fixing damaged spots, and removing loose paint, stuff like that. She's in her ugly phase now, but she's going to look beautiful in the end."

"I can't wait to see it all done."

"Me either. It will also be nice to have furniture." I laugh.

She laughs too. "There is that. Is Coco okay?"

"She is. She'll be fine, just needed some vitamins." The relief I felt when Jake brought her back into the room and told me she was going to be all right ... it shifted something inside me, something toward her, myself, and him too.

"Oh, that's good. I was worried for you. But tell me, what did you think of Jake?" She wiggles her brows, and I roll my eyes.

"It wasn't actually the first time I met him," I tell her as I grab the napkin in front of me and start tearing it.

Surprise crosses her face, and she leans back against her seat. She doesn't say anything, but she doesn't need to. I know she's just waiting for an explanation.

"He came by on his boat a couple of weeks ago, yelled at me about being on private property, said I needed to leave. I had been about to toss some lettuce into the water for Jessie, so he technically caught me red-handed."

She gasps. "Tell me you didn't."

"I didn't. He very disapprovingly informed me that it's illegal, which I didn't know." Shifting, I cross my legs, and my foot involuntarily starts bouncing.

"It is," she says, very sternly.

"So imagine my horror when I show up to the vet with Coco and there he is. Let's just say I wasn't the kindest to him at my house." A twinge of guilt flickers through my chest.

She laughs again while I continue murdering my napkin. Talking about him for some reason makes me antsy.

"I'm sure he's just fine. Was probably good for someone to give him a little lip—the people around here think the Hawthorne brothers walk on water. But, from what I know about Jake, he's good people. I know his brothers Garrett and Bauer a little bit more as Bauer's a lawyer and handles real estate law, probate, things of that nature, and well, you know Garrett. But as I mentioned, it's a small town, so gossip travels."

"I thought about Garrett when I saw the last name outside Jake's practice. Lawyer, veterinarian, general contractor—seems like an ambitious family. What do the parents do?"

"His mother stayed at home to raise them, but his dad is a lawyer too, and he used to be the town mayor, so their family is a little like royalty around here. These days they're retired and traveling around in their RV, but they'll be back here in the winter months. Their family has deep roots in this town. This will always be home."

"Are there more of them, or just the three brothers?"

"I'm told they have a younger brother named Hayes who went to live in Denver. Apparently the mountains always called to him more than the beach. Hayes leaving made him a bit of a black sheep, but good for him for following his dreams, right?"

"Absolutely. So, what's Jake's deal?" I almost cringe asking. Really, I don't care to know about this guy, or any guy for that matter, so I'm not sure why I did.

"Why are you interested?" She beams at me suspiciously.

"Ah, that's a hard no." I lean farther back into the booth to put a little bit of distance between us. It wasn't intentional; I just reactively moved. "I'm not interested in anyone, nor do I plan to be. I've just only met a handful of people, and unfortunately he was one of them," I say, but somehow that feels wrong. I am grateful to him for being so kind to Coco and helping her.

"Well, since you're not interested or anything," she teases, "I'll tell you what I know. Rumor has it, his fiancée left him standing at the altar."

"Like at the physical altar? She didn't end it before it got to that?" I'm horrified for him.

"Nope. Obviously with his dad being the former mayor and all, Jake is beloved. Like I said, all of them are, so you can imagine how packed the church was and how scandalous it became as the minutes ticked by while everyone was inside waiting and she never showed. Even the bridesmaids had made their way down the aisle and were in place."

My jaw drops.

"That's awful." A pang of sadness for him hits me, and I feel the betrayal deeply.

Then again, maybe it was a blessing. I'm sure it's a tossup as to which is worse, being left at the altar or being left during the marriage, but if I had my vote, it would be the altar.

"Right? I mean how humiliating."

She says this without comprehending my situation and how humiliating things were for me. I find I suddenly feel a little protective of this guy, for no reason at all other than we both share being part of an unfortunate, emotionally taxing experience.

"As for him getting on to you about Jessie, well you already know he's a veterinarian, but he also volunteers with the state river park and with different manatee rescue groups. Chuluota Springs is home to a lot of manatees come winter time, so he stays pretty busy helping those who've been injured, mainly by boats, and need to be rescued and rehabilitated."

"That's pretty selfless of him."

"Yeah, he's always doing these kinds of things. In a couple of weeks, after the season has started, he'll start organizing a shoreline cleanup. One halfway through the season, and then another at the end. You should come with us."

"Like a volunteer thing?" I glance out the window and look at the river. The thought of it being polluted in such a way turns my stomach.

"Yep. The season brings in all kinds of tourists. Some stay in town, but most travel just for the day. Boats all go out together, and whether it's all friends or a collection of families, it doesn't really matter—litter inevitably gets in the water and washes up to the shoreline. Sandwich wrappers, plastic bottles, chip bags, all kinds of stuff. Things blow off the boats when they're cruising around, and as thankful as we are for the increase in businesses, this is still work that needs to be done."

"Sounds good to me. I've always believed strongly in community service, so you can count me in."

"Great! I'll sign you up once he releases the plan and then text over the details."

"What are y'all talking about?" Corrie asks as she slides into the booth next to Natalie with all of our goodies. My eyes land on what I know is mine, and my stomach growls, rejoicing.

"Jake's shoreline cleanup," she replies, reaching for her coffee and inhaling deeply. On top there is a cute design in the foam of the milk. "Mmm, butter rum coffee, my favorite."

Corrie looks at me. "Like I told you before, my mother doesn't believe in an espresso machine, but what she does is flavored coffees. We have amaretto to butterscotch to vanilla nut and everything in between. And, yes, you should totally come to the cleanup day. We provide coffee and pastries in the morning to get everyone fired up and ready to go."

"Really? That's amazing. I'm definitely in for the cleanup, and next time I'll have to try one of those flavors."

"You totally should," Natalie chimes in. "I'm not sure how they roast these beans, but the coffee is heavenly."

"Well, if it's anything like this iced coffee, I'm certain I'll love it." I grin at them both.

Corrie's smile grows, and then it slowly slips off her face. Looking around, she leans closer to me across the table and quietly says, "For the record, I didn't believe any of the things all those people said about you."

Just like that, my heart sinks, and so does my appetite.

"Oh, well that might make you the only one," I tell her.

$\mathcal{I}$t's been a week since I met Natalie and Corrie at the cafe. I'd like to say I left feeling empowered to be out and making new friends, but I didn't feel that way at all. I tried to shake off Corrie's words, but they sank into my fragile heart and left me alternating between feeling exposed and angry. So, I did what I've done since I arrived: I threw myself into another project in the house, hoping to exhaust myself to the point of not caring. This round is the floors.

After reading article after article on how to refinish wood floors, I decided to ask Garrett to come spend part of the day with me, and we both agreed mine needed a full refinishing. If the home was newer, we probably could have gotten away with just a screening where we sand off the thin top layer then coat with polyurethane, but since the home is older, we could not. The floors are worn down from spills, drops, shifting furniture, grit tracks from shoes, marks that look like claws from pets, the weather, and, well, age.

What I learned is if you don't move the sander at just the right pace and in just the right pattern, it can remove more wood in one area than another and make the floor uneven. So, he brought in a certified sander and finisher. Together we removed the baseboards from all the rooms and moved the few pieces of furniture and the painting from the library, and I tied up the curtains. While the professionals used the sander, I went behind them and filled in any holes or gouges with wood filler and worked on removing the loose dust with a shop vacuum and a dry mop, which is how Jake finds me.

Just like last time, I don't hear him approach. Granted, the shop vacuum is super loud, but then there he is, standing tall, looming in the doorway with inquisitive eyes as they scan over me and around the room.

"You scared me!" I yell as I clutch my chest then bend down to turn off the vacuum. Dust particles float in the air between us, and behind me in the kitchen, Coco calls out "Ryla!" at my sudden outburst.

"Sorry, I did knock." He smiles at me apologetically while pointing with his thumb over his shoulder to the back door. His smile briefly stuns me as it's such a contrast to how I picture him in my mind from the morning on the dock, and I drop my gaze. Today, he's wearing light blue shorts, a gray T-shirt, and flip-flops. He looks casual and nice at the same time. I would be lying if I said I hadn't thought of him over the last couple of days, especially since Natalie told me his story. Then again, I only know six people here: Natalie, Jake, Willow, June, Corrie, and Garrett. It's not like I have much else to think about, and I refuse to think about what brought me here.

"I can't imagine why I didn't hear you," I respond jokingly, moving the vacuum out of the way and kicking the cord to the side.

"Sorry to just come by unannounced, but I made this for Coco and thought I would drop it off." He holds up a white paper bag, the top of which has been neatly folded over.

"What is it?" I wipe my hands across my shorts and push up

the protective eyewear Garrett is forcing me to wear. I'm certain I'm a filthy mess, but he doesn't seem to have noticed.

He walks over, hands the bag to me, and takes a step back, and then I watch as he again looks around the back half of the house, at each of the visible rooms. There's an odd expression on his face, and his brows furrow when his eyes catch sight of the black plastic covering the piano legs that are sticking out under a large drop cloth. Garrett and I talked about moving the piano outside during the renovation of the floors, but in the end we decided not to for fear of throwing it off key somehow or possibly getting it weather damaged. Instead, we wrapped it in cellophane and covered it with cloth.

"Odd, right?" I say to him. "I was under the impression that the house hasn't been lived in for a really long time, but when I got here, there were several things left behind from the previous owner. I can't imagine why they didn't want these things, and that piano is a very expensive one. I looked it up."

He carefully walks past me and stops in the doorway of what I've decided is going to remain the parlor room or be known as the living room. He studies the piano like it's the oddest thing he's ever seen then turns to look at me. The blue of his eyes against his tan skin catches me off guard, causing the pit of my stomach to unexpectedly swirl.

"Do you know how to play?" he asks.

"As a matter of fact, I do. The piano wasn't mentioned during the purchase, so it was a complete surprise the day the realtor showed me the home. She didn't disclose the items left behind, but they were a welcome revelation, to say the least."

"Well that's something." He seems pleased for me, as he follows me into the kitchen.

"Natalie Wood was my realtor. She was great to work with." I chuckle on the inside like I do every time I say her name. Placing the bag on the counter, I open it. Inside is a large sealed plastic bag filled with a frozen chopped-up vegetable-berry blend.

"Ah. She's somehow found her way to be the go-to person for the pricier properties around town," he says while looking around the kitchen.

It's bright today. I didn't realize how dirty the windows were until the restorer repaired and cleaned them. Now the natural light of the sun pours in. I look up from the bag to Jake, and the light is so bright I can see freckles dusted across his nose and upper cheeks.

"Somehow found her way?" I say incredulously. "Maybe it's because she worked hard to get there," I tell him, supporting my friend.

He holds his hands up in defense. "I meant nothing by that. Yes, she does work hard—I just meant of all the realtors, she's found herself in a great spot."

I watch his face for any type of mocking, but he sounds sincere, so I let it go. Looking back down at the bag, I know Coco is going to love this.

"This is great. Thank you." I turn to look at him, and his hands are now in his pockets.

"I called a friend of mine who specializes in exotic birds, and he told me what to make for her. This should last you a while. You can keep it in the freezer, and when you run out ..." He pulls his hand out of his pocket and looks down at the folded piece of paper he's holding, then hands it to me. "This is what the mixture is. Next time you can just make it yourself."

I glance at the recipe and then at him. "Dr. Hawthorne—"

He laughs, cutting me off. "Please, just call me Jake."

The sound of him laughing is lovely, and I find this side of him is completely contradictory to the brooding, scowling guy I first met. Again the smile is back, and it unnerves me. *What is wrong with me?*

"Jake." His name rolls off my tongue easier than it should. "Thank you."

He gives me another smile, and I think maybe he's not so bad after all.

Grabbing a bowl from a drying towel next to the sink, I take it and the blend to Coco's new large glass aviary. Behind her, through the window, the river is gleaming and crystal blue-green. Coco's watching me as I approach, and she fluffs her wings. I realize Jake is standing behind me, and they're staring at each other.

"Hello, Coco," he says, gracing her with one of his nice smiles too.

"Hello," she says back, and his smile stretches more to a grin.

He holds up a hand and points to me—"Ryla"—and then turns his finger toward himself. "Jake. My name is Jake."

Coco just yells out "Ryla!" again, and I beam at my sweet girl.

"Well, you're definitely looking better today," he says, pleased, and Coco nods her head up and down.

I move to open the aviary door, and she spots the new food blend and squawks, "Hungry!"

"How many words does she know?" he asks as I place the bowl inside. She moves to it and immediately begins inspecting.

"I'm not sure. I read once that they can learn up to 1500 words and have the intelligence of a five-year-old and the emotions of a two-year-old. They are spot-on about her acting like a two-year-old."

His brows rise. "That's pretty impressive. What made you decide to get her?" He reaches his hand in and runs it down her back. She shifts toward him for more petting while keeping her face in the bowl.

"She was a gift."

By the look on his face, he's remembering when I said

Carter's name. He nods in understanding then takes a step back from Coco and me. "So, I see you've been busy," he says as he again puts his hands in his pockets and glances around at all the dust on the floors and the bare walls.

"Yes. This has been pretty time-consuming. Last week, I finally finished stripping the wallpaper, and yesterday the contractors finished the third round of sanding with an 80-grit pad. Both the upstairs and the downstairs have been done, so now it's just me trying to remove all the dust so we can get ready to apply the sealer and the stain."

He leans down and swipes his fingers through the dust and over the smooth floor.

"Do you need any help?" he asks almost tentatively as he stands back up.

"Why? Are you offering?" I tilt my head to look up at him, curious and teasing at the same time. Pieces of his dark hair have fallen onto his forehead. Cheese and crackers, he is good-looking.

"If you need it, yes." His earnestness sweeps through me, along with the heat of a blush. I can't imagine what it would be like to have him here in my home every day. He's slightly intimidating, and I'm not sure why.

"Thank you. I really appreciate it, but I think we've got it. Garrett has been great, but if something comes up, I'll let you know."

He nods as his gaze travels over my face, and a long pause settles between us. I wouldn't say it's an uncomfortable pause, but I feel like he's using some secret power to peek into the weak spots of my full-body armor. I feel exposed to him for no reason at all, and it's a strange sensation.

"Garrett treating you okay?" he asks gently.

"He is."

"Good." He hesitates. "I really am sorry about how we first met. I didn't know, and I shouldn't have assumed."

"No worries," I tell him, and I mean it. "And I'm sorry too. I'm not generally a rude person, and I was to you," I say, eating crow.

He presses his lips together and gives me a closed-mouth smile. Just like that, we've both moved on from bad first impressions.

"People have always taken an interest in the property," he says, hoping I'll understand, and I do.

"It's a beautiful home with a beautiful view." I shrug and look past him through the far window, down toward the boathouse and the river. I do love the river.

He turns and follows my line of sight. "So, have you seen it yet?" he asks as he takes a step away from me and moves to the window.

"Seen what?" I reply, knowing exactly what he's asking. Moving to stand next to him, I glance at the new potted plant on the porch outside the window, a pineapple plant. I'm so excited to grow one. The most I've ever grown is herbs on the balcony of the Chicago condo.

"The light at night on the dock," he says. It's then that I notice the smell of him over the dust-filled air: coconut, sandalwood, and laundry detergent.

I want to lean over and breathe him in, but instead I say, "Nope," with a pop to the P.

"But you've heard about the ghost?" He glances down at me.

"Ghost—I love how you say that like it's singular. I've been hearing there are ghosts all over town." I move away from him and back to the counter where I seal up Coco's new food. The bag is cold; it's been kept in the freezer, so I'll have to take it down to the boathouse.

"Yeah, there is that too. Do you think it's true?" He turns to face me with curiosity stamped on his face.

"Before moving here, I would have told you absolutely not. But now ..." I shrug. "One story here and there is questionable, but this town, from what I've heard, is apparently very haunted, and everyone I've met has told me about the ghost of Mrs. Easler. Why? Do you think it's not true?" I lean against the counter.

"That's a tough one. In general, I believe in facts, science. I think there is an explanation for everything. However, there are quite a few strange occurrences around here that can't be explained. I know about Mrs. Easler—everyone does. I've seen the light, the light at the end of the dock. I grew up here, and she's been a part of the stories for decades."

He's seen her light. Shock sweeps through me as I think back to Willow's words and how a ghost will show themselves when they want to connect. Why him? Why not me?

"Well, I haven't yet. I have explored the dock to try to come up with what it might be from. There has to be something that causes a random light, right?"

One side of his mouth quirks up, and small wrinkles form on the outside corners of his eyes. "Give it time. I'm sure she'll make her appearance soon."

"I hope not," I tell him, and he smiles.

Together we walk through the rooms downstairs. I excitedly give him a tour and point out different features of the home and all the changes I want to make. We talk about what decoration ideas I have, and he offers a few suggestions and an estimate of how long the overall project might take. It's nice to be able to share my enthusiasm for this house with someone, and he seems to genuinely want to hear it.

The last space we enter is the living room. Whereas he just paused in the doorway and looked at the piano when he arrived, this time he walks over, and my insides clench as I watch him pick up the lone picture frame lying on top of it. I want to tell him not to touch it, but it's too late and that would be rude. After all, it is sitting right out in the open, and I feel the blood drain from my face.

He stares down at the six-by-eight gilded frame for several heavy seconds then looks back up at me. His gaze is incredulous and tinted with his own anger on my behalf, and although appreciated, it's not wanted.

"Is this for real?" He holds up the frame.

I know I should've left it in the box, the box I never should have brought, but lately I've felt more loss than anger. I needed to remind myself why my life is the way it is, so this morning I pulled it out. It was never meant for another person's eyes, because in every way, it sums up the biggest failure of my life, one I'm trying to move on from.

I don't answer him; I just swallow. I mean really there's nothing to say and the words won't come. I nod my head once and his anger immediately turns to pity. I'm so embarrassed and instantly dragged back to that moment and the events that led up to it.

It was early last November, in Chicago, and although the temperature was mild, the winds were fierce. Last minute, I changed my plans for the day and decided to walk to one of our newer boutique hotels to sort out how many Christmas trees and what kind of decorations I needed to order. Walking into the hotel lobby, I stopped in the middle to get a 360 degree look at the vision I'd brought to life, and I couldn't help but feel a pride so deep and rewarding. It had taken seven months for us to acquire the space, strip it, redesign it, and execute it. Mixed with the dark blue and gold colors of the Crest Hotel logo, I modernized their appearance to keep the rich and opulent look of a luxury hotel. It was gorgeous and featured in magazines around the world.

"Mrs. Crest." A woman from behind the registration counter

called my name to grab my attention. I'd seen her several times over the last couple of weeks as I'd been finishing a few final details, though other than pleasantries, we'd never really spoken.

"Good morning." I approached her smiling. She glanced down and began typing on her computer. "And how are you today?" I asked, looking over the setup behind the counter and at her black uniform, which was pristine.

"I am lovely, thank you for asking." She swiped a room key, put it in an envelope, and slid it across the counter to me, leaving her hand on the top. When she lifted her eyes to mine, there was worry, regret, and determination in them as she put on the fakest smile I had ever seen, her dark red lipstick glaring as she very quietly said, "It's wonderful you are here to meet your husband for lunch today."

I jerked back, shocked. "My husband?"

"Why, yes." She lowered her voice. "He's been here every day for the last two weeks, just working *so* hard." There was an edge to her words, and tingles started firing in my brain as the air in my lungs seized. Her stare was so deliberate. Not once had Carter mentioned to me that he'd been repeatedly visiting this property. To my knowledge, he'd spent his days at the corporate office in the Loop.

"Two weeks you say?" I asked, just barely able to get the words out.

She sympathetically nodded.

Looking down at the key, she slid her fingers away, and as if on autopilot, I reached up and pulled it to me.

Rarely are there moments so poignant and definitive. She knew and I knew that what was going to happen in the next five minutes was going to change the course of my life.

Taking a deep breath, I found the courage to look up at her one more time. There were tiny lines creasing her forehead between her brows, but her lips pressed together in a closed-mouth smile. To anyone passing by, our conversation looked like any other, but we both knew the implications that would occur, especially due to her lack of discretion.

Sliding the key into my pants pocket, I laid my bag on the counter and pulled out a business card. "If I don't see you again, please let me know if I can be of *any* assistance to you. My email address is on the card."

She took it and, with pity and regret, said, "Thank you. The Lake Michigan suite."

I gave her a nod and turned for the elevators. With each step, my heart pounded harder in my chest, and breathing became almost impossible as my adrenaline was spiking.

The Lake Michigan suite was my favorite of the rooms in the hotel. It is one level below the penthouse and shares the floor with the Michigan Avenue suite. Both overlook the lake, but one shows the north side of Chicago, including Lincoln Park, and the other shows the south side from Navy Pier over Millennium Park to Soldier Stadium.

Once in the elevator, I scanned my key and pressed the button. It shot up quickly and arrived, and the doors opened.

I'd like to say the entire scenario was a complete shock to me, but as I stood outside the closed door, I wasn't so sure. For a split second, I told myself it didn't matter, I had a really good life with Carter, and although he'd suddenly felt the need to warm others' beds, he still chose me to spend his life with. Then again, has this been happening all along? But then I thought, *That's great for him, but is this the life I want to live? For the rest of my life?* Deep down in my soul, I knew the answer was no, it wasn't. I deserved better.

The suite is 1500 square feet, so when I scanned the key over the pad and the lock unclicked, no one heard me enter. Very quietly, I slipped in, praying more than anything that he really was here alone and working, but as I saw the trail of discarded clothes, my dreams of forever and happily ever after evaporated and my heart broke.

My Carter.

My husband.

How could he?

Walking toward the bedroom on the thick plush carpet, I heard him; I would recognize the sounds he made anywhere. It was the feminine ones I didn't. With my heart pounding, my ears throbbing, and my eyes blurring, I stopped in the doorway to see what my heart already knew. There under the covers— covers I'd picked out—was my husband breaking his vows and me in the process.

I cleared my throat, they both froze, and Carter's head whipped around to find me leaning against the doorframe with my arms crossed.

"Ryla ..." he sputtered.

Our eyes stayed locked onto each other as I watched shock, fear, and then anger move over his face. Seriously, what did he have to be angry about?

Spinning around, I began making my way to the door, and he called my name again. I had seen enough. I mean what could he possibly have to say to me in this moment to make any of it okay?

"Ryla, wait," he said for the third time.

I stopped. I don't know why, but I did. At this point, I didn't owe him anything else, but something somewhere deep down in me had to hear what he needed to say. Turning, I found him scrambling from the bed, completely naked, condom still in place, and my stomach rolled over.

I was going to be sick.

"Who told you?" he all but demanded, coming to stand in front of me and finally covering himself with his hands.

"Who told me? That's what you have to say to me right now? Unbelievable."

It was then I thought to glance over at his partner, and I couldn't help but gasp. As if one heartbreak wasn't bad enough, I now had two. I saw the pale skin covered with freckles I'd stared at most of my life, wild auburn hair, and familiar green eyes.

"How long?" I asked her, and she turned her head to the side to dismiss me. There was my answer: long enough.

I wasn't sure which betrayal hurt me more, my husband or seeing his infidelity with one of my oldest friends. After all, she was a bridesmaid in our wedding. How utterly and completely cliche.

Needing to get out of there before I embarrassed myself with a massive emotional breakdown, I very calmly turned and walked to the door.

"Wait! We need to talk to you," he said.

We?

But I didn't wait. I walked out of their room, out of the hotel, and turned right. I walked through the fierce wind until it got dark, until my feet and my heart couldn't take any more, and then made my way home. I had no idea if he would be there or not. My guess was no, but what I did find on the hall table next to the bowl where we dropped our keys was a stapled packet of papers and a purple Post-it over my favorite wedding photo of us that said, *I want a divorce.*

I guess he changed his mind. He wasn't choosing me to spend his life with after all.

11

———

$\mathcal{D}$isconcerted with a strong mix of melancholy.

That's how I feel today after Jake saw the Post-it still stuck to our wedding photo. I never removed it, instead I left it there for those moments when I wanted to mourn. It was a stark and immediate reminder of why I shouldn't, even though I did.

Embarrassing isn't a strong enough word, and every time I replay the shocked expression on his face, my insides want to wither up and die. I've never shown or told anyone about that note. It was humiliating and cruel in the worst possible way, and as an outsider, I can only imagine how he's judging me, wondering what type of person Carter was for me to marry. But that's the thing—Carter was never cruel, at least not until that moment.

Two steps forward, five steps back. Jake felt those four little words, I saw a visceral reaction in the way his head jerked in shock, and in turn I felt them too, all over again. Obviously the sting isn't as sharp as it was the first time, but that didn't change the fact that I felt like I'd been ripped open to be raw, exposed, and pushed back to square one. Jake left immediately after this, with my closed off demeanor he could tell I was done with our social call. He didn't ask for an explanation or even a piece of the story, not that I would have given him one. And it didn't even matter that I've been thriving here in this new place doing a new thing, as a result, I haven't left my house in days.

The timing of the floors project couldn't have been more perfect, and other than the contractor and Garrett, who stopped by to inspect our progress, I haven't had to be social with anyone else. Grocery delivery is an amazing thing.

Seal the wood. Stain the wood. Hide from reality.

I'm sure he, like most would, is wondering why I kept it, and honestly I don't have an answer. At first I couldn't look at it. Every time I did, my breath would catch and a fresh slice would whip through and wound my heart, but then after a while, I couldn't stop staring at it, couldn't stop wondering about it. Was he in a rush when he wrote it? Was this his plan all along, or did he think of it at the last minute? I've traced the letters, watched them blur through the endless tears I've shed, and used them to fuel the direction of my life. It's why I got it out of the box, a reminder on the same day I met Carter five years ago that my life will go on. It is continuing on, and I'm proud of how far I've come.

There are conflicting views about how many stages of grief there are when it comes to a divorce. Some say seven, some say five, and well, as I wanted to get past this as quickly as possible, I chose to go with five: denial, anger, bargaining, depression, and acceptance. While there are a ton of infidelity and divorce statistics out there, the one I looked for the most was how many never saw it coming. I think this is what I have the hardest time with, because I didn't. I never saw it coming. There were no tells in his behavior, his personality, or even how he looked at me. Apparently, it's 26 percent of men and only 14 percent of women. That means 86 percent of women knew it was coming, felt it deep in their bones. I wonder if that makes the whole process easier or harder. I guess I'll never know.

That morning, the day I found him with Veronica, he had snuggled up behind me in bed after our alarm went off and told me he couldn't wait for the day to be over so we could be together again. I've replayed every minute and scene, examining the things he said, how he moved, the way he looked, and I can't come up with anything, not one thing. We snuggled, we took a shower, we got dressed for work, we had breakfast together, and he kissed me outside our building while telling me to have a good day.

Where were the tells? I still can't find them, and that makes me feel stupid, naive. He played me, and in the most horrible way.

The denial phase lasted all of twenty-four hours. After I found the Post-it, I had the worst night's sleep I've ever had. I ended up at my parents' front door at the crack of dawn, distraught in a way that made me not recognize myself, and I told them what happened. While I said repeatedly, "I can't believe this is happening to me," that quickly turned into an anger so fierce I saw red for days thinking of the betrayal carried out by my friend and my husband.

How can someone who claims to love you go behind your back and be that person? Where was the respect? I was at least owed that from the person who took the leap of faith into marriage with me. If he knew he didn't want to be with me, knew he was having feelings for her, he should have stepped up and ended it way before then. But then again, he was sure ready to go with those divorce papers. I never asked him, but I always wondered when he had them drawn up. How long had he known?

The next morning, while I was at my parents' house losing myself, Carter and Veronica stepped out onto Michigan Ave hand in hand. There was zero consideration for me and how bad the backlash from the media would be. The media loves scandals from the rich and famous, and instead of finding out the true story, some spun it where he was the villain, breaking my poor heart, while others reported that she was saving him because I was ruining him and the Crest family name.

Me ruining him.

What a joke.

My life as I knew it was over. No husband, no lifelong friend, and ultimately, no job. Although I run my own company, all of my projects at that time were contracted with Crest Hotels, and there was certainly no way I could go back and finish them. Of course they understood, paid me for what I had completed, and then hired one of my recommendations to finish what I had started.

Two days later, movers came in and packed up his belongings. While some rooms were left exactly the same, others like his office were wiped clean. It was as if he had never even been there, and it was while sitting in the middle of the floor in the empty room that I skipped over bargaining and went straight to depression.

Along with the loss of my husband, I lost my best friend. That's what he was to me, and it broke me to realize that wasn't what I was to him.

For me, cheating is a dealbreaker. There's no coming back from it, no reconciliation, just sucking up my pride, knowing I deserve better, and that's it. But I wasn't ready to move on. My heart hadn't caught up with my brain, I still loved him, and I certainly was far from being ready for acceptance. I needed to grieve. I needed to forgive myself and get to the point where I realized this wasn't my fault and there was nothing wrong with me. Moving on implied I was ready to let go of what I had, and how could I be? When I said forever, I meant it.

But then again, what are words anyway? Spoken, they are just a collection of sounds strung together to invoke a feeling, lost in the wind easily enough, and on paper they're just letters formed to create a unit of language that can be conveniently washed away, which is what I'm doing now—washing them away.

As I lie on my stomach on the edge of the dock, the sky is cloudy, as if it recognizes my poor damaged heart, and the tide is high. The tips of my hair are dragging in the water, and with my small Tiffany's notebook in front of me, one by one, I remove each Post-it Carter gave me, stick it to my finger, and then drop it into the river to wash the words away. It's so easy too. Once the paper becomes saturated, I just swipe my thumb over the wet surface, and the letters erase themselves as if they never even existed.

It's a strange feeling to literally wipe away memories. Part of me wonders if I should stop, but then I ask myself why? Why do I need to keep these? What is the purpose? By pulling each one out and reliving the words, I am allowing myself that memory, acknowledging the time we shared, and then wiping it away to allow for new space and new memories. I'm letting go.

The first Post-it Carter gave me was found the morning after we met, on the front door of my friend's summer home. It said, "Ryla, I really hope you'll call me ... Carter," and his phone number was written underneath. I remember feeling so excited and so hopeful. I hugged that note, hung it up on my refrigerator when I got home so I could see it whenever I passed, and—obviously—I did call him.

From there, Post-its became our thing. He would leave them in random places for me to find, and he always said the most endearing and loving things. Well, occasionally there were a few dirty things he wanted to do to me when he got home, but mostly they were little notes about me and our life together. I cherished these notes. They were priceless to me, which is why I kept them in a notebook with the date and, if applicable, a note about what we were doing and where we were to go along with it. My intentions were to one day show our kids this sentimental piece of us. How foolish I was.

This current Post-it is standard yellow, and written on it is, *Remember that time we road-tripped to the wineries in southern Michigan? You wore a light blue dress, and I felt like the luckiest guy in the world.*

Just another ruined memory and a lie. Maybe he did mean that at the time, but as he so effortlessly changed his mind, I realize it's all fleeting too.

As I swirl the paper around, a warm breeze blows across the water, and I watch as the words loosen, bleed off, and float away.

Beneath my fingers, the tall river grass is visible. It sways back and forth, and, ominously, it's too similar to a hand waving the words goodbye. The river absorbs my tears, tears that feel good to let free. So many moments, so many final goodbyes.

Goodbye, *Meet me at Gibson's steakhouse at seven o'clock* for our first Valentine's together.

Goodbye, *Your smile makes my heart beat harder.*

Goodbye, three Post-its of 25 things he loves about me for my 25th birthday.

And goodbye, *Please make me the happiest man in the world. Marry me?*

I guess it is only fitting that he would ask for a divorce this way too, but with him knowing how much all of his Post-its meant to me over the years, I've yet to understand why he took this away from me too. I get it, he didn't want to be with me anymore, but did he have to tarnish our time together and our love in such a callous way?

It makes me question if he ever truly did love me.

Months went by after he moved out. Chicago had one of the

worst winters it had had in decades, and with the city being snowed in, the paparazzi were ferocious with their need to find content on our failed marriage to exploit, exaggerate, and distort.

They camped outside my condo building. They followed me anywhere I went, and every picture they posted made me look like a madwoman. They also followed Carter and Veronica and made her look like an angel. I can't imagine a time in life where things could be worse than that, and as much as I love Chicago, I needed to leave. I felt unable to move on with my life, and I so desperately needed to.

The water ripples against my hand, and it evokes a soothing feeling in me. It does that; I don't know why. Maybe it's the steady temperature, maybe it's the sounds it makes, or maybe it's the view. I love looking out over the clear waters and allowing it to hypnotize me.

Lake Michigan was visible from our condo and there's the river that runs through the middle of downtown, but I can't say I ever gave either much thought. Having a water view or being near water never mattered to me before, so I'm not sure why it does now. I just know this river calls to me, and I'm happy this is where I chose to be.

"What are you doing?" comes from behind, startling me.

Quickly wiping my face, I turn and see June standing there watching me. I was so lost in thought I didn't even hear her approach.

That's a good question—what am I doing?

Washing away years of lies.

Erasing memories and moments from my past.

Silently pouring my heart out to the river and allowing it to take away my sorrows.

Saying goodbye.

Shifting to the last phase and giving in to acceptance.

Soaking in the beauty that is around me.

Letting go.

"Nothing much," I tell her.

Coco, who is sitting in her travel cage next to me, stares at June like she is an intruder. It might seem strange to most that I brought her out here with me to witness this, but she's my moral support, and she was there with him too.

"You aren't littering into the river, are you? Because if you are, my mama will not be happy with you." She places her hands on her hips and glares at me.

I grin at her. "No, I'm not littering." I point to the pile of soggy Post-its so she can see I'm stacking them up.

Her forehead wrinkles in confusion. "Grown-ups are weird."

"Yeah, we can be." I turn to sit up, brush off my clothes, and push my wet hair away from my face.

"My mama wanted me to ask you if you'd like to come over and visit for a while. She said to tell you she made a fresh pitcher of sweet tea, and she used her special sun tea vodka."

Sun tea vodka ... never heard of it.

"How can I say no to that?" Just like that, the emotional turmoil I've been struggling with releases its grip, and I feel like I can breathe. Finally.

One deep breath in and one long-overdue exhale out.

I'm ready.

I know I'll never accept the way Carter ended things or what has happened since, but this week, after Jake seeing that Post-it and the releasing of the memories I've held on to so tightly, I do feel a shift in myself that is more peaceful, calm, less lonely. The mental and physical exhaustion I've struggled with for months ... it feels like it's time to rest, time to heal. It finally feels like it's time. I've made it through. I'm okay, and I smile to myself because, for the first time, I know when I speak those words to someone, I'll mean it.

12

$\mathcal{A}$fter cleaning myself up, I grab a bottle of wine I had delivered in my most recent grocery order and take it to dinner. Just like last time, when the front door opens, I am embraced by the delicious scent of food.

"It smells so good in here," I tell June as she flings open the screen door for me to come in. It smacks a painted rock that's used as a doorstop, and I smile to myself.

"Yep, Mama decided to make fried chicken. Just wait until you taste it—dee-lih-shuss," she says exaggeratedly.

"Hey, Ryla," Willow calls out from behind her, open and friendly, just what I so desperately need. She's wiping her hands across a waist apron as she walks into the hallway toward us.

"Your boot is off!" I blurt out, excited for her.

She glances down at her slipper-covered foot then shakes it out in front of me. "Yep, just in time for the season to start tomorrow. I can't believe it's already here."

I noticed on the walk over that the dock has been cleaned up and decorated. There are potted flowers, chairs set up for waiting guests, and a new sign under the awning explaining the pricing.

"Does it get that busy?" I ask her as June runs off and leaves us, and we shift into the small foyer.

"So busy. Believe it or not, I make most of our annual income over the next three months. Just you wait, boats will be lined up outside the dock and floating in your inlet waiting for their turn."

"Well, that's great for you." She literally works from home, and the people come to her. Sounds like a good gig to me. I kick my shoes off.

"You say that now." She chuckles. "But eventually you will want your solitude back. The river gets busy, the town is busy, and it's just crowded everywhere." She shakes her head. "Come on back." She gestures backward. "Dinner is almost ready." Turning around, she makes her way into the kitchen.

"Thank you for the invite—the company is much needed tonight," I tell her, not making eye contact.

On the stove she has a large cast iron Dutch oven filled halfway with oil. She pulls an apron off a hook and hands it to me to put on, and I set the bottle of wine down next to the sink.

"I saw you earlier on the dock, and then again later, so I sent June over. You all right?" she asks, concern laced in her eyes.

I think about her question as she turns back to the counter, picks up a piece of chicken, and drops it into a brown paper bag. She hands me the bag and motions for me to shake.

As I nod my head, it's with the same clarity I found on the dock that I realize I am. I shift my shoulders and notice the weight I've been carrying around feels lighter. I feel lighter. I still feel sad, but then again, today was an emotionally taxing day. "I think so," I tell her, and as she studies me, she can see I mean it.

Eye to eye, we look at each other in understanding. I don't need to say more, and she approves of what she sees in my expression. Her eyes quickly drift over my shoulder to something, and then she turns to the bag she's made for herself and we begin shaking. I glance back to see what caught her eye, but there's nothing there.

"Sounds like we need to celebrate," she says, nodding toward the wine.

"And we will be with all this fried chicken." I look at the plate she's already fried up, and it looks golden, crispy, and incredible. My stomach growls.

"Fried chicken, fried okra since the oil was already hot, and yellow corn."

"I might have to move in," I declare, and she laughs. I've never had fried okra, but I can't imagine it doesn't taste incredible. To me, Willow seems like the kind of person where it doesn't matter what she makes—it's going to be amazing.

"Well, I was thinking more about that bottle of wine you brought. The wine opener is in that drawer over there." She points to the one next to the refrigerator. "And if anyone is moving, it's us to you. What are you going to do with that big house?" she asks as she takes the bag from me and drops the few pieces of chicken into the oil.

"Not sure yet, but it's coming right along on the inside. You sure you want this now? I hear there's some sun tea vodka."

"I say wine now, and we'll drink that next." She smiles at me, and I smile back. It's going to be one of those kinds of nights.

I find the wine opener and remove the cork. "I was thinking of heading into town tomorrow to look for some paint colors." I glance at her, and her brows rise. I've actually wanted to look at paint colors all week. I just couldn't bring myself to go, but after today, I feel ready.

"Tomorrow is not the best day. The festival starts, and the streets will be blocked off." She moves to the cabinet, pulls out two glasses, and sets them down in front of me.

"Oh, that's right. Natalie mentioned something about it, asked me if I wanted to go."

"You should. You should see your new town all decked out in its finest. June and I will make our way over at some point, and there's a parade at eleven and tons of great food." She picks up a large slotted spoon and rolls the chicken over.

My heart sinks a little. I have always loved festivals and street fairs, one of my favorites being the Old Town Art Fair. There's something about the atmosphere of being outside with beautiful weather and happy people not in a rush to get somewhere.

"I don't know," I tell her. The thought that I might be recognized and the commotion that would ensue because of it is almost too much of a deterrent.

"You'll be fine," she says assuredly.

But I'm not so sure. At just the idea of all those people surrounding me, anxiety rears its head and my chest starts to tighten.

"Do you know who I am?" I ask her quietly as I pour the wine.

She stops what she's doing and turns to look at me, like really look at me. I can't tell if she does know or not, and I find that I hope she does. I want her to know. Maybe it's because I feel like I'm somehow hiding or lying to her, or maybe it's because keeping it a secret and not really opening up makes me feel more alone than I am.

"You're Ryla, and all I need to know is what you tell me," she says assuredly.

"Unfortunately, not everyone thinks the way you do." I pick up my glass and take a sip.

"What they think doesn't matter."

"They will sneak onto your property to get pictures of me. They will come to your door and offer you money for any type of information about me that you'll provide them. They will hover and invade, and we'll lose our peace here."

"Is June in danger?" she asks, tension moving over her facial features as if her safety hadn't occurred to her.

"No. Absolutely not. Vultures they might be, but there's no threat to her or you."

She considers what I'm saying, the grease popping in the pot in front of her. "Well then ..." She shrugs. "It's a good thing I know how to use my shotgun, and if we need to fire it off a few times a day, we will."

I can't help but laugh at her bluntness. My guess is the city reporters would near mess their pants at being fired at.

Over the next several hours, I tell her my story, and she opens up about hers. Fortunately, she has never heard of me. Crest Hotels, yes, but not Carter and me. She laughs and tells me she has zero time for gossip fodder and would never waste her money on tabloid magazines. I might shed a few tears over this. Did I have friends in the city? Yes, but once I became married to Carter, they mostly became acquaintances. Ivy has always been my friend and confidant, but Ivy isn't here. I didn't realize how much I needed people, and it feels so good to be able to talk about my life and not be prejudged as if they already know us or me based on something they read or saw on television.

As for Willow, she was never married to June's father. He always had plans for leaving Chuluota Springs, and she didn't. This was her home, and when the opportunity arose, he left and never looked back. There's something about having had your heart broken by someone you went all in with that creates a kinship between two people, this thread that connects damaged hearts with a profound understanding and sews them up together. It's as if a little piece of the burden is shared, and with it comes relief. Tonight, Willow and I are stitched together.

It's dark out by the time we both decide to call it a night. There's only a slight mugginess of humidity clinging to the air as gentle breezes drift up off the water. The clouds from earlier have receded, exposing the moon and the stars, and I find it pleasant, just like my soul. There's a calmness that comes with letting go, and I know I'm going to sleep well tonight.

Using the flashlight feature on my phone, I begin to make my way down the path that leads back toward my house. I'm not sure what compels me to look up, but I do, and that's when I see it. Shock and adrenaline burn through me like a wildfire, and I swear my heart stops beating.

There, off in the distance where my dock should be, is a yellow glowing light.

"It can't be," I mutter, walking a few more paces forward. Shadows, shrubs, and trees block my vision so, very carefully, I move off the path and make my way to the muddy water's edge.

If I hadn't been told about the light, I probably wouldn't have thought much of it. A reflection, a solar-powered bulb, an illusion—it could be anything, but something way down in the pit of my stomach tells me it's none of those things. After living on the dock for the last six weeks, I know it like the back of my hand, and I know there is nothing that could be producing that strong of a glow. It's not in the middle, it's on the opposite side of the dock from the boathouse, but still, it's there, and I know without a doubt I'm staring at the ghost light of Mrs. Easler.

"Well, what do I do now?" I whisper to myself.

Not being one to scare easily, I find my insides are a mixture of fear, curiosity, and awe. It's not like I think I'm in any danger; it's just knowing that the light isn't supposed to be there. It's defying reality—well, the reality I thought I knew.

Creeping my way back to the path, I resume making my way home with my attention divided equally between not tripping over anything and the light that doesn't seem to flicker at all. As I cut into my yard, call me crazy, but I think it's shining brighter.

I slowly move down the dock, the boards creaking with my

weight as I come to the intersection at the end: left to the boathouse, right to the light.

Facing the light, I stare at the finite details of an old hurricane lantern that I can just barely make out. It's simple really. It's rectangular and all glass except for the edges, the base, and the top. There's a curved handle, but no one is holding it. It's somewhat transparent—I can see the trees behind it—but the large candle inside burns so bright I have to squint.

How can this be?

It isn't floating high, maybe about chest level, but the entire scene before me is so odd. My brain is trying to reconcile what it is seeing with what it knows, and as impossible as I would have thought this to be, there it is, proof, right in front of me.

Feeling a surge of intrigue and braveness, I take a step closer. The light seems to flare brighter just for a second as it hangs suspended in midair, and as I reach my hand forward, it disappears.

Poof.

Gone.

Blackness surrounds me, and although it isn't cold outside, a chill runs straight down my spine.

13

———

How does one get a good night's sleep after seeing something so extraordinary, unexplainable, and, in many ways, frightening? Well let me tell you, they don't. I thought I was going to have the best night's sleep ever, but of course I didn't, and it wasn't even because of the loud bird.

It's not that at any point in time I feared for my life; it was just that knowing there was a possibility Mrs. Easler was lingering outside my door was unsettling. Half the night I lay there trying to convince myself I hadn't really seen what I saw, and the other half I stared at the doorknob just waiting for it to turn and open. I know it was just a light, but if what everyone says is true and it is her light, this means Mrs. Easler can't be far behind, right?

I think about how, when the light went out, the cicadas stopped whirring, the tree frogs went silent, the birds refused to call to each other, and Coco's feathers seemed to ruffle and stay ruffled. It was a solid answer to my question of whether or not she was gone—she wasn't. It's as if even Coco knew or felt something in the air as well, and she was on guard for if or when something might happen.

So of course, after another terrible night's sleep, while I was lying there wide awake and fully alert taking in every single noise I heard and shadow I saw, I decided it was time to move out of the boathouse and into the main house. It's not as if I'd accumulated a lot of belongings, so after four trips using my laundry basket, the transition was done. Although I haven't started on the renovations for the upstairs yet, aside from the floors, I went ahead and moved into the master bedroom, and next time I talk to Garrett, I'll have him bring in the mini refrigerator to use until the kitchen is done.

The bedroom is large, and like the kitchen and eating nook, which it's directly over, it's very bright. The morning sun pours into the room, warming it, so I know the windows in the bedrooms facing the river will need darkening shades. As for the doors, which lead to an outside balcony, I'll have to think about it. There is something calming about still being able to see and hear the river, even if it's just through the small window panes or by the crack of the door. The view of the dock is also obstructed, which means if Mrs. Easler returns, I won't be able to see it.

I ended up caving and texting Natalie just as the sun was starting to rise, saying I'd go to the festival with her. I'm not sure if it's because Willow talked me into it or if I was wanting to get away from the house, but either way, I was ready to go at 10:30 when she picked me up by boat. She claimed this way I have no way of backing out or leaving early, and she's probably right.

"Good morning!" Natalie calls out from the inlet, waving and smiling from ear to ear.

The thickness of the summer morning air clings to my skin as I jog across the yard and down the dock to meet her. In typical Natalie beach chic Southern fashion, she's wearing a yellow sundress with brightly painted dangly beaded earrings and gold flip-flops. She looks beautiful, and for the life of me, I don't understand why she's still single.

"It's so strange for you to pick me up this way," I say as I climb on board and laugh.

"You'll get used to it. My guess is it won't be long before you buy your own boat once you see how easy it is to get around, especially downtown." She grins at me.

She's not wrong. While exploring the little town, I noticed most of the places I would want or need to go are on the river with boat parking: the grocery store, the hardware store, the little town, and a few restaurants.

"I suppose," I tell her, thinking she might be onto something. It's not like I can't afford a small one.

She puts the boat in drive, and we slowly pull out of the inlet. I glance toward Willow's and see June running across the yard and waving. Of course I stand and wave back dramatically as if in a movie.

"I'll see you later!" I call out.

"Bye, Ms. Ryla!" she answers. Such a sweet little girl.

It's then I look back at the dock, my dock. It looks so ordinary, like any other dock you'd see anywhere else: faded brown, weather-beaten, warped wood. Only, I know it's not like others. Even so, I can't help but think that even if the haunting had been disclosed during the purchase as is required in some states, I still would have bought it.

"So, what changed your mind?" Natalie asks, glancing at me as I shove the edge of my large sun hat under my legs to keep it from flying off the boat.

"Willow told me I should go, said I would love all the food." I twist my hair at the base of my neck, securing the ends under the strap of my dress. I should have brought a hair tie.

"The food is my favorite part. Just you wait, I'll have you so stuffed on scallops you won't be able to eat for two days." She smiles over at me with a knowing look.

"Sounds good to me. I've never met a scallop I haven't liked." I laugh as I settle into the seat to enjoy the ride.

This is the first time I've traveled the river, and I'm giddy and greedy as I take in as many details as I can. The stretch near my house isn't too wide, but it's passable and safe enough for boaters, kayakers, and people floating in inner tubes at the same time. The water is still clear blue-green, and the swaying grass can be seen underneath. Small houses line the riverbank, each one eclectic and charming, and then about half a mile down, there's a sign that says, *Tubers Exit Here.* How fun would it be to float the river?

"Where do people rent the tubes?" I ask, genuinely curious. I've never floated in an inner tube before.

"At the state park just up the river. They have trams that take people three miles north, and then they let you out. It takes about two hours to float it."

"Sounds lovely. I'll have to take my sister when she comes to visit." Ivy may be a fashionista, but she's also adventurous and would love to just float by.

"Any plans for her to come yet?" she asks, tucking the loose hair blowing around her face behind her ears.

"No, but once the house is more occupiable, I'll invite her down." The thought of seeing Ivy has me longing for her. It's been six weeks since I left Chicago and saw my family.

"I look forward to meeting her. We'll have to plan something fun when she comes."

I've thought about this too. Maybe I'll have a girls' night at my house and invite Natalie, Corrie, and Willow. I want her to love it here like I do, and I also want her to see that I'm doing okay.

Eventually, the river opens wide, and the color of the water darkens as it deepens. We pass a few motels, a resort, and a few smaller marinas then come up to the town on the left. All in all, it took maybe 15 minutes to get here, about the same amount of time as driving.

There are boats everywhere. Big ones, small ones, pontoons, speedboats, sailboats—you name it, one can be found.

"Are you sure there will be somewhere to park today?" I ask, looking at the very congested marina in front of us. She's focused and seems to know right where she is going.

"Yep. This is Corrie's family boat, and they have their own spot at the marina. Trust me, trying to find a place to park a car today would be worse, but the marina runs a taxi service, so even if the public docking is full, you just give them a call, anchor up, and someone zips out to pick you up."

"That's convenient and so nice of them to let you borrow it."

She nods her head as she slows to a near crawl, weaving her way through the anchored vessels. As we get closer, the hum from the noise of the crowd grows, and I stare at the endless number of little white-tented booths lined up and down the river walk. There are people everywhere, and my stomach turns uneasily as it fills with nerves. I'm glad I brought a large floppy hat and big sunglasses to cover me. I don't think I'll be recognized, but the what-if still makes me unsure.

"They are nice. Last year, I helped out in the diner during the festival. Corrie needs the help first thing when they open, so I've been up and working since six. People are so excited for the festival, coming in droves at the crack of dawn to make sure they get parking and first dibs on booth items. It's just easier for me to zip over and pick you up this way."

"Wow! You've been here since six? Does she need any more help?" *Please say no. Please say no.* The thought of actually having to talk to people has my stomach pulling into knots.

"No, she's got coverage the rest of the day, which is why I'm here with you." She glances over and smiles. "First thing in the morning, it's hard for her to get the baking done and man the walkup window and the customers inside. She has two wait-resses on staff, but on mornings like this one, she needs a third."

She slowly slips into her targeted spot, and a teenage boy runs over to meet us and grab the tie-up rope from Natalie. Once the front rope and the back are secure, we hop off and make our way up to the street.

"You're going to love the festival. It's so much fun." She grins at me while grabbing my arm and squeezing it tight.

"If you say so. If you've seen one, you've seen them all, right?" I tease, grinning widely back.

Turns out, this festival is nothing like I have ever seen before. Yes, we have the Taste of Chicago and smaller neighborhood festivals, but this one is themed with a caricature of a happy scallop jumping out of its shell, and even though the sun is beating down with all its force, it's as if the whole state and then some is here.

"Wow, this is crazy!" I say to Natalie as I take in all the activity. The streets are packed with people, and booth after booth lines both sides of Main Street, the river walk, and the smaller side streets that connect the blocks across town.

"I told you it's a big deal. You'd know this if you left your house more and joined us for breakfast or lunch sometime. The signs on each light pole advertising the festival have been there for weeks."

I look at the ornamental light poles lining the street. Each one does have a dark teal announcement flag with the logo, the festival title in white, and the dates. The flag is super cute, and I imagine the town swaps them out seasonally, like for the Fourth of July and Christmas.

I don't respond to her comment about me not leaving the house, just humming in acknowledgment. She and Corrie have invited me out a few times, and as nice as it feels for them to include me, they know why I'm apprehensive. Maybe next time I'll just invite them over to my place instead.

"I guess I have seen them, I just wasn't expecting all this. It's incredible. I'm so happy for the town."

"Most of the festivals in Florida are in the winter since it's so nice outside. This is one of the few you'll find in the summer, and it draws people from all over the state. Just wait until we get to the food tents—I hope you're hungry."

Come to think of it, I am.

Slowly, we walk down the street, passing each booth, taking in all the local arts and crafts. Natalie knows so many people, and where I had been hoping we would blend into the crowd, unfortunately we don't. True to her word, she lets me be invisible, and instead of her introducing me, I wander into the booth in front of us. I have no doubt that since I'm walking with her, people know who I am—the one who bought the house—but I'm left alone, and I appreciate it.

Eventually we make our way past the "kids' sanctuary" of activities and to the waterfront park hosting the food vendors.

Turning a baffled look to Natalie, I tell her, "I don't understand."

There is only one normal food tent announcing corndogs, turkey legs, and fried elephant ears. The rest are all small, very individualized, and serving seafood.

"Yeah, the festival committee only allows the one outsider, and that's really for kids and those who are allergic to shellfish. The rest are meant to enjoy the reason for the season and are by the locals. Many of the vendors are from restaurants in the area, and some are just individuals passionate about cooking. Plus, they're all being judged, kind of like pies at the state fair. It's who serves the tastiest scallops." She rubs her hands together excitedly.

Walking by the vendors, I see there are many choices:

various grilled scallop salads; fried, grilled, or blackened scallop tacos; seared scallops with bacon and oranges; scallop ceviche; scallop chowder and other soups; scallop po-boys; baked scallop au gratin; spice-crusted scallops; bay scallop fritto misto; scallop pastas; scallop sliders—the list goes on and on. There's even a tent promoting scallop ice cream. Some might say when in Rome to that one, but I'll pass.

"So where should we start?" Natalie asks, and I point to the taco truck. *Yum.* Is it even possible to make a bad taco? I think not.

Once we gather a collection of food, we find a shade-covered bench under a tree in the park, and while digging into a large cup of fried scallops, I can't hold it in any longer and decide to tell her. "I saw the light."

Natalie's hands freeze as she's lifting a slider, surprise stamped on her face. "You did?"

"Yep, last night. I can still see the hovering lantern. It's as if it's now burned itself into my memory forever."

She frowns. "Is that why you were coming out of the house and not the boathouse?"

"Yes. Moved right on up there this morning." Although I don't think I would have stayed there much longer anyway. Even though I love the boathouse, I was starting to feel a little cramped, and it's so hot during the day. The poor little portable air conditioner just wasn't cutting it.

She hums with understanding while eating the mini slider.

"I just don't understand—why now, after all these weeks? It was so bright too. It's not as if it was there other nights and I didn't notice it. I definitely would have. Other than the moon, there isn't any outside lighting. Hard to miss a random glow coming in through the window."

"Well, I've never seen it, so I have no frame of reference." She grabs a napkin and wipes her mouth. "But it does make me wonder too—why now? Why after all this time? What happened to make her appear? I think that's the strangest part."

"Right! Because if she didn't want me there, she would have appeared immediately after me arriving to try to scare me off, and I feel like if she is just haunting the dock, she would have appeared sooner and consistently. I don't know, the whole thing is confusing and surreal. I mean we're talking about a ghost."

A ghost that, up until yesterday, I didn't believe in. But then again, when I think about Natalie's words, *what happened*, I can't help but wonder if her appearance had anything to do with my Post-it ritual and the deep sorrow I released into the water.

"Maybe you're just overthinking it. You're looking for a reason when there isn't one. Many, many people have reported seeing the light over the years, and I don't think there's anything special about her showing up now. I just think it's sad. Can you imagine loving someone so much you remain stuck in between worlds? She's waiting for someone who will never come."

She looks over my shoulder and out to the river. Her face is solemn as her mind has drifted to somewhere that's not here. My friend has a mysterious side to her, and I hope maybe one day she'll tell me about it.

"No, I can't imagine. Just look at me and Carter." I shake my head as my heart pings, not for a love I no longer have, but for all the emotions I was consumed with for months. I loved him, but I know for a fact it wasn't that kind of love, at least not on his side, and maybe not even on mine. Some people mourn the loss of their marriage for a long time, but for me, I think I more mourned the idea of what I thought we were. That's been the hard part to reconcile. How much of it wasn't real? How much of it was a lie?

"Well, from what I've seen and what you've told me, it seems he just loved himself the most."

Maybe that's it. Maybe that's the missing piece. He loved himself more.

I don't confirm or deny her statement, just tilt my head from side to side as if that's a thought and continue eating.

After lunch, we end up stopping in front of a booth at Jake's office, and the hairs on my arms rise as I feel his gaze land on me. Even behind the sunglasses we are both wearing, I would swear he is looking me straight in the eyes and it makes me feel all kinds of anxious, but not in a bad way. He nods and gives us a small welcome smile, and I can't help but wonder if he's thinking about the Post-it. Is he thinking about my reaction to him seeing it and how I not-so-subtly asked him to leave by claiming I needed to get back to the floors? Does he feel sorry for me? If the roles were reversed, I would feel sorry for him. I know it seems insensitive, at least to others, to end a marriage the way Carter did, but it is what it is, and deep down, I understand why he felt he needed to do it that way. Do I agree with him? No, but that's just how it goes sometimes.

"Welcome to our booth, ladies," says the guy standing next to him.

He is a little bit taller than Jake, has the same dark hair and the same shade of skin, and is also built like he should be standing on the line for some NFL team. Where they differ is in the shape of their face—his is more angular—as well as their personalities. Knowing Jake has brothers, I'd bet the house this guy is one of them.

Grinning, the guy says, "I hope you've come to empty those pockets for our manatees. As you know, manatees are under the protection of the Endangered Species Act, and we are doing our part to help keep them safe and healthy. With every donation, we're giving out these reusable metal straws and bracelets made of recycled water bottles." He holds them both up and waves them excitedly.

No one says anything, and no one moves. A silence falls over us as I take in the two of them, both wearing a teal-colored shirt with white writing that says, *Save the Manatees*. Jake is looking at me. Natalie glances from the guy to Jake and then at me. The guy next to Jake looks at all three of us, with me being last. His smile slips just a little as he tilts his head in confusion. They're all looking at me, and I suddenly feel the need to flee. Being near Jake already made me feel some kind of strange nervousness, and now I feel worse, like I'm being studied under a microscope. I hate it. It's then that I involuntarily move to take a step back, but Natalie grabs me to hold me in place.

I know Jake knows me, but does he really? After the Post-it, did he find out who I am? And this guy, his brother—wrinkles have formed between his brows as he takes in the three of us. Even with the big hat and sunglasses disguising me, the thought that someone might recognize me has instilled a level of anxiety that's lingering and growing instead of dissipating.

Shifting in place, Jake clears his throat, puts his hands in the pockets of his navy blue shorts, and takes a small step back even though he's behind the table. It's a disarming move as clearly he sees I'm skittish. He's reading me like I'm one of his animal patients, and I can't decide if I appreciate this or if it makes me angry.

"Are you enjoying the festival?" he asks, breaking the silence. Sweat rolls down my back from the heat, and I glance at his arms: broad shoulders, tanned and muscular. The perfect kind of arms to fall into.

Wait. What? No.

What is it about this guy that has my mind drifting and has me unnerved at the same time?

His brother whips his head to look at Jake and then back at me. He's trying to figure out if we already know each other, or if Jake's just being polite. His head then shifts, so I know he's looking at Natalie. Beside me, she shrugs one shoulder as they silently communicate.

"I am," I tell him, and I really am having a good time. I let out a deep breath and think about how amazing some of the artwork and the food has been.

"That's good," he replies, giving me another small smile. "What did you buy?" he asks, glancing toward the large paper shopping bags.

Glancing down, I set them on the ground, and from the first I pull out a wind chime. There's nothing too fancy about it. It's constructed with six brushed aluminum tubes, and hanging from the bottom is a large shell with a scene of the river painted on it.

"They said it's weatherproof and won't rust," I tell them.

"Did you buy it from Charlene?" the guy next to Jake asks.

"Yes, she did," says Natalie.

"Then she's right, it won't rust. I got one as a gift a few years ago, hung it up in a tree in my yard, and it still looks and sounds great." He beams.

"It's supposed to sound more like a garden chime versus a church chime, so we'll see," I say with a smile.

"Where are you going to hang it?" Jake asks as I pack it back up in the bag.

"Downstairs porch near the breakfast nook." I think it will be nice to hear in the mornings, or when I'm in the kitchen. Plus, I think Coco will like it too.

He nods in agreement.

Next, I pull out two of the four black and white photos I bought. All are the same square size and shape, so they will look great hung together.

"Since my home was one of the originals, I thought it would be kind of cool to hang these old photos of Chuluota Springs in the library. There are four, and I bought them from the historical society. They said they're all dated from 1885 to 1925."

Jake takes one from me; it's actually a photo of my home on the river. The boathouse hasn't been built yet, and the Easler fishing boat is docked. Some of the trees are smaller, and the beach is bigger. He stares down at the photo for a few moments, smiles, and then hands it back to me. "These will look great in the library."

Jumping into the conversation, Natalie wraps her arm around mine. "Right! And isn't it also great that I finally got her out of that old house? All she's done for the last month is work, work, work," she says, exaggeratedly but endearingly.

"Wait, you're the new owner of the house?" the guy asks, standing up straighter and looking even more intrigued than before.

People are moving all around us. I can feel them behind us, stopping to look at the booth, but then they keep going, and I'm glad. I have to believe donation booths are the least visited.

"She is," Jake says. "And from what Garrett says, she's working rather hard too."

The compliment hits its mark—me—and I let out a breath that leaves me feeling proud.

The guy next to Jake lets out a long low whistle, and my cheeks heat under the perusal from the three of them.

"What she's done looks amazing. You should stop by and check it out some time," Natalie says to the guy and Jake, not knowing that Jake has already seen it, and just a few days ago.

"How about tomorrow?" Jake asks calmly, as if going to my house is no big deal and something he does all the time.

"I'm not available tomorrow," the guy says disappointedly. "My name is Bauer, by the way." He slaps his hand on top of Jake's shoulder and squeezes. "It's a good thing this guy here works with animals—he has the social skills of a goldfish."

I can't help the small laugh that escapes me as Jake frowns. At least I'm not the only one who thinks he's sometimes off-putting.

"He's not so bad," I tell Bauer, coming to Jake's defense since he's taken such good care of Coco, and Bauer's brows shoot straight up.

"Is that so?" he asks as if he's just figured something out, and surprisingly Jake's cheeks dot pink.

Cutting off his brother's teasing, Jake asks, "Will Garrett be there tomorrow?"

"He should be. Since they started, he's been there at some point every day to check on the progress."

"That's good," he mutters, and I pick the bag back up and put the two pictures in it.

"Hey, I've done all right by myself," I tell him, thinking about the tile I laid the other day in the downstairs bathroom.

"I'm not saying you haven't, but it would be nice if the home was a little more inhabitable for you."

All eyes fall on me, and no one says anything. He's not wrong, and although his comment before felt great, this one feels more like he's worried or concerned. Does he worry about me? The thought evokes tiny butterflies and their wings brush up against my insides.

"Agreed. I'm ready to order some furniture and get my kitchen up and running."

"You know what they say about your boathouse, don't you?" Bauer interrupts, changing the subject.

"Yep, that it's haunted."

Not wanting to continue on about the house or have Natalie announce what I've seen, I open my purse and grab a fifty dollar bill. I drop it into the jar, and both guys stare at me as I shift the bags to one hand then grab Natalie's arm to move on.

"It was nice to meet you, Bauer. See you tomorrow?" I ask, pausing to look at Jake.

His voice is smooth and sure as he says, "Looking forward to it."

Bauer's head again whips over to look at him, and at the same time, those butterfly wings stretch and my heart thumps hard in my chest.

Oh my.

14

———

*B*ang, bang, bang.

Instead of a bird calling to all of its friends, this time it's the sound of a hammer that wakes me.

Bang, bang, bang.

With muted morning sunlight creeping into my room, I roll over and pull the pillow over my head. I know Garrett said he would be by today, but it's Sunday, and given that the sun isn't making the room feel like it's bursting with brightness, it's early.

Bang, bang, bang.

I thought moving into the house would mean I'd finally get a good night's sleep, but I guess I was wrong.

Bang, bang, bang.

Groaning, I glance at my phone and see it's almost eight. These days—well, except for yesterday—I'm barely up and moving at this time, but back in Chicago, eight would be late. If this were a normal week day, I would have already exercised and made a protein shake, and I'd be getting ready for work.

My heart pings a little at the thought of my old job. I loved it, and where we lived downtown, my last project was within walking distance. I guess here I'm within walking distance too considering I'm working on this house, but it's different. Yes, I'm still designing and decorating, but the biggest obvious difference is the lack of external energy. It's very calm and very soothing, and I would be lying if I said it hasn't been an adjustment. I'm used to people; my whole life I've been surrounded by them, and now I'm not. Yes, this is my choosing, but it feels different than I thought it would. Not necessarily different in a bad way, just different.

Chicago in the mornings is go-go-go: people hustling to work, people out running, the trains are overcrowded, the coffee shops overflowing, busy sidewalks, cars clogging the streets, et cetera. There's a buzz in the air from so much movement, and here there isn't. Here there is a stillness, a sense of tranquility. That is until the birds or the banging kills the mood.

Bang, bang, bang.

Throwing the blanket off of me and onto my blow-up mattress, leaving my hair a mess, I scramble down the stairs, stomping as I go.

"Garrett, it's too early for banging," I say as I throw open the back door—only, it's not the dark hair on the top of Garrett's head I'm looking at. It's Jake ... Jake with his well-defined arms filling out another long-sleeved sun shirt, Jake in a pair of low-slung athletic shorts that perfectly rest on his hips, Jake in a pair of work boots with white socks peeking out at the top.

"Oh." I pull up, startled, and take a step back.

Lowering the hammer he's holding, he straightens, and since he's a few steps lower than me, we're eye to eye, his blues to my hazels. My stomach dips.

Looking me over, his gaze quickly trails down my front. I do the same to see what he sees and realize I'm standing here in a pajama set Ivy sent me that consists of very short pale pink shorts and a tank. His brows pull down as his eyes again find mine.

"Do you always answer the door dressed like this?" The timbre of his voice is deep, and although I like the sound of it, I don't like his tone. Feeling self-conscious, I smooth my hair back off of my face then cross my arms over my chest and glare at him.

"What are you doing here? And where's Garrett?" I look past and around him, not finding him, just the stillness of the river. The air is calm and already a touch sticky from the imminent humidity.

He props one foot on the next step up. "I told you I was going to come by today. He sent me a text saying he's running to get some more wood and would meet me here. We're working on the steps and the porch." He waves his hand toward a small pile of lumber sitting on a pallet.

I'm excited to know they're starting on the back porch. They've already repaired the upstairs porch on both sides of the house, the large columns in the front, and the framing around each window. After this, I believe the house will be painted, returning to its splendor in white.

"When you said you were stopping by, I didn't realize it would be for this. Why are you working on the house?"

Running his free hand across the back of his neck, he says, "I lost a bet."

My jaw drops a little, as does a piece of hair from the messy bun on top of my head. I blow at it, and it slides to the side. "What kind of bet?"

"The kind where he caught more fish than me. It's a standing bet every time we go out. Winner can claim what they want, when they want. Bauer mentioned to him last night that I was going to come over today, and now here I am replacing these stairs and sections of the porch."

"Sounds terrible." I wince at him and drop my arms.

He shrugs his shoulders. "I don't mind. When he wins, it's usually construction-related, so I know what I'm in for. Besides, I like spending time with him," he says sincerely.

I get it. There isn't much I wouldn't do if it meant spending time with Ivy as well.

"What about when you win? What do you make him do?"

"Depends on the time of the year. Up the river there's a state park"—he raises the hammer to point in the direction—"and in the educational center there are aquarium tanks with local fish and species. Last month, he had to help me clean a few of them, including the ones with snakes."

Snakes! Oh my God. Just no.

"Are you serious? Don't they have like hired staff for that?" There is nothing about handling snakes that sounds like fun to me. I amend my earlier thoughts—that might be one of the few things I would not do to spend time with Ivy. At the most, I would watch her and stand to observe from afar.

"Most of the employees are retired or school age. I'm the resident wildlife veterinarian, so I volunteer my time."

"That's nice of you." I grimace. I mean come on, snakes? And who knows what else he's got in there.

Somehow following my train of thought, he presses his lips together and gives me a closed-mouth smile.

Letting out a deep sigh, I point over my shoulder to the kitchen. "Well, now that I'm up, I'm going to make a cup of coffee. Would you like one?"

"Sure. Thank you." He sets down the hammer as I open the door wider. Cool air rushes over us.

"Come on in. I'll meet you in the kitchen."

"Sounds good," he says, his eyes briefly glancing over me one more time.

Racing back up the stairs to my room, I dig around in the

laundry basket where I've been keeping my clothes and pull out a pair of running shorts, a sports bra, and a T-shirt. Right at this moment, I'm feeling extra grateful for my new washer and dryer. It's not that I'm trying to impress him, just that my clothes are pretty gross after working on this house all day every day.

Quickly, I brush my hair and my teeth, and then I head down to the kitchen.

"Sorry, just thought I should change first."

He's standing next to Coco's cage and turns at the sound of my voice. "No worries," he says, taking in my new outfit. "Although I wouldn't have complained if you chose to stay in the pajamas." He smirks.

"Yeah, I bet," I fire back with sarcastic teasing, and he shrugs as if to say, *Can you blame me?*

We fall into a comfortable silence as he stands at the kitchen bar and I run the coffee pot. I also have a package of blueberry muffins from the grocery store bakery and set two on a plate. He nods his head in thanks, picks one up, and eats it.

"Sorry, I don't have anywhere for you to sit yet. My goal is to shop for each room entirely when it's ready."

He looks around the space, and then I watch as he glances toward the piano in the music room. The picture is gone, back in its box where it belongs. I should probably apologize or something for how I ended his visit that day, but I just can't. I don't want to bring it up, and I don't want to be asked questions. I feel good. I've transitioned to a place of moving on, so there's no need to go backward, just forward. That was there, and now I'm here.

His eyes come back to find mine. They're a little wary, but whatever he finds in my expression has him letting out a contented sigh.

"But you've moved into the house?" he asks as I set his cup in front of him. No sugar or creamer for him, just black. I can't help but wonder if everyone knew I was living in the boathouse.

"Yeah, I decided it was time."

I look past his shoulder and down to the dock, to the second piling on the right. Jake turns to see what I'm looking at.

"You saw it?" he asks, turning back to face me. He's genuinely curious, and I nod while taking a sip. There is nothing like a good cup of coffee in the morning. "What did you see?" He shifts his weight to lean his hip against the counter.

"Just the light, floating in midair."

He lets out a chuckle. It's a nice sound. "I bet that was fun for you."

"Not really, and I've seen it two nights in a row."

"So, are you a ghost believer now?" he asks.

"I'm not sure." And that's the truth. I know what I saw, but then again, what did I see? I keep thinking there has to be a logical explanation, but what is it?

"Bauer has always been into the ghost stories of this town. It's why he asked you yesterday. You should talk to him—he might be able to shed some light on the situation, pun intended," he says while smiling. "He runs the town river ghost tour, does it once a month during the year and once a week during the season. You might find it interesting."

"A ghost tour? Like one of those you find in a city like Savannah?" I ask, tearing off a piece of the muffin and eating it.

"Yep. He takes the tourists down the river walk and then to a ferry boat. He rents it from one of the daytime excursion companies that take people out to see manatees. It's got a glass bottom. People love it, and being on the river makes the tour unique."

"There are enough places for him to make an actual tour?"

Jake chuckles, and a piece of hair falls onto his forehead. "Unfortunately, yes."

"Maybe I will then." My curiosity is piqued.

"Honestly, it makes me feel better to know you aren't out there anymore. Not that I was overly worried or anything, it's just ... well, the house is safer."

I can't argue with him there. As much as I needed the escape of the boathouse when I first got here, I was ready to move out of it. The new air conditioners alone enticed me to move inside.

"I just need to stop working downstairs for a bit and take care of my room. The floors are sanded but need to be finished, the walls, the lights, redo the bathroom, all of that, and then order some furniture. A real bed would be nice."

"What are you sleeping on now?" he asks, taking a sip of his coffee.

"A blow-up mattress."

He chokes and starts coughing. "Sorry. Did you say blow-up mattress?"

"Yes." I grin at his blatant horror.

He sets the coffee cup down. "That's what you've been sleeping on all this time?"

"It's not that bad. Besides, I've gotten used to it."

"It is that bad, and what happened to all of your furniture from your home in Chicago?"

I hesitate before saying, "I left it there."

"I see," he says, reading between the lines. "Well, how about I help you up there today instead of the porch, and we'll get it moving along." He walks around the island to the sink and rinses out his coffee cup. I can't help but notice the muscles in his back as they move under the shirt.

"What about Garrett?" I ask as I shift next to him and do the same. The scent of cocoa butter, sandalwood, and dryer sheets floats my way. It's not the first time I've noticed the way he smells, and I like it. A lot.

"He can help us too. What do you want to do?" He turns so he's facing me, but he doesn't move away. I have to look up at him, and with his blue eyes looking down at me, those butter-flies return, swirling against my insides at our nearness.

"Strip the bathroom bare, except for the tub, and empty out the closet. There are two built-in cabinets, I'm assuming a his and hers, but I'll have the closet custom done, and the shelving in them needs to go."

"You want to leave the tub?" he asks, his brows pulling down, and a giggle escapes me. I'm certain he's imagining some stained, old, small, dirty tub.

I take a step back to put some space between us. "Yes, it's brand new. Strange too. No one knows why. It was another one of those things left behind, but it's beautiful and I love it."

Uncertainty flits across his features, but then it's gone. "If you say so."

I can't help but smile widely at him.

Once in the room, I do my best to ignore the way it feels to have him in here. The sun is now fully pouring in, giving the space a buttery hue. It may be a blank slate, but it's still my bedroom, and I notice that he glances toward the air mattress.

Jake, who grabbed tools out of the back of his truck, heads to the bathroom to start removing the old tile on the floor, and I move into the closet to take down the two five-foot cabinets that are stuck to the walls. I thought about leaving them just because, but I don't like where they are placed and am already drooling over how I want my closet designed.

Inside each cabinet, there are shelves on the top and drawers on the bottom. They don't inspire me, so they've got to go.

When I pull on the first cabinet, it wobbles a little, and using my phone flashlight, I slip it into the space between the cabinet and the wall and see there are two brackets with cables anchoring it. How they got it this tight, I'll never know, and the only thing I can think of is to rip it off and repair the wall.

Back and forth and side to side I teeter the cabinet. Eventually it budges, and I yank hard. Together the cabinet and I fall to the ground, me letting out a loud *oomph*. I get it, it's original to the house, but like the wallpaper, I swear the materials they used then are so much better than the ones they use today. Hearing the noise, Jake wanders in and assesses what's going on.

"You okay?" he asks, picking the cabinet up off of me. Of course he makes it look super easy and light.

"Yep." I stand up and shake off the dust that fell out. "This sucker wasn't budging."

"I can see that." He grins.

We're both now standing in the closet, and the space seems to have shrunk. What is it about this guy's presence that makes me so off-kilter?

I shove it with my foot, and the bottom drawer has fallen out; that's when I spot the corner of a piece of paper. Bending over, I run my hand along the inside of the drawer, and there on the top is almost like a hidden ledge. It may be about four inches in depth, definitely large enough to hide things. I slide my hand across the ledge, and there lying in what I thought was an empty space is an old newspaper. Pulling it out, I see it's an old *New York Times* from 1917. I can feel my jaw dropping. I mean how often are things like this found? The pages are yellow, faded, and folded in half. As I use the top of the cabinet to gently flatten it, my eyes nearly bulge out when I see the headline: *Easler Fishing, More than Just a Catch*.

Holy moly! I let out a small noise of excitement.

They were featured in *The New York Times*! I have to frame this and hang it up!

"What is it?" Jake asks.

"Look at it, it's amazing." I move to the side so he can see, and he comes to stand right behind me. Heat from his body brushes against mine, and his brows kiss as he absorbs what it is, and his eyes flash to find mine.

"An article in *The New York Times*," he mutters in awe.

"Isn't it incredible?" I whisper. "I had no idea the fishing company was that well known or famous."

His gaze lingers on mine and drifts over my face for just a heavy second, and then both of us look back at the paper. My stomach swirls at him looking so closely at me, but I simply ignore it as I stare down. The words of the article can't be made out. Some are faded, others smudged, and as we attempt to open it, the brittle pages either stick together or begin to tear, so we stop. Maybe I won't be hanging it.

"I bet the *Times* has an archives section where we could look up the article," he says, not even realizing he said the word 'we'.

"From what I've been told, Mr. Easler was well known for his fishing business, but he must have been so much bigger than I thought." I glance at Jake, who picks up the paper and, with no success, tries to manipulate it.

"This is a seriously nice find," he says, handing it back and moving a step away from me.

"Right? The house keeps presenting me with all kinds of things." I smile, but his wavers. Does it worry him that things were left behind? Does he think someone is going to come for them, like the painting and the piano? "Did you look at the logo?" I ask him, hoping to change his train of thought.

Although we can't read the words of the article, there is a picture of the company logo in the middle of the column. The words Easler Fishing are in a block font, but on the left side there's a fish jumping over the word Easler, and on the right there is a conch shell.

"I know the logo. I'm pretty sure everyone who was born in this town does. The marina was the original Easler fish house where they processed all of the incoming haul. If you have time, you should stop inside. They've kept the building plaque, and it hangs on the wall. Although it should probably be in a museum somewhere, it's not."

"Wow, I think I will," I tell him, feeling more excited than I have in a long time. Well, I will when I feel more comfortable going out during the daytime, and while I'm down there, maybe I'll stop by to see Corrie for an iced coffee.

15

———

Surprisingly, it takes ten minutes for me to find a place to park my car, and eventually I give up and just park in the lot for Jake's veterinarian office. I thought by sneaking down here at night I'd feel more hidden, but with how crowded the town is from tourists, it may as well be midday. If Jake has a problem with this, well, I'll cross that bridge when I get to it, although I don't think he will. It's been a week since I've spoken to him, and surprisingly I'm a little saddened by this. I don't know why; I'm certainly not looking for any type of relationship, so maybe it's the loneliness. It was nice to have him over last weekend.

Then again, I don't think I'm lonely. I think it goes back to the slow pace and quietness of this way of life, and also because, for the first time in my life, I'm on my own, truly on my own. Yes, I still talk to my parents at least once a week, and they are following along with the blog posts and website updates. My father has shared plenty of ideas, but he's been surprisingly content to just let me be. And yes, I talk to Ivy just about every day, but talking over the phone is different than physically being with them. The minute the call ends, the silence settles in. It's a nice silence, though. It's allowed me to think and to be able to hear myself versus the world around me.

My bedroom was completed yesterday, and the closet and bathroom will be this week. I finished the wood floor and laid the tile in the bathroom, painted the walls in both rooms, and hung heavy drapes, and Garrett had a plumber install a new toilet while his electrician added recessed lighting and put up a ceiling fan. It took a little creativity with the wiring, but he made it happen. Furniture starts arriving tomorrow, along with the materials to complete my vision of a walk-in shower, his and hers bowl sink vanities, and large ornate mirrors for the wall. My inner interior decorator is beyond giddy with anticipation.

In a few days, my toes will sink into the new large area rug, and at night, I will finally sleep in a bed. A real bed.

Weaving my way through the couple of blocks it takes me to get to the river walk, I take in the shops, the activity, and the energy on the streets, and I find at this moment I'm content. The sky is clear, the stars are bright enough that they're winking, and the moon is just high enough over the trees on the eastern side that it can be seen. It's a beautiful night to be out, and I'm humbled by how right it feels to be here. Of all the places in the world, this little place on this night feels like mine, and my heart feels calm.

Giddy with anticipation for what I might learn about the town tonight, I quickly make my way to the riverfront and then to the hardware store where the tour is set to begin.

The tour is exactly what I expected it to be—that is, full of tourists, mostly older, with a few kids. There must be at least fifty people, and it seems everyone is feeling just like I am: eager but anxious. From the store, Bauer walks out. He's wearing all black with a black cape, and his hair is slicked back. He looks ridiculous, but judging by the grin on his face, I think he's just as excited as all of the people here are.

"Good evening, everyone," Bauer says in a creepy but funny voice. Chuckles resonate through the group as the thrill to hear the stories about this town ripples throughout the crowd. "Welcome to the Chuluota Springs ghosts and hauntings tour."

Peeling my eyes off of him, I slide them over the group, and I can't help but be elated for him and this crowd. Off to the side, standing not too far away from Bauer, I spot Jake. He's smiling at his brother, and it's an easy expression, full of familiarity, just like I would give Ivy. The thought of her gives me a slight pang of longing for her company; it would be fun to do this with her. No, it will be fun to do this with her when she comes to visit.

Feeling someone looking at him, Jake's eyes skip over the crowd and land on mine. I give him a small wave, and he smiles at me. I feel that smile sink into me from head to toe.

"Before we get started, the first thing I want to explain to you is that there is a difference between a ghost and a haunting. While most people use those terms interchangeably, they mean something different. A ghost wants to get justice. They have a story to tell, and they linger around until it's told and people have discovered what they are trying to say. Whether it's because of a murder and they are wanting their killer to be found or there's a message they need passed along, they are not happy with or accepting of how things ended. I mean who doesn't want a ghost to appear in their home and lead the way to a hidden treasure?"

Light laughter moves through the crowd.

"Now, a haunting has more to do with a lingering. It's not always unfinished business. After all, tragic things happen, from illness to sudden death and murder, but what experts have discovered is that when this happens, energy presses upon the atmosphere and an impression is left behind. Most hauntings take place where they were happiest. The best example I can give you of this is a playhouse or theater. We've all heard stories about theater hauntings, and over ninety percent of the time, the ghosts seen or reported are former actors, directors, and stage-hands. They are there not because a calamity happened, but because it was their favorite place to be. Can a ghost stay behind by choice? Who knows. But in our little town, we have a combination of both, and tonight, if we're lucky, we'll see one."

"What are you doing here?" I whisper to Jake as he slips in next to me.

"Support. This is the first tour of the season and the biggest one he's ever done."

"Really?" I look up at Jake to see him smiling proudly at his brother. I then look down and find him in a black T-shirt, a pair of well-worn jeans, and running shoes. His dark hair is a little damp, like he recently took a shower, and his jaw is covered with a day-old shadow. He's seriously handsome. I wonder if he knows how much so.

He nods. "He's fascinated by the history of this town and loves to share it with others."

"And he's a lawyer by day?" I remember Natalie telling me this.

He glances at me curiously then answers, "Yep."

"Oh, well, I guess do what you love and love what you do, right?" A warm breeze blows up off the river. I can't help but lift my face to the sensation as I take in the tepid southern night. The smell is salty and briny with a hint of fish. I love it.

His eyes cut to me again, and the corner of his mouth turns up.

"I can't think of anything worse than what he does. He's a general practice attorney, so he sees it all, from real estate to civil issues. So much paperwork." He shakes his head.

"Yeah, I'm more likely to decoupage the furniture or the wall with the paperwork than read it." I smile up at him, and he smiles back.

"How have you been?" he asks.

"Good. My room and the bathroom are almost finished, and I've started painting the rooms downstairs. It's coming along nicely."

"I'm glad to hear that." His gaze is warm and sincere. "So, you decided to come?" He stuffs his hands into his pockets as the group starts making its way down Main Street toward the marina.

"Yep. Just thinking of it as research. Plus, you told me I should come check it out."

He lets out a low hum of understanding and nods. "I think you'll like it."

"By the way, I parked at your office," I say nonchalantly. "The streets were full, and I got tired of looking."

His expression is amused as he looks down at me. "No worries. You can park there any time you want."

"I appreciate that." A feeling I haven't seen too much of lately sparks through my veins: happiness.

Just before the marina, Bauer shuffles the group so we stop in front of Dockside Diner.

"Our first stop is here at Dockside Diner. This diner, or should I say the building, is as old as the town. It housed the original restaurant in Chuluota Springs, and when it opened in 1841, it was primarily a fishing tavern. It's also the location of the first recorded town ghost sighting. Although Chuluota Springs wasn't really a town then, there were inhabitants who worked the sugar mill, which is just up the river and one of our stops."

"He sounds very believable," I whisper.

"He does. But then again, growing up here, there's no way to not believe the stories. We've heard them all our lives, and in many cases, we've seen things firsthand."

"Every night since the first night I saw the light, it's returned. Every single night," I tell him. Just saying it out loud makes me feel like I'm crazy, but I know I'm not. I know what I've seen, and it was there.

"I'm not surprised," he says assuredly.

I turn to face him. "Really?"

He takes in the surprise on my face and chuckles. "Well, not that you've seen her—I know you have. Once a ghost manifests itself, that's when the haunting begins and never ends. A lot of people know about or have seen Mrs. Easler's light. I mean, your home is a stop on this tour."

I suck in a gasp of air and take a step away from him. "What?"

His brows pull down as my reaction has surprised him. "You didn't know?"

I shake my head and stare at him, while still trying to hear most of Bauer's story about a lost game of cards, a horse that was for payment but turned out to be lame with a limp, and a pistol duel in the street. Apparently, the guy who won the game, Mr. Graddy, was the one who took the bullet and died. His ghost is seen mostly just as the sun is setting, and he paces up and down in front of the diner, angry, waving his gun, like he's looking for revenge. That or his new horse.

"No. I guess it makes sense, everyone I've met has asked me if I've seen her, I guess I'm just surprised is all. I'm not sure how I feel about my home being paraded in front of a bunch of strangers."

"It was in the tour description." He looks at me warily, and then his expression relaxes. "He doesn't pull up in front of the house, just stays in the river. It's not as bad as you're thinking, and it's more about the story."

"If you say so," I say cautiously, feeling uncomfortable about a group of people staring at my home.

Bauer continues, "It's recorded that most didn't believe the tale, that it was just the ramblings of drunken fishermen after long days on the water and late nights in the tavern, but then one early morning before the sun had risen, about fifty years later, Mr. Easler, who was a founding member of the town, was meeting his fishing crew to head out for the day when he saw him. He was discovered not by the marina where he should have been, but standing right there"—he points toward the intersection of Main Street and the riverfront—"in the middle of the street. He came face to face with the ghost of Mr. Graddy, and as each of his crew members arrived and joined him, they all saw the ghost, from his angry expression to the details of the clothes he was wearing. Since that day, the ghost of Mr. Graddy became something of a legend."

The group is quiet as they process what Bauer just told them and look up and down the streets. Obviously, there is nothing there, but the scallop festival banners, hung on the light posts, flap loudly in the breeze coming off the river and cast moving shadows onto the street.

Without saying another word, Bauer turns and walks the group to the marina. People are whispering loudly to their companions as we board a large glass-bottom boat. Like Jake said, it's a tourist boat used to take people out during the day to look at the manatees and fish.

Murmurs have once again started amongst the tourists. They clearly liked the first story, and their yearning for more is palpable. I make my way toward a seat in the back, Jake follows and sits next to me, Bauer quickly goes over the rules of the boat, and then we're off.

The next story he tells is one about the river. Like any body of water, when it comes to death, there are mysteries and murders. Rivers can especially leave people feeling unsettled as they travel around them. With hidden inlets, blind bends, springs, the weather, and the creatures that live in the water, inevitably there are deaths, some explained, some not.

He goes on to talk about Captain Walters. He is the resident river ghost who can be seen traveling up and down the river in a small boat. He wears a dark fisherman's hat and jacket, and he stands holding a lantern, searching for crew members who were lost at sea. Whether he realizes he was lost at sea too, who knows, but he's there, and residents of the town mainly see him during the long summer months. Unlike Mr. Graddy, Captain Walters is seen mostly late afternoon, after a midday shower has blown through, and into the night. He appears like a mirage, and then he's gone again. Or is he?

We all watch enraptured as Bauer leans down to light a lantern I hadn't noticed is sitting next to him. He's standing at the bow of the boat but then turns to put his back to us and raises the lantern, holding it up, as if to reflect the light off of the river.

I glance over at Jake; he's smiling at his brother, whereas I have chills from the eeriness and quietness of everyone on the boat, the only sound being that of the water splashing against its edges as we advance up the river. I can't help but wonder if I've seen this light and not paid any attention to it because I didn't know. After all, how many nights have I sat on the dock and stared out at the river?

Jake bumps me with his shoulder as he looks down at me.

"You've seen this river ghost?" I whisper to him.

He nods his head, and his smile shifts more to a grin.

"Don't worry, he stays on the river—he doesn't sway into inlets," he teases.

I frown. Seriously, one ghost is enough. Having another show up might force my hand into packing my bags and heading back north.

"Our next stop is up here on the right at the Chuluota Springs Resort." Bauer sets down the lantern and points toward the large resort. I follow and look at the property, and he's quiet as we make our way to the destination. Other than the day of the festival when Natalie drove us down the river, I haven't really seen the resort up close. I knew it was here—it's advertised every time I open any social media app—but I haven't been able to explore it.

The main building, which is four stories tall, stretches along the river in the shape of a U so the rooms can look out over the water. It is beautiful and looks not only simple but elegant. Although it's dark, lamp posts and lights have it glowing under the moonlight. There are strategically placed palm trees, a blue glow from where the pool must be in the center, and hammocks swaying along the river's edge.

"Is anyone staying at this property?" he asks, and a few hands go up. I'm not surprised. Yes, there are other motels and bed and breakfasts in and around town, but this one screams comfort.

"That's what I thought. There are always a few." He grins conspiratorially. "The resort was first built by two Sicilians who were wanting to entice fellow family members to immigrate to the United States and work at the property, to help build up the town. As you know, the rivers are naturally spring fed, and like their Midwest counterparts, people believed the mineral properties of the springs to be healing. With rave reviews of the river's turquoise and deep blue colors, word spread faster than the transportation it took to get here. People from the west, the next largest town being New Orleans, and from the north came in droves to stay at the resort. I mean really, if the options are snow or a mild 72 degrees in the middle of January, I know which I'm going to pick every time."

The group chuckles.

"Have you been there yet?" Jake asks, leaning over.

"No, but it looks beautiful." Each room has a balcony with a pair of rocking chairs. How lovely.

"You should stop by. They have two restaurants that are open to locals. One is a little fancy and features upscale Southern fare, but the other is out by the pool and serves some of the best fried grouper and citrus slaw around."

"Citrus slaw?" I turn to look at him. Even though the chairs are all evenly spaced apart, he feels so close to me. My stomach dips with his nearness.

"Yes, it's delicious. Instead of mayonnaise, it's citrus vinaigrette based, and there are chunks of pineapple in it. It's good."

I smile at his enthusiasm over the food, and he smiles back. The moon is higher in the sky now, and although there are shadows on his face, I can still see the paleness of his eyes as they are not guarded but friendly with me.

Here Bauer goes on with the story about suicides and mysterious drownings. He talks about how hotels are notorious for strange occurrences, but here at this location the one that is talked about over and over again is the ghost of a little girl named Mary. She drowned while swimming in the spring, in front of dozens of people.

"They say drowning is a silent killer, and it really is. Once you slip underneath the water, there's no splashing and no sound. No one knows why she drowned. She was apparently a good swimmer, and how devastating that she wasn't discovered by anyone until it was too late."

He pauses here as the heaviness of losing a child sinks in for all of us, and then he proceeds to step up the creepy level by ten.

"Since her death, many sighting reports have popped up over the years. People will wake up in their rooms at night and find her standing next to the bed looking at them. She only ever says one word: Mama. And it isn't a particular room. She's been spotted in almost all of them, as if she's searching for her mother."

Frowning, I look at Jake and find him with his lips pinched together as he's trying not to smile.

"What is wrong with you? Why are you smiling? That is terrible. I will never stay in that resort now."

"You should have seen your face," he sputters, then throws his head back and silently laughs. I've never seen him laugh like this, and it's a sight to behold. Just when I thought he couldn't get more handsome, he does.

Facing forward, I find Bauer looking at us. With his brother laughing and me scowling, his face splits into a huge smile too.

A few people ask questions, and then soon enough we're off to our next stop with Bauer beginning his next tale.

"Before Chuluota Springs became a town, the area was already known for the Molinaro Castle. Angelo Molinaro owned almost seven thousand acres and ran the largest sugar mill in the state of Florida. Originally established in the 1840s, it operated for decades and was a stopping point for people who were on the trade route from New Orleans to Tampa. Everyone knows Ellis Island was a huge immigrant port to the United States, but most forget about New Orleans. The New Orleans port was a sought-after destination for Italians, primarily Sicilians. They were fleeing their homeland, which had fallen into a corrupt, dangerous, and unlawful state, and in the 1880s, word caught like a storm surge that Tampa, more specifically Ybor City, had become the cigar capital of the world. Factories were going up left and right, and it even surpassed Havana, Cuba, not only in its quality, but in its variety. Factory workers in Ybor City were hand-rolling cigars in 36 different shapes and sizes.

"The calendar crossed over to 1900, and then there was Prohibition, which took place from 1920 to 1933. Can anyone guess what happened to our sugar mill during that time?"

The boat slows, and off in the distance we can see limestone ruins of the mill and, behind it, what looks like a looming old Italian countryside villa, one straight out of Medieval times.

"Moonshine," someone calls out.

"That's right. Traditional moonshine is a non-aged spirit distilled from a combination of fermented sugar and grain. The sugar is what makes it different from spirits like whiskey. Whereas moonshine ferments with the combination of sugar and grain, whiskey ferments with one hundred percent grain. Who here has had moonshine?"

Two people raise their hands.

"Well, you're in luck, because I brought some today for you to sample."

Murmurs rise, as does the tourist excitement. Bauer reaches down into a bag next to the lantern and pulls out a gallon glass jug of liquid and a large package of clear eight-ounce plastic cups. He hands the package to the person closest to him, she takes a cup, and she passes it along.

"Where does he get that from?"

"He makes it." Jake smirks.

"Isn't that like illegal or something?"

"Nah, it's no different than brewing your own beer. He's not selling it or distributing it for mass consumption, so it's fine. After all, he's the lawyer, so he should know."

"Now it's the 1920s, our little fishing town is established, the trade route is becoming more congested, World War I has ended, and people are angry about Prohibition. You can imagine that the sugar mill became a hotspot and a destination for all different kinds of people. Rumor has it, Molinaro's son became involved with the American-Sicilian mafia in New Orleans and used his father's sugar mill to supply moonshine to their organization. Many people claim to have spotted the transactions and transportation of the alcohol by boat—after all, that's the quickest way to go back and forth to New

Orleans. It's also common knowledge that law enforcement in this area turned a blind eye to the activity at the mill. Strange accidents would occur if someone poked too hard, snooped too much, or in general caused a ruckus. People would show up at the castle and then go missing, if you catch my drift, which makes what is left of our castle and sugar mill a very haunted place."

"Can you go into the castle?" someone asks.

"Yes, part of it is open to tours, but most is closed off to the general public. Unfortunately, the son of Mr. Molinaro and his family were victims of the supposed organized crime he was involved in, and the end result was devastating for Mr. Molinaro. Of all the locations here in Chuluota Springs, what you should know is that the castle is the most haunted. Ghosts have been seen at all times of the day and night. Visitors have reported feeling the temperature around them drop, the hairs rising on their arms, brushes of air against their skin, distorted visions, wavering lights, blurry images, and whispers in their ears. If you're looking for paranormal proof, visit the mill and spend some time there. It's not a matter of if you see or experience something abnormal, but most definitely when."

The murmurs of the crowd increase in volume.

From there, Bauer takes us a little farther up the river to the state park. The river has narrowed, and old cypress and pine trees canopy overhead, blocking the moon. I can see why this tour is such a huge hit with the tourists; the stories are intriguing, and the ambiance is perfect. Here Bauer talks about the land before it was settled as a fishing community: the Seminole Indians, their ceremonial grounds, and the spirits who are still felt and present today. Afterward, with a quiet and contemplative group, he turns the boat, and we head back toward town.

"So what do you think?" Jake asks quietly, his shoulder and leg brushing against mine when he leans over.

"I think he's doing a great job. You were right, I do like this tour, and I've loved all the history he's thrown at us too."

"What was it you said—do what you love and love what you do?" He smiles at me, and I can't help but smile back.

"Our last story this evening takes place at the Easler Mansion. Well, not at the mansion, but on the dock in front of it. The Easlers were one of the original founding members of what is now our thriving little town today, and the ghost that resides there is one of the most mysterious in Chuluota Springs."

The boat slows as it turns and hovers in the entrance of my inlet. I'm not sure how I feel about my home being so on display, but Bauer and the tour really aren't doing anything wrong. The waterways are open to the public.

"What makes this situation unique is no one knows if she is a ghost with a message or just a haunting. See, Mr. Easler founded Easler Fishing Company in 1899. He was apparently brilliant at steering a ship and navigating the ever-changing weather we have here off the coast of Florida, but one night in 1917, he didn't return. Poof—vanished. The story told is that Mrs. Easler would sit waiting on her dock all day and then with a lantern at night, just praying they'd gotten it wrong. She was adamant about being on the dock and refused to leave it, so the boathouse was built for her. It's the light of the lantern that can still be seen today, letting generations of town members know she's still waiting for him to return.

"Now, we all know it's not uncommon for grieving ghost widows to be found all up and down the eastern coastline of the United States, but it's the skeptic in a lot of us who've heard this story that can't help but wonder if there was something more. Was it a freak accident? Or was it murder? And if so, why?"

Murder. A cold chill sweeps down my spine. It never even occurred to me to think that. I just assumed he drowned during a storm; that's what Natalie said. Am I living in the home of a murdered man?

"Now, there are reports of Mrs. Easler claiming there was foul play, saying she just knew this wasn't an accident, but people ignored the rantings of a grieving woman. The Easlers had also lost their oldest son in 1915 in World War I, and apparently she suffered from bouts of what we now call depression, so no one took her seriously."

Just then a faint light appears on the dock, and people all around us gasp in awe. Even Bauer has turned to look at it. The group is quiet until the shock wears off and murmurs emerge among passengers traveling together. In front of us, the woman leans over to her friend and whispers, "I bet that's fake. The light just magically appeared as we arrived?"

"I don't know," her friend answers. "Looks pretty authentic to me. There are no cords or lines running over the dock...it's as if the light is just floating there."

And it is. I know it is, because I've seen it, night after night.

Bauer turns back to look at me, his face excited like he's thought of something more he wants to add, but whatever expression he sees on my face changes his mind. In my peripheral vision, I see Jake also shakes his head no.

"Do you think he was murdered?" I quietly ask Jake.

"I don't know. Seems logical, though. Greed has a way of turning the best people."

Greed. I toss around that word, thinking about how there could be a connection.

"Do you think there's more to just her light lingering behind? Do you think she has a message?"

"I don't know that either."

"I thought she was just kind of there—it never occurred to me that she might be lingering for other reasons as well. I'm not even sure how I would decipher what she's trying to tell me. It's just a light."

Just a light.

People now have their phones up, trying to take pictures of the light, and surprisingly this bothers me. As this is my house, in a way, she's now my ghost, and I feel somewhat protective of her. If she is grieving, do these people really need to immortalize her pain in a photo?

After a few more minutes, Bauer turns the boat, and we head out of the inlet and back to the river. As the content of the tour is now over, people are asking him questions, but I can't hear them. I'm so lost in my head over the thought that her poor husband might have been murdered, and I almost don't register the wave of heat down my right side.

Shaking out of my thoughts, I turn to find I'm leaning against Jake and my hand is being held by his. I'm not sure if I reached for him or if he slipped his hand in against mine, but it feels foreign, like something that hasn't been done in so long. Actually the entire interaction is puzzling to me. Yes, my family hugged me when I said goodbye, but I've spent so many months alone, with just me, that this kind of closeness has me reeling.

I look down, he lightly squeezes my hand, and I stare at the sight of it being engulfed by another man. A blush burns up to the surface of my skin, and my heart starts pounding harder in my chest. What is happening right now? Should this feel wrong? Does it feel wrong? I can't decide if there's a rightness to this or if it's uneasiness I feel. I just know I feel something, and it isn't until Jake squeezes my hand again that I realize I'm still staring. Jerking away from him, I pull my hand free.

"Sorry," I mutter.

In a relaxed manner, he leans back in his chair and drapes his arm over mine. "No worries."

I feel like an idiot.

Actually, I think I feel confused more than anything else.

For the remainder of the ride back to the marina, we listen to Bauer answer questions and tell more stories about the town, and once we return, I realize Jake and I haven't spoken to each other at all. Maybe he's leaving me to my thoughts, or maybe he doesn't know what to say to me. Regardless, I should say something, but he beats me to it.

"Tomorrow, a bunch of us are going scalloping. Bauer will be there with a few of his friends, and Garrett will probably invite Natalie. You should come. It will be fun."

16

———————

Stepping out of the back of the house, I pull the door shut tight behind me to find Jake has already arrived and is slinging a rope around one of the dock posts to settle the boat. I can't help the small smile that finds its way to my lips at just the sight of him, and I remember the first time I saw him there almost two months ago. Originally, I thought there was no way I would ever want to be friends with him, yet here we are, and it turns out he's not so bad. Not so bad at all. Reaching down, I grab my bag and the small cooler I packed and make my way down to him.

"Morning," I call out, feeling giddy. It's a new day, the sky's the perfect shade of blue, and I'm about to head out and try something new.

"Morning." He answers without looking at me, his voice deep and rough like it's the first time he's using it this morning. He's wearing another long-sleeved sun shirt and swim trunks, just like the day I met him, along with sunglasses and a baseball hat flipped around backward.

Yanking on the rope to make sure it's pulled tight, he climbs out of the boat onto the dock and stops abruptly as he faces me.

My sister, who decided I wasn't attired appropriately for a Florida lifestyle, recently sent me a huge box of clothes, and maybe I'm wrong, but I thought the sundress I picked out to go over my bathing suit was cute.

"What? Is it too much?" I ask as he stares at me without speaking.

"No." There's a small shake to his head. "You look beautiful."

Heat flares in my cheeks at his words, and the vision of him holding my hand last night flashes through my mind. I told myself I wasn't going to think about that today, and I wouldn't be awkward; I would just be me and enjoy this new adventure. Seems I need to remind myself again.

"Thank you." Looking down, I run my free hand over my hip to smooth down the dress. It's a pale blue, like his eyes, and I've paired it with a plain pair of rubber flip-flops and the large sun hat I wore to the festival.

"Here, let me get those." He walks forward and takes my things.

"I packed us lunch, just in case. I wasn't sure how long we would be gone," I tell him, and he grins.

"I packed us some food too. Usually we stay out until we get tired or sunburned, sometime midday. Did you pack sunscreen? You're going to need it," he says, his head tilting as if he's glancing at my arms.

"Don't make fun of my poor pale midwestern skin," I say jokingly. "I've acquired a little bit of color since I've been here."

"That may be." He smiles over his shoulder at me as he climbs onto the boat.

Setting down my things, he turns and holds his hand out to help me climb on. I take it, and his palm is warm just like last night.

"You look tired," he states, assessing my face, pulling me from the thought.

"I am. There's a loud bird who likes to make itself known in the early hours of the morning, and I have no idea how to make him or her stop or fly away. I swear it's like it sits up in the tree closest to the house and screams on purpose." I move to the bench across from where he'll be driving the boat and take a seat.

He laughs. "Those birds are called limpkins, or the crying bird. They call out like that when it's mating season, or when they feel the need to be territorial because they spot a predator like an alligator." Just as quickly as he tied up the boat, he unties it from the dock and pushes us off.

"Are there alligators in the river?" I realize my voice is a little louder than necessary, but it never occurred to me that there would be alligators. I mean sure, it's Florida and I know they live in the lakes, but this river empties into the Gulf.

He takes a seat and looks at me, his lips turned up slightly as if I amuse him. "Yes, but they won't bother you if you don't bother them."

I hum in disapproval but make a mental note to scan the edge of my property when we get back.

Smiling, he turns the boat toward the river, moves us out of the inlet, and then throttles the engine so we take off.

This morning, the river looks so different than it did last night. While it was still beautiful, it was ominous in an eerie way. Now, it looks serene and enticing.

We pass the resort and the marina, and before I know it, half an hour has gone by as we exit the river and weave our way through the small barrier islands that dot the water near the shore. How he knows where he's going, I have no idea, but as we pass cluster after cluster of others who appear to be out scalloping too, his relaxed demeanor never changes. He loves being on the water, it's evident, and I wonder if I've ever loved a place as much as he loves this one.

Eventually, he spots whoever it is he's looking for. There's a large black and white pirate flag hanging off one of the boats, and he sits up a little straighter as the boat begins to slow. I'm nervous; I know there's no reason to be, but I can't help it. If someone recognizes me, things will change. I know it, and I'm not ready yet. Picking up my sun hat, I slide it on to hide my face for now.

There are three other boats, and someone yells "Jake!" as he kills the engine and we glide right up to the one closest to us. Moving past me, he raises his hand in acknowledgment and opens a cabinet for an anchor. He easily throws it over, the guy on the other boat throws a rope to connect us, Jake wraps it back and forth around a silver hook, and just like that we're settled.

"Morning, newbie," I hear called out, and I look over to see Bauer smiling at me from two boats over. It's then I realize everyone is staring at us, or I should say me. Each boat has two or three people on board, and other than Bauer, I only recognize Natalie, who is with Bauer, not Garrett. She's grinning at me and waves when I glance at her. Anxiety about being discovered by the rest of these people rips through me, and I take a deep breath to try to calm it. I raise my hand and wave back.

"Morning," I answer him.

"How'd you like the tour?" Bauer asks. He's wearing a short-sleeved button-down, the buttons undone so the shirt is flapping open, and swim trunks. I glance at Garrett, who already has his shirt off and is just standing in his trunks talking to a guy and a girl on his boat that I don't recognize, and I mentally shake my head. These brothers are something else, and then I remember there's a fourth one too, in Denver.

"Loved it," I tell him, and I really did. He did a great job, even if I did mildly freak out at my house.

A huge smile splits his face. "I can't wait to pick your brain, but what was your favorite part?" He moves from the back of his boat to the front so he's standing closest to me.

"Watching you walk around in a black cape," I tease. His friends from the third boat, the furthest from me, immediately start ribbing him. Bauer laughs too, but I turn away, hoping to end the conversation and move the attention off of me.

Pulling my dress over my head, I neatly fold it, put it in my bag, and pull out a long-sleeved pink sun shirt, similar to Jake's. I smirk at him as I slide it on. "Who needs sunblock now?"

He grins. "You do, snowflake." He walks over and hands me a bottle to spray my remaining exposed skin.

"I thought I would take one from your playbook today." I pull at the sleeve of the shirt.

"You'll be glad you did. The sun can be brutal, especially out here on the water. People don't realize the UV rays reflect off of the water too, increasing your chances of getting burned."

"Well, I definitely don't want to get burned," I mock, peeking up at the sky to see there are not many clouds.

"No, we wouldn't want that," he says. Even through our sunglasses, I feel his eyes locking with mine. He has such an intense way about him all the time, and my stomach dips. "So, you've never scalloped before, right?" he asks, breaking the moment, moving to the benches that run along the back of the boat, and lifting a padded seat. Underneath is storage, and he pulls out two mesh bags then closes it up.

"Nope, I have no idea what to do." I glance at the other three boats to see what others are doing. A few people are chatting, and a few are putting on headgear.

"It's pretty easy. I'll dive down and find one while you put this on." He hands me one of the bags, and inside it is a pair of flippers, a mask, and a snorkel. After dumping his contents on the bench, with just a mask on, he leaps over the edge of the boat into the water and disappears. I lean out and look for him.

The water isn't deep and it's clear, so I watch as he reaches down and grabs something. Kicking his way back to the top, he swims around to the back of the boat and climbs on board, soaking the floor.

I consciously have to make sure my mouth doesn't drop open as a wet Jake walks my way. *Oh my.* Running his hand through his hair, he shakes it out, pushes the mask up to his forehead, and then wipes his face to remove the excess water. The shirt clings to his skin and leaves nothing to the imagination. Lines, indentions, and the bumps and valleys of the muscles layering his body, each one making itself known, and he's completely oblivious as he stretches his arm out and hands me the small shell.

With effort, I try not to make it obvious I've lost my breath, I tear my eyes away from him and stare down at the brown and white object. "So this is what I look for?" I ask, hoping I don't stutter or shake as I reach out to take it.

What is wrong with me?

"Yes. It's slack tide right now, so swimming will be easy and the seagrass will be standing straight up. Although the colors of the shells vary, you'll see them tucked into the grass easily enough."

"Are there things down there that will bite or sting me? The fish?" I look up at him. The mask is propped up on his forehead, his blue eyes now visible and crinkling in the corners.

He chuckles and the sound wraps around me. "No, not today. It's shallow here, and with all the boating activity, most biting and stinging things have made their way elsewhere."

"Don't make fun of me." I lightly shove him as he smiles at me. This smile is soft, warm, and if I didn't know any better, I would say affectionate. "How many should I look for?" I ask as he slips his mask off and goes about hooking on the snorkel.

"As many as you can find. Bay scallops are small, like the

ones you probably ate at the festival. Most likely the bivalve of the shell will be open, so don't be surprised if it snaps shut and moves away from you."

"And these won't bite either, right?" Why I'm nervous about this, I don't know. I just am.

He grins again. "No, but I wouldn't recommend getting your finger stuck in the shell."

Great. Now I have an image of my finger being chopped off.

"Why are there so many here?" I ask, copying what he's doing with his mask and snorkel.

"Because fresh water from the river runs into the gulf, creating the perfect environment of fresh and salt water for the scallops to thrive. If the water is too salty, they will die."

My face dips in surprise. Interesting.

Sitting on the bench, he slides his flippers on, and I do the same.

"Should we stop somewhere when we're done and have the scallops shucked? My next-door neighbor claims to be the best and the fastest in the area."

He leans backward and stretches out his long legs. His arm reaches across the back of the bench where I'm sitting, and he watches as I finish buckling the flippers around my heel. "I would agree that she is. She's sort of a legend around here, but one doesn't grow up in Chuluota Springs and not know how to shuck a scallop."

"Oh, I suppose not." It didn't even occur to me that this is something everyone knows how to do.

"Don't worry, I'll teach you." He gently pulls on my ponytail then stands up.

I follow, and he hands me the mesh bag the equipment came in and then proceeds to hook his over his wrist.

"Are you ready?" he asks, still amused by my wariness.

"As ready as I'm going to be."

He nods then sits on the edge of the boat and falls over. I follow what he does, welcoming the temperate water as I sink below the surface and float over the grass, searching for anything that looks like the shell he brought up. Finding nothing, I resurface to blow the water out of the snorkel and to get more air, and to my left I see Jake coming over with another one in his hand.

"Where did you find that?" I'm animated, and his lips tip up.

"In the grass."

Letting out a groan, I leave him, diving back down, and much to my delight, I find one. Only, as I approach it, I see two rows of light blue dots lining the edge of the shells. Mesmerized, I slowly reach out to grab it, but it snaps shut and zigzags away from me.

What the ... ? I'm annoyed, because although he doesn't realize it, Jake and I are in a competition to see who can find the most.

Heading back to the surface, I find him sitting on the ledge on the back of the boat, waiting for me.

"What are the blue things?"

"It's eyes," he answers, and my mouth drops open.

"Oh my God. Are you serious? Can it see me?"

"Sort of. It's a survival thing, from food to predators. Their eyes aren't built like ours, and scientists don't actually know what the scallop is perceiving when it sees something."

"Now I feel bad for catching them."

"Don't. They don't have brains—you aren't hurting their feelings. Besides, they are so good to eat."

They are good to eat. I think about the fried scallops I had at the fair, the perfect mix of crispy, salty, and sweet.

"Okay. How many have you found?" I look for his bag. He has it dangling in the water, and when he pulls it up, I see there are four.

Without thinking, I let go of the boat, put my hand on his leg to keep me afloat, and grab the bag.

"How did you find these already?" I look up at him. Water drips off the mask and from his hair and runs down the side of his face.

He shrugs one shoulder, smiling at me.

Letting go, I kick backward and give him a look that says, *Game on.*

His lips pinch together as he's still smiling at me, but his brows rise in acceptance. Diving down, I remember what June said: "It's like Easter egg hunting." *Let's go hunting.*

Hours later, with two full bags of scallops, we've decided to stop for lunch. Jake and I each counted our bags as we tossed the scallops into a five-gallon bucket, and with blatant satisfaction, Jake beams at me as he's in the lead by 13. I assure him that 13 is peanuts and I'll pass him after lunch, but he just laughs.

Bauer and Natalie decide to join us, bringing their cooler over, and with the radio on, the four of us kick back and load our plates with food. Garrett said hello to me but mostly steers clear. I want to ask why, but I'm pretty sure it has to do with Natalie.

"So, you're from Chicago?" Bauer asks, stuffing his face with a large sub sandwich.

"Yes." I shouldn't be surprised that he knows this between his brothers and the small town, but I find that I am. I also can't help but wonder if he knows anything else.

"What did you do there?" he asks, now shoving a few potato chips into his mouth.

"I was an interior designer and decorator." I look away from him and down to the hummus and vegetables I packed. Picking up a carrot, I swipe it through the dip and take a bite.

"That's cool. Do you plan on doing that here as well?" he asks. Jake is watching me. My shoulders are tensing, and I can't tell if he notices or not, but I hate this line of questioning. I get it, he's curious, and to most these are innocent questions, but to me they feel loaded.

"Technically, I already am. One of the reasons I bought the house was to challenge myself. Up until now, I've mainly done hotels, and there's quite a different feel of the space between a hotel and a home."

"You got me there. What are the other reasons?" He leans back, eyeing me almost suspiciously.

I glance at Natalie. Her eyes have gone large; she knows how this is making me feel.

"Bauer," Jake says, just the one word effectively telling him to knock it off. Jake knows about the divorce, but I've been pretty private about it, and he hasn't pushed. Then again, maybe he realizes if I talk about my past, he'll have to talk about his, and quite frankly I'd rather risk swimming with the alligators.

"What? Everyone is wondering—that's not a secret. I'm just apparently the only one to ask." It's the lawyer in him. I know he can't help it—he's a truth seeker—but still.

"They don't ask for a reason." Jake's words are weighted, but this somehow makes me feel worse. Does he know who I am? Who I was married to? He can't know. Who would have told him? After all, if he Googled the name I've given, he won't find anything. But at the same time, omission is still a lie. I know this, and although our friendship is new and evolving, I'm not ready to tell him, lie or not. Status, money, attention, gossip—they change things, always. I've seen it happen over and over my whole life.

"It's fine," I tell the two of them as they wordlessly communicate and scowl at each other. "I visited the area once with my family, and I liked it here. Randomly, I came across the house and thought, *Why not?*" That's the answer that has seemed to work for everyone else so far.

"So you up and moved, just like that?" he questions, his brows pulling down underneath the edge of his sunglasses.

"Yes." I give him a smile I'm certain he and Jake can both tell is fake.

"Huh," he mutters.

Saving me, Natalie leans over and asks him about some paperwork on a listing she has. They begin talking, but Jake and I do not. I'm sure he knows there is more to my story than just the divorce, and I'm sure he wants to hear about it too, but I just can't tell him. Not yet.

Suddenly not feeling hungry anymore, I grab the mask and snorkel, loop the now empty bag back on my arm, and dive back in.

17

————

$\mathcal{I}$t's midafternoon by the time we decide to say goodbye to Jake's brothers, Natalie, and their friends. Both our scallop bags have refilled to the top, my skin is faintly pink even though I repeatedly slathered on the sunblock, and I'm sea drowsy, the kind of drowsy that only can come from the gentle rocking of the boat on the water, the salty air, and having hours of a good time with good people.

My mother once told me the older we get, the harder it is to make friends, true friends, but so far I think she's wrong. Maybe that's true in the world I came from, but not here. These people have no one to impress and nothing to prove. They are kind to everyone, coming across as wholly themselves, and when Jake invites me over for dinner, I immediately say yes.

We make a quick stop by my house so I can shower and change, and then we're off to his. He parks the boat at the dock outside his office. I already knew he lived upstairs in the house over the veterinarian practice, but I wasn't prepared for how renovated and beautiful it would be.

We took a private set of stairs up the back of the house and entered into the kitchen. You would never know it's the second

183

floor of an old bungalow home—the floor plan is open, light, and looks like it's a new condo straight out of one of my father's urban buildings.

Jake leaves his cooler and our bucket of scallops in the kitchen and me to explore while he takes a quick shower himself. My interior decorator heart glows at all the details I find, from the white and black marble island countertop to the subway tile backsplash; the dark brown, gray, and blue accent colors; and even the old and comfortable-looking blanket tossed on the end of the couch.

Everything looks new, but it also looks just like him. Masculine, relaxed, but in depth with its features. There's a wooden boat on the mantel that looks like he built it, and the base of the lamp on the end table is filled with shells I'm assuming he's found.

"Your home is beautiful," I tell him as he comes back to the kitchen. He's now wearing a pair of jeans and a light blue T-shirt. His hair is wet, not that it hasn't been all day, but he looks casual. He looks so good I have to turn away.

"Thanks. Garrett did it," he says as he moves the cooler, repositions the bucket of scallops, and has Alexa play some music.

"Wow. Well, I'm glad I hired him then—it seems we have similar tastes."

"Yes, he has talked incessantly about your house and all the dream features it has. It's like contractor heaven for him." He smiles faintly while thinking of his brother and moving around the kitchen. He pours us each a glass of ice water and sets one in front of me.

"What made him become a contractor? You and Bauer took the studious routes, seems he would have been guided that way too." I move to the chair at the end of the island to get out of his way and take a seat.

Grabbing a large colander, he dumps half of the scallops in and rinses them. His sink faces the window, so I'm presented with his back, and my eyes glide over his shoulders and the muscles there. He's quiet as he contemplates his answer but then says, "Garrett is dyslexic. School was really hard for him. He loves to learn, that was never the problem, just … well, you get it."

I never would have known. Every time we've looked at plans, notes, or contracts with other vendors, he's never said anything or gotten anything wrong.

"I do. But, I've known a lot of contractors, and not all of them can do what he's done."

In my peripheral, I see Jake smile at the compliment for his brother as he places the bowl over a pot on the island next to me to catch any water that still needs to drain. He grabs another bowl and two knives then pulls his garbage can closer to us.

"So here's how we're going to shuck the scallops." He hands me one of the knives. "A lot of people use a scallop knife. However, I've always been just fine using a butterknife." Reaching into the bowl, he grabs a scallop for himself and hands one to me. "Do you see how each side is a different color? One side is dark and the other is light. We want the light side up, and do you see this notch here?" He points to a notch near the hinge of the two shells. "We want this on the right side, with the hinge facing you."

He moves the shell around so it fits perfectly in his hand, and I match him.

"Next, we're going to take our knife, slip it into the little opening right next to the notch, and begin moving it across the shell, twisting it up. Now, there's a muscle here"—he points to the left side of the hinge, which is next to his thumb—"which is our ultimate prize, and it holds the shell together. We want to cut it as close to the upper shell as we can so we don't lose any of the meat." He wiggles the knife back and forth until it's all the way through, and he opens the scallop.

"Looks disgusting," I tell him.

He grins. "We're going to throw away the top half of the shell." He tosses it into the garbage can. "We'll loosen the innards and scrape them off." This goes into the garbage too. "And then voila! What we're left with is the scallop meat."

I stare down at the nickel-sized scallop just sitting there all by itself. How someone first figured out that this gorgeous little scallop was under all that, I'll never know. He frees it from the shell and tosses it into his mouth.

"Wait! Shouldn't you cook it before you eat it?" I ask, alarmed.

He grins at me, his blue eyes framed by his dark eyelashes, all warm and friendly. "Nah, can't get any fresher than this. Sweet and tender—you're going to love them. Now you try."

Looking at the shell, I flip it so the lighter side is up then go about opening it the way Jake did. It isn't hard to slip the knife in and wiggle it across, but what I do discover is that the edge of the shell is sharp. Working my way to cut the muscle, I move slowly, and then the shell gives. I think I thought it would be harder than this, but as I push the little white scallop into the bowl on the counter, I realize the hard part is the time it's going to take to shuck all of these to have a decent amount to eat. Jake was right—find as many as you can, because you can't have too many.

"Try it raw. Tell me what you think," he says after opening another one and holding the meat out to me.

Hesitantly, I pick it up, lock eyes with him, and slowly put it in my mouth. It's a little salty, but overall I think it's kind of sweet and super tender. He's right, they're tasty this way and would make a great ceviche.

"You were right. They are good like this." I smile at him, and he smiles back. It's easy to be with him and surprisingly very comfortable.

I pick up the next one, and side by side we begin to shuck the large bucket of scallops. I don't know what I thought would happen when I moved here, but meeting a guy wasn't it. Somehow though, here I am. Here we are becoming friends, and I feel relaxed, like I can just be me and not worry about saying or doing the wrong thing. With Carter, I'm starting to realize maybe I had morphed into what I thought he needed me to be versus being the me I was when we met. I was the perfect polished wife and socialite instead of the girl he met on the beach who was carefree, had braids in her hair, and ate cotton candy until she was almost sick while watching the sunset. Whereas I thought we were growing up together, adulting, he was losing interest in me.

Still though, we were married, and he should have talked to me instead of cheating.

Taking a sip of the water, I clear my mind and glance back up at Jake, who's flying through these scallops at a pace I could never keep up with, which is a good thing seeing as how he found more than me and technically won. I don't understand how someone could leave this guy standing at the altar. What a horrible thing to do, and especially to him. I'm sure he has flaws, but I haven't found them yet. He's such a nice guy.

Seems we both deserved better.

"Where's the dog?" I ask him, looking around.

"What dog?" He looks up at me curiously.

"The one with the prosthetic leg."

Understanding drifts over his features. "Oh, that's Betty's dog, my receptionist. Beamer was hit by a car, and I tried to save his leg but couldn't."

"That's terrible. Did you build the leg for him?" I pick up another shell and slip in my knife.

"Ah, no. She took him to see a prosthetist in Tampa. I would have no idea where to begin with that." He flings an empty shell into the garbage.

"Gotcha. Although, as a lover of animals, I'm surprised to see you don't have any pets."

One side of his mouth tips up. "I actually do. Dash is around here somewhere." He glances past my shoulder at what I assume is Dash's normal lounge location but then shrugs.

My brows rise. "Dash?"

"My cat." He grins. His teeth are darn near perfect, as is his mouth. My stomach swirls at the thought of his mouth on mine.

The cat hears his name, and a meow sounds from the other side of the living room. I turn, and there sauntering out of Jake's bedroom is a large hairy orange tabby cat. I don't know why, but I never considered him to be a cat guy, which is ridiculous—after all, he's a veterinarian and loves all animals, but still, this is unexpected.

I look at the cat and then at Jake. Whatever expression he sees makes him laugh.

"Dash was a patient of mine, and unfortunately his owner passed away. We've estimated that Dash is about fifteen now, and he's missing an eye—what was I to do? No one wants an old cat like that, and I didn't have it in me to put him down."

"How long have you had him?" The cat saunters into the kitchen and over to Jake. He rubs up against his leg, and Jake bends down to quickly scratch him behind the ears.

"About three years."

"How old are you?" I ask him.

"Thirty-two." Jake stands back up then rinses his fingers off before resuming the shucking. "He smells the scallops and knows dinner is going to be grand tonight."

"You'll feed him these scallops?"

"Why not? Cats eat seafood." He shrugs as he grabs one out

of the bowl and gives it to Dash. The cat eagerly takes it and scampers off.

"I guess I've just never thought about it. You surprise me, Jake, all the time. Just when I think I have a little bit of you figured out, you prove me wrong."

"What do you want to know?" he asks, his eyes locking with mine.

I think about his question, then quietly but brazenly say, "I think everything."

Silence hangs between us as we look at each other. His eyes roam over the details of my face, and my skin ignites like a feather is being brushed over it. Breaking eye contact, I look down as he lets out a deep sigh. I don't think it's in frustration or resignation, but more like finality. "Okay," he says, in a low but tender voice.

"So, what's your story, Jake the veterinarian?" I ask, not looking at him but picking up the next shell and prying it open. We're almost done, and I'm glad because my stomach has started to growl.

He chuckles. "Shouldn't I be the one asking you? After all, I'm not the new person here—you are."

"Well, you're new to me, and there's not much to tell. I needed a change of scenery. You already know about the divorce, so I'm sure you understand."

He nods as he thinks about this, and a pang of guilt hits my chest. In a way, it's a lie. There is more to tell, but the truth is, none of it is relevant to him or what may or may not be between us. This is us, and that is not.

"I grew up here. Chuluota is my home. I know it's not much for most, just a small town, but I've always loved it here and always saw myself growing old here. Plus it's where my family is."

This makes me think of my family and how I so easily left

them. They don't fault me for needing to get away, but over the last two months, I haven't really given any thought to when or if I'm going back.

"What made you decide to become a vet?"

"Like the town, I've always loved animals too. Aside from domestic pets, there are a lot of other animals here that sometimes need help as well. Living here on the river and the gulf, we see a wide variety, like birds, sea turtles, manatees, and occasionally a dolphin. I work closely with the Clearwater Marine Aquarium when one is sick and in need of rehabilitation before it can be released."

"That's amazing. I've seen dolphins in the wild, but you've probably hugged them, haven't you?"

"Something like that." His lips tip up.

"What about Jessie? Have you hugged him recently?" I tease.

He lets out a laugh, the sound sending flutters to my heart.

"No, I just keep an eye out for him. He's lived under that dock for so long, and no one knows why—usually manatees migrate."

"Maybe he's keeping Mrs. Easler company." I think back to last night, the light, and Bauer's story.

"Maybe," he says thoughtfully.

"Do you think what Bauer said is true? Do you think her husband was murdered?"

"I don't know. It seems plausible. There was one surviving person on that ship."

My eyes whip up to his. "There was?"

Little lines form between his brows. Maybe he thought I already knew this, but I didn't, and now I have to know.

"Mr. Thomas Greene. He was Mr. Easler's main skipper, and he was found washed ashore some estimated twenty miles south, but the ship never turned up. He claims he fell overboard during the storm and somehow made it to land, but no one remembers there being a storm that bad on that day, and there's no record of one."

I let that sink in as I grab the last scallop from the bucket and go through the motions of prying it open. I definitely find myself siding with the skeptics here, because how does one survive a terrible storm and make it from who knows how far out in the water to land?

"Was he found with driftwood or a boat or anything?"

"I don't know. If he was, it was never mentioned to my knowledge. From what we learned as kids about the history of the town, people rejoiced that there was one person who survived while mourning the loss of the others. Mr. Easler and Mr. Greene were both beloved."

"Huh." I throw the last shell in the garbage as he takes the bowl to dump the scallops back in the colander then rinse them off in the sink.

"Would you like a glass of wine or a beer?" he asks, looking over his shoulder.

"Sure. Do you have white wine? After being in the sun all day, I'm thinking a cold wine sounds delicious."

He bends down and opens the door of a wine cooler that's built into the island. This has me thinking about the closet located under the stairs at my home. Converting that to a mini wine cellar is the perfect thing to do with that space, and I make a mental note to tell Garrett. Jake pulls out a bottle, pops the cork, and pours us each a glass.

"Any requests on how we cook these babies?" He returns to the sink and shakes the colander again to drain off more water.

"Nope."

"All right. I hope you like lemon and garlic butter." He glances at me to see my reaction.

"That just happens to be one of my favorites."

He smiles as he moves about his kitchen with ease, grabbing

a large frying pan and a pot to boil water for pasta. He's smiled more today than any of the other times we've been together, and I really like seeing him smile.

"So what happened to the fishing business?"

He looks over at me. "It should come as no surprise when I tell you the skipper took over the operation, and it continued to thrive for decades."

I suck in some air as I start to put pieces of this town's story together. I think about Greene Park and a few other landmarks with that name and not the Easlers', and an irrational anger stirs inside me. How convenient for Mr. Greene.

"If he was murdered, maybe Mrs. Easler's ghost is trying to tell us something. Maybe that's why she's still here and hasn't crossed over or left or whatever it is ghosts do."

"Maybe, but then again, maybe it's just a light. That's all we see. People have watched and studied the light for years to try to determine if there is anything to it, but nothing. Nothing has ever come of it or changed."

I hum quietly. He's right, it is just a light, but I have one thing all those other people don't ... the house.

<h1 style="text-align:center">18</h1>

<hr>

Three nights have passed since Jake dropped me off on the dock after our day together, and three nights have passed where I sat for hours at the end of the balcony outside my bedroom and stared at the light.

I've tried to track its patterns, and at first I thought I was reaching for something that wasn't there, but then I noticed the light would react to me and flicker off. It never moves, always stays two posts to the right. Occasionally I think it may bob up and down, but if I move as if I'm going back inside, it disappears.

This got me thinking about all the other times I've seen the light. It only shines when I'm looking directly at its location on the dock. When I go back into the boathouse, the light will fade. When I'm in the kitchen and going about different things, if I glance at the dock, it comes on, and if I move through the room, it's gone. Same with on the balcony—when I'm sitting in the lawn chair I've dragged up here, the light is there, but when I move or look away, in my peripheral vision, I can see it's gone.

All of this leads me to believe she knows when I'm looking and when I'm not, and if she wants me to see the light, I think there's a message somehow too. I'm just not sure how to discover what it is.

"What are you doing right now?" Ivy asks. "You sound out of breath."

Ivy has taken to calling me every day to check in. It's not at any specific time, and we usually don't talk for long, but I love that she calls. I know they're still worried about me, but as time goes by, it seems they are getting more comfortable with me being here. After all, I'm doing all right, plus I'm certain seeing the progress of the house on the blog helps.

"I needed to get out of the house for a bit, so I'm walking up and down the driveway."

Walking and sweating. Natalie told me August is the hottest month of the year, and although it's still July, I can't see how it can get any hotter than this. I may be under the shade of the trees, but with the humidity, sweat is rolling straight down my back.

She laughs. "Why?"

I wipe my brow with my shirt. "Well, I guess I wanted to stay close to the house, and I just needed to stretch my legs. Garrett is installing new baseboards today, and between the saw and the nail gun, it's all pretty loud." I had hoped to get the downstairs painting finished first, but that didn't happen.

"If you say so, but I know you, and you only pace when your brain is working in overdrive." There's the faint hum of music in the background; she must be in her shop.

"I received an interesting email through the new website yesterday from an editor with *Southern Living* magazine. They'd like to do an article on the house, before and after, including the history of the home and mentioning the town."

"Really? How did they find you?"

"Must be through social media for the new account. I have an Instagram page and a TikTok page. I've tagged and hashtagged all the images and videos, so it would be easy enough if they're looking for content."

"Do you think that's a good idea?" The concern in her voice is evident.

"I'm not sure, but I love the way the house is coming along. It should be shared with the world, and then there's the town—if it brought in any new tourism, that would be great."

I think about Corrie and her family, Bauer with his tour, and the marina. Although this place has grown and prospered over the years, it is still a fishing town at heart. Maybe people will come just to buy the fish, or maybe they'll charter tours. It could be great.

"I understand all this, but are you ready for what this might do to you?"

Seagulls fly overhead and squawk at each other as a hot breeze brushes against me and rustles the leaves on the trees. I pause as I think about her question. I've been in Chuluota Springs for two months now, and although I've made friends, I'm not certain how the discovery of who I am will be received. Yes, Natalie and Corrie know, but then there's Jake, Garrett, his crew, and even Bauer. How will they react? Will they even care?

Turning around, I stare at the house through the trees. It really is such a magnificent house, and I'm proud of it. I think like anyone with their job, when you're proud of something, you want people to recognize that, and the magazine reaching out has made me—the designer me—feel so good.

"No. Definitely not. But who knows ... if I did say yes, maybe there would be a way to leave my name out of it. Or by the time the article comes out, maybe I'll be out and discovered anyway."

"Maybe, but you should still think about it a bit more. I feel like the paparazzi manhunt for you has shifted to a whole new level. Veronica is still crowing about you to anyone in the social scene who will listen. It's quite pathetic really."

I let out a long sigh. "I'll think about it." Just picturing her face has my stomach souring, but surprisingly the dull ache that usually accompanies it isn't there. I look down at my hand, at where my wedding ring once sat, and a small smile slips over my lips. Healing—it's about freaking time.

"Now, the most important thing we should be talking about, and the real reason for my call, is Jake. I read the scalloping post you put up yesterday, and I saw the pictures." The glee is one hundred percent evident in her voice. "You've never mentioned his level-ten Southern hotness."

That small smile now stretches to a large one. He is so good-looking. Sometimes it hurts to look at him because I feel physically and emotionally shifted when I do. Carter was handsome in that white collar, rich, WASPy, yacht club kind of way. Jake is just something all on his own, and I find every time I'm with him, I like him a little bit more.

"There's not much to tell you. We're just starting to be friends," I tell her as I resume walking and wondering if this makes me happy or not. He hasn't said or done anything to make me think he would want something different or more, but then again, he doesn't have to spend time with me, which he chooses to do.

"Sure you are," she teases.

"We are," I say a little more firmly, but she just laughs.

"Oh, sister of mine. Whatever you say. I look forward to hearing more about him."

"Don't hold your breath."

"For the record, Rylie, I'm proud of you."

My heart thumps hard in my chest. After so much negative noise over the last year, one forgets what it's like and how much it means to hear the good stuff too.

"Why? What do you mean?" I again stop to hear what she has to say and stare off into the trees of my property.

"Well, I love seeing what you're doing with the house. It looks amazing, but it's more than that—you're not hiding. You've made friends, you've started a life there, and from everything you've said, it sounds like a good one. I was so worried about you after everything went down…it was just uncharted territory for all of us. You've handled it all so well, and you're doing so well."

My eyes prick with the telltale sign of tears. It's not that I need a pat on the back, but hearing this releases some weight I've been carrying. They were so disgruntled when I said I was coming here, but it has been good for me, I am doing okay, and it means something to me to hear her say this.

"Of course I love you and I miss you," she adds. "But, I'm happy for you. You deserve all that you're finding there."

"Come visit me." The longing to see her pierces the composure I hold so tightly to.

"I'm planning on it once Fashion Week is over." Fashion Week happens twice a year, February and September, which means she'll be here sometime in October.

"Perfect. I'll make sure your room is all set up for you." I've been mentally planning her room for weeks and have been browsing websites for a really large gilded ornate mirror that will be the focal piece. Ivy isn't necessarily vain, but fashion people have a tendency to stare at themselves in the mirror a lot.

"I look forward to my welcome basket." She laughs.

"I bet you do, and by basket you mean wine." Ivy has an undeniable love for all full-bodied cabernets.

"You know me so well." I can picture her smiling, and it makes my smile grow just a little larger. It feels good to smile, and these last few weeks have definitely brought it back out.

I do know her, and she knows me too.

After we end the call, a silence falls over me as I stand under the trees and look up. Through the long branches, the sky is so blue, the perfect shade of the color, and in this moment I feel something good—I feel that happiness. It may be fleeting, but I can recognize it, and my heart seizes it. With my arms open wide and my head thrown back, I spin in the driveway, watching the world around me, a kaleidoscope with swirls of dark green, blue, and white from the clouds. Feeling like this, it really does make me believe I'm healing, and I do want to, more than anything.

As dizziness overtakes me, I stop, and there tucked into the trees, about thirty yards away, I see what looks like a shed. Natalie never mentioned one, but I'm assuming it's mine as my house is the last on this street. I don't know why I didn't think to look over the entire property before, because of course this house would have a shed, a barn, or something since a fishman once lived here, before cars were a thing.

Leaving the driveway, I make my way through the trees, and as I get closer, I see the shed actually looks more like the size of a small barn, and directly to the right of it is the remains of a trail that leads down to the inlet.

Turning around, I look for the house, because how is it possible I didn't see this before? It's not that it's that far away; it's just with the bend in the driveway and the trees, it's obscured. There aren't even any traces of a former trail to the house like there was to get to Willow's. I wonder if Garrett knows it's here.

As I look back at the barn, every movie I've ever watched where there is an old abandoned rural building slips into my mind. Wild animals, snakes, spiders, squatters—who knows, and it's with extreme trepidation and excitement that I step toward the door, lift the wooden handle, and slowly open it.

The heavy fluttering of wings echoes around the space, and I duck as birds whoosh over my head and fly out. Dust from the ground is stirred up into the air as I pull the door the remaining way open, sneeze, and stare at a mostly empty space. Taking a few steps in, I let my eyes wander over every detail of the forgotten structure. The ceiling has a large hole in the back left corner, the walls leak light between the boards, and there are partitions that lead me to believe there were three animal stalls at one time.

This barn is most definitely dilapidated and probably termite-infested. It's beyond repair and will eventually need to be torn down, but I can't help the thrill that runs through me. Fishermen from the turn of the century were notorious for finding rare things, mostly from shipwrecks that washed ashore or during fishing, and with all the pots, hand tools, large tools, and knickknacks on the shelves here, I wonder if any of it is valuable.

Walking to the side wall, I lightly run my fingers over a long wooden workbench, leaving streaks in the heavy layer of dirt, and stare at the space. Each item holds a memory from a time long forgotten. Curious, I squat down and look under the bench. In the closet cabinet there was a hidden ledge, and sure enough, behind the dropdown lip of the edge of the table, which disguises the surface to look as if it's four inches thick, is another hidden ledge.

Using the flashlight on my phone, I shine it at the ledge, and behind loose old cobwebs is a small wooden box.

My heart starts to race.

There has to be something in it; the ledge would be empty otherwise. As I pull the box out from underneath the work table, items rattle inside it, and I swipe my hand across the top to remove the dust. There are flowers etched into the wood, making it a very feminine object, and I immediately know it was hers, not his.

Setting it down on the table, I slowly lift the lid, and I gasp as I stare down into it. Now, I don't know much about guns, but I do know I'm staring at a very old Colt revolver.

Along with the gun, there are bullets scattered throughout

the box, a note, four pinkish stones, and one piece of jewelry: a brooch with small diamonds and the pink stones.

Lifting out the gun, I marvel at how old it looks but also how new at the same time. I can't help but wonder where it came from and how much it could possibly be worth today. Afraid I might somehow be damaging it, I place it back in the box and gently pick up and open the note, which is only folded once.

Scribbled in faded old cursive handwriting, it says, "Take care and be safe, my love."

Chills race down my arms.

19

———

Today is my wedding anniversary. Well, my ex-anniversary. Although I know the date should technically be irrelevant now, it's just not, at least not today. Maybe one day it will be, but until then I can't just wipe away the feelings and memories this day holds for me.

I would be lying if I said I hadn't been dreading this day, because I have been. People always say your wedding day is the happiest day of your life until your first child is born, and they aren't wrong. It was the happiest day of my life. I can't even argue that, and if I were given the opportunity to go back in time and tell that girl on that day what's coming, all the things I know now, I don't know that I would. There are so few days where we experience that kind of joy, that kind of love in its purest form, and I don't think I would ruin it for her.

We were married in the gardens at the Art Institute of Chicago, and our reception was held at the Chicago Yacht Club. The trees were the perfect shade of green, the boats were stacked and shiny in the marina, and the smiles on the faces of our family and friends...I will never forget it. Everything went off perfectly, from the gorgeous summer weather, the music, and the laughter to the fireworks at the end of the night. It was the perfect day, and I was certain I was with my perfect guy.

"What do you think, Coco? Is today going to be a good day?" I ask her as she bobs her head up and down. She's sitting next to me on the kitchen island, and we're sharing a bowl of strawberries. Of course she doesn't answer me, but I let out a deep sigh as if she has. Today is also our gotcha day, the day I was given Coco.

Don't get me wrong, today is a good day, and it really is. The sun is out, I'm sitting in a stunning home I'm renovating and decorating, and the river is sparkling in the morning light. I think my heart is just bruised; how could it not be?

I'm startled and pulled from my thoughts as knocking sounds on the back door.

My heart leaps.

Turning around, I glance down toward the dock to see if Jake's boat is there. I shouldn't be this hopeful, but I am. It's been a week since I last saw him, and sure enough, there it is parked in the same spot as always.

Have we talked? Yes, a little. He's texted a few times here and there, but mostly about nothing, just checking in on me. Flutters dance against my insides, and a smile slips onto my face before I even reach the door. When I pull it open, there he is, and I somehow believe he must have known I needed a friend today. With his messy windblown hair, day-old scruff across his jaw, and blue eyes staring back at me, those flutters pause mid-tango and settle in the bottom of my stomach.

He blinks, one side of his mouth quirks up, and his brows rise in question as I stand there staring at him, and I realize I'm grinning.

"Morning," he says.

Gah, his voice, that rough raspy morning voice.

I shouldn't be affected by it, shouldn't be affected by him, but

I am. It's like he's slowly casting a spell over me, and I'm all right with it.

"Morning," I parrot back, rocking up on my toes in happiness.

His smile grows. "What are you doing?" he asks, clearly amused by what I'm assuming he thinks is strange behavior.

"Oh, um ..." His question makes me pause. What was I doing? I certainly can't tell him I was reliving and wallowing in my failures. "Having breakfast with Coco. Would you like to come in?" I open the door wider.

"Don't mind if I do." He moves up the steps, and I move back, allowing him to enter. He stops just over the threshold and looks up. "The chandelier is gone?"

"Yes. Both of them actually." I look up too, at the empty space. With them gone, both foyers feel so much larger and vacant. "Garrett knows a guy who is restringing the wiring in them. As pretty as they are just hanging there, I would love to see them lit up. They shouldn't be gone too long."

I give him a brief smile then turn to head back to the kitchen. I find Coco right where I left her, on the island with the strawberries, and she dances in place when she sees me. Jake has closed the door behind us and hums with delight as he enters the room and spots her.

"Hello, Coco," he says soothingly.

"Hello, Jake," she responds, hopping over to see him.

Jake's surprised gaze flies to mine with delight, and I can't help the large smile that splits my face.

What do you know, my wedding gift from Carter has unknowingly given her stamp of approval and added another layer to this day. I'm not sure how she remembered his name, maybe from me mentioning it in passing, but I love that she greeted him by name. He strokes her back as she pushes her body into him, and he looks around the kitchen.

"Wow, I can't believe how much you've gotten done. It looks amazing."

It really does. Garrett called Monday morning after the scalloping day to tell me my cabinets and countertops were in. They didn't take long to install, and while some of his men were putting the baseboards in, we finished the kitchen. It's just beautiful. Distressed white cabinets, stainless steel appliances with a powder blue Lacanche range, the vintage-looking blue and white tile backsplash, lighting that makes me drool, the new farm-style kitchen sink, and the waterfall white and gray marble island top—this room is officially my favorite in the house. We even painted Coco's new cage to match the cabinets.

"Thank you. I'm in love with how it's turning out. The kitchen table will be here this week, and I just know it's going to look perfect." I glance toward the sunny nook. Coco's cage currently occupies the space, but both will fit nicely. The table just seats four.

"Next time we are definitely eating dinner here," he says, and heat blooms in my cheeks. He's thinking of the next time, a next time with me, and a light vibrating sensation thrums underneath my chest.

"Absolutely. I'll cook up a good midwestern meal for you."

His brows rise. "Really? Like what, a Chicago-style hot dog?"

"If that's what you want, but I was thinking more along the lines of homemade perogies and butter cake cookies. You aren't a food snob, are you now?" I ask teasingly. It's crazy how just his presence has changed my entire morning and the mood that was accompanying it.

He chuckles. "No, if there's food, I'll eat it, although I can't say I've really ever had either. My mom might have given us perogies out of a box as a kid."

Clutching my chest, I fake shocked horror. "Well, that just won't do."

He chuckles.

Reaching for my coffee cup, I'm about to offer him some when he asks, "What's that?" He's looking at the old wooden box on the counter.

"I found it in the barn."

"Barn?" He looks at me curiously.

"Yeah, it's back on the far corner of the property. You can't really see it from here as the oak tree on this end of the house blocks the direction it's in, and I guess no one ever really thought to explore that area. It's pretty large. I love letting my mind wander with what it was used for."

Walking over to the box, I pick it up and run my hand over the top of it. I carefully cleaned it after I brought it home, trying to remove as much dust and dirt as possible without removing the integrity of the stain. I set it in front of him and watch as he opens the lid. Confusion and awe fill his face as his jaw drops a little.

He doesn't lift his head, but his eyes glance up at me through his ridiculously long dark eyelashes. "This is a really cool find. I can't believe you just found it."

"Right! And look at the note."

I move closer to him, pick up the piece of paper, and hand it to him. He takes it from me and gently pulls the page apart to not wear out the crease. His brows pull down as he studies it.

"Do you think it was meant as an endearment or a warning?" I ask, although the more I think about it, the more I think it's a warning.

"I don't know," he says quietly as he very carefully refolds it, puts it back in the box, and then runs his fingers over the old piece of jewelry and the gun. "Where exactly was it?"

"Under the workbench. There's not much in there, and I have no idea what most of it is, but there are gardening pots and a few tools I recognize. I don't know why I did it, but I ran my hand under the edge of the table. Turns out the edge was a lip, and tucked into a secret slot was the box. Just like the shelf in the closet."

"Do you think it's loaded?"

"I have no idea." I pick up the gun and rotate it around to see if there is a way to look into the bullet chamber. There's not. Before this one, I'd never held a gun before. I hand it to him, and he does the same before returning it with the barrel facing away from us.

Leaning back, he pushes the box back toward me and gives me an amused look. "Maybe I should start calling you detective instead of snowflake."

"Ha-ha. I don't know about that," I say a little sheepishly, but I still feel very proud at the same time.

"You found the newspaper and now this. I'm certain you'll uncover other things as well. Old houses love to tell stories, especially old Southern ones."

"We'll see." I look around at the rooms of the house visible to me. "I love it, so I can only hope there's more."

Coco, deciding she's done being left out, squawks at him and calls his name. He glances at the box again and then at her, giving her his full attention.

"What are you going to do with it?" he asks, resuming running his hand over the back of her head and down her back. She looks so blissed out, and I imagine if he ran his hands over me, I might feel the same way—which makes me pause and question myself. *Do I want him to run his hands over me?* And as we spend more and more time together, I'm thinking my answer might be, *Yes.*

"I have no idea. Right now I just keep staring at it."

It's one of those things where, although I found it after the purchase, it doesn't quite feel like it rightly belongs to me, only, I don't know who the previous owners are. I'm not sure Natalie would either.

"Can't say I blame you. I'd stare at it too," he says, rubbing the back of his neck with his free hand. "So, I stopped by because I was wondering if you have plans today." He shifts from one foot to the other.

Today, a day I thought would hold such a dear place in my heart forever.

"Not really. Just working around here," I tell him, working hard to keep the bruise from being pushed on. Again, it's not that I miss the actual marriage after the affair and the months following; it's the symbolism of what today meant to me that aches.

"How do you feel about getting out of the house?" he asks.

With a gratefulness I can't even explain to him, my heart sighs at the reprieve from being lost in my head for endless amounts of time and at the idea of spending another day with him.

"What'd you have in mind?" I ask, almost a little too excitedly.

"I'm going over to the state park for a few hours. I check on the animals monthly, drop off food, that kind of stuff, and I was wondering if you wanted to go with me."

"I think that sounds great. I would love to go. Is there anything I should bring?" I move to rinse the coffee cup and the bowl and set them both in the sink.

"Nope. I've got everything loaded up, so whenever you're ready, we can head out."

"Okay." I glance at Coco. Usually I'm nervous about people handling her, but I know Jake would never do anything to hurt her. "Do you mind putting her away while I change my clothes?" Currently, I'm wearing a pair of yoga pants and a T-shirt.

His gaze drifts down over me quickly before he gives me another smile and says, "Absolutely. Do your thing."

I'M NOT sure what I thought the Chuluota Springs State Park would be like, but it certainly wasn't this. In many ways, it's a small zoo, except this zoo is mostly filled with animals who've been rescued or are being rehabilitated. Of course there are standard animals one would presume to be in a Florida zoo, such as a black bear, a Florida panther, red wolves, Key deer, and manatees, but it's so much more than that. They have a reptile house, alligators, tons of birds and fish, and a hippopotamus. That's right, a hippopotamus. Jake thinks he's in his thirties, roughly, as he's been with the park for over twenty-five years.

"I can't believe all these animals are here." I wrap my fingers around the fence and stare at the black bear lying in the grass, rolling around on his back, and basking in the sun.

"Yeah, this park has been here for a long time. The land was originally purchased after the sugar mill closed down to help rebuild tourism, and it doesn't hurt that it's such a wonderful place for the animals. Most that have come here stay here, because we believe they wouldn't survive if reintroduced to their natural habitat. Take Apollo over here." He leans his head toward the bear, who also looks in our direction at hearing his name being called. "He came to us as a cub. He was four pounds, abandoned by his mother—who knows why—and now after all this time, he's imprinted on humans. He isn't afraid, and if anything he thinks everyone wants to feed him. So, you can imagine how well it would go over if we were to release him."

"He sure is cute." I watch as the bear eyes Jake. He knows him, there's recognition, and I think it's sweet.

Jake chuckles and puts his hands in his pockets. "Most days he is. Some days he's just a menace," he says affectionately.

"So we are at a state park, but this is more like a zoo. Who works here?" I ask as we continue walking down a path to check in on the red wolves.

"You're right, the park is funded by the state, so although it is called a park, it's a zoo too. Semantics." He shrugs his shoulders. "The main staff of the zoo is made up of the zookeeper, who manages the day-to-day necessities of the animals like feeding, exercising, and bathing. Next is the animal curator who is in charge of the big picture for the animals, such as shifting them from one location to the next, the requirements of their environments, breeding, applying medicines—just their overall needs. There are the zoologists who are in charge of the educational aspects like lectures, and then there's me, a volunteer wildlife veterinarian."

"So, you're not paid to come here?"

"No. I don't need to be paid. I just love animals, and this is one of the ways I can give back to my community. Yes, I'm on call for the park, but mostly, I'm not needed. Injuries don't occur too often, and really I just help the animal curator prevent illness, preventative medicine."

How amazing is that? A small smile slips onto my lips as I think about how the more I learn about this guy, the more surprised I am. He's such a good person and selfless in so many ways. Natalie said his family is treated like royalty in this town, and I can see why if they are all like him.

Which in turn makes me think of Carter. It's not that I'm comparing them, because I'm really not, but the differences between them just keep stacking up. Carter never did anything charitable unless he knew someone was going to know about it. He loved the spotlight and big grand gestures, but Jake couldn't care less. It never bothered me the way Carter went about giving his money, not his time, but maybe it's because I really didn't know the difference. My mother volunteers with various organizations, but again, it's mainly financial donations, not time.

"Sounds rewarding." I look up at him and feel this new wave of admiration sweep over me.

Feeling me staring at him, he looks down, and his eyes lock with mine. "It is."

Not hesitating, he slips his hand over mine, threading our fingers together, and we start walking. Staff at the park look at us curiously, or I should say they look at me, and for the first time in a long time, I don't feel like hiding. Do I want to jump out and have a flashing neon sign say, "Look at me! Here I am!" No, but I feel proud to walk with this man, a man who is making a difference in the world, not because he needs recognition or feels he has to, but because he wants to.

During the months following the exposure of Carter's affair and the divorce proceedings, I was on a mission to end the pain and heartache. I didn't want to appear weak and devastated, even though I was. I wanted people to believe I was strong enough to push through it all and was better than the situation I had found myself in. Believe me, humiliation by someone you love—it's not a good feeling, even though I had nothing to feel humiliated about as he was the one who couldn't keep his pants on.

So, I started reading empowering books and articles. As I poured myself into the stages of grief, just hoping to push myself through them as quickly as possible, I jotted down inspiring quotes, I redecorated, I leaned on my family, and through it all, I gave myself hope. Bad things happen to people, but life goes on.

One Chinese proverb I came across said, *Be not afraid of growing slowly. Be afraid only of standing still.* I didn't want to stand still anymore. I needed to do something, which is how I found myself on the internet and searching for a new place to live. Was I looking to hide from the paparazzi drama? Yes, but I was also looking to throw myself into a project I could feel good about, and maybe find myself a little. I was lost, floundering in my day-to-day routine, and now, here in this place with these people, I feel like I'm a better version of me, finding my footing, and definitely healing. I'm growing, and my heart feels grateful.

I am thankful for today, today of all days, and it's become one of those days where I ask myself how I got here. Not in a bad way, but a way where I'm proud of myself. For so long I've lived a certain lifestyle and been in the spotlight, and I was wrecked when my life was disrupted. I've mourned the loss of it all and worried I'd never get it back when the truth is, coming here, I'm reminded that the world does go on and the way we lived isn't the only way. I'd forgotten that, and today is just another reminder. That humbles me.

As the day winds down and we pull up next to my dock, we're quiet as he ties us to a post. It's not an uncomfortable silence, but more of a contented one. He gives me a hand, helps me out of the boat, and follows, and together we make our way to my back door. It hadn't occurred to me that this might qualify as a date, but right at this moment, it sure feels like one, and I find I'm not frightened by the prospect of it, but more anxiously giddy and nervous.

"Thank you for today," I tell him, and he rewards me with a small, pleased smile.

"I'm glad you had a good time." He brushes his hair off of his forehead and swipes it to the side. His eyes land on mine, and I feel almost breathless as this handsome guy looks reverently and tenderly at me.

"I'm even more glad that you left the snake tank cleaning for Garrett," I tease.

His head tips back just a little, and he laughs. The column of his throat is tan like his face and inviting. I wonder what it would be like to tuck my cheek against it and feel the vibrations rumbling through him. It's such a good sound, and I feel bathed in ease and comfort.

As I glance down, the words slip past my lips before I can pull them back. "Today was my wedding anniversary."

In front of me, he settles into a stillness, and tension slowly rises through Jake's muscles as he lets out a sigh. I look back up at him, and his shoulders are squared, his jaw hardened, but his eyes only show concern, not annoyance at me mentioning it.

What does he think about this? Did I ruin our day? I hope I didn't; I found it to be profound and good for my soul.

Moments pass, and I wait for him to respond. His gaze has moved to a whole new level of penetrating as he searches for any tells about how this announcement makes me feel. Eventually, he breaks the silence.

"You good?" he asks, and I genuinely think he wants to know.

I nod my head. "Better than," I tell him, and I mean it.

His expression softens as he stares at me, and I revel in the nearness of him. Gently he pulls on the bottom edge of my shirt, and I sway toward him. He's not touching me, but the heat coming off of his skin sinks into mine. Turning his head, he lowers it and kisses my cheek, his lips just barely brushing the corner of mine. I can't help the sudden intake of air I need to fill my lungs, and I'm rewarded with his signature scent of sandalwood, fabric softener, and sunshine.

His brows furrow a little as he leans back and looks down at me. There's a wariness in his eyes, but also curiosity. I'm not sure what he sees, but if he could read my mind, he would know how momentous this whole day has been for me. He might not have kissed me on the lips, but he may as well have. Today, I was kissed by another man for the first time in over five years, and on my ex-wedding anniversary date.

"I'm not sure if you're planning on going to the concert next weekend, but if you'd like to go with me, I'll swing by and pick you up," he finally says.

I realize I'm staring at his mouth, and my gaze shifts up to his. There's heat behind the blue, reminding me of the hottest part of a flame. My stomach clenches.

"Concert?"

He's still holding on to my shirt, and I wish I had the courage to reach over and do the same.

He clears his throat. "Yeah, it's actually one of my favorite events of the year. Up and down the river, businesses and home-owners put balloons on their docks to notify boaters they have music, and people cruise around and listen. Each dock usually has something different. There's country, pop cover bands, eighties rock, folk, Irish music—one guy drags his piano out and plays it, and at the end there's a fireworks show. I think it's nice." He shrugs one shoulder.

"Sounds wonderful. Do you usually go with friends or something? I wouldn't want to get in the way of that."

He drops my shirt and takes a small step back, my body sways after him, still craving the closeness. Where he's standing, the sun is directly behind the trees behind his head, and his dark hair glows.

"Nope. Well, I mean I have in the past, but the last two years I've gone by myself. A little time on the boat with some great music ... I don't need much more than that."

That does seem like something he would do. As much as this town loves him and his family and all the friends they have, he's perfectly fine in his own skin and doing his own thing, including attending a concert by himself.

"Okay, I'd love to go."

I'm rewarded with a small heartfelt smile.

20

———

*S*ince my day out with Jake, the world seems brighter.

It's crazy how differently things are perceived based on how you are feeling. Because come on, the world isn't brighter; it's the same—I'm the one who feels different.

I'm not so naive as to think I didn't have some eye-opening personal growth happen, because I did, and it feels really good. I've played my music a little louder, sung a little stronger, and received looks from all the workers, including Garrett, although his looks were less suspicious like I had gone crazy and more like he knows why I'm feeling the way I am.

And you know what? I'm okay with that.

I feel alive, not like I'm just passing time, and it feels great.

The marina is surprisingly quiet as I slip into the building. It's Wednesday night and it feels as if there is a lull in the summer crowds, and I'm grateful for the slow afternoon. As I wander through the building, I take time to look at all the photos lining the walls and showing the history and progression of the marina since the beginning.

Unlike my house, this marina is a historic landmark, as it was the original fish house for Easler Fishing Company. The bronze plaque outside is hung proudly, and although I'm not related to the Easlers, I can't help but feel pride for their family too. It's been recognized for its significance to the town, and I can see why. In the beginning, according to the plaque, the fish house was a place to support any fisherman who came this way. Buying bait, having a place to sell their catch, and, in the 40s once freezers were invented, buying ice—they could do it all here.

Over the years, it's turned into a retail shop, a small waterfront cafe, and now the main marina for the town. Yes, there are a few others that dot the river, but this one is at the heart of downtown. The pictures show it was once about the size of a small house, one way in and one way out, but now it's a rather large building broken into new addition sections, and where I'm currently standing is the retail store. There are all types of fishing supplies and boating gear, and it's here you can sign up for one of the river tours. It's also here that they have the old Easler Fishing Company sign, my main reason for coming in.

A lot of business signs from that time period were painted. The letters were hand drawn or traced with a stencil then painted with bright colors. On this one, however, each letter and detail is carved individually from wood then mounted on a backboard. At some point, the letters were painted what looks like maybe black, but now they are faded and weather damaged. Just like the logo from the newspaper, there's the fish jumping over the first half of the name and the conch sitting at the end. Both have remnants of faded paint too, the fish gray and the conch orange and pink.

"Great sign, right?" a voice says to my left.

Startled, I turn to find Bauer walking toward me and smiling. He's just as striking, large, and handsome as his brother, but I have zero flutters and only a friendly penchant for him.

"It really is." He stops next to me, and for a few long seconds, both of us stare at the sign. "Do you know what kind of fish it is?" I ask.

"I believe it's a sturgeon."

I take a peek at him; he's holding his phone, and he's dressed in a white button-down with the sleeves rolled up and a pair of dress pants. Such different attire from that of his brother, but it suits him perfectly.

"It's a jumping fish. They love rivers like ours because they cycle through both fresh and salt water," he says.

"Is it good to eat?" I ask, wondering if I've ever had it and wasn't aware.

"It's not my favorite, but people love to make a smoked fish dip out of it, or just fry it. Their eggs make good caviar too."

A smoked fish dip sounds good to me. Add in some crackers, capers, red onions, and lemon juice ... yum.

"And the conch shell—why is that in the logo?" I glance at him. The brown color of his hair is a smidge lighter than Jake's, and I wonder if it's naturally that way or if it's just from being out in the sun. It looks freshly cut, short on the sides, but the top looks as if he's been running his hands through it all day.

"There's always been a huge demand for conch meat, although now it's illegal to take a living queen conch, and the United States prohibits the import of the meat from a lot of countries in order to make an impact on preservation. The queen conch is on the endangered species list, not that it is endangered, but there are efforts in place to help prevent it from becoming endangered due to trade."

"I see." I return my stare to the wooden sign. To spend a day aboard one of Easler's boats ... how fun and different would that be?

"I have no special talent, I am only passionately curious," Bauer states.

"What?" I turn to look at him again, confused.

"Albert Einstein." He grins. "I read a lot—hazard of the job, and you were curious." He shrugs his shoulders.

A job I imagine he does very well from what I've seen. He loves details.

"What are you doing here?" I ask him.

"Securing the boat for Friday night. I have another tour," he states proudly.

"That's great! I know they'll all love it. You really did a great job—I was completely sucked into your stories."

"Stories or facts?" He raises one brow. "So, what are you doing here?" he asks in return.

"I just wanted to see the sign. Now seemed as good as any to avoid the crowds, plus I can't help but feel compelled to want to know more. Maybe it's because I live in their house, maybe it's because of Mrs. Easler's ghost, I don't know. I just have this feeling their story isn't over yet. You know what I mean?"

He looks at me thoughtfully, as if he's trying to understand me or come up with the right words. I get it—I'm not from here, and I have no connections to or real investments in this town other than the house, so I can see how he views me as an outsider possibly sticking my nose where it doesn't belong, assuming there is even anything for me to stick it into.

"You should head over to the library," he finally says, tucking his phone into his pocket. "They've got an entire section on local history. Anything you're interested in, they've got it, from the Seminole Indians and how to grow tropical plants to cookbooks with local recipes."

The library! I totally forgot about the public library. Garrett mentioned it too.

"Ghost stories?" I ask playfully, trying to lighten the mood.

He cracks a smile so similar to that of his brother, and my heart pulls with fondness.

His smile stretches to a grin as he takes a step away from me.

"Oh, most definitely," he says, winking at me just before he turns to meet with a guy at the counter.

After walking a few blocks through town, I find the library and am shocked to find it's so big. It's not what I was expecting, Chuluota Springs isn't that large of a town, but immediately upon entering I'm engulfed in that recognizable smell of wood, glue, dust, and vanilla. This library is vast with its rows and rows of books, a children's section, and public computers.

"Hello, there," calls an older man from behind the information counter. He's shorter, wearing thick glasses and suspenders. He smiles widely at me, and I can't help but return it.

"Hello," I reply, making my way toward him. There's something about libraries and bookstores, the way they feel, the knowledge they contain, and excitement bubbles under my skin at the thought of what I might find today.

"I've been waiting for you to come in," he says. His thinning gray hair is swept to the side, his face is shaved, showing off his pale skin, and his smile is inviting and kind.

This surprises me. "You have?"

"Of course. Everyone in town knows about you. For months, there've been all kinds of speculations and rumors, and I see at least one of them is true." His eyes sparkle in that old man kind of way.

"Really? What's that?" Unease slips in.

"That you are young and beautiful."

Heat floods my cheeks as I stare at him, and he continues to smile.

"Come this way," he mumbles as he makes his way out from behind the counter and toward a large bookshelf that has a reserved sign on it. "The Easler house, as you know, is famous in our little community, and you're the first and only new owner it's had in a really long time." He grabs a stack of books off the shelf and turns to hand them to me.

I take them from his outstretched arms.

"There's no way anyone could buy that house and not want to know more. I pulled these for you as they all make references to the family and the impact Mr. Easler made. Maybe if you start here, you'll find what it is you're looking for."

"What am I looking for?" I ask as if he's onto some secret I should be in on as well but am not.

He leans forward, and with his voice just barely over a whisper, he says, "You'll know when you find it. The more curious you are, the more secrets will be exposed."

I think about his word choice, exposed versus revealed. Revealed is more of to make known, but exposed feels like there is something larger behind it, something that was to remain hidden but is now visible.

"My name is Mr. Williams. If you need me, you know where to find me." He grins and then shuffles back to the counter.

Making my way over to a table, I set down the stack of books and look at each one. There's a wide variety: *Haunted Chuluota Springs*, *Sunken Treasures of the Gulf of Mexico*, *Rare Gems of the South*, *Fishing Tales of the Southeast*, *Small Towns in Florida*, and the one I start with first, a sepia-toned book that can be found in just about every city: *Images of America: Chuluota Springs*.

Flipping through the book, I see it's filled with black and white photos depicting life in the late 1800s and into the mid-1900s. Just after the introduction and chapter 1, which speaks briefly about the sugar plantation, there's chapter 2, titled *Gulf Coast Fishing*. Below it is a three-by-four image of what I am assuming is the original Easler fishing boat since there is a large E painted on the side, and in front of it are five men, each one wearing a hat, dark pants, a gray button-down with the sleeves rolled up, and suspenders. The caption reads: *The main source of Chuluota Springs' prosperity was fish from the Gulf of Mexico. Fish-*

ermen seen here worked for Easler Fishing, the first in the area to commercially sell its catch.

I look at each of the five men. They are all roughly the same height and look so similar. Two are smoking cigars, and I realize despite all the photos I've looked at up until now, I'm not sure which of the men is Mr. Easler, if any of them. Then I find him a few chapters later, his portrait as he was named the first town mayor in 1899. Dark hair neatly combed to the side, dark eyes, high cheekbones, full mustache, and sitting in a three-piece suit. He looks so handsome, and a wave of loss for Mrs. Easler rolls through me. So sad.

Flipping through the pages, I stop reading the captions and just stare at the images. There are so many of the people and the town as it began to be built up. All the locations Bauer mentioned in the tour, from the saloon to the springs resort before the storm, are in this book. Tourists vacationing in the springs of the river, little boys fishing off a long dock somewhere, the riverwalk made of dirt before it became what it is today ... the images are fascinating, and there is even a picture of a social event at my house. The women have swept-up hairdos and are dressed to the nines in evening gowns despite the weather here in Florida, clothed in materials you know they are sweating through underneath.

It isn't until I spot an image of Mr. and Mrs. Easler together that I pause. She was a tiny thing, barely coming up to his chest, but she has her arm through the crook of his elbow and they are smiling at each other. The adoration is evident, and also the brooch, the same one I found in the barn.

The adrenaline of recognition sweeps through me.

How surreal is it that I'm looking at a piece of history, the same piece that sits in my house? But I guess the house is also history too. It's strange to me to know that I live in these people's home, that I'm modernizing it and changing it from the vision and love they had to make it my own. Do I think they would mind? No. I've kept the integrity of the house, haven't structurally changed it. All I've done is clean, modernize, and decorate.

"What happened to you?" I mumble as I stare at Mr. Easler and drag my finger over the two of them. In every photo he's in, he seems larger than life, and to think he might have drowned in a storm … that doesn't feel right to me. I mean, I guess it's feasible—lots of people have drowned, and definitely many due to bad weather—but I just don't know.

"Miss." I hear a loud whisper breaking through my thoughts, and I look up to find the librarian smiling at me. He's holding a pocket watch connected to a chain and tapping on the face. "It's time for us to close, but if you would like to check those books out, I'd be happy to create an account for you."

I push my chair back and stand up. "That would be great. I would love to take these home and read over them," I tell him as I close the book and stack them up.

"Library policy is three weeks, but if no one has requested them, you can extend that." He gives me a big knowing smile.

Together we move to the desk, and I pull out my ID. Maybe he doesn't notice, or maybe he doesn't care, but I wait to see if he catches the difference in the last name I've used around town and the one on the card. He doesn't, not even hesitating a bit.

"If I wanted to request a specific article from the archives section of *The New York Times*, could I do that here?"

He looks up at me, his bushy gray eyebrows rise in surprise, and one side of his mouth quirks up like he knows exactly what I want to see. "You sure can. Just tell me what it is, the date if you have it, and I'll send off for it."

Well then.

That was easy.

21

For several days, I've pored over the books, photos, and stories about Chuluota Springs. I've memorized details about the town's timeline as well as the intricate particulars in the photos, looking for any clue I could find to connect the story to something greater. I didn't understand what *Rare Gems of the South* had to do with my house or the Easlers, but I thumbed through it all the same.

Jake was right—although they don't come out and say Mr. Easler died, in 1917, Mr. Greene, who seemed to be just a step behind Mr. Easler in the earlier photos, starts gracing more of the pages in more of a prominent position, dressed in finer clothing and surrounded by the same men who seemed to follow Mr. Easler. The E that was painted on the front of the boat becomes a G, the sign that now hangs in the marina is removed, replaced by one that reads Greene's Marina, and in one photo, he's standing with a woman who is also wearing a brooch. It's so similar to Mrs. Easler's that I was certain it was until I compared the two. The design is exactly the same, but the center stone on Mrs. Easler's is significantly larger. I thought it was strange that, for such an unusual piece, there would be another one, an almost identical one. Maybe Mr. Easler and Mr. Greene were together somewhere when they bought those brooches. Who knows, but it does appear that all these years later, Mr. Greene stepped right into another man's life.

Which makes me wonder ... if I can pull archived articles from the *Times*, can I for this town too?

"What are you thinking about so hard out here?" Willow asks as she sits down in the rocking chair next to me. I wandered over to her house after hearing June's laughter float across the inlet and have been sitting here watching Willow down on her dock for the last twenty minutes as she's finished working with a family of four. They had two bags of scallops that shrank down into one clear plastic bag of meat. It still feels like so much work for so little reward, but they sure are tasty.

I also can't argue with how much money she has made this season. She is quick, referred by many, and has a large set of returning customers.

"That I'm extremely grateful our houses face the east," I tell her, chuckling as I turn my gaze toward the late afternoon light sparkling on the water like a river of floating golden diamonds. The sun, which is behind us on the other side of the trees, was not kind today, and the bugs have had no qualms about speaking out against it as well.

"Amen to that," she says, leaning forward and removing the apron around her waist. In it she keeps a few tools, the money people pay her, and a towel to wipe her hands.

"Business still good?"

"Yes, but it's going to start slowing down here over the next few weeks. Local schools will go back, and then the northern schools not too long afterward. It's been a good season, though. I can't complain."

I think about how simple Willow's life is, and how happy she is. I'm not saying this in a bad way—after all, she still has adulting to do like owning a home and raising a daughter by herself—but I've never heard her complain or wish for anything different. She seems content, and her skin radiates with a healthy glow, lacking the lines of stress that are present on so many faces.

And then I think about how it's the same for Jake.

All my life, I've been surrounded by people who want more, more, more. What they have is never enough, whether it be status or material things, and the idea of "keeping up with the Joneses" is a real thing. Here, these people ... they just seem to live their lives, and they're satisfied.

Don't get me wrong, I know Willow and Jake aspire to things. After all, Jake does have a very successful practice, a new boat, and things like that, but his boat isn't the largest, he isn't flashy, and neither one of them carry a single bit of arrogance or pretentiousness.

My mind drifts to Carter, who wore arrogance and pretentiousness well—so well. Although he and his family sit in the upper one percent of the population, people still wanted to be friends with him. He was jovial and definitely a trendsetter versus a follower, but then again, that's all he knew.

That's all I knew too, yet here I am, seeking something different and something better, at least something better for me.

"June." Willow calls for her, and the front door is propped open so she can hear us through the screen door.

Her little feet come pounding toward us as she skips over and peeks her head out. "Yes, Mama?" Dark curls fall around her big caramel eyes.

"Darlin', be an angel and get us some of the special sweet tea, please."

Without another word, the screen door snaps shut, and she heads back into the house.

"I'm hoping what you mean by special is that delicious sun tea vodka you made." I grin at her.

"You know it."

"What's she doing in there?" I bounce my head in June's direction.

"Probably painting. That child would paint my whole house if I let her," she says, pushing on the floor so her chair begins to rock back and forth.

"That's not a bad hobby to have." I smile at her and do the same.

She smiles back, and it's warm as she thinks of June. "No, it's not. She's been working on images of the river. They're quite good too. I told her if she makes enough of them, maybe next year we can get her a booth at the festival and sell them. Art is art, right? And if priced right, I have a feeling people will love the fact that a child made them. We can put it toward her college fund."

"I think it sounds like a great idea. If she's serious about it, I can help with a little website for her, just so people can find her."

"I'm sure she'd love that. She's way more into technology than I am."

The pounding of feet returns, and June bumps the door open with her hip. "Here you go." She hands each of us a glass.

"Thank you." I give her a wink and a smile, and she grins back at me as the screen door again snaps shut.

"Speaking of finding ..." Willow takes a sip of her tea. "Have you found anything new about your house?"

"No, not much. I'm still reading the books from the library, and although they don't say anything at all about Mr. Easler's disappearance or the possibility of it not being an accident, I still don't have a good feeling about it. Did your grandmother ever mention a man by the name of Mr. Greene?"

I shift in my chair to look at her, and the expression on her face changes from surprise to one of anger.

"Yes. But then again, anyone who's from here knows the Greene family." She says the name with disdain.

"I know there was a Mr. Greene who seemed to take over after Mr. Easler died, I know the park downtown is named after him and at one time the marina, but other than that, I haven't done much research on that family yet."

"No need. Everything you need to know is summed up by saying Mr. Greene was a crooked man. Green fits that man to a tee, as he was always green with envy. He was one of those people who was never satisfied and always wanted what everyone else had, including Mrs. Easler."

I gasp.

"How do you know that?" I'm certain my eyes are wide with shock.

"My grandmother. She used to love to talk about stories from when she was a girl. She loved to tell this story about how she would hide in the trees and watch as Mr. Greene would go to the dock to see Mrs. Easler and shout at her. Once her husband died, he really had no business being over there, but for years he would return, and so would the shouting."

"That's awful." I think about poor Mrs. Easler grieving the loss of her husband, and this person who was supposed to be her husband's friend coming over and being unkind to her.

"Wasn't he already married?"

"Yes, but rumor has it he stepped out on her all over town."

I try to think about the truth in that statement. I know how bad rumors can be when they are spread, and I also know how false they can be. But then again, what was he doing bothering her on the dock and yelling at her?

"I'm not surprised, though," Willow offers up.

"Why?" I ask, looking over at her.

She takes a sip of her drink and then says, "June's father is a Greene too."

I almost choke on the tea as it goes down the wrong pipe, and I start coughing.

She stops rocking her chair and assesses me to make sure I'm alright.

"I know. Don't go giving me any looks—I knew better. Tigers don't change their stripes no matter how many new cubs are born."

"So the Greene family is still here, in Chuluota Springs?" I ask, surprised.

"No. He was the last of them. The thing about character is, people can see straight through sweet to find the sour. That whole family was sour, and over the years, they lost their footing around here. Their family tree—instead of it growing, it rotted, dwindled, and Trent was the last of them. Just like the others, he was ambitious and never satisfied."

She pushes off the ground and begins rocking again.

"How did you and he even start?"

"We grew up together, went to school together, and then one day, I saw him over at your house looking around. I confronted him, and he just grinned. That boy was so pretty to look at even a nun would find it hard to resist him, and once he turned on the charm, I was done for."

"Did he say what he was doing there?" I ask, curious as to why the Greene family members keep showing up at my house.

She shrugs. "He said he was dared by some of his friends to go into the house."

"What for?" I'm so stunned I can't tear my gaze off of her.

"I didn't think about it much at the time—after all, his friends weren't there, so how would they know?—but looking back, I'm almost certain he was looking for something."

"Like what?" I ask, still shocked.

She tilts her head. "What do you know about conch pearls?"

"Not much. It never even occurred to me that conch shells make pearls."

The creak from her chair resonates with me, and I push off and start rocking back and forth as well. It's lazy and slow, unlike this conversation, which has my head spinning.

"Oh sure they do. Any mollusk is capable of producing a pearl, although only those that have shells lined with nacre produce pearls that are used in the jewelry industry. Nacre is what most call mother of pearl, that iridescent layer on the inside of the shell. Conch shells, however, don't have nacre, so they're not actually pearls, they're just called that. They think the pearls are formed from an irritant or a piece of a shell that gets stuck inside near where the meat is, and over time, crystals build up around it. The pearls come in a variety of colors, but the pink and red ones are considered to be very rare and highly valuable."

"Wow, I'm not sure I've ever seen a conch pearl before." This must be why Mr. Williams gave me the gem book. I flipped through it but didn't pick up on the conch pearl. I think back to all the pearls I've seen in my lifetime. Pearls have always been a favorite of my mother's, and she has white, yellow, black, pink, brown, taupe, and even a greenish pair surrounded by diamonds to make earrings. All those pearls look the same, not like they were made from a different kind of shell.

"I'm pretty sure you have. Didn't you tell me there was jewelry in that box you found with the gun? Was any of it pink?"

A small gasp leaves me as my mind runs over the details of the brooch.

"Those are conch pearls," I say, more to myself than asking her the question, but she answers anyway. They were not perfectly round, basically oval shaped, and the pink color reminded me more of a grapefruit or salmon pink than a pastel Easter hue.

"I'd bet tonight's dinner they are."

"But why would she hide them and not have kept them in a jewelry box?"

"Who knows. They must have meant something to her. Why does anyone hide something? Maybe she thought someone was going to try to steal it."

"Maybe, but I wonder who."

I'm staring out at the river, the golden diamonds more of an orange color now. Willow's silence has me glancing her way. She has one eyebrow popped and is giving me an *Are you kidding?* look, and I can't help but laugh.

"Well, all fingers do seem to be pointing that way," I tell her, taking a sip of the tea.

I think about the Easler Fishing Company logo and the conch shell on the bottom right. If he was harvesting the conch meat too, he was most likely finding pearls as well. Was he selling those too? If so, I wonder how much they were worth. Enough for murder?

It seems Mr. Williams knows more than what he is letting on, and that's all the more reason for me to look into this further.

"Speaking of dinner, what are we having?" I ask with a hopeful expression.

22

---

*R*ight on cue, today at four-thirty, an afternoon thunderstorm rolled in. I should be used to them by now since we've had one every day since the beginning of July, but I'm not.

When the first storm—unexpectedly to me—swept through at the end of June, I was anticipating something much worse than what we got. The sky darkened to a shade of gray so deep that if light black was a color, that would have been it. The air was hot and sticky, and then all of a sudden as the darkness approached, a breeze kicked up off the river, ruffling the leaves on the trees and dropping the temperature at least ten degrees. It was a glorious reprieve from the sweltering humidity until the rain hit, and as the days passed, the storms seemed to get worse and worse.

Sheets of rain pour down from the sky with a ferocity I've never experienced before, pounding everything underneath, and the lightning is insane. I've always heard Florida is the lightning capital of the United States, and now I know why. If we were anywhere else, I would say we are engulfed in a massive daily monsoon, except these storms come and go in a matter of minutes, as few as 10 and at the most 30. The storms sweep in from over the gulf, soak the hot dry earth, and just keep moving on as if they didn't just wreak havoc on everything in their path.

Today, as it approached, I sat in a lounge chair on the upstairs porch off of my bedroom to watch. The river water turned gray to mimic the sky. At first it was still, and then it became choppy, pushing the edge of the river further up the bank. As the wind blew in, a wall of water falling from the sky rounded the bend of the inlet and quickly neared. I remained in my chair until the rain was so close my skin was dusted with mist, and then and only then did I get up and go inside to call Ivy.

"What are you doing?" she asks, knowing something must be on my mind if I'm calling her at this time of the day.

"Watching today's storm blow through." I'm still standing by the doors to the balcony. The rain is coming down so hard I can't see the inlet, and interestingly, the anxiety that comes from not being able to see what is in front of you resonates with how I'm feeling and settles in deep.

"That sounds very ominous, why?" she asks.

"I don't know. I'm going out with Jake tonight, and I think I'm second-guessing myself." I'm proud that I'm able to accurately voice what's making me feel off.

"You're thinking too hard about this."

Of all the times Jake and I've been together, I'm not sure why, but tonight feels like more. Unlike the state park, it's definitely a date, something I didn't think would be happening for me for a long time, if ever. Dramatic much? Yes, but there's something about being burned in a marriage that doesn't make the injured party eager to do it all over again. At the same time, I'm ready—at least I know I'm ready with him. The idea of putting myself out there on a dating site to meet just anyone new is a big fat no, but with Jake, it just feels right. I think that's what has me hung up, because maybe it should feel wrong. I mean, how long should someone like me wait before they move on? I'm certain most would say immediately, don't wait at all, but what does that say about me and the love I supposedly had for him? Because I did love him.

"I know I am, I think I'm just nervous," I tell her as I start pacing in front of the window. She'll know I'm pacing, and I half expect her to call me out on it, but she doesn't.

"Why? You've been around him plenty of times." There's music in the background, meaning she's still at work or she's out shopping. I always forget that we now have a time difference. Even though it's only one hour, she's central time, sometimes that's a lot.

"I know, but for some reason this feels different, feels bigger. Am I ready for this?" I need her to tell me what to do. I need her to tell me it's going to be all right. Dating should be fun, right? This is not a Stockholm syndrome situation where I'm subjecting myself to the same torture I went through before.

"Listen, that's the fear talking, and you have nothing to be afraid of. Life goes on, you're moving on, you know this. You're living your life, and you only get to live it once. So what if it feels bigger? Maybe it is, but you are definitely overthinking this. I get it, Carter hurt you, in the most unforgivable way. I still have things I want to say to him, even though it doesn't make a difference, not anymore. That chapter is closed, and you're writing a new one—a new one with a hot guy who you happen to like and who likes you and wants to take you out. Go for it. I know you're on this journey to find happiness, but Rylie, it comes in many forms. Whether it's from having cold fingers after a fun day of snow skiing, licking the icing off a maple-glazed donut, shopping in Bloomingdale's, taking a bubble bath, or having a hot pair of lips attached to yours, take it, feel it, own it, and let this go. Enjoy your night out. From what you said in your text earlier, the concert sounds amazing. I promise as you're reliving what that man is going to do to you later, you'll thank me."

I stop pacing. "What's he going to do to me later?" I all but whisper, feeling a curious anticipation settle low in my stomach.

She laughs. "I'm not sure, but I can't wait for you to tell me tomorrow."

I groan. "I hope you're right."

"I know I am, so get out of your head and into that white sundress I sent you last week. His jaw will drop when he sees you in it."

She is right, I know she is, and I'm so glad I called her. And his jaw does drop, along with his eyes, when I open the back door to greet him.

"Wow," he says roughly. "I'm not sure what to say, other than you look beautiful."

Heat hits my cheeks at his compliment, and then the scent of clean soap and sandalwood hits my nose as he leans forward to kiss my cheek. My eyes momentarily drift shut at his nearness, and every bit of nervousness I was feeling evaporates. He grounds me, calms me, and I sway toward him, seeking more of his steadiness.

"Thank you," I reply as he pulls back, runs his hand down my arm, then smiles down at me, dark lashes hanging low over his gorgeous blue eyes. "You clean up well yourself," I tell him, taking in his navy blue shorts, light blue button-down with the sleeves rolled up, and brown flip-flops. His hair looks like he might have attempted to style it, but the wind from the boat ride over here has it standing up everywhere. His face is freshly shaved, and I find I want to drag my finger over the edge of his jaw and then his full lips.

"Are you ready?" he asks, taking a step back to give me more room on the porch.

"Yep," I reply, closing the back door.

He holds out his hand, and I take it as we walk down to his boat.

This is definitely a date.

"How was your day?" he asks as he helps me climb in. Other than a few short text messages confirming tonight, we hadn't really talked much today. Of course I read into that a little too much, but then again, I had to remind myself he's not a super chatty guy.

"Good. This morning I finished putting up the new wallpaper in the breakfast room, and I hung curtains. Some real exciting stuff is happening over here. How about you?"

He unties the ropes and pushes us away from the dock. "I took a hook out of a pelican's gular pouch."

A small gasp leaves me. "Is that its mouth?" I watch as he sits behind the wheel and slowly guides us toward the river.

"Yes, the sack that hangs underneath the bill."

"How did it get there?" I move to sit in the chair next to him instead of on the bench in front of him, and I cross my legs to keep my dress tucked underneath and not blowing around. His eyes skip toward my legs briefly and then move back to the river. My insides coil and tighten, and I bite the inside of my bottom lip to keep from smiling.

"A local was fishing off the marina pier, and the hook was still attached to the fish it decided to eat. The fish bit through the bait, and the bird swooped in."

"That's crazy. How did the pelican get to you?"

As we enter the river, he picks up speed, and I'm mesmerized as his hair and his shirt flap against him in the wind. He's so handsome I can't help but stare.

"Fishing net. It made a loud noise, and the fisherman saw the blood. He threw the net over and dragged it in."

"Oh man. He's lucky he didn't swallow it. It'll be okay though?"

"Yes. It happens and it sucks, but it'll heal."

"Well, you definitely had more excitement in your day than I did in mine."

He looks over at me, and his mouth ticks up on one side into a lopsided grin. I feel that grin all the way down to my toes.

Seriously, what is happening to me?

One would think I've never been around a good-looking guy before with the way I'm reacting to every word he says and every move he makes. Raising my hands, I press them lightly to my cheeks to see if they're warm and then run them over my head to smooth any flyaway hairs that might have escaped my ponytail.

The river is crowded, and any remnants there might have been from this afternoon's storm are long gone. There are zero clouds in the sky, making this the perfect night. For two hours, we cruise up the river and then back down, listening to all kinds of music. I've never seen a concert like this before, and this is quite possibly one of the best nights I've ever had. Jake says hello to more people than I can count, and each time they look at me curiously. I find that tonight I don't care. I'm proud to be with him, and this makes me feel good. It confirms what I already knew was happening: I'm letting go. At some docks, we sing along with the performers, and at others, he takes my hand and we dance with the swaying of the music and the boat.

It's romantic and fun, and I'm so glad I didn't back out. Ivy was right—this is me living my life.

After we make our way back toward the marina, Jake idles the boat and throws the anchor over. Instead of sitting on the bench seat, we made a picnic on the ground in the front of the boat with the towels and the food he brought along. That's right, food. He thoughtfully went to the grocery store and prepared snacks for tonight. I'm touched and aware that with each passing minute, I like him more and more. Around us are other boats setting up to watch the fireworks show, there's music drifting across the water, and above us the stars are starting to glitter in the night sky.

"Do you know what conch pearls are?" I ask Jake as he picks up a piece of cheese and tosses it in his mouth. Our flip-flops are long gone, and with our feet bare, his legs are stretched out in front of him and crossed at the ankles, and mine are tucked up underneath my skirt while I sit cross-legged next to him.

He looks at me, and confusion crosses his features as he chews. "Yes, and so do you. They're in the brooch you found in the barn."

Picking up a cracker, I spread on some scallop dip—that's right, scallops instead of shrimp—and hold it up in front of me. "Well, I didn't know those were a thing until Willow told me. I just thought they were some kind of pink mineral stone like jade or a rose quartz or something." I plop the cracker in my mouth. This dip is seriously so good.

"Yeah, conch pearls are just one of those things. I mean I've always known about them, and my grandmother used to have them. A lot of people around here did, fishing community and all."

"I guess so." I reach for my wine and take a sip. What he's saying does make sense, and I can see how it is regional/local knowledge. I'm certain if I put my mind to it, I could come up with quite a few midwestern things he's never heard of.

"You don't see them as much anymore. With the ban on fishing for conch, they aren't as common. Why do you ask?"

"I went to the marina the other day to get a good look at the sign. With the conch shell in the logo, I'm assuming Mr. Easler was known for conch meat as well. I mean why else would it be in such a prominent, important place? I can't help but wonder what they were doing with the pearls they found. Was that part of the business? Did he sell them, or did he keep them? If he had a lot of them, there's a motive for murder."

He picks up his beer, takes a sip while staring at me, and then grins. "You just can't help yourself, can you?" The blue of his shirt is making the blue of his eyes that much more striking, and seeing them kind and soft toward me makes me want to paint the inside of the whole house this perfect color.

"Nope." I smile back. "You may have known some of these things your whole life, but I haven't, and I'm fascinated. I can't help but lie in bed at night and come up with different theories." Mentioning the word bed to him has heat climbing up my chest. I'm not sure if he notices, but Jake does seem like the kind of guy who's aware of all the little details in front of him.

"Well, if you need a partner for sleuthing, I'll be your side-kick," he teases, and I shove him in the shoulder ... his very solid and muscular shoulder.

"Mock me now, but just you wait, I'll figure it out," I declare confidently while secretly loving this laid-back version of him.

After we finish eating and playing a game of twenty questions to get to know each other more, we clean up the picnic and move to the rear of the boat where we can lean back and kick our feet out in front of us. Jake wraps his arm around my shoulders and gently pulls me in at his side. I willingly go, just wanting to be closer to him.

"So what do you think of our little town?" he asks, linking the fingers of his free hand with mine and tilting his head so he can see me better. His thumb rubs back and forth across my hand, and my heartbeat slows. It's so easy, and it feels so comfortably normal to be wrapped up with him like this; one would think we've been together for years.

"I love it. I was so focused on the house when I bought it that the town and the community didn't even occur to me. But, so far, it's amazing. The people are kind"—I flash him a look that says I'm thinking of the day we met—"mostly"—he chuckles—"and I find myself surprised. Living in a large city, I think it's easy to forget that there are other ways to live, other places to live well, and this is definitely one of them."

"Good." His gaze trails over the details of my face, and the deep timbre of his voice takes on a tender tone, giving me butterflies.

Above us, the first firework lights up the sky, and the crowds on the water and lining both sides of the river cheer. One after another, the bright colors fill the night, the booming of each echoing through the air and sinking into my bones.

Minutes pass as we enjoy the show, slowly drifting closer and closer to each other, the heat from his body filling the small space that's left between us, along with the salty fresh soap smell of his skin. Turning to face me, he moves his hand from across my shoulder to the back of my head, where he tangles his fingers through my hair. I'm shivering, and definitely not because of the weather—it's still so warm and humid out—but because I can't control my nervousness or anxiousness. I'm half convinced I'll disintegrate into dust if he continues touching me and half convinced I will if he doesn't.

"Ryla." His other hand drops mine and wraps around the side of my face. When he tips my head backward and toward him, my eyes slip shut, but very quietly he says, "Look at me."

Soulful deep blue eyes stare into mine, heavy-lidded with a want to taste me as much as I do him, but also with a hint of vulnerability present that lets me know this isn't just a random first kiss to him. It means something.

"You are so beautiful," he whispers, lowering his head so his breath shares space with mine.

The fireworks continue to go off over us, and although we're surrounded by others watching the show, it's as if we are the only two here.

Boom. Pop. Sizzle.

Colors explode one by one, and with each thunderous burst,

my heart reverberates in my chest, that is until his lips settle on mine.

Then the world goes still.

Leaning into him, I raise my hand and wrap it around his face, mirroring the placement of his on mine. His skin is soft, not at all rough like I would expect to find if he still had day-old stubble. My thumb swipes across the corner of his mouth as it's touching mine, and he lets out a rumbling sound while tilting my head and parting our lips to deepen the kiss.

Oh. My.

The taste of him is unexpected. It's exquisite and indescribable. I want to drown in his flavor, and as his lips press and his tongue brushes against mine, I feel as if I'm having an out-of-body experience.

If there were a way to die and be reborn in the same second, the same moment, it would be this. This kiss is so different from any I've ever had, and because of it, I somehow feel different. I feel changed in a way that means I never want to return to my prior self. It's insanely romantic, and there's no denying the blazing desire he has for me. He's not tentative at all; he's consuming and thorough. He's not rough—in fact, his lips are soft and loving—and he's not desperate. He's taking his time as if the only thing that would stop him would be me, and that's not happening. I'm captivated and so deep into what he's doing to me and the way he's making me feel like I'm the only thing in the world that matters to him, and I barely hear the cheers of the crowd as the grand finale of the show lights up the night sky beyond my eyelids.

I ache on the inside as he slowly ends the kiss, and his gorgeous blue eyes find mine. I want to beg him for more, but at the same time, that first kiss was so perfect I know I will be reliving this moment for the rest of my life.

He leans his forehead against mine, and no words are said as he lets out a sigh and smiles. We both know the night is coming to an end, and I reach for his hand to hold on to him for a moment longer. Affection settles over his expression as he leans forward, kisses me chastely, and then stands, pulling me with him.

By the time we make it back to my house, I'm one hundred percent drowsy and drunk on this entire night. Affection, intimacy, love … it's all such a strange thing. Each has so many layers and comes to us in so many different ways, and I know, no matter where life takes Jake and me, after tonight, there will always be a part of me that feels deeply for him. He found a crack in the very thick cast that's been concealing my damaged heart, and he infused it with a piece of himself. He's filling my buckets without even realizing it, and he's freed me in a way I knew I needed but didn't know how to make happen. Now I feel like I can soar.

He slides the boat up next to my dock, and it hits the bumpers as he steadies us then ties it to a post. Instead of walking me to my door, he takes my hand to help me off the boat then wraps me in his arms to give me one last searing kiss. The warmth from his body, the soft command of his lips, the feel of his hands as they run over me and into my hair … I feel useless and like a puppet. He could pull my strings any way he wants, and I'd willingly be at his mercy.

Grinning because he's completely aware of how he's turned me into mush, he runs his hands down my arms to capture my hands. "I'm on call tomorrow night, so I'll be busy with emergency appointments, but are you free the night after?"

I look up at him, the darkness of the night turning his eyes silver. "Are you on call a lot?" I never considered how the life of a veterinarian would be.

"Usually twice a week. There's not a 24-hour animal hospital here, so myself and three other vet clinics in the area share the night duty."

"Oh, that's nice and convenient." I lean against him, breathing him in one more time.

"It is. We share an on-call service, keeps it simple." His hands tighten around mine, and he pauses as he takes in a breath. "Thank you for spending the evening with me," he says, his words vibrating from his chest into me.

I pull back to see his face. "Are you kidding? I'm the one who should be thanking you. Tonight—" I swallow, trying to push the emotion back down. "Tonight was amazing. I will never forget it. Ever," I tell him, and he hears the sincerity.

"So ..." He quirks a smile at me.

"So, I was wondering if you'd like to have dinner with me. Not tomorrow night, but the night after? I should be free," I ask, winking, teasing and hopeful.

His smile stretches just before he bends down and kisses me again. His lips are damp and warm, and I could get seriously addicted to kisses from him.

"I'll be here," he says with his lips against mine, and happiness from him pours through me and from me to him.

I can't bring myself to leave the dock as he climbs back onto the boat and heads out to go home. Halfway through the inlet, he turns and raises his hand. Giddy, I wave back and blush from head to toe.

Wow.

This guy.

Faintly, in the corner of my visual field, the mysterious light on the dock appears. It slowly grows, getting brighter and brighter. I'm not surprised. She's right on cue, and of course she waits until Jake has pulled into the river, now out of sight, and that's fine.

Until it's not.

From the light, a whisper of a voice floats through the air, and I stop breathing as fear and instant chills shoot straight down my spine.

Did the light just speak? To me?

No, that can't be possible. I must be mistaken, and I take a step back—then I hear it again.

"Where the light shines."

I'm so startled I jump. My already racing heart comes to a complete stop as the light grows brighter than I've ever seen it, and I'm face to face with none other than Mrs. Easler.

I know it's her; I've seen her picture. All these years, people have speculated about what the light is and who the light is from, and they were right. She's shorter than I expected, but with her dark hair blowing wildly in the nonexistent wind and the lantern she's holding down by her side, the same lantern I've seen for weeks, I find I'm transfixed. She's not completely transparent, but she's not solid either. There's a shimmer to the outline of her, as if she's being projected in front of me and could suddenly disappear.

This can't be happening. I must be hallucinating after Jake messed with my pheromones, hormones, sanity—something.

But there she is, still standing in front of me and staring at me as if I can solve all the world's problems.

"Mrs. Easler," I whisper, completely aware that I'm attempting to speak to a ghost and after this am certainly going to need psychiatric help, but she doesn't answer. She's staring at me as I'm staring at her, though I get the feeling she doesn't really see me but knows I'm here.

The glow of the lantern wavers, and she raises it just a bit.

"Where the light shines," she says again after a long moment.

And then just like that, she and the light are gone.

My ears start ringing in the silence, and I'm again holding my breath in shock. It's pitch black out other than the moonlight, and the temperature around me is so cold I'm shivering. I know I should move, know I should do something, but while my heart races, I can't seem to stop staring at the now empty space.

Desperately, I try to come up with a rational explanation, but I can't.

The shivers turn to shudders as the temperature slowly warms.

I would say I'm less fearful and more flabbergasted than anything. Because really, I don't understand.

What just happened?

23

———————

The sun has barely peeked over the trees on the far side of the river, casting a burnt orange glow on the edge of the water, and I can't wait any longer. Trying not to run, I walk fast and weave my way down the barely-there path to Willow's and find myself panting on her front porch. Before I even have a chance to raise my fist to knock on the door, it flies back, and she's standing on the other side of the screen wrapped in a bathrobe and wearing a pair of old slippers.

"I swear, you were tearing through those woods like a herd of elephants," she whisper-shouts, the hinges on the screen door creaking as she pushes it open. "Come on in, I just made a pot of coffee." Then she looks me over from head to toe. "Although I'm not sure you need any."

Turning, she makes her way back to the kitchen. Leaving my flip-flops on the porch, I follow. The scent of coffee is strong in the air, and I'm instantly craving a cup, even though I already had one.

"June isn't up yet, so keep your voice down. My guess is the little miss stayed up way too late on her electronics last night," she says as she reaches into a cabinet next to the refrigerator and pulls out two mugs.

I think about how I stayed up way too late last night too. Between the kiss from Jake and Mrs. Easler speaking to me, if I managed more than a few hours consecutively, I'd be shocked. Even after all that time lying there and staring at the ceiling, I still have no idea how to say what I'm about to say. I know it sounds completely one hundred percent ridiculous, but if anyone is going to believe me, it's going to be Willow.

"Lawd, spit it out. You're like a beehive that's about to burst," she says, looking over her shoulder at me as she pours the coffee.

"I saw her." The words rush out of my mouth, and it's such a relief to tell someone that I already feel like I can breathe better.

She hands me my cup, pours some creamer into hers, and takes a sip, pausing as my words sink in. Her eyes have sharpened as she's studying me, but then they seem to smile as they relax and little wrinkles form in the corners.

"And here I thought you were coming to tell me all about Mr. Jake Hawthorne." She takes another sip and stares at me over the rim of her cup.

She's teasing me? After what I just told her? Did she not hear what I said?

And wait   Jake?

"How do you know about him?" I ask, slightly flustered that she doesn't feel the same level of excitement and awe as I do. I mean, I saw a ghost—my ghost. This feels like a really huge momentous thing. I pick up the creamer and add some to my cup.

"Honey, who in this town doesn't know about you and him? Y'all have been spending an awful lot of time together lately, and you were spotted together last night."

I let out a groan. We have been together a lot, and out in

public, so I guess it's not a secret, but still. "We can talk about him next. First we need to talk about Mrs. Easler"—I whisper her name—"and how I saw her."

Setting her coffee cup down, she moves into the living room, and I follow suit. Pulling an old photo album off of a bookshelf in the corner, she opens it up to a certain page then hands it to me. I can't help but gasp.

"Is this who you saw?" she asks.

The photo is small, black and white, and indicative of developed photos from a previous generation, but in the image is Mrs. Easler and a woman who looks so similar to Willow it's eerie. The pair are sitting on the porch of this house, drinking what looks like lemonade, and playing cards.

"Yes, but she didn't look like this. This is kind of how she looks in the books from the library too, just less fancy." I lightly run my finger over the photo. It's tucked tightly behind a piece of clear covering that's sealed with adhesive, and it's amazing to me that it's still sticky after all these years. I remember Willow saying her house has been here almost as long as the Easler house, but I guess I never considered that they would have been friends. That's completely dumb, because if the town was as small as everyone said it was and her husband was a fisherman and gone for periods of time, of course they became friends. How could they not? And this picture is the proof. This image shows true friendship, smiles that are given through love, not because they were forced for a photo.

"They were friends," I state more than ask as I look up at Willow.

"They were. She was actually Mrs. Easler's housekeeper, but from the stories my grandmother told, it was never about a working relationship, but a deep love of two friends."

I glance back down at the photo and stare at the two women. A wave of relief overtakes me as I am so grateful for this woman, her confidant. All this time I had been thinking Mrs. Easler was all alone, but it seems she wasn't. Not entirely.

"What did she look like?" she asks, tilting her head to try to better understand what I'm saying about last night.

"Older. Lost. She definitely wasn't happy like this." I lay my hand on the photo and feel a surge of emotions. I don't know Mrs. Easler, we aren't related, yet I feel a kinship toward her that's unexplainable.

A beat passes before she nods like she understands and takes the album from me to return it to the shelf. I want her to leave it out, want to flip through the pages and see if there are more pictures. I find I desperately want to discover more of her and more of her life.

"Tell me what you saw," she says as she retrieves the coffee cups from the kitchen and hands me mine. She sits on the couch, and I flop down in the large chair across from her.

The chair is overstuffed and comfortable, so I pull my legs up and wrap both hands around my mug. "She was wearing a white dressing down, her dark hair was loose and blowing around, and of course she was holding the lantern. She wasn't put together like she is in all of her photos...she looked desolate."

Willow looks out the window toward the river as she thinks about what I've told her. From here she can see her dock, which is great as she can see if she has any customers waiting.

"That makes sense." She looks back at me. "Remember she lived out there for so many years. I imagine night after night, she sat out in her night clothes with her lantern waiting for him to come home."

Leaning forward, I look directly at Willow and tell her, "She spoke to me. She said, '*Where the light shines.*'"

Willow lets out a small gasp, her eyes widening. "She spoke to you."

"Yes, and that was all she said. Twice. What do you think it means?"

"I think it means she has unfinished business," she says matter-of-factly.

Flashbacks of Bauer talking during the tour come to me, and I remember him saying the same thing, that a ghost is different from a haunting because it usually has unfinished business. It's seeking revenge, has a message to pass along, doesn't believe its life has actually ended.

"What kind of unfinished business?" I ask, almost panicked. Now that I've seen her once, am I going to be seeing her all the time? Up until now, it hasn't occurred to me that she might move off of the dock. Is she going to follow me? Anxiety starts to creep in, and I take a deep breath to exhale it. I'm getting way ahead of myself, and for no reason.

"Now how am I supposed to know that?" She laughs. "You're the one she manifested to." She takes a sip of her coffee and hums with satisfaction as if this news pleases her.

Well, it doesn't please me.

Following her lead, I take a sip of my coffee and look around the room. June's paintings are perched all along the wall, and there are children's novels lying on the coffee table. Carter and I never talked about having children. I think it was assumed we would one day, but then again, maybe he thought differently.

"So, what do I do now? Are there ghost experts who need to be contacted?"

She laughs. "No, there aren't any ghost experts for this. If she showed herself to you, most likely it will remain that way. I can't help but wonder if she feels connected to you because you both suffered from a heartache. Anyway, I wouldn't worry about it too much," she says.

Don't worry about it? I'm not sure that's even possible. The entire scene and situation have me reeling.

"And what about Jake?" she asks, openly curious and pulling me from my thoughts of this transparent floating woman following me around my house while she still thinks it's hers.

I hesitate, because I'm not really sure what to say. I like spending time with him, I do, but where we go from here, I have no idea.

"I see," she eventually says. "Ryla, life is short. If he makes you happy, what difference does any of that other noise make?"

The difference is that everything I've gone through over the past year creates a new type of reality. The fairytale bubble has popped, and it's forced me to reevaluate and speculate on everyone with caution. She was a lifelong friend, and he was my husband. Shouldn't you know the person you're married to? Shouldn't you know someone you've been friends with for two decades? But then again, do we ever truly know someone when we're constantly learning about ourselves? It's the masks we wear, them and us, and maybe it's the fear about what others will discover under them that has us tightening the straps. But when it does fall away and they're standing in front of us completely bare, what happens then?

I can't help but wonder if I ever truly saw Carter bare. I thought I had, but it seems he was selective with what he chose to share with me.

"All I'm saying is eventually everyone moves on no matter what brought them to their low point, and well, if he makes you happy, there's nothing wrong with moving on with him. He's good people, and so are you."

Moving on.

I've spent so much time trying to let it all go, I guess I never thought about what came after. Moving on ... at this point I'm not even sure how, or maybe I've already started. Jake's smile and the adoration I sometimes see in his eyes when he looks at me come to mind, and my stomach clenches, the good kind of clenching where the butterflies fill the empty space and flap their wings.

After coffee with Willow, I decide to head into town and get another cup from Corrie. Yes, this is my third cup today, but since it's iced and paired with the most delicious blueberry muffin, I'm calling it brunch.

Not surprisingly, this little town doesn't have a jewelry shop. Sure, you can buy a few things here and there at the boutique shops, but not anything of real value. What I do find is a pawn shop.

Although I've never been in one, I push the door open, and it's exactly what I expected to find: clutter everywhere. You name it, they have it, from old fishing gear to household goods to designer bags. It smells like an old closet, and the sounds of Motown permeate the air, emanating from a record player swirling a black vinyl record around. As I approach the single sales counter in the back, I'm surprised by the amount of jewelry displayed in a large glass case.

"Welcome. Looking for anything particular?" an older woman asks from a reclining chair next to the back wall, startling me. I didn't see her and jump a bit.

As I shift in her direction to get a better look at her, she smiles kindly. Part of me wonders if I should be asking about the conch pearls or showing off the brooch. I've only looked at a few historical photos from the library books, and this brooch is in several. It's possible she might recognize it, and the last thing I need is to draw unwanted attention. But, my curiosity to learn more is too great.

"Hi there." I smile back and warily approach. "I was wondering if it might be possible to find out the value of something. There aren't any jewelry stores in town, and I see that you have quite a bit." I glance back at the case.

"That I do," she says as she pushes up out of the chair and

slowly makes her way behind the counter. She's wearing a nice pair of dress slacks and a blouse, and her hair is pulled into a bun at the base of her neck. "Are you looking to sell it?" she asks inquisitively, her eyes drifting over me from head to toe, lingering on the diamond studs in my ears.

"Nope, it's an old family heirloom, and I'm just curious," I tell her, bringing her gaze back to mine.

"All right, let's see what you've got." She grabs a dark green velvet board and places it in front of me on the glass case.

Reaching into my bag, I pull out the small running sock I've been using as a bag. My fingers brush over the individual pearls, but I grab the brooch and lay it on the board. The woman's eyes lock onto it, and for just a moment, she doesn't move.

Then she lets out a low whistle.

"Heirloom, you say?" She glances back up at me speculatively as she gently picks it up. It makes me wonder what kind of people she gets coming in here.

"Yes, ma'am," I tell her, hoping she doesn't see through my kind-of lie. Technically it is an old family heirloom. Maybe not my family, but still.

To me, the brooch looks like what you would expect. It's not round, instead oval in shape. It looks almost like a flower with the petals symmetrically placed around a centerpiece. There are sixteen alternating petals, eight of them conch pearls and eight of them diamonds. The pearls start at the top and are the prominent points of the brooch. To complete the design, the center pearl is the largest, and it is ringed with diamonds. The whole piece is set in gold.

Off to the side, she grabs a loupe to examine the diamonds one by one, looking for any inclusions or imperfections to prove that they are in fact diamonds and not costume jewelry.

"Do you know what these pink stones are?" she asks, never taking her eyes off of the piece.

"I do, they're conch pearls."

She hums and nods her head. Flipping the brooch over, she continues to use the loupe to examine all the details.

"Have you thoroughly looked this over?" she asks, glancing up at me.

"I have," I tell her confidently.

"Then you saw the signature?" She rises up and lowers the piece back to the board.

"Signature? No."

She hands me the loupe, I pick up the brooch, and there on the inside of the gold lip, at the anchor of the clasp, is a capital block cursive C, and next to it is 00109 with a space then 12.

My eyes flip up to hers. "I didn't see this before."

"I was thinking you didn't." She moves out from behind the counter to an old bookshelf. Finding the one she wants, she pulls it out and brings it back to the counter.

"Do you know what it means?" I ask her.

Slowly, her lips tip up, and tiny wrinkles form in the corners of her eyes.

"Are you sure you're not looking to sell this?" she asks, her smile still growing as she holds the book tightly.

"No, I'm not. And given your reaction, I definitely shouldn't be."

She laughs and sets the book on the counter. Opening it up, she finds the page she wants and turns it around so I can see.

"This is one of the stamps used to mark a piece for Cartier."

I can't help but blink at her with a blank stare. Did she just say Cartier? Like the expensive globally known jeweler? I stare down at the page and look at other pieces that have the same brand as mine.

"Do you know what the numbers are?" I look back up at the woman who is ardently gazing at the piece.

"I'm pretty sure the longer number is a serial number and twelve is the year it was made."

"1912," I say, my voice just barely over a whisper.

That does fit the timeframe of the Easlers, and given the fact that there are conch pearls in the setting, I have to believe he had this piece custom commissioned for his wife.

"So, I'm guessing you don't know how much this is worth?" I ask her.

"No, child, but I can tell you this—a nice conch pearl ranges from four to seven thousand dollars per carat, and an exceptional one can be upwards of fifteen thousand per carat. I know each of these is well over a single carat. As for the center pearl ..." She lets out another whistle. "Along with the diamonds and the maker, if I were you, I'd be buying and installing a built-in safe or storing this in the bank."

Closing my fingers around the brooch, I pull it back toward me, suddenly feeling overwhelmed. "Thank you for looking at it. I appreciate the information you've given me."

"No, thank you. That brooch is the most exciting thing I've ever seen come into this store. Please do come back and tell me what more you find out about it as I'd love to know. And don't worry, I'll keep this between us. Heaven knows there's been enough strife in this town throughout the years over those pearls."

"The conch pearls?" I ask, confused.

"Yes. This is a fishing town. It's illegal to pull those conchs out of the water now, but it wasn't always. I think they passed that law in the 70s, but I'm not sure that's actually stopped them. Those pearls are worth a pretty penny, and people get a little crazy over them."

"How crazy?"

"Real crazy," she deadpans.

24

———————

$\mathcal{I}$’ve found myself back on the dock today, alternating between lying on my stomach, dragging my fingers through the cool clear water, and staring up at the towering tree line and the sky. Although it's now August, for some reason the humidity is low this morning, and the sky is covered in clouds like rows of cotton balls.

Over and over, my thoughts are on repeat, and I can't stop mulling over four things.

Conch pearls.

The ghost of Mrs. Easler.

Where the light shines.

But mostly Jake.

After I left the pawn shop, he called to let me know he would be out for the night to assist another veterinarian with a dolphin. He tells me dolphins love to follow bottom trawlers and steal the fish from bottom nets and long lines. Unfortunately, more often than not, they get caught, tangled, and injured. This particular dolphin got its fluke tangled in the rope, and it almost ripped off. I can't even imagine. He's also on call tonight and tomorrow night as one of his colleagues is out of town, so unfortunately, it'll be a few more days before I see him again. Surprisingly, or maybe not so surprisingly, I feel sad.

Since then, where I thought I would mostly be ruminating over conch pearls, ghosts, and mysterious people from generations long ago, I've found myself lost in conversations Jake and I have had, the way he makes me feel, and how I ended up here.

For almost a year, I've lived feeling jaded. I let Carter, the trauma, the stories, the lies, and the stress take over, and I believed it all. I let those things belittle and define me. Even though I felt justified for feeling that way, all it's done is weigh me down. Being here over the last couple of months, little by little, I've felt that disappointment and misconception about who I've defined myself as slip away. I know I'm not a jaded person. It might have taken me longer than others to realize this, but now I do, and I feel lighter, freer. Plus, it's making moving on so much better. Because Willow is right—it is time to move on.

Do I think moving on is something that happens overnight? No, but allowing the acceptance of what has happened and the emotional place I'm trying to arrive at to fill more of the space inside me, inside my heart, feels like life, and that feels so good.

It feels like hope.

It feels like happiness.

I know happiness is defined as an emotional state that symbolizes joy and fulfillment. While I am working on getting to a place where I feel all these things all the time, I am certain in my heart and deep down in my soul, I feel more positive than I do negative, and with that I feel peace.

Well, maybe not peace all the time. Just thinking of Jake and what he did to my mouth has me blushing and my insides zooming up and down like on a rollercoaster. Is Jake a huge part of this happiness and joy I'm feeling? Absolutely, but I think the difference is that, with Carter, I needed him, and with Jake, I want him.

Carter and I were picture perfect for the life we were raised into. I needed him in a way where we conquered that life and upheld society's expectations of us. The thought of living a different kind of life with a different kind of person never even occurred to me. Did I feel like I fit in? Not always, but I knew how to play my part.

With Jake, I just want him. There are no expectations, no preset rules I have to follow. We don't have to be anyone but ourselves, and I find that freedom gives me the most joy.

For the last couple of weeks, I've been so worried about telling him who I am, but he sees me. He sees the me I am without all the fanfare, the me I want to be, and I really like the way he looks at me.

I'm proud of myself for moving on, and I'm even more proud of myself for embracing the gift of this person I've been given and for opening my heart to the possibility of love again. Do I know what will happen between us six months from now? No, but nothing can be worse than how things ended with Carter, and I survived. I'm moving on.

Looking back at the river, a river I love, I'm reminded that it's like the heart and has its own rhythm. Just like the heart, it keeps going, never stopping, just like me.

And then I realize what has stopped—the crying bird. I'm startled by this and don't even recall when it happened. Maybe it found its mate too.

The familiar sound of heavy tread on the dock has me looking up and seeing Garrett in typical work attire of cargo shorts, a Hawthorne Construction polo, and work boots. He smiles at me as I stand and wipe off my clothes.

"You know, if you need something to do, I'm sure I can come up with something," he teases, running one hand through his hair.

"What makes you think I wasn't doing anything?" I tease back, placing my hands on my hips.

He gives me a knowing look as he glances down at the dock then back up at me. I can't help but laugh, even though I know I was doing something. My heart was healing.

Pulling on the screen door, he holds it open wide so I can move in and sit at the little picnic table.

"Today is a big day," he says. There's mischief in his eyes.

"Oh really? How so?"

On the table he lays out ten large swatches of white paint. "You get to pick the new color of the outside of your house."

When I told him I wanted to keep it white like the original, I expected him to make an executive decision, but nope. In front of me are the colors marshmallow, snow, heron, Chantilly lace, linen, cotton, dove, cloud, paper, and plain white. Immediately the heron shade jumps out at me, and I point to that one.

He gives me a nod and leans back. "Well, that was easy."

"Which one would you have chosen?" I ask him.

He points to the Chantilly. It's nice too, and I wouldn't have complained. Then again, I wouldn't have known the difference.

"Garrett, do you ever wonder about this place?" I look up, and his eyes lock with mine. His features are so similar to Jake's but not at the same time, especially his hazel eyes.

"What do you mean?" His brows pull down in confusion.

As much as I trust him, I never did get around to telling him about the brooch, the gun, or the newspaper article. I'm not sure if Jake mentioned them or not, but something tells me no as he's never brought any of the items up. I don't know why I didn't tell him; I just feel like the house is telling me its secrets, and I'm not ready to share them with everyone yet.

"Oh, I don't know ... like what really happened to the Easlers? Did he drown or was he murdered? What ever happened to the daughter? Who's the owner of the trust? All these years, why didn't anyone ever work on the main house, yet they maintained the boathouse? Just questions like that."

He runs his hand over the back of his neck and looks back up at the house.

"Well, I don't know anything about murder, but they say after the oldest son died, the second son met a girl at the resort during Prohibition and followed her north when her family left. When he was older, apparently he was the one who repaired the boathouse and started the upgrades. Maybe he was planning on retiring here, I don't know. The daughter stayed close by but never claimed the house after her mother died. I heard once that Mrs. Easler died from an influenza outbreak. As for the owner of the trust, doesn't Natalie know?"

"Not that I'm aware of. If she does, she didn't let on that she did."

He hums in understanding as he looks at the boathouse. Natalie would have told me. I know deep down in my gut she would have. She's as interested in this place as I am.

"It's in the trust that the boathouse is to be updated every five years until the property is sold."

I'm a little bit shocked and lean back from the table. "What? How do you know that?" I ask him, almost accusatorily.

"Because my company maintains it. We're the ones who had it ready to go when you arrived." The electrical, the new toilet, the ceiling fan ... all of those things were his doing.

I feel frozen, and as I take a closer look at him, I suddenly feel justified in not telling him about the things I've found. I feel like he's kept secrets from me, so it's only fair I keep them from him. I mean really, I don't owe him anything.

"Why didn't you ever tell me this?" Why didn't Jake mention any of this?

"Didn't seem relevant, and you never asked," he states matter-of-factly. I'm shocked. Maybe Jake just thought, as the owner of the house, I knew, and I should have known. Garrett should have mentioned it when I first met him to discuss the project. I mean why didn't he? He certainly could have used that to his advantage, having familiarity with the property and all.

"Didn't seem relevant …" I'm looking at him now as if he has two heads and I don't know him at all. "Why?"

He shakes his head and shrugs one shoulder. "I don't know. I guess I just figured Natalie told you and that's why you came to see me about the renovations."

Natalie … she never mentioned it either. Then again, we never really talked about the terms of the trust. At the time, the purchase was between mine and whoever held the one here. The less that was said the better.

Then a thought occurs to me. "Did you install the bathtub upstairs?"

"Yep." He pops his lips just before he frowns.

"Why?" I ask, so desperately trying to piece together all the unknowns of the puzzle.

He lets out a deep sigh. "Honestly, I'm not sure."

I'm confused by his answer, and I match him, a frown for a frown.

"Did you bring in the piano?"

"No. One day I went in to do an inspection, and it was just there."

It was just there.

"Who hired you?"

He tilts his head like I should already know the answer. "Bauer. Didn't you know he was the attorney who handled the sale for the trust?"

I think back to the paperwork. I was still in Chicago, I handed everything off to my attorney to review, and once she gave me the thumbs-up, I just signed where I needed to sign and wrote a check. Natalie mentioned that he handles the real estate documents for her, but it never even crossed my mind that he did my house as well, but it should have.

I don't answer his question. Instead, I look at him directly as wariness drifts over his features, and I say, "So, I'm assuming he knows who the owner of the trust is."

"I assume he does."

25

"Wow, I can't believe how different it looks in here," Jake says as he comes in the back door, kicks off his flip-flops, and stops at the entrance of the library. His eyes are large, and his grasp on the handles of the plastic to-go bag he's holding tightens. I move into the room to turn on the lights, and his eyes wander over the details while mine wanders over him.

I really missed him.

This nighttime look just might be my favorite of his: hair freshly washed after a long day but windblown from the boat ride, a worn pair of jeans that look so soft and fit him so well, and a basic solid-colored T-shirt. Tonight it's light gray. He looks comfortable, familiar, and I want to wrap myself around him.

I can't wait to wrap myself around him.

When he texted me first thing this morning asking if he could bring over dinner instead of me cooking, I thought I was going to jump out of my skin. Minutes on the clock have never ticked by as slowly as they did today, and I'm so happy he's finally here. I laugh on the inside, feeling wonder at how I ever lived without him.

Tearing my greedy eyes away, I look around the room. Over the last couple of days, while he was working and on call, almost all the rugs and the furniture I've ordered for the house have arrived. Some might think I'm crazy for ordering everything online without seeing it, but I know what I like, and I know the manufacturers I purchased from.

"Right. It's starting to feel like a home. Not that it didn't before, but I love how everything is coming together. It feels like it's mine, you know what I mean?"

Here in the library, I painted the bookshelves and the wainscotting white and chose to wallpaper the remaining space with a formal lace damask pattern. It's two-toned with an ivory and almost hazelnut color, perfect to add some warmth to the room but also keep it light enough. I decided to leave the old navy curtains that frame the painting in the library. They may be faded, but they're original to the house, and I just love them.

I bought a large thick multicolored area rug that's heavier on the blues and four camel-colored leather chairs. They face each other, two on one side and two on the other, with a table between each pair and oversized ottomans to put your feet up. With new light fixtures, a couple of throw pillows, and four soft blankets, this room is ready to go. After all, if I'm reading, I want to be completely relaxed.

Jake walks in and runs his fingers over the back of one of the large chairs. Each is outlined with bronze nail heads, and I wonder if they're warm after his touch. I know I would be.

"I do," he says, his voice deeper, rough.

Is he imagining himself sitting in one of these chairs and reading? Because I'm imagining that. I would be lying if I said I didn't buy these chairs with him in mind—a little on the masculine side, large, and sturdy.

He takes a long glance at the painting and then at the four pictures I bought at the festival. I hung them on the wall opposite the bookcase and placed a vintage bar cart underneath. An unfamiliar expression drifts across his face, and then he isn't looking at the room anymore; he's looking at me. Like really looking at me. There's an energy behind his gaze, and his blue eyes have darkened. A tightness unfurls in my stomach and slowly makes its way to my arms and legs.

It's one hundred percent crazy how this guy makes me feel with just one look. With Carter, I always felt like we were a team, but here, right now, I'm realizing that's not how Jake views me— not as if we're a team, but more along the lines of me being something he wants to win, to claim.

Clearing his throat, he says, "You were right, the black and white photos from the festival do look great in here." His eyes flit to them. "Seems like the only thing missing ..."—he turns back to me and grins—"is books."

Heat burns through my cheeks.

"Yes, well, can I even call this room a library if it has no books?" I smile back at him, feeling like he's a magnet and I'm a magnet and we're being pulled together by an unknown force.

"One day it will," he says, his eyes lingering on mine and soaking up the details of my face.

"One day," I say softly back.

For months I've focused on just trying to get through one day and to the next, and for as much as I've tried not to think long term about what will happen or where I'll be, I can't help but recognize the draw deep within me that wants to tether me to this place, this home ... him.

A buzz sounds in the air, breaking the spell, and Jake pulls his phone from his pocket. He reads the incoming text, glances at me quickly, and says, "I'll be right back." He leaves the room and makes his way toward the kitchen. Work calls and texts frequently come in from his on-call service as well as people who have his personal number. He takes them all, and if he feels they need to be seen, he refers them to the after-hours line. Only once that I know of has he gotten up in the middle of the night to see a patient when he had the night off. Of course it helps that the practice is just down the stairs from his condo.

While waiting for him to return, I wander into the sitting room across the hall, which houses the large piano. It is so beautiful and still just as much of a mystery as it was on the first day. Aside from Mrs. Easler and her message—which I still haven't told Jake about—I'm just mentally stacking up all of these mysterious pieces, and I can feel I'm getting closer. Closer to what, I don't know yet, but eventually all of it will start clicking together.

Sitting at the bench, my fingers lightly slide over the keys with familiarity. In many ways, playing a piano is like riding a bike. Once the routine and repetition are instilled, they never truly go away.

The beautiful sound echoes around the room as I play the opening of "Clair de lune," by Claude Debussy. I find it ironic as I once read this title comes from a French poem in which the author depicts the soul as somewhere full of music where birds are inspired to sing by the sad and beautiful light of the moon. I'm lost in thought about this and the melody when all of a sudden, the room bursts with light. Closing my eyes, I take a moment to let them adjust and then slowly open them in awe as I see Jake slightly dim the brightness with a dial on the wall in the foyer.

Jake has turned on the chandelier in the back of the house, the same chandelier I didn't even notice they'd reinstalled today, let alone was working. I also didn't realize how dark the house is at night. Not only is this chandelier a striking centerpiece for the back of the house, but apparently it's the main source of lighting, and my heart feels like it's exploding.

Moving to the foyer, I stand next to Jake, with both our heads tilted back, we stare up. It's so beautiful my eyes water from complete euphoria.

"I think I was so used to seeing it here, it didn't even occur to me that they were both back and hung. How did you know to turn it on?" I glance at him, and he looks down at me.

"I didn't. That was Garrett who texted me. He asked what you thought of the chandeliers, and considering they were both off, I assumed you didn't know."

"I didn't. It's just breathtaking. No wonder so many people would come here years ago—this piece is a showstopper all on its own."

We both look back up at the light fixture. A moment of silence passes as we take in how stunning it is, admiring all the tiny rainbows dancing across the ceiling from the reflections of the crystals.

"It really is," he agrees.

Is this what Mrs. Easler meant by *Where the light shines*? Was she talking about this light? Does this answer seem too quick and easy? It's not a secret that she loved these chandeliers; they're talked about in two of the books from the library that I have and no telling how many more.

Next to me, Jake turns a little to face me, and he reaches for my arm. Warm fingers slide down over my skin to my hand, and it's as if the thoughts in my head instantly shut off like a tonearm scratching across a record. His fingers link with mine.

He's touching me.

All hail, praise to the light gods.

"So, should I tell him you like it?" His voice is rough, but his brows are raised in a playful way, and a small smile tips the corner of his full lips.

"Yes, but maybe later." I shrug one shoulder and then bite my bottom lip. For days I have been wanting to see him, talk to him, be with him, and call me selfish, but I want this time for just the two of us.

Turning toward me, he wraps his free hand around my face. His fingers tangle in my hair, and his thumb swipes back and forth across my cheek. His eyes are a rich blue, and as they travel over the features of my face, I feel as if he's painting me. My lips tingle as his gaze pauses, and then he lets out a sigh, almost like a surrender.

"I missed you," he says, and my poor, shriveled-up, wounded heart floods and expands as he rehydrates it with his words.

There's a wariness to him that I don't want him to feel, so I take a step closer and breathe in the scent of sunshine and fabric softener. Gently, I place my hand on his chest and say, "I missed you too." Because I did, so much so that I felt almost a little crazy.

His heartbeat under my palm is strong, and the heat from his skin seeps through the fabric as if searching for me. I love it and am quite certain I am falling for him.

"I can't stop thinking about you," he whispers, his lips slipping to the sensitive skin just below my ear.

"I can't stop thinking about you either," I say, leaning farther into him and allowing my hand to drop so it can slide up under his shirt to the warmth of the skin on his back. The muscles ripple, and his fingers grip my hair tighter.

His lips glide, and in that brief second before they brush with mine, I realize I'm completely at peace with what is now my past. The inner turmoil is gone, the anger and the disappointment. I knew I was almost there, and it's a great relief to know I now am.

Is it because of him? Yes and no. I will never let another man define me again, but that doesn't mean I haven't opened myself up to him. I have and I am, and it's exciting. I'm proud of the person I've become here. I'm proud of the friendships I've made, and I'm super proud to know that these people appreciate me just for me.

"I've been wanting to do this again since the moment I left." His lips press into mine, and I smile against him.

"Took you long enough," I mumble, and he smiles too, until his tongue brushes my bottom lip as he takes it between his teeth and ends our conversation.

Jake kisses like a Hollywood movie star. He's thorough, and it's insanely hot, so swoon-worthy he makes me weak in the knees—knees that brush against him as he pulls me closer and holds me to him.

Wow. Just wow.

Breaking the kiss, I take a step back, pull on his hand, and move toward the stairs.

He follows, and his gaze never leaves my face. It's as if he's as mesmerized by me, as if I am the light shining from the chandelier.

I take another step back, and he takes two, closing the distance between us and linking our fingers together again.

"Are we skipping dinner?" he teases, his thumb now running along the inside of my wrist. It causes me to shiver.

"Are you hungry?" I ask, because if he is, I'll definitely steer us in a different direction.

"Not for food," he says, his gaze heated.

Fervor races from the very bottom of my stomach, over my chest, and up into my cheeks.

I thought if we got to this point, I would be nervous. In fact, I wasn't sure if or when I would ever be ready, but as I lead Jake up the stairs to my room, I find I am not.

"Are you sure you want this?" he asks, as his mouth trails down to my collarbone and his hands squeeze my butt, pulling me flush up against him.

"I don't know if I'll ever stop wanting this," I tell him, with my fingers tangled in his hair.

He pulls back to look at me.

"Ryla," he whispers, as he looks at me so ardently and runs his thumb over my swollen bottom lip. "Sometimes the things you say to me, I feel like this can't be real, but it is real, isn't it?"

He states this as a question, but I know it's not. It's more of a wonder, almost dreamlike. Bringing his mouth back to mine, he slowly, effortlessly and gently, one piece at a time, removes our clothes.

What does he see when he looks at me? I know what I see when I look at him, loyalty, passion, kindness, and a giving heart. I also see inches and inches of golden skin that trembles as I trace each and every indention, every line.

What does he taste as his mouth explores every part of my body? I taste sunshine, salt, and a flavor so good I know I'll always crave more.

And what does he feel as his large hands memorize every peak, every curve, and every hidden place on my body? I feel a man who's strong, guarded, and carries his love close to his heart, but who also shares it freely with those to whom he gives himself.

And he's giving himself to me.

How did I get so lucky?

I also feel what it's like to be wholly consumed by someone, someone who just wants me, all of me, from what he knows of my messy past to the person I am when I'm sweating and laying tile. Just like I want all of him. All the time.

The smell of his skin. The feel of his hips as they settle against mine. The size and delicious weight of him as he stares down as if I am the most precious thing in the world. The words he whispers in my ear as he pushes inside, and I become his and he becomes mine.

We become one.

Minutes, hours, all through the night, we take turns giving and receiving. Like the tide moving in and out, our bodies undulate together. No part of us is left untouched or unexplored. He's not shy and neither am I. My fingers grip his shoulders, his waist, his hair. His hands pin down my hips, own my body, and reverently hold on to my head. Our mouths drink from one another, our sounds are swallowed by the other, and over and over we find our way to shared raw bliss.

This moment, it's ours.

It's passionate, vulnerable and healing.

It's moving on.

It's starting new.

26

Slowly, I become aware of his fingers gently tracing circles across the sensitive skin of my hip under the sheet. The morning stillness I've come to love so much about this place is content around us, and with my eyes still closed, the only sounds I hear are the whirling of the ceiling fan, the lapping of the water against the shoreline, and Jake's breathing. It's warm and steady as it moves across my neck, and with his solid body curled tightly behind mine, my heart seems to have suddenly found an unfamiliar rhythm. It's new and quick, one that wants to match his.

Reaching for his hand, I pull it so he wraps his arm around me. With his palm pressed against my stomach, he scoots closer and easily eliminates the remaining space between us. He's warm and perfect, and although we're both awake, neither of us has said a word. Right at this moment, words seem unnecessary.

With Carter, it was so easy to fall in love. It was like we slid right into it. We were young, carefree, excited to begin this thing called adult life, and happy. He instantly became my person, and the rest was history. But with Jake, it doesn't feel so easy. It took growth, patience, and vulnerability. I wouldn't necessarily say I've fought it, but it's been unexpected, especially after our first meeting. I wasn't looking for it and never thought I would find it here, but then again, isn't that when they say it happens, when you least expect it? This feeling, the one I have for him, while it is exciting, it feels less about the excitement and instead burns. The two are completely incomparable, and I feel as if his mere presence has somehow set my soul on fire and my heart free.

"What are you thinking about so hard this morning?" he asks, his voice rough and his breath moving through my hair.

It's as if I can physically see the book of my life laid out before me and the last page of a chapter has been flipped so a new one can begin. The content is unknown, but the chapter heading is there, and it's titled with his name. Jake. I love seeing it written in my story, and although I shouldn't wish it too hard for fear of jinxing it, I'm hoping he's present in many chapters to come.

Upon my hesitation, he props himself up on one elbow, and I roll to my back.

My breath catches as I look up at him. Just seeing him here like this with his hair falling over his forehead and the fresh stubble across his jawline, I can barely maintain my composure under his bright blue stare. It's an open sky that holds a promise. His eyes are intense, fearless as much as they are endless, and full of devotion. His openness is present; he's handing it to me with transparency, wanting me to see he's giving it all to me. It's there for the taking, and with whispered words from his body to mine, he's begging for me to give the same.

"Talk to me," he says, concern gracing his gorgeous features.

It would be so easy to withhold from him the enormity of how I'm feeling. Vulnerability is an emotion I rarely let others see, and after the failure of my marriage, in many ways I've felt defective when it comes to being loved. Of all the people in the world, Carter was supposed to love me and accept me the most, but in the end he didn't. I've always felt different from others, and whereas I've always viewed this as a gift, one where I'm unique, this past year it's felt more like a curse. I've always felt like one of a kind, which isn't necessarily a bad thing, unless it's viewed as a flaw.

Does he view me as flawed?

I don't think he does.

Maybe he sees me as damaged, but damaged things can be fixed or admired for their scars. I know I have scars, ones he still seems to find beautiful regardless.

I give him a small smile that says I'm almost ready to bare it all. My hand runs down the length of his torso, brushes against the top of one of his legs and wraps around him. His features smooth out and soften as he understands what I'm not saying but wanting to show him. And it's as he's leaning forward to place his lips against mine, I tell him, "I sleep deeper with you next to me."

27

_D_ays have passed.

Days spent in complete happiness as we navigated finding a new routine where we were together more than we were apart. We went out to dinner, I helped him with the volunteer beach cleanup he organized, and we spent many hours riding around on his boat chasing dolphins, watching the sun set, and getting lost in each other. As for the nights, I offered to meet him at his place, but he said he liked being at mine more, said it's bigger and he enjoys being in a home, the home I've made. How could I say no to that?

We talked about our families, the differences in where we grew up, our paths to where we are professionally, and all of our favorite things from foods to movies. We talked about the Easlers, the brooch, the gun, the progress on my house, and the website I created (which he went and read every word of), and together we sat on the dock waiting for Mrs. Easler to return. She didn't; only the light appeared, which is still a sight in itself, and we pondered whether it was because of him being present, or maybe it never happened at all, and I was just crazy and imagined the whole thing.

I've thought about asking him if he knows who the owner of the trust was, but I don't really know what the point would be, and he would most likely direct me to Bauer. Then I'd have to explain to him that I don't want to discuss trusts with Bauer because it would lead to questions about mine, like why I purchased the house with one versus just my name, and I'm still not ready.

Which leads to the one thing we've yet to talk about: our exes.

Except, with every day that passes, I feel more and more trapped under the weight of an identity that is no longer me. At first I was being an ostrich and burying my head in the sand, but now, after all this time and so many conversations later, I really don't have a reason not to tell him fully about who I was married to and what has happened over the last year. Then again, he hasn't told me about his. What I need to do is just rip off the Band-Aid. It's not like I think it will change how he feels and maybe he'll feel like he can then open up to me. Am I the reason he hasn't said anything? Is he worried that I'll feel I have to share too? All I know is that eventually, the noise will catch up to me, to us, and he's going to find himself smack dab in the middle.

Jake left early this morning to go home, feed Dash, and get ready for work. He mentioned he has a full day of four-legged patients but will be back late this afternoon. He gently kissed me on the forehead just before he walked out, and I rolled over to grab his pillow. His side of the bed was still warm under the covers, and even though daylight was filtering its way into the room, it lulled me back to sleep.

Just like I found it profound to kiss another man after all these years, as I was getting ready to meet my friends for breakfast, I also felt this strange out-of-body sensation thinking about how I now sleep curled up in bed with another man too.

Part of me is shouting, "Who are you?" and then the other part is cheering, "Way to go!"

Either way, I like who I've become here, and just thinking about his fingers as they drag across my skin leaving streaks of heat and his mouth as it skims down my neck to the dip between my collarbones, my stomach clenches with awe, vulnerability, and anticipation for next time, knowing how good it will be.

I immediately find parking on the street, and with the sun shining and the seagulls flying overhead, I'm not sure I could be more content than I am at this moment.

Walking into the cafe, I see it's not overly busy, and I quickly find Natalie and Corrie already chatting in a booth overlooking the riverwalk. Some of the foot traffic from the tourists has started to slow down. The local schools are back in session, which means soon the northern ones will be too. I look forward to the little town being sleepy and quaint.

"Good morning, ladies." I smile at both of them while they eye each other knowingly. There are already three coffees and three muffins on the table. My stomach growls, and my mouth waters at just the sight.

"Apparently, it's a real good morning for you," Corrie teases as I slide into the booth next to Natalie.

"What do you mean?" I ask her, unable to contain the smile stretching across my face. I pick up the coffee and take a sip. It's delicious.

"So, there's a rumor floating around that a certain boat has been spotted at your dock all hours of the night and early in the morning over the last week," Corrie says while she wags her brows.

I roll my eyes, that smile growing larger.

Natalie gasps and shifts to face me better. "You didn't tell me he was spending the night! This is the best news!" She claps her hands together.

"It's only been a few nights, and you guys ..." I press my palms over my cheeks as the heat of a blush crawls into them. "There are no words." I squeeze my eyes shut.

Natalie squeals and squeezes my arm.

"Jake's always been such a good person. He's salt of the earth, if you know what I mean," Corrie says, and I do.

He is fundamentally wonderful. He's loyal, low maintenance, hardworking, and straightforward. What you see is what you get. There's no drama, and he leads a fairly simple but wildly successful life. He's kind, and when he goes all in, there's no questioning it. Just like with me, I know he's gone all in. Where we're going, I don't know yet, but it feels good to know he's next to me.

And I'm so happy.

When I moved to Chuluota Springs, I figured I would make a friend or two after a while, but I wasn't looking for it, didn't think it was necessary. I was so focused on hiding, escaping, and trying to deal with the mess that had become my life, and I had forgotten what living life is like. These people—Jake, Willow, Natalie, Corrie, and so many others—they've reminded me and made it so that all I've done recently is live, from having these wonderful friends to becoming a part of the community to meeting a guy who makes me feel like anything is possible. I feel on top of the world, but then I remember my other life, and worry sets in.

"So, what's the problem?" Natalie asks, seeing in my face that my mind has wandered to the dark side.

"He doesn't know." Shame prickles under my skin, and that weight on my chest pushes down.

"You haven't told him?" Natalie asks. Confusion and shock appear on their faces.

"There's never been a reason for it to come up. He knows I have an ex-husband named Carter, but I'm pretty sure he doesn't know who Carter is, or who I really am outside of Chuluota Springs." I bite my bottom lip in a grimace and then frown.

"Why don't you just tell him? I'm sure he'll understand and not think it's a big deal," Corrie says, leaning over and placing her hand on my arm.

"I hope not, because I don't know. Everything is still so new, and once I'm found"—I put air quotes around found—"things will be different. I just wanted him to know me."

I wanted to know myself too. In a way, it's like if I didn't discuss or remember that time in my life, it never happened. It removes that layer of identity while allowing me to let what's underneath and buried rise to the top.

"I hate to break it to you, but it hasn't been that new for a while," Natalie says. "I saw the way he looked at you at the scallop festival, and that look pretty much said *mine* then. That was weeks ago." She pulls her hand back, tears off a piece of her muffin, and pops it in her mouth.

Weeks, not months. To me, weeks still feels pretty new.

"You're going to have to tell him sooner or later, because if you don't, he'll hear it from someone else," Corrie says.

"I know." I reach for the muffin and pull the paper down. It's something for me to fidget with. "I don't know why it makes me so nervous—it's not like I've done something wrong. The media … eventually they'll move on too, right?"

Corrie pulls her phone from her pocket and places it on the table. "I set it to receive notifications every time your name pops up." She swipes down to show me her notification center; it's filled with pings from all different sources.

My heart sinks.

"Instead of 'Where's Waldo?' it's become 'Where's Rylie?' It's really only a matter of time before someone says they've seen you here," she says sympathetically.

Letting out a groan, I drop my head to the table. I'm not

embarrassed by my past or regretful. I was who I was, but that doesn't change the fact that I just want to be seen for who I am now, someone who is creative and independent on her own, who has her own identity and is unique from others. Did I receive money from Carter? Of course, but I had my own too.

"Morning, ladies," says a deep voice. Natalie stiffens next to me, and I look up to see Garrett standing at our table. I didn't even notice he had walked in, but here he is, and he's smiling, but not really. I mean what is that look on his face? It's like a cross between a starved animal and a clown. He's dressed in his usual work attire of boots, faded jeans, and a polo. His dark hair looks freshly combed, and if I didn't have eyes only for his brother, I would think he looks pretty darn good.

Except for the strange expression.

"Morning," Corrie says, being her usual chipper self. She slides out of the booth, offering up her spot as she smooths down her apron.

Garrett nods briefly at her but doesn't take the seat. His eyes are only for Natalie.

Corrie glances at me, and her eyes widen in a *What's going on with them?* kind of way. I just shrug in return. It seems I'm not the only one who has secrets.

It also seems like I've been too busy worrying about my own life when I should have asked them about theirs. This is something I hope I'll be rectifying soon.

Very soon.

28

————————

After leaving the coffee shop, I wander over to the library to return the borrowed books and see if Mr. Williams ever received the *Times* article we requested. At the time, he told me he would forward the email over to me, but it hasn't come.

While trying to do some more research on the Easlers at home, I came across several websites that were digital newspaper archive companies, but each required a subscription, and in the end, the few I looked at really didn't have a whole lot in regards to this little town. At the time, I'm sure there were only a few hundred people living here. Even now, all this time later, there are only a few thousand. Like all small towns across America, I'm certain this one wasn't recognized or remembered.

I've thought a lot about the owner of the home and the trust. The thing is, trusts are set up to protect one's assets, and they give someone else, the trustee, the power to manage it. The most common type of trust is a living trust. It usually isn't funded until there's a death. Afterward, there are instructions on how the assets are to be distributed. I could be wrong, but this is what makes the most sense for my house. I think once I tell Jake who I am, I'll ask Bauer. The truth will be out there, so I won't have anything to hide.

After all, no one has lived in the house, just the original family. In the *Images of America* book, I found a photo of the Easler daughter as a toddler. Her birth year was listed next to her as 1903. Assuming Mrs. Easler left it to her once she died, it doesn't matter, because generations and generations have passed. I Google-searched and looked for a record of a sale transaction on the home, but there isn't one, not that I really expected there to be. Chuluota Springs is a very small town, and this house was old and run-down.

If there is someone attached to the trust who profited off of the sale versus the money being gifted to a charity, shouldn't they be the ones to receive the brooch and the gun?

"Good morning!" Mr. Williams says when he sees me come through the automatic doors, his face lit up with excitement.

"Good morning," I say back as I make my way to the counter and place the borrowed books on it.

He glances at his watch then back at me. "Well, almost afternoon, but regardless, I'm glad you're here." He picks up the books and moves them to a cart labeled *Check in* then shuffles over to his computer, pushes up his glasses, and begins typing. "I have your article. I have for a bit, but I think I typed in your email address wrong." He begins spelling it out, and sure enough, where there should have been an S is a five. "Well, that explains it."

He types a few things then reaches under the counter to pull out a few sheets of paper.

"I went ahead and emailed it over to you, but here's a printed copy as well. I must say, I very much enjoyed this article. I may be just a librarian, but at heart I'm a historian too, and I love this town. Yes, every town has its stories, but this one continues to fascinate me even all these years later."

"So you're my go-to person for town information?" I wonder how much he really does know about the Easlers.

He grins. "Yep. But then again, most of the things I know did come from books. All it takes is a little creativity, and most stories link themselves together in one way or another."

I ponder this, thinking he's right. There are the photos of the Easlers, the book on jewels, and the one where I found a mention of his ship sinking. Nowhere did I find any conspiracies, but it doesn't take a genius to wonder if they are connected.

He slides the printed copy of the newspaper article across the counter, and with shaky, excited fingers, I take it. This time as I glance down at the page, the title—*Easler Fishing, More than Just a Catch*—stands out to me large and bold.

"If you have any other questions, please let me know," he says.

"What about microfiche of *The Chuluota Springs Tribune*? Maybe from 1900 to 1920?"

"Unfortunately, Hurricane Hugh came through in 1952, and some of the buildings didn't make it. The library flooded, and the *Tribune* building was not spared. Also, microfiche wasn't invented until 1961. I so wish we had the articles and stories from the town's earlier days. I would love to have read about the stories from passing famous visitors."

I suppose that would be interesting to some. They would have had to stay at the resort, or maybe at the Molinaro castle.

After thanking him for the article, I find a large overstuffed chair to sit in, take a deep breath, and read it.

Murder? Mystery? Foul play?

Plenty of theories, speculations, and investigations, but not one definitive answer. What has happened to Mr. Easler? This is the lingering question in the recent disappearance of John Easler, owner of Easler Fishing Company in Florida.

In the world of fine jewelry, Mr. Easler is a rare and precious gem.

He is known to the greats, especially to none other than Pierre Cartier himself, the greatest of the greats. Cartier, known around the world as "the jeweler of kings and the king of jewelers," has most recently graced our pages with images of the several brilliant tiaras ordered by King Edward the VII and the sale of the magnificent Hope Diamond.

As many know, the prestigious French jewelry company opened in New York City in 1909, then in 1917 moved to 653 Fifth Avenue, a Neo-Renaissance mansion owned by his close friend Morton Freeman Plant, son of railroad tycoon Henry B. Plant. Cartier purchased the property from Plant for $100 in cash and a double-stranded natural pearl necklace valued at the time at one million dollars. The necklace, one of the many romantic gestures made by Plant for his wife, solidi-fied this as one of the most legendary real estate transactions of all time.

After the sale of their mansion, the Plants headed south. Mr. Plant built the Tampa Bay Hotel, and for many, its reputation precedes its name. It is the quintessential place to be seen for socialites. Each year in February, it serves as the venue for the Ye Mystic Krewe of Ye Gasparilla Coronation Ball. While many towns have their festivals, Tampa Bay's Gasparilla celebration rivals that of Mardi Gras in New Orleans with its swashbuckling pirates of the Ye Mystic Krewe, their invasion of the city, and the parades and balls.

The event, named after legendary pirate José Gaspar of the late 18th and early 19th century, began in 1904. Gaspar was a Spanish aristocrat by birth, a Spanish naval officer turned pirate, and known for terrorizing the West Coast of Florida. Legend has it there is buried treasure along the coast, but it has never been found.

Treasure is what led Mr. Cartier to Mr. Easler.

Mr. Easler was commissioned to provide conch pearls for the next coronation crown. The two gentlemen had met at a previous ball, and it was Mrs. Easler's stunning conch pearl drop earrings that captured the jeweler's eye. Since then, the pair has been seen dining at the hotel on several different occasions, and Mrs. Easler has been photographed wearing a brilliant diamond and conch pearl brooch. Sources tell us Mr. Cartier designed and created it himself in exchange for a dozen conch pearls. It would seem there is a trend with Mr. Cartier and pearl transactions.

The rare and beautiful conch pearl.

While many view natural pearls to be as prized as gems, such as rubies and emeralds, it's the conch pearl, which comes from the queen conch of the warmer waters of Florida and the West Indies, that is sending jewelers and buyers on a frenzy. With their unique colors such as pink, orange, and brown, their shapes, and their lack of availability, the conch pearl continues to be one of the most sought-after gems in the world.

Which brings us to Mr. Easler, a well-known commercial fisherman from Florida.

He served in the Spanish American war then settled with his wife in the small town of Chuluota Springs. For almost 20 years, he has provided restaurants along the east coast with fish, shrimp, scallops, and conch meat. Odds are you've eaten some of his catch and didn't even know it. Which leads us back to our original question: what happened to Mr. Easler?

What is known is that Mr. Easler was scheduled to meet Mr. Cartier at the Tampa Bay Hotel at three o'clock but never showed. He was traveling by boat when apparently a storm came in and the boat sank. While there were only a few passengers, all but one died. Mr. Cartier claims they were meeting so he could retrieve the conch pearls for the crown and purchase others to add to his collection. Passersby at the hotel claim Mr. Cartier was greatly disturbed by the no-show and disappearance of his friend, as well as one particular expected conch pearl, which he said was purported to be the largest in the world.

One cannot help but wonder how many people would have wanted to get their hands on the largest conch pearl in the world. Murder? Mystery? Foul play? We can't help but think there's more to the story, and if that's the case, what has become of the coveted pearls?

What happened to the pearls?

This question resonates with me and rings loudly between my ears as I lean back in the chair and drop my hands, holding the article in my lap.

Are there more pearls? Did they go down with the ship? Did they hide them? Did they suspect there might be an evil plot working against them? I just don't know.

And what about the largest found in the world?

Digging my phone out of my bag, I search the internet for the largest conch pearl. There is one expert who mentions knowing of three conch pearls over one hundred carats, but mostly the ones for purchase on the market today are in the forties. All sites request contact for inquiries and no prices are listed. I do, however, find an article about a conch pearl, enamel, and diamond bracelet designed by Cartier in the late 1920s. It was said to be from the personal collection of Queen Veronica Eugenia of Spain, and it sold for almost three and a half million dollars at Sotheby's Geneva in 2012. Otherwise, it seems most of the spectacular pieces are now found in museums.

Feeling excited and completely overwhelmed, I glance toward Mr. Williams and see a knowing look on his face. He winks at me as if saying he'll keep my secrets, secrets only a few people know. The lady at the pawn shop was right—I need to get a safe or head to the bank. There's no telling how much this brooch is worth.

29

———

*L*ife is good.

And with just the thought of those words, I know I've cursed myself. I didn't mean to think them this morning, but I did, and now I know it's just a matter of time before the universe says, *Hold my coat.*

Every night this week, Jake has come over after work. If he gets done early, we cook dinner together, but if it's later, I have dinner waiting for him.

It's so easy to be around him. We laugh and tell stories from our life, and we've talked ad nauseum about conspiracies regarding Mr. Easler, Mrs. Easler, and the conch pearls. Did the pearls sink, or are they hidden somewhere in the house? If so, where might they be? I feel like we've checked every inch of the place, including shaking the painting that was left on the wall to see if they were sealed inside and going over every nook and cranny of the old grandfather clock. At this point, I think I've resigned myself to the fact that they aren't here. Someone must have found them, or perhaps they did in fact go down with Mr. Easler to the bottom of the gulf.

But this morning, just after he kissed me goodbye and I

285

heard the door shut, I did the unthinkable and thought those words. Immediately after, thunder rolled over the house like a bad omen. Not once in the several months I've been here has it rained in the morning, only in the afternoon, but not today. Rain poured out of the sky, and with it the impending feeling of dread. It wasn't a matter of if the other shoe was going to drop; it was when. So, as he picked me up after work late in the afternoon to run to the grocery store and that feeling kept lingering, I wasn't surprised when something compelled me to stop at the end of the aisle instead of joining him in the checkout line.

Unbeknownst to him, I watch as Jake tenses all over then slowly picks up a magazine. He stares at the cover then flips it open. I'm not sure what he's looking at, but deep down, fear stirs, and my heart starts racing in my chest. I'm no stranger to the cover of a tabloid, especially before I moved here, but it's been a while. The world should have moved on. Other people out there have done other things to grab the media's attention. Why is it still me?

Snapping it shut, he shoves the magazine back into the rack and shakes his head as he looks at the ground. My stomach bottoms out, because with that betrayed, devastated look on his face and the expedited rate at which his chest is rising and falling, I know he's seen something about me. As much as I wished otherwise, it's too late.

I should have just told him.

I tried to this week. I thought over and over about how I would broach the subject, but I could never find the words. I really did want to tell him. I'm ready to tell him—I just didn't. It would have changed us, I know it would have, and I wanted to live in the bubble we created together for a little bit longer. Now, with sudden clarity, it feels like my world and that bubble has popped.

This was my biggest fear, him discovering I'm not exactly

who I say I am, and now he's formed opinions based on something he saw versus the truth I could have told him.

This is bad. This is so, so bad.

Slowly, I approach him with the remainder of our things as he turns to face me. There are accusations in his expression, in the way his brows are pulled down and his lips are pressed tightly into a thin line. I glance toward the magazines, and there on the one in the middle is a picture of me in a formal gown with my head thrown back laughing, and I look crazy. On the cover in a huge font is the word *MURDERHEIRESS*.

Oh no.

The words pound through my head as the anxiety I've now had for weeks about him discovering this part of my life comes rushing to the surface. My skin is burning, I feel like I can't breathe, and my heart is thumping so hard it aches.

At this moment, the world around us has stopped. I know people are moving, progressing through the checkout lines, and talking, but I can't hear or see any of it, just him standing next to me, so tense it's kind of scary.

"I can explain," I whisper as I stare at his handsome face, but as his eyes, which are already blue, turn to ice then narrow and his cheeks flush red, I realize they're the wrong words to say.

Frost flings my way as he turns, completely ignoring me as if I'm not here, and he quickly begins to unload his basket. I say nothing and do nothing, for what is there to say with all these people standing around? The checkout girl says hello to Jake—after all, most people in this town know him—but when she looks my way, recognition strikes her features as her eyes widen and her jaw drops open just a little. I know Jake sees this as he takes a step away from both of us. The girl says nothing, and neither do I. I feel like I'm dying on the inside as the three of us check out in complete silence except for the beeping of the scanner. He pays for our groceries, and I know now is not the time to say anything more.

Grabbing the bags, he nods to the girl who's still staring at me in awe, and another surge of anger flashes over his features as he abruptly turns and makes his way to the door.

I know Jake, more than he thinks I do, and I know this is going to send him reeling. He's an honest guy, and while we haven't had the talk yet for either of us, I know that truth and trust mean something to him. I know I probably should have told him, but I didn't have to, and up until recently, I didn't want to. The girl in that photo is my past, one I've worked really hard to say goodbye to over the last few months, and quite honestly, I haven't felt like it was anyone's business—not even his.

Have I pushed him to tell me every single secret and detail of his life? No. Do I think he owes me anything other than who he is now? No, so why should I owe it to him? It shouldn't make a difference who I was before I came here, and quite frankly, if it does, maybe he's not someone I should want in my life. But just that thought sends a piercing pain through my heart, and I involuntarily reach up to rub the spot on my chest.

Exiting the store, I'm walking behind Jake, still grappling with how and what I'm going to share with him, when a flash-bulb goes off accompanied by the sound of a shutter clicking on a camera. A random guy has come out of nowhere; he pushes into our space and starts throwing out questions. Jake freezes at the sudden onslaught then moves right past him, because it isn't him he wants, it's me. Of course this has to happen at this moment. What are the odds and could it be any more incon-venient?

As I try to follow him, I trip, and my hands scrape across the ground.

"Rylie Crest, why did you go into hiding?"

"Did you think you could escape the truth?"

More flashes go off, and my eyes fill with panicked tears. I have no idea how he found me, and my heart hurts so much as I right myself and stare straight ahead at Jake's retreating back.

"Is it true you killed him so you could keep all the money?"

And there it is, the one thing everyone thinks the most.

Jake briefly stops walking as those words have, unknowingly to the reporter, hit the wrong target. His whole body has jolted, and before I can reach him, he resumes walking.

No. No. No.

It's funny how up until Carter's death, I never cared what people thought of me. I knew who I was, and so did my friends and family. But this, this slash of character the media has created, sunk its teeth into and run with—it completely unsettles and crushes me. Plus, they're using Carter's death as a sales headline, as clickbait, and I continually wonder what is wrong with society. Shame on them.

People have stopped all over the parking lot and just inside the store. They are staring at us, at me, and just like this morning, the bad omen returns and thunder rumbles overhead.

Without acknowledging them, without saying even a word, I follow Jake, who's quickly walking to his boat. The questions stop as I didn't take the enticement to respond, but he's there, close behind, still taking photos. I can feel it, and I know Jake can too.

Jake climbs aboard, puts the bags down, and then holds his hand out to assist me. I take it, feeling the warmth of his palm against my sore damaged one, and that's when I realize I'm shaking, because he is steady.

His eyes are molten, the blue part of the flame as they briefly land on me, and whatever he sees on my face has his brows pulling down and the muscles ticking in his jaw. He releases my hand, takes a seat behind the wheel, and cranks the boat on. In an instant, he whisks us away.

"Jake." The wind is whipping around us, and he doesn't respond. He doesn't even acknowledge me as he drives the boat back up the river to my house, and I feel this impending sense of doom. I'm not sure if what I say is going to matter to him. Right at this moment, it seems he's made up his mind about me, and I feel completely soul-crushed.

Usually in horrible situations, time creeps by, but it's as if today the boat has another speed altogether, and we arrive at my house in the blink of an eye.

I've had months to tell him, or at least how I wanted to form and shape the conversation, but now that the moment is here, I just don't know, and I can't help but wonder if it will matter.

He parks the boat, again takes my shaking hand to help me up onto the dock, and then about-faces and quickly eats up the distance to the house with his long legs.

White light streaks across the sky and splinters out. A second later, the boom of the thunder claps loudly. The air has turned humid, and the strong scent of rain permeates the air.

Closing my eyes, I take a deep breath and follow behind as if I'm marching to the guillotine, until we're both standing in the kitchen.

This is a mess, a complete mess, and without even saying anything to him, I have this foreboding sense of catastrophe.

"Jake." I say his name again to attempt to get his attention, but he doesn't say anything, just shakes his head no and holds up his hand to let me know he's not into talking, his steely gaze locking onto mine. He stares at me, and more than anything I wish I knew what he's thinking. I wish I could crack open his head to see what it is he's seeing, feel what he's feeling, hear the words racing through his brain. Then I might be able to find the right words to make this better.

Letting out a harsh exhale, he breaks his eyes away from mine and takes a long, slow look around the kitchen and over to

Coco's cage. She's watching us, and she knows something is wrong.

I wait patiently as his gaze trails over the little details of the kitchen that mean something to me, but maybe not to someone else. I'm not sure why he's looking around—maybe he's collecting his thoughts—but his eyes wander out of the kitchen to an old vintage map of the river I bought and hung in the dining room, back to the light fixtures that dangle over the kitchen island and the glass doorknobs I used on the French doors. It's sudden when he turns on his heel without one word or backward glance at me and walks out the back door.

I can't help but follow.

"Just wait! Where are you going?" I call after him as he reaches the start of the dock. The birds have gone silent as they are hunkering down to get ready for the second storm of the day.

He comes to a stop, and without turning to face me, he asks, "Did you murder him?"

Is that what he thinks? He's known me for months. Have I ever given off vibes that I have it in me to kill someone? Isn't he smart enough to know not to believe what he reads on the cover of a tabloid?

"How could you even ask me that?" I am completely offended, and my heart is racing so fast it again feels hard to breathe.

He turns toward me, and every muscle in his face down through his shoulders is rock-solid tense. "I don't know ... it seems like a legitimate question. Seems like there's a lot I don't actually know about you, Rylie, details you chose not to tell me."

I'm certain there is still a lot I don't know about him as well, things he chose not to tell me, but I'm not getting mad about that. It's his right to choose what and when he wants to share.

"Perhaps, but that life isn't my life anymore." I've come to stand directly in front of him, and on the inside I'm pleading for him not to do this, to listen to me and understand me.

"You sure about that?" He waves his hand in the direction of the grocery store. I understand what he's saying—they've found me and now brought that life to our door.

Letting out a deep sigh and trying to diffuse some of his anger, I calmly say, "No, I didn't kill him, and no, I wasn't out for his money."

He tilts his head to the side as his eyes narrow. "How much money are we talking?"

I recoil then shrug my shoulders. "Does it matter?" I have my own money. I always have. Carter's just became an excess that is collecting dust in my bank account.

"Of course it does!" he says animatedly, and I flinch.

"Fine." I throw my hand out. "More than whatever number it is that you're thinking."

He lets out a deep, shuddering sigh, his head drops, and he closes his eyes.

My shaking has returned.

"But I'm not sure why that is relev—"

"How long do you plan on staying here?" He cuts me off as if he hasn't heard me talking.

"What do you mean?" I ask, noticing that although it was dark outside before, now it appears and feels even darker. There's no moon and no lamp light. All I have to see by is the light leaking out of the back of the house from the chandelier. It traces a path down the dock to the inlet, casting its glow across his face. He's agitated, distressed, and I watch as his chest rises and falls at a rapid rate, his hands squeezing into fists.

"How long before you decide to go back to your old life? Chicago?"

"I haven't decided what's next. I've just wanted to focus on the now, here, the house … you." Isn't that what he's doing with me? Living in the now, this new relationship, day by day?

"Right," he says, taking a step back and stuffing his hands into his pockets.

How was that the wrong thing to say? If he were to tell me he's living in the moment with me, I would be thrilled. Or is it that he's upset about something else?

"I didn't lie to you, Jake. The only thing about me I chose not to tell you was my married name. Because why is that relevant? I stopped being that girl almost a year ago, the day I found them together, and now, what you see is what you get. I am who I am, and I'm not going to apologize for it. I don't owe anyone an explanation, not even you. This is my life."

He mulls over what I've just said while watching me.

"What I see is what I get, huh?"

"Yes!" My chin quivers.

Breaking eye contact, he looks back up at the house, and I watch as a myriad of emotions play across the features of his face. He shakes his head, and instead of talking to me more, he again turns toward his boat.

He's going to leave, and my soul fractures.

I'm so stunned I reach forward to grab his arm, but he's faster than me and I stumble over the unevenness of the dock planks.

"You don't understand," I yell.

"You're right, I don't," he fires back.

"Jake, will you please just wait a minute?" I'm begging, and I'll continue to beg if he just stays and talks to me.

He stops next to his boat. He doesn't climb on, but he doesn't turn to face me either.

"Every day I wake up and I'm angry at him." I clasp my hands together and pull them up tight against my heart. This hurts—all of this hurts.

Slowly, Jake shifts so he can see me.

"I'm so angry about what he did to us, to me." I point to my chest. "But then I remember he's dead, and I feel guilty for being angry, because what is the point? He was my husband, I loved him, I gave all of myself. And even though that wasn't enough, I would never wish him to be dead. Ever. I feel like a horrible person."

He pierces me with a look that says he thinks I'm horrible, and my insides both cringe and rebel at the same time. I also gave myself to Jake, but the way he's looking at me suddenly makes me feel like he doesn't think I'm enough either.

"Really?" I whisper. "Unbelievable." I shake my head and take a step away from him. I should have known. There really is nothing worse than the feeling of guilt, but right at this moment, feeling stupid has taken a prominent second place. Why did I ever think I would be able to have a relationship with someone who saw me just as I am, just me? I don't live in a world where I can go unjudged by others, and stupid, stupid me romanticized the idea that I could. I thought he was different, and I guess he's not. He's just like all the others, and at this realization, a large lump forms in my throat, my nose burns, and my eyes fill with tears. All it took was hearing a name and knowing I have more money than he thought I did for him to completely dismiss who I am.

Not liking whatever expression he sees on my face, he asks, "Why are you angry at me?"

"Because ... Did you not enjoy getting to know me? Do you not like who I am? I thought we were friends. Actually, I thought we were more than that, but color me surprised, you're just like all the rest." I tighten my arms and now wrap them around me. The happiness I felt over the last few weeks dissipates like tendrils of smoke and evaporates into the air. I can't help but wonder if happiness is just a fickle emotion and why it is I came here chasing it, desperately looking for it.

He jerks back as if my words have stung him, and then he leans forward. "Friends." He breathes the word out, and it slices me. "Well, I did like who I thought you were, and now that the truth is out, I'm not sure I ever did know you."

"And what truth is that?" I ask him, genuinely curious as to how a single name, two words, *Rylie and Crest*, changes who I am and who I've been with him.

"That you are a liar—a fake."

I suck in a sharp breath as if he's punched me in the stomach, and my heart feels like it has been cut in half. I was never fake with him. I was more myself with him than I think I have ever been with anyone else. I came here, to this town, raw, and I've worked so hard on peeling back my layers and smoothing them out. I was me, every step of the way, and right this second I don't think there is anything more hurtful he could say to me.

The tears stinging my eyes slowly overflow, drip out, and land on my cheeks, and there's a bright flash and another clap of thunder overhead. I should have jumped at the quick, loud noise, but I'm too lost in my own head and broken heart, repeating his words.

Wind rushes through the trees, pushing the leaves out of the way, and wraps around us. My hair flies up and whips around. The water has turned slightly choppy, and he and I both know he needs to go now if he plans to beat the storm. Whether or not he sees the tears, he doesn't acknowledge them or how he's just broken my heart. Instead, in the span of a long, slow blink, he's gone.

He's left me here, on the dock, all alone.

It's not that I mind being alone—after that conversation, I need to be—but being called fake by someone who means so much when it's my character that I value about myself more than anything ... it's left a Jake-sized hole in my heart that feels irreparable.

How could he say that to me?

I thought dealing with one heartbreak this year was going to be impossible, but now dealing with two, I feel one hundred percent pulverized to smithereens.

I should have told him. I know this, but I thought he would understand. It's not like I've lied to him about anything else, just my name, and well, maybe my past through omission. But I talked about my life with him, didn't shy away from the details for fear of him not liking them or understanding, so why should I have to feel bad about a name? It's my business, my life, and who I choose to share that with and when is up to me. It's not fair for him to be mad at me about this. I didn't do anything wrong except marry a guy who clearly didn't love me enough, at least not as much as I deserve. I do deserve to be loved fully and completely by someone.

Next to me, the light on the dock appears, and it grows so bright under the stormy sky I have to squint, until there in the middle is Mrs. Easler. She's devastatingly beautiful, and if my already wounded heart could hurt any more, it does for her too. To be stuck here, in the in between year after year, waiting for someone who's never going to come—just tragic.

"Where the light shines," she says to me, her white dress blowing around her legs and in the breeze.

Ice-cold drops of rain begin to hit me as I stare at her. She doesn't look that much older than me, and there's a beauty about her that is rarely found. Why is she back? Why is she telling me this now? Out of all the nights I've sat out here and awaited her return, she picks tonight, the one night I just can't deal with this too.

One after another, the drops increase in speed. I feel repeatedly stung until my skin is drenched, my hair and clothes are soaked, and warm steam floats up from the wood of the dock.

"Where the light shines," she says again, but after everything that's happened over the last hour, I feel speechless, broken, numb, and I find I can't say anything to her in return.

30

Carter died on a Tuesday.

Our divorce was to be final that Thursday.

Carter didn't like confrontation. While he was ruthless as a businessman, he lacked confidence when it came to those he kept closest to him. He was a people pleaser and couldn't stand the idea that someone wasn't happy with him. I'm not sure what made him that way since the world adored him from the day he was born, but nevertheless, he constantly worried about people being unhappy with him.

Which is why he had texted me earlier that day to see if he could come over.

My guess is he was looking for some type of private closure between the two of us, even though I'd closed that chapter of my life the day I found him literally with his pants down. While he was constantly needing assurance from others, I did not. I've always known my worth. Maybe that's what attracted him to me, who knows, but in the end it wasn't enough to keep him. Then again, if it was so easy for him to walk away, maybe I never had him.

When I opened the front door to our condo and saw him on the other side, I remember my brows pulling down because he looked terrible. We hadn't been in the same room since the day I found him that fateful day, one because he moved out and on, and two because there simply was no need.

"What's wrong with you?" I asked, as I stepped aside and let him enter.

"These days, I'm not sure anymore." He took his phone and his keys and placed them on the console table, just like he had every night when he lived there. I saw the moment he recognized the habit and paused briefly. I also wondered if he remembered that was the spot he left our divorce papers and sealed our fate.

Turning around, I walked back into the living room and headed for the kitchen.

"Would you like something to drink?" I asked him.

"Water would be great, and some Advil too, if you have any."

Not saying anything else, I nodded and moved to grab him the drink and pills while he took off his suit coat, draped it over the back of the couch, and sat down on a stool at the kitchen island.

Words were not said. I wasn't even sure what there really was to say.

As I placed the drink in front of him, I expected there to be an uncomfortable tension between us, but there wasn't, just him rubbing his head with his eyes squeezed shut.

Carter had always had bad headaches. They were infrequent enough that he never went to see the doctor for them, but when they hit, he would be down for a few hours, occasionally the day. Toward the end of our time together, they had seemed to increase in frequency, but I just attributed them to stress about the affair once it was exposed.

"How have you been?" he asked, opening his eyes and looking at me.

"As well as can be expected." The media had not relented at all regarding our demise. At first, they made her out to be the villain, then it was him, and now it was me. Apparently, I had a drug and alcohol problem. The truth never matters, just headlines that will sell stories, which sells magazines.

"I am sorry. I want you to know that. I know my words probably don't mean much and they've been uttered hundreds of times by people, but I mean it when I say I never meant to hurt you."

And that's the thing about my people-pleasing soon-to-be ex-husband—I truly know this, although I'm not sure how he ever thought the situation wasn't going to hurt me. He broke his vows, our marriage, and my heart.

I turned away from the counter and went to make myself a glass of water. As angry and upset as I was with him, it sucked that he was putting me in this position.

"If you've come here looking for forgiveness, you're not going to find it." I turned back around to face him, and he was again rubbing his head.

"I'm not asking for forgiveness. I don't expect you to forgive me, I just … I just needed you to know I really am sorry. I do love you, I just … well, it doesn't matter anymore." He closed his eyes and scrunched up his face, the pain obviously getting significantly worse.

I heard what he was saying: he loved me, but he wasn't in love with me anymore.

Letting out a deep sigh, I took a mental picture of him sitting there, knowing it would most likely be the last time. It had been good while it lasted, and I suppose if asked, I'd say I have no regrets.

"Ry," he said, his voice cracking and his eyes opening to find mine. "I don't feel well. I think you need to call 911."

While he was speaking slowly, his words began to slur, and I watched as the left side of his face began to droop. Panic like I had never felt before fired on all synapses, and my skin started burning. Grabbing my phone from the counter, I made the call, uttered the words ambulance and hurry, and watched as he fell off the stool and dropped to the floor.

At that moment, it was as if the last three months and all the problems that had led us to this moment disappeared. Fear like I had never known slammed into me.

Throughout life, everyone has heard of someone having a heart attack or stroke. We all know the signs to look for—chest pain, tingling and numbness in the left arm—but what no one really teaches is what to do if we find ourselves in these situations, and at twenty-six, it certainly wasn't something I'd ever thought of before.

Everything happened so fast. I could hear the operator through the phone, but all I could do was scream that something was wrong with him. Eventually I dropped the phone; I knew they would find us, and Carter needed me. He was panicking about what was happening to him. His words became unintelligible, though I could make out that he was saying he couldn't feel part of his body. He quickly lost part of his vision, and after that, everything seemed to just stop. I was begging him to stay with me, telling him help would be arriving any minute. Hysterical tears were pouring from my eyes and dripping onto him as I hovered over him. Then he closed his eyes, slurred out, "... do love you," and stopped moving.

Carter was unconscious when the medical team arrived, and shortly thereafter, at the hospital, we were told there was no hope for recovery. He would never wake up again. As his spouse, it was technically my decision when to tell them to turn off the life support, but I defaulted to his parents.

Turned out Carter had something called moyamoya disease. This stupidly rare disease is a vascular blood vessel disorder that causes the carotid artery in the skull to become blocked or narrowed, reducing blood flow to the brain. It may occur at any age, though symptoms most commonly occur between ages five and ten in children and between ages thirty and fifty in adults. One year shy of thirty, right there in front of me, he suffered an ischemic stroke, hemorrhaged, and essentially died.

Did you know that every forty seconds, someone in the United States has a stroke? Or that every four minutes, someone dies from a stroke? It's the fifth leading cause of death for Americans. I think I always thought things like strokes were an older person's issue, certainly not something we had to think of yet, but boy was I wrong. Carter's time of death might have been pronounced at the hospital, but for the rest of my life, like an old movie, I'll be able to rewind and play the moment I believe he died on my floor.

I thought I knew pain from the affair, but grief pushed me to a whole new level.

At the funeral, I sat with his parents in the front row while my family sat behind me and toward the rear. His mother was inconsolable, and she clung to me as if she didn't realize that in a different scenario, two days earlier I was set to legally no longer be her daughter.

The church was packed. Everyone knew about our pending divorce, but no one mentioned it. Carter was beloved by many, and despite our current marital circumstances, condolences were showered over me.

At the gravesite, the priest calmly and fluidly spoke the words we all know so well from the *Book of Common Prayer*, and with each breath I took, my heart crumbled to ash and dust alongside his.

"Forasmuch as it hath pleased Almighty God of his great mercy to take unto himself the soul of our dear brother here departed, we therefore commit his body to the ground, earth to earth, ashes to ashes, dust to dust, in sure and certain hope of the Resurrection to eternal life, through our Lord Jesus Christ, who shall change our vile body, that it may be like unto his glorious body, according to the mighty working, whereby he is able to subdue all things to himself."

A week later, I met with my attorney, who informed me that I wouldn't just be receiving the assets allocated in the divorce prenup, but all of them, the full estate, as legally I was still his spouse and documented beneficiary. His parents were in agreement with this, not that they could really dispute it, but on the other hand, Veronica had quite a bit to say, which stirred the media into a frenzy.

It didn't matter that there was a medical diagnosis through autopsy; overnight, I became a gold-digging murderer. His condition was manipulated, twisted, and some even went to say falsely planted by the family, and the person who spoke the loudest was her.

Since they were together, she felt wronged and wanted what she felt she was owed. She wasn't called or notified, and she heard about his death like everyone else, through the media. She wasn't invited to sit with the family, because even though she considered herself a member, she wasn't, and not one piece of his life was left to her. It all came to me.

In the end, instead of being able to somewhat reconcile with one of my oldest friends over our shared grieving, I ended up getting a phone call from the Crest family attorney letting me know they'd issued a cease and desist to her on the basis of slander. The family, who didn't approve of how he'd handled things between us, had had enough of her running her mouth. Too bad they didn't have the ability to shut off the first amendment and stop the tabloids too.

Three months later, as I was packing my belongings to be moved to storage, I found Carter's wallet under the living room couch that sat closest to the kitchen. It must have fallen out of his suit coat when he took it off. Inside it, along with all the tiny mementos of him, was a single pale blue Post-it that said, *I'm sorry.*

31

The river is gray today.

I've somehow found myself back at the end of the dock, which my feet are hanging over, my toes just skimming the surface. I'm not sure why I'm here, but this is where I feel called to be when my soul is sad.

The sky is dark as remnants of last night's storm lingers. Humidity fills the air, and the birds are quiet this morning after a sleepless night. I glanced down to see if Jessie was nearby, but only shadows beneath the surface looked back at me. The river is unsettled, and instead of its usual welcome appearance, it feels standoffish and troubled. I know there's no correlation between the two, but there's froth and foam, and with them come memories of Jake's eyes, his words, and his touch. All twist and turn just like the stormy waters in front of me.

I was warned about the river. They said if I listened just right, I would be able to hear it speak. Whispers would float up to the glassy clear surface when least expected, sometimes with words for the heart, other times secrets stolen from the soul. It's always giving and taking, and just like the ebb and flow of the current, it's always changing.

Just like life.

Many hours have been spent here pouring out my heart and cleansing my soul. Whereas then I found the salty air and cool waters healing, now I feel as if it's mocking, cold, and saying *I told you so.*

I should have told him.

I waited too long.

Carter was the first person close to me to ever die. A couple of my grandparents died when I was younger, but I wasn't old enough for it to really make an impact, to feel that loss.

Not like Carter.

I had already mourned the loss of our relationship. It was traumatic, but can finding your husband with someone be called anything else? By that week in February when our divorce was to be final, I had accepted our fate.

And then he died.

Right in front of me.

That type of grief was less traumatic and more life-altering. My insides felt shifted. This person who had become a part of my makeup, woven into the fibers of my being, was suddenly gone, and I felt hollow, vacant. It took me a long time to adjust to the fact that he would no longer be walking the earth. We may have not been together, but there was some type of stability knowing he was still out there somewhere.

Not anymore, though.

They say the last stage of grieving is acceptance. With acceptance, hope rises out of the ashes like a phoenix giving new purpose to the world. It's not that the pain from losing Carter has disappeared; I'm just not mentally trying to change the outcome anymore.

I can't even remember how many nights I lay in bed and wished to wake up from this nightmare, from all of it. One emotion warred with another, and living in the same condo we bought together, where we created a shared life together, and then where I watched his life leave this world ... it became too much.

Yes, the media and paparazzi were relentless. Yes, Veronica spoke to anyone anywhere that would listen to her side of the story. But it wasn't so much the noise around me that drove me to leave Chicago. It was the idea that if I could move somewhere else, I would be able to move on. The condo felt like a tomb, and I felt like I was suffocating in it. No one understood me, and I needed to find a place where I could breathe and learn to be me, the me without the expectations and the accusations. If you hear something long enough, eventually you'll believe it, and I just couldn't succumb to that.

So it was with a hopeful heart that I found this house, packed up the few things I wanted, and drove all day and half the night like a bat out of hell. I was certain if I came here my life would move on. That gave me hope.

Although, I don't feel hopeful now.

Did I move on? Yes. I found a happiness that felt less like something I desperately needed and more like something I wanted just for me. It felt organic. It felt real.

Which is why this loss, the loss of Jake, doesn't feel traumatic or life-altering. It makes me feel shattered in a different way that has damaged my quintessence, and the only way for it to be repaired is to find myself in his arms.

Arms that chose to judge me, belittle my character, and leave instead of slowing down to listen and truly hear what I had to say.

This isn't what I wanted.

I wanted to be free. I wanted to find an easier life without all the pretentious expectations and the drama. I wanted to find a happiness that was real and just for me.

And I thought I had. I allowed that hope to give me wings.

It's as if I laid myself bare at his feet and invited him, someone else, to break me all over again. And he did. This vulnerability, this place I've somehow again found myself in—it's not what I planned or wanted for myself, and now I don't know what to do.

Am I going to leave? No, at least not right now. I came here for me, found this project that has given me new life in a career that I love, and no guy is going to run me out. I will keep moving forward, just like I've been doing for the last year, and be proud of my accomplishments.

Despite my broken heart.

That's the thing about grief—it feels so bone-deep, like a permanent chronic ache, but this—how he left, the lack of confidence and faith in me—the pain feels acute. It's real time, and I feel trampled down.

Letting out a sigh, I stare out over the rippling water.

I know happiness is found within. It's not something that should be dependent on someone else, and I am happy here, truly I am, happier than I ever thought I would be. This right now just sucks.

Next to me on the dock, my phone buzzes, and I see that my sister is calling. Natalie, Corrie, and Willow have all called, but I'm not ready to talk to them yet. Soon, just not yet.

"How are you holding up?" Ivy asks. Late last night, she started texting me nonstop with photos that had been released online. There were a slew of images of Jake and me coming out of the grocery store, his face angry, mine covered by my hand. Of course they fully disclosed where I am, discovered who Jake was, and gave a full write-up on him. His name is everywhere. Some of it is not favorable, but most of it's just curious as to what this new guy means to me and what I'm doing here in this town.

"About as well as can be expected." Three seagulls fly over me and head for the trees.

"We knew this day was going to come eventually. I'm just surprised you made it this long. Have you seen any paparazzi around the house?" The familiar sounds of Chicago echo from the background. This is one of the things I love when she calls me in the morning. I instantly recognize the sounds of a police whistle; she must be at a crosswalk based on the rumble of a city bus as it goes by and just the murmur of other conversations. While these sounds are lovely and nostalgic, I find I'm not homesick for them.

Turning my head, I scan the riverbank surrounding the inlet. "No, but that doesn't mean they aren't out there. Willow fired her shotgun once—she must have been warning someone."

"Oh my God."

We were not raised with guns, so the concept of using one to scare people off is foreign to us, but at the same time, I love it.

A small grin curves my lips. "Right? Best neighbor ever."

"What did Jake say?" she asks, not realizing he's already removed himself from the equation.

I don't answer her, and through the phone, I hear her gasp.

"You never told him. I can't believe you! Why, Ry? Carter dying is not some little thing that happened to you. It's essentially the biggest!"

Her tone has my hackles rising.

"Is it though? We were already done. He left me and moved on, so whether he died that day or fifty years later, I mean what difference does it make?"

"The difference is on that day, you still loved him," she says matter-of-factly.

I hear what she's saying, I do, and I have thought about all of this more than anyone could ever imagine. Weighing the two, comparing and differentiating, compartmentalizing.

"I guess I just can't reconcile one because of the other. He left me, and now it's technically twice." Grief pushes me down. I still feel the physical loss of him. Death is such an unforgiving final thing.

"He did, and I'm sorry he did that to you."

I'm sorry too. Closing my eyes, I feel my chin quiver as I try to take in a breath to calm my emotions. I am sad; there is no other way to put it.

"He called me a liar and told me I was fake," I whisper, feeling as if my chest wants to cave in.

"Who did?" she asks defensively.

"Jake," I murmur. Just his name hurts.

"Oh, Ry." Her voice is low and full of sympathy.

"Yeah." What more is there to say?

"He'll come around. All of this just ambushed him. From everything you've said, he seems like a pretty reasonable guy."

"That's what I thought too, but now I'm not so sure. You should have seen his face last night. It isn't that he was just mad at me … it was something more. I just don't know what."

"Nothing is insurmountable. Give him some time and let the shock wear off. I know Crest is just a name and has nothing to do with who you are as a person, but it is overwhelming. Even you can admit that."

"Maybe," I tell her, hanging on to her words and allowing them to fill some of my broken cracks a bit.

It's midafternoon when I see movement through the window, and my heart catches as I realize it's Bauer and not Jake. It's not that I thought he would be coming back, but that feeling of hopefulness had unwantedly made an appearance. I watch as he ties up his boat, turns around, and stares up at the house. His head tilts back as he takes it all in, then he shakes it as if he's bewildered and makes his way up the dock.

My eyes drift over to the spot where Mrs. Easler appears. I've been so caught up in my emotions I haven't really thought about her popping up again. Do I find it completely insane that a ghost has shown herself to me twice now? Yes, but I don't know what any of it means. I don't understand what she means—"*Where the light shines*"—so I feel at a loss. On another day, I'm sure I'll revisit it all, but today is not that day.

Setting down the paintbrush—I've been busying myself with working on Ivy's room—I climb down the ladder, make my way downstairs, and take a look around. It's a little messy, but it doesn't look that bad, and I'm proud of the work I've done, the decorating, and how the house is coming along.

I greet him at the back door as he walks up the steps. He's come directly from work and is wearing navy dress slacks, a light blue button-down with the sleeves rolled up, and a matching brown belt and shoes.

"Hi, Bauer. What brings you out here?" I ask, wiping my hands on my shorts as I try to give him a genuine smile but can't. It's forced, and he sees it.

I am happy to see him. He's a piece of Jake, and stupidly I need this more than I care to admit.

He props his hands on his hips and gives me a once-over. His lips are pursed instead of smiling, and my stomach dips.

"I thought I'd come out and see what you've been up to," he says, his voice low.

"Really?" I ask, my eyes finding his gray ones. They aren't bluc like Jake's, but they still feel similar, and my heart thumps hard in my chest.

He pauses, shifts his weight, and then says, "Actually, no, not really."

Yeah, I had a feeling. I mean he's never come here before, and I've lived here for months.

"Well, come on in. I'll show you around anyway."

Room by room, we walk through the house. I turn on both chandeliers, and he comments on some of the details he likes. With each one, a new surge of pride wraps around me, and he unknowingly gives me a few ideas for blog posts, like a tutorial on how to herringbone tile a wall.

Once we reach the kitchen, he leans his hip against the island and crosses his arms over his chest as he looks at me. "You need to understand something about my brother. He's a one-and-done kind of guy, and when Rebecca left, we all just assumed that was it."

Rebecca.

Jake knows I know she left him at the altar, but other than a few passing comments, we haven't brought her up. New love doesn't want to be weighed down by an old one, but the thought of her breaking his heart makes me so irrationally angry, I'd love nothing more than to hunt her down and give her a piece of my mind.

"And then he met you," he says, watching me closely.

A long weighted pause descends upon us. What does he want me to say? Quite frankly, none of it is his business.

"I didn't lie to him, or to you. What you see is what you get." I toss my hands out, worrying he might be upset with me too.

He looks at me disbelievingly.

"Bauer. You don't know what I've been through. None of you do." I let those words hang in the air. "Why is it so bad to want people to know me without the name, the title, the money? I just wanted a fresh start. I want people to see me without the head-lines. Wouldn't you?"

He pauses as he thinks about his words to choose the best ones. "Thing is, he's the most loyal guy I know. Once you breach the walls and you're in, you're in."

My shoulders fall. "Well, after last night, I guess we know I was never truly in." I break eye contact and look past him to Coco. She's watching us but hasn't said anything.

Bauer doesn't say anything either. Instead, he paces around the kitchen then stops in the doorway of the breakfast room.

From here you can see straight through each room to the back of the house and out the window.

"I'm not so sure I agree with that," he says without turning to face me.

"Well, I wouldn't know," I say sadly.

Although I thought I did. Did we declare our feelings or intentions with each other? No, but what we had didn't feel like a summer fling or something to pass the time. It felt like the beginning of something that could have been great.

"You know, I never did think he'd sell this house, and look at it now." He runs his hand over the doorjamb as if he's fondly remembering something. "What you've done with it is amazing, and how ironic that he sold it to you."

The hair on the back of my neck rises, and my eyes narrow. "What do you mean?"

He turns to look at me and says, "Jake."

Ice-cold shock sweeps over my body as a surge of adrenaline nearly knocks the breath out of me. I take a step away from him, suddenly feeling uncomfortable and completely out of sorts.

His brows pull down.

"Are you telling me this was his house?" I ask, totally flummoxed and flabbergasted.

He tilts his head to the side and sticks his hands in the pockets of his pants, confusion gracing the features of his face. "He didn't tell you?"

"No. The purchase was through a trust. A trust you handled. I was never told who the previous owner was."

"Really," he draws out, suddenly realizing he said something he shouldn't have.

"Yes! And now it all makes sense." I start pacing the kitchen. "Your family's long history with the town, why Garrett maintained the house, why you handled the trust, and why Jake was so curious about all the plans and changes I was making. I asked

Garrett about it once, about the strange things like the bathtub upstairs, and he told me he installed it but didn't know why. I thought he meant it was just a random installation with an extra tub."

"He probably meant he didn't know why because we all knew Rebecca was never going to live here. Don't get me wrong, she was sweet and we all loved her, we just knew this wasn't going to be enough for her," he says as he defends his brother, but all I heard was the word Rebecca.

Rebecca.

My stomach drops, and suddenly I feel sick. How did I not put all this together sooner? I never even considered looking harder to find the family tree to see who might have owned the home, and really, I'm surprised Mr. Williams from the library never mentioned it.

I feel so stupid. All the things about the house I talked about, gushed over, and planned with him ... it's as if she walked out of the spot and I walked into it. He was able to pick right back up and move on.

Feeling claustrophobic, I move away from Bauer and his knowing gaze and begin to walk through the house. Anxiety, embarrassment, and disappointment course through my veins, making it hard to breathe. Stopping in the sitting room, my eyes land on the piano—the piano he must have bought for her. Natalie told me she plays in an orchestra. No wonder he stares at it like he does when he comes over.

I feel so foolish. All this time I've been fixing up a house he had planned to build a life in with someone else.

How ironic indeed.

32

Fueled by adrenaline, I make it about one hour after Bauer leaves before I get in my car and drive to Jake's office. I have no idea if Bauer called him to let him know what happened, but I don't care. With each minute that passes, my humiliation doubles, and with it comes anger.

How could he not tell me?

I understand not having the ex talk, but for months we've been together in the house—his house. Seems like he could have provided me insight, something, and if I'm honest with myself, I would have found fixing it up together endearing. It would have meant more and become sentimental in a way I wasn't aware of when I first bought the home, and I feel robbed of that.

Why didn't he tell me? I don't understand. We've talked so much about so many things, but coming from him, this would have been the biggest.

Moments of us together flash through my mind, moments I missed that should have raised red flags. There was the way he walked around the home like he knew it. I thought he was just taking in the changes I'd made, but it was more than that. He knew things like where the bathroom was, where the laundry room was, and the location of the electrical panel, and in hindsight, he didn't seem all that surprised when I told him about the barn, just surprised that I found something in it, and let's not forget about the piano. If I had to guess, I bet it was meant to be her wedding gift. It's insanely high quality and obviously brand new. It's the kind of piece that's meant to last a lifetime, a lifetime he was preparing to spend with her.

Parking outside, I notice the lot is empty as I storm up the steps and through the front door of the practice. It accidentally slams behind me. I didn't mean for it to be as loud as it was; I am conscious of the fact that he might still have patients even though it is after six. Betty, his receptionist, looks up, sees the expression on my face, and just points down the hallway toward his office.

"I'll just see myself out," she says, quickly gathering her things, shuffling past me to leave, and calling Beamer the three-legged German Shepherd to go with her.

I don't even remember moving down the hallway, but as I find myself standing in the doorway, there sitting at his desk, working on his laptop in a pair of black scrubs, is Jake.

Just the appearance of him is disarming with his messy dark hair and stormy blue eyes, but as his brows pull down and the tightness sets in his jaw at the blatant displeasure in seeing me, the anger that's been building inside flares.

"It was your house and you never told me. Why?" My heart is pounding ferociously in my chest, and I squeeze my hands into fists to try to release some of the excess energy coursing through me.

His eyes narrow, and then he shrugs his shoulders, shoulders I've had my arms draped over and my face buried against. "Didn't feel it was relevant," he says, all calm and collected while I'm a firecracker whose fuse is about to run out.

"Not relevant! Are you joking?" I'm so worked up I'm vibrating.

His eyes drop as he looks me over, and then they rise to again find mine. I'm still wearing the same clothes I had on earlier while painting Ivy's room, shorts and a tank top, and I feel like I've just been lasered by his gaze. I'm burning hot.

Leaning back in his chair, he flattens his hands on the desk in front of him and says, "No. After all, what were your words again? Oh, that's right, my past is my past. I don't have to share it if I don't want to."

Air rushes from my lungs. He's mocking me.

Splinters rip through my skin and pierce the deepest parts of my soul.

The thing is, he didn't know about my past or that I had left out big details. He thought I was just a normal girl who had gone through a normal divorce like what happens to fifty percent of the people willing to say "I do," but he unquestioningly chose to walk through the halls of my house and sleep in my bed without clueing me in to that one very large piece of information.

"This is not the same thing and you know it. This is not tit for tat. You can't compare the death of my husband and me working so hard on healing myself to owning an old family home, an inanimate object. It's not the same. Not even close."

He flinches and at least has the decency to look a little bit contrite.

Needing a moment to compose myself, to attempt to stop the shaking, I break eye contact and look around his office. It's neat, organized, and fairly simple. It's painted a very faint pale blue, which unfortunately makes his eyes brighter. The furniture is black wood and black leather. On the wall to my left hang his framed professional certificates and accolades, to my right is a large window that looks out over the river, and behind his desk is a wall of black shelves. They are filled with different types of medical books, pharmacologic books, random trinkets, and picture frames. I study each picture; they are all of his family, but then I see one directly behind him that is of me.

I'm shocked.

It's small, four by six, but it's there. Me and Coco standing on the dock. In it I'm laughing, and I have no idea when he took this. Not only that, he took the time to print it, frame it, and display it. My heart splits in two at the thoughtfulness. I'm so confused, and as he realizes what I'm looking at, he lets out a deep breath, drops his eyes, and reaches up to rub the back of his neck.

Without looking at him, I break the silence. "That first day, when you showed up and yelled at me about feeding Jessie the lettuce, you already knew I was the new owner, and yet you still asked me to leave. Why?"

I look back at him, and this time he's walled off his emotions and stares at me blankly.

"Actually, I didn't know you were the one who bought the house. The lawyer who handled the transaction said the buyer wished to remain anonymous, and I was fine with that. I was letting the house go, so I guess it just didn't matter who bought it."

"You mean your brother the lawyer," I deadpan.

He blinks as he processes my words, and then his eyes widen and he flinches again. There's my answer—Bauer did not call him and warn him in advance. Or if he did, Jake just hasn't received the message yet.

He doesn't answer. He just stares at me as if we're in a faceoff.

My eyes burn at the betrayal I feel from him. Actually, I don't even know if betrayal is the right word. I feel like all our time together at the house, working on it and living in it, somehow now feels disingenuous. It meant so much to me, but what did it really mean to him? Clearly not enough for him to let me in on this one giant six-thousand-square-foot secret he was keeping. After Carter's infidelity, I didn't think it was possible to be so hurt again, but here I am.

He's hurt me, and I'm devastated.

The tears brimming in my eyes free themselves and track down my face. I need them to plug up my heart as I feel like holes are being drilled into it.

"You made me feel so bad last night, calling me a fake and a liar. You stepped all over my character, the person I've worked so hard to move past over the last couple of months and the person I gave to you. I get it, I should have told you, and I was there. I was ready to go back and tell you all the horrid things that have happened over the last year—I was just trying to find the right time. It's hard, it's humiliating, and above all, it's just sad. But you know what I didn't do? I didn't bring you into mine and Carter's home, withhold a very big piece of information from you, pretend he never lived there, and play house with you. You've been to my house how many times now? You've helped me make the changes, watched me play her piano, slept in my bed, cooked meals with me, made memories that meant something to me, and you never said one word. Not one."

I swallow hard, trying to push the massive lump in my throat away.

"You've made me feel like the substitution for the life you wanted before and didn't get. I mean how convenient that I bought it and not some older married family. Did you have fun? Did you have fun playing house with me? I just don't get it. If you cared about me, truly cared, how could you? How could you do what you did with me, make me feel—" I cut myself off and shake my head. "I let you in." My chin wobbles. "I trusted you." The tears now race away from my eyes, spilling all over my cheeks. "Even after everything that's happened to me recently

..." I take an extremely shaky breath as his face falls. "I tried so hard—" I almost choke on the words as I hold in a sob that wants to rip through me.

Slipping the bag I brought with me off my shoulder, I reach in and pull out the ornate box I found in the barn. Taking a step toward him, I place it on his desk. His brows have furrowed, he's breathing hard, and there's color high on his cheeks. He knows inside is the gun, the pearls, and the brooch.

"These belong to you," I tell him, and for the second time in my life, I turn away from a man I love and run. I run down the hallway, throw open the front door, and head straight for my car. I just can't face him anymore.

"Ryla. Rylie, wait!" I hear through the window. Jake has followed me and is now standing in front of my car, but I can't. My heart is cracked open, and along with the tears, it is bleeding out all over the floor.

Putting the car in reverse, I back out of the lot and pull away without looking at him.

What is it about me that makes others think it's okay to deceive me? What have I done in this life or maybe a past one to deserve so much heartache?

I just don't understand.

33

Not wanting to be in the house, a house I have come to love more than any other home I've lived in, I wander down to the dock. With my feet dangling over the edge, I lie down to gaze up at the evening sky.

The river seems more calm tonight than it was this morning, or even over the last couple of days. Then again, if all our secrets are out in the open, it has no reason to be troubled—unlike me. Well, I'm not even sure that's true. I've spent so many months worrying that people, mostly Jake, would find out who I was and that I was here in Chuluota Springs, and now that it's out there, I feel weary and depleted. Clearly I did have a reason to be concerned; look at the outcome.

Exhaling, I feel an exhaustion unlike anything I've ever known. In Jake's office, I was ready to battle until death. Now, I just want to go to sleep.

The air is humid tonight. For some reason the afternoon shower skipped today, and my skin feels sticky. There's a salty, earthy smell to it, and I'm reminded of the day I arrived, stepped out of the car, and breathed it in. It's interesting because I've often asked myself if I would have done it if I'd known then what I know now, and the answer in regards to Jake is one hundred percent yes. Carter, I'm still not so sure, but I have zero hesitations about Jake. Even though things are not as I was hoping they would be, I have no regrets.

For the first time in my life, I am confident in who I am. Once I settled in, I never really worried about whether or not the people here would like me or accept me. I was just me regardless, and I've loved finding out new facets about myself. Was I concerned that things would change once they all knew who I used to be? Yes, but I think it was more about what would happen to the town and the people surrounding me once they knew. How would the community react? Would I be chased or followed? What kind of disruption would it cause that would inevitably change people's opinions of me? But the truth is, up until now, things didn't change. Natalie, Corrie, Willow—it never mattered to them who I was married to, and with Jake, his glasses weren't rose-tinted; they were crystal clear.

He saw me.

He saw me grieving. He saw me healing. He saw me growing. And he still liked what he saw.

I felt appreciated by him, and even loved. From my quirkiness to even my attitude, he embraced it all and never asked for me to be anything different. He never made me feel like I had to be perfect; instead I felt adored. He showed me what it's like to be in a relationship with someone where the spotlight isn't one-sided, where we shine together. He showed me what I can have and what I deserve, and with that thought, tears slowly leak from the corners of my eyes, dripping down the sides of my face and into my ears. I don't even have the energy to wipe them away.

In the distance, the hum of a boat's motor echoes as it enters the inlet, and then it goes silent as the engine is brought to slow speed. My heart rate picks up as it leisurely comes closer, and I close my eyes, not wanting to see him. I wasn't sure if he would come after me or not, and as upset with him as I am, I'm still glad he has. He became my person, and I just hope he doesn't crush me even more. I'm not sure how much more I can take.

The boat bumps against the bumpers on the pilings, and I listen as he goes through the motions of tying it up, climbing up onto the dock, and walking toward me. Sitting down next to me, he too dangles his legs over the side, and I feel the moment he lays on his back to face the sky as heat from his shoulder and his arm brushes mine. Minutes pass as more unwanted tears continue to leak from my eyes and run down my face.

Silence falls over us, and with each breath he takes, the tension that was wrapped around him earlier dissipates. He's exhausted too.

Breaking the silence, he begins talking. The edge to his tone is gone, and the familiar tenor of his voice reaches out and soothes me.

"This house has been mine my whole life. From Mrs. Easler's daughter then generation after generation, it's been passed down to the oldest child, and I have no idea why no one has seized the opportunity to live here. They just didn't. My grandparents married and moved into a house on the same property as my great-grandparents, and my parents, well they wanted to live in town. There's also the fact that it was completely rundown and needed more work than most people wanted to do or could invest in it."

He is related to Mrs. Easler's daughter. He is related to Mrs. Easler! My ghost. I don't know why I'm shocked by this, but I am. I knew his family had roots here, but I had no idea they ran that deep.

He pauses as he thinks about his words, and I listen to him breathing. It's a sound I listened to night after night when he stayed over, and I find it comforting and reassuring.

"I've always known this house was mine, and all I have ever done is dream about what it would be like to live in it one day with my family. I know a lot of people have dreams that are bigger than staying in their hometown and settling down, but I didn't. I loved growing up here, and I love being close to my brothers. I created a vision for my life with traditions and memories so vivid I was certain Rebecca would help me make them come true." He lets out a deep sigh. "Even though she always told me she didn't want to live in Chuluota Springs.

"I never told her about the house ... it was meant to be part of my wedding gift. After all, you saw it when you got here—it wasn't exactly someone's dream home. When we first got together, I was doing an internship at the Florida Aquarium in Tampa. It was exciting and new, and I guess you could say we lived a city life. She plays the piano for the pit orchestra at the Tampa Center for the Performing Arts. She always knew my plan was to settle down here in Chuluota Springs, and it turned out she was living more in the moment than imagining a life with me."

In the moment—so similar to what I said to him about living in the now, and my heart aches for him. I can see how he would be hurt by this. He was giving his all, only to be made to feel as if he was again a temporary thing, not worth someone taking that leap to go the distance for. More tears leak from my eyes. I never wanted to cause him any pain, and that's exactly what I did, even if it was unknowingly.

"As timing would have it, before we were to be married, the veterinarian who used to be in my practice was ready to retire. I took out a business loan and bought the practice from him. She was excited for me, even for us, I think, until she started to make the drive and spend time here. She suffocated. Small fishing town, narrow roads, seafood shacks for restaurants, mosquitos, slower life—none of it was for her, and in the end, not even I was."

She is the dumbest person in the whole world. I can't imagine someone not wanting him. He's kind, generous, ambitious, thoughtful, patient, and quite possibly the best person I know.

The sound of his hair moving against the dock lets me know he's turned his head and is looking at me. I still can't open my eyes, for I know seeing his beautiful blue eyes and his handsome face so close and magnified just might rip me in two.

"You are not a substitute for her," he says softly. "Did I love her, yes, but after spending these last couple of months with you, I now understand."

"Understand what?" I whisper, my heart rate suddenly picking up pace.

"What this is, what I want, and what I deserve." His warm breath brushes across the side of my face. Like Icarus, I want to turn toward him as if he is the sun, but I fear melting, falling. What if he doesn't catch me?

I faintly shake my head. "I'm not following."

"Rylie—"

"Ryla," I cut him off. I like this person who I've become, and I want her to stay. He pauses as he thinks about this, but then continues.

"Ryla, I fell for you. Hard. It was effortless and exciting, and you've never made me feel like being myself is somehow wrong. With you, I'm just me, a small-town veterinarian, a low-maintenance simple guy, and it felt good. Up until yesterday, I never felt I had to be someone else in order for you to like me or want to be with me. I know who I am."

It's funny because these are the same things I felt about him too, or at least what I thought, and it seems I'm not the only one afraid of not being caught when I fall.

"I know who you are," I tell him, just barely over a whisper.

His fingers brush against mine, and then he gathers my hand in his, linking our fingers together.

Letting out another sigh, he says, "I never felt like I was enough for Rebecca. Yes, she loved me, but I always felt she loved the idea of me more. I always felt on edge. If I wasn't careful, I would say the wrong thing or do the wrong thing, and even though I knew that wasn't healthy, I did try my hardest to be what she needed."

"What about what you needed?" I ask, finally opening my eyes and turning to look at him. There's a desperation written on his face in the stress lines of his forehead and in the tightness of his jaw, but his gaze is resolute. He's certain of the outcome, and it's not going to matter what I say. I want to slip into the river and drown myself in my heartache.

He pinches his lips together in a firm line, and his eyes wander over my face. Is he memorizing my details like I'm memorizing his?

"Want to hear the funniest thing?" he asks.

I nod, because I do. I want to keep him talking as long as possible before he decides it's time for him to leave.

"She doesn't like animals." He tips his head back and laughs.

"What? How is that possible? Who doesn't like animals?" I ask, anger lacing my words as I soak up his sound.

His eyes return to find mine. "I don't know, but she doesn't. It completely baffles me. I was going to marry the one girl in the world who doesn't like animals. Animals! The biggest single defining factor of my life. That's why I don't have any pets. Dash came to live with me shortly after things ended with her, and I just decided to wait until he dies to get a dog. For so many years,

I've wanted a dog of my own, but I met her when I was still in school. I didn't feel it was the right time to own a pet, and she has horrible allergies. I always had to shower before seeing her, and I had to keep my clothes separate from hers."

My mouth is hanging open because I am horrified for him.

"I don't know what to say. I've always admired that you give so much of yourself to your job, to all the animals. I honestly can't see you doing anything else, and it's one of the things I love the most about you."

His eyes widen just a bit then slowly glass over with unshed tears. How many years has he wanted someone to say this to him, someone he cares for? Letting go of my hand, he shifts so he's more on his side and facing me.

"Ryla," he says, his voice rough. "I honestly had zero interest in ever finding someone else. My entire relationship with her, down to her leaving me standing at the altar, can be summed up in one word: mortifying. I never wanted to put myself in a situation like that again. But then I met you."

He swallows, and I watch the lines of his neck move.

"When I saw that magazine cover and connected the dots about who you are and the type of life you come from, every single old fear and insecurity surfaced. I wasn't good enough for her, my life here wasn't good enough, and I felt pushed straight back there. I even asked if you plan to stay here, and you told me you didn't know. I probably could've handled it better, but in my mind, what I heard and what I felt was that I am in love with another girl who has no plans of staying with me. How did I find myself in this situation twice?" Pain streaks across his features, and I hate that I'm part of the reason why it's there.

"Jake—"

"I'm sorry I said those things to you," he rushes out. "I don't think you're fake or a liar, and I do understand, I really do. Do I wish you had felt you could tell me, yes, but I would be a hypocrite if I said otherwise. And I am sorry for not telling you about the house. I wanted to. I was going to." He exhales sharply. "It's just this house ... it was always just a house, and I watched you make it a home, one I wanted to belong to with you." He pauses and then says, "I really don't know what held me back."

Listening to this beautiful man pour his heart out to me, I want to be a sponge and soak up every single thing that has ever hurt him, want to wipe it away so it doesn't exist anymore.

"You need to know," he says, his gaze imploring me to hear him, "I don't care about who you were married to or how much money you have. All I care about is you."

Hope glitters my vision as I stare at him.

"I know that, and I care about you too." I reach over and lay my hand on his forearm.

"But not enough," he mouths, the words just barely moving past his lips.

"I never said that. You did," I say, not defensively, because I now understand where he's coming from, but more firmly because he needs to hear me too.

Rolling to face him, I pull my knees up and scoot closer. With one arm under his head, he wraps the other over me. We might be lying outside on the dock, but right now, we are the only two people to ever exist.

"You asked if I plan on staying here, and yes, I answered with I don't know, because I didn't know. I moved here because I needed to move on with my life. For months, all I could focus on was one day at a time. I threw myself into this project with no intention of thinking about what came next. There was enough going on in my world and swirling around me outside of it, and I just needed to live in this bubble—a bubble you slipped right into. Do I know what the future holds? No, but I wasn't just living in the moment. I was imagining a life with you. What that life looked like, I didn't know, but I guess I thought we'd figure that out together."

There's devastation on his face at my words. I can't tell if it's because he heard something he needed to hear or because he didn't. Fear grips me as my chin quivers and more tears begin to fall.

Reaching up, he wipes a few off my face, and then he leans forward to rest his forehead against mine.

"Please don't cry. I can't bear it," he says, his voice pained and his warm breath brushing against my skin.

"I'm not leaving you. Stay with me. Be with me?" I whisper against his lips. I'm only going to ask him this one time. After all, I shouldn't have to beg someone to want to be with me, but after hearing him tell me a little bit about Rebecca, I know words matter, and he needs to feel like someone is fighting for him, needs to know we are in it together and it's not one-sided.

He pulls back, looks me in the eyes, and gently runs his finger down the side of my face to tuck a few pieces of hair behind my ear. I know he feels the depth of those words, the true meaning behind them, as there's another level of intimacy two people share when they are being completely vulnerable, and he nods his head. His wordless answer burns through my skin and begins mending my poor frayed heart as it knows he's just said, "Always."

Closing the distance, I place my lips on his and breathe in the subtle scent that is him. It's familiar, it's therapeutic, and I want to bottle it up until the end of time.

Jake's arm tightens around me and pulls me even closer into his body. He returns my kiss with one of his own that is slow, deep, and wildly affectionate.

"I'm sorry. For all of this," he eventually whispers, and I tilt my head backward so I can see his handsome face and full, swollen lips.

"I'm sorry too," I tell him, because I am. I don't ever want to keep anything from him again. I want to give it all to him.

Silence falls over us as the warm summer night clings to our skin and the sounds of the water gently brushing against the dock float our way.

Eventually he asks the question, the one question we've yet to bring up.

"So, Rylie Crest, huh?" he asks, almost wary like he does and doesn't want to know, but also because he's not sure how I will react.

I let out a deep overdue sigh.

"That is legally my name," I tell him, frowning. After all, it is just a name.

The lines around his eyes soften, and he reaches up to smooth the hair back across my forehead. With this touch, he acknowledges what I'm saying, and in the depth of the deep blue sea that is his eyes, I find empathy, compassion, and most importantly understanding. And isn't that the thing I most wanted from him? For him to see me, the real me, to understand and accept me, just as I am?

"You know I love you, right?" he says, a small smile lifting one corner of his mouth.

"That's good, because I love you too." This truth has released me from an emotional place I never intend to return to.

"Where you go, I go, okay?" he says and asks at the same time.

I know this is his way of saying he'll leave Chuluota Springs if that's what I want, but it's not. I do want to stay here with him.

"Okay," I whisper back. "But where you are, is where I'll stay."

His small smile grows and stretches across his beautiful face.

Letting out a groan, he wraps me in his arms and rolls us until he's on his back and I'm straddling him and lying on his chest. We lie here for some time as the sky deepens into twilight, his hand runs up and down my back, and I listen to his beautiful heart, a heart that calls to mine no matter where we are and feels like home.

34

It's been two weeks since Jake and I laid our hearts bare down on the dock, over the water. I told him all about my relationship with Carter, from beginning to end, and he listened with sorrow gracing his features for the life experiences I've already endured. For so long, I was worried he would judge me, but he didn't. He just embraced me and then gave me a new memory to help replace one of the old. Occasionally, I find myself glancing that way, remembering, and then blushing as visions of what we did afterward flash through my mind.

We talked a lot that night and the nights after. We talked about his life, my life, and what we want out of life together, but it should be noted that Jake also has a way of speaking with his hands, hands that make me feel treasured, appreciated, and loved. I didn't know love and intimacy could feel this way, so consuming, so complete. I loved Carter, but it never felt like this. This feels whole, like we are a whole together, and have dropped the weight of the past. We're shackle-free, and our future has begun.

When I first moved to Chuluota Springs, Garrett mentioned

in our introductory meeting that the people here look after each other, and he was right. As it turns out, they consider me one of them, and the citizens don't take kindly to strangers invading their town with the sole purpose of spying, stalking, harassing, and falsifying information about one of its residents. Hotels and motels have denied them occupancy, restaurants refuse to serve them, and the local police have followed them incessantly. It's been made clear they are not wanted here, and one by one, they've left. After all, there's no more story for them, at least not one they're looking to tell.

A few new people have stopped by to welcome me officially: the mayor, the police chief, and the ladies from the garden club. While I found it kind and appreciated the sentiment, I think it's more so because they're in love with what I'm doing to the house. People are proud of this little town, and this house means something to them.

Of course Jake is always there, beaming with pride, though for him it's not about the home, but the girl who's put her heart and soul into it.

Letting out a contented sigh, I gently close my laptop. I'm sitting in the library with my feet up. I had hoped to get some content done for the blog, but I'm distracted, and pleasantly so.

My eyes wander out the window, back down to the dock and to the place where Mrs. Easler resides. The water is crystal blue-green today, and it reflects my mood: bright, clear, not muddied, and at peace.

I've thought a lot about Mrs. Easler's phrase, *Where the light shines*, and I think maybe it's less of a place, less literal, and more of a feeling. It would be symbolic that, of all the houses I could buy, I find the one that has a ghost who is trying to teach me a lesson. I came here looking for happiness, and I found it in myself and with the people I've chosen to surround me.

Tearing my gaze away, I move to stand, and that's when I see it.

My breath stills in my chest as I stare down at the tiny round object lying on the floor.

How can that be? My heart starts to flutter as the speed at which it's beating rapidly increases. There's an unknown pressure building in my chest, and I blink in complete stupefaction.

Looking around the room, I see I'm still here by myself and nothing has changed, but at the same time, everything has.

Easing out of my chair, I kneel down on the floor and slowly pick up the pink gem.

I don't understand. Where did it come from?

I run my hand along the floor and push the curtains to the side; it's then I feel the weights at the bottom. When I was redoing the floor, I didn't think anything of it, but now, my heart is pounding so hard in my chest I can barely breathe.

Picking up the bottom edge of the curtain, I see there's a small tear in the corner, and when I stick my finger into the hole, it brushes against what feels like a small rock. It was common a long time ago for people to weigh their curtains with rocks to keep them from flapping around in the wind. Nowadays, we use penny weights or chain weights, which are sewn into the bottom of the curtains. Removing my finger, I slide my hand along the bottom of both curtain panels and feel the little tiny bumps.

Jumping up, I run into the kitchen and grab a pair of scissors and a plastic sandwich bag to put the conch pearl in.

Returning, I slide down on the floor, tearing the skin on one knee, and slowly lift the curtain to reveal the bottom crease in the hem. Slipping the scissors in the hole, I snip to make it a little larger and then put them down on the floor.

Tipping the curtain panel like I'm squeezing toothpaste from a tube, I slowly and meticulously work my fingers to push anything that might possibly be inside the hem toward the hole.

One by one, rocks, pebbles, and dirt fall out, along with three more conch pearls. I'm so stunned by what I've found and what's lying in front of me that I don't even remember snipping a hole in the other panel until four more conch pearls hit the wood floor and disperse among the pile of rubble. Eight conch pearls total.

Eight.

Holy moly.

They vary in size, shape, and color. Two are orange, one is brown, another is yellow, and the other four are various shades of pink. While they aren't exactly round, instead more oval-shaped, each one is roughly the size of a green pea or larger, and knowing what I do now, I know they are worth a ton of money.

One by one, I pick them up, gently wipe them off with my shirt, and drop them into the baggie.

I think about so many details of the pearls I've read about over the last couple of weeks, and I'm just in awe. I am staring at the most rare and most expensive type of pearl in the world. They say the probability of finding even one is one in ten thousand, and even then, the chance that it is gem quality is less than ten percent.

And I'm staring at eight.

Looking up at the window, I see the sunlight is pouring in. "Where the light shines," I whisper, shaking my head in awe.

Standing, I brush off my poor knees, clutch the bag to my chest, and then race out the door toward Willow's. I barely feel the ground underneath my shoeless feet as adrenaline pumps through me and takes me through the trees and to her front door.

Of course she heard me coming and is waiting for me. She ushers me into the family room where I unload on her what just happened.

"Did you say you found them in the curtains in your home?

The old navy blue ones?" she asks as I'm pacing and she's rolling them around in the palm of her hand.

"Yes."

"Do you think there are more somewhere else?"

I stop, turn, and look at her. "I don't know. It seems possible. I've found them in two places and now have twelve total, but where would the others be?" I toss out my hands.

Willow looks down at the pearls, looks back at me, and then moves to the bookshelf. She removes the photo album she showed me before and begins flipping through the pages. There, three quarters of the way through, sits another photo of Mrs. Easler and Willow's relative. This time they are sewing what looks like the quilt on Willow's couch. Both of us look toward it and then back at the photo.

"I wonder," she says, laying the book down on the chair she's standing next to. Gently, she peels back the clear plastic page and lifts the photo. On the back in old scripted handwriting, it says, *Seek and you will find.*

The hair rises on the back of my neck.

I let out a gasp as Willow stands up straight, shock hitting her spine. Turning the photo back over, we look and see that both ladies are similarly hunched over the quilt and working on the same block, a solid one that is next to another with small white flowers. Since the photo is black and white, we look at the quilt and find the patterned one first. Willow picks up the quilt and there, faded but most definitely the same, is the navy blue fabric of my curtains.

"This can't be coincidental, right?" I ask as our eyes find each other.

She doesn't say anything, but she does look over my shoulder, and her eyes widen.

I turn to see what it is. "What are you looking at?"

She doesn't answer me, just lays the quilt down and moves into the kitchen to grab a pair of scissors. I watch as she flattens the quilt out over the back of the couch and runs her fingers over the navy blue block.

"Feel this," she says to me, and I do. I run my hand over the fabric and realize this block is thicker than the others.

Taking the scissors, she very carefully snips along one edge, next to the seam. Sticking her fingers in, she pulls out another piece of fabric that's been folded several times.

"I always wondered why this piece was like this. Now we know." She lifts her hand and holds out the fabric for me to take. "I think this belongs to you."

"This is crazy," I say to Willow as my trembling fingers take what she is offering.

I open the fabric, and there, painted on instead of written, it says, *Seek and you shall find a love that never dies. Like the ticking of my heart, it will stand the test of time. Where the light shines is where my soul resides.*

I can't move. I can't breathe. I'm so overwhelmed I feel like a balloon that's about to pop.

Willow grabs the photo album again, and we both look at the other small picture that shares the page. Here the two women are standing in the doorway of the back of my house with the foyer visible behind them. There against the wall, under what I know is the chandelier, is the old grandfather clock.

Seek. Find. Ticking. Time. Light. Resides.

It can't be.

"We looked in the clock," I say to Willow, my eyes rising to find hers.

"Guess you didn't look hard enough," she replies, and then we both burst out laughing because what else is there to do?

Picking up the baggie, she and I both move to the door. I have to know, especially after all of this. But as we slip onto the porch, a customer pulls up to her dock and waves to us, and for Willow, duty calls. We exchange a look as she heads in one direction and I head in the other. Instead of racing back to the house, I find myself wandering at a slow, surreal pace. The anticipation shocking my system is almost more than I can bear. After all this, what if they aren't there? Then again, what if they are?

For weeks I have been wondering if the chandeliers had anything to do with the light. They shine so bright and were such a prominent part of the house when the Easlers lived there. Maybe the light isn't the window, or maybe it is. All of this is just so confusing.

The boards creak as I make my way up the back steps and stop just outside the door. I turn to glance over at where Mrs. Easler is always on watch, willing her to be there, but she's not. It's still daytime, and not once have I seen her in the sunlight.

Are the pearls supposed to be in the clock? Or are they possibly under the floorboards where the clock used to sit? I have thought that maybe they were in the floor somewhere, but as all signs are pointing to the clock, I guess I'll find out. I don't know why I'm surprised, after all it is one of the few pieces that were requested to always remain with the house. What I didn't consider is that the clock was moved. I don't know why I always thought it was in the room I found it in, but the proof is in the photo. There it was, just waiting for me to give it a second look.

Walking inside, I find the place in the foyer from the picture where the clock used to stand. Getting down on my hands and knees, I examine the wood for any inconsistencies. Granted we have resurfaced the floors, but even then I don't remember any of the boards in here being loose or different from the others.

Here in this place, each rectangular board is face-nailed in tight to the floor joists. Which leaves only the clock.

Moving into the parlor room, I stop in front of the old grandfather clock and gaze at it. More than once, I've thought about doing a blog post on this clock, and I most certainly will now.

It's at least seven feet tall, roughly a foot and a half wide, and maybe a little less than a foot in depth. It doesn't take up too much room, and although it is a pretty piece, it definitely looks like an antique. It's made of mahogany, it must be wound every six to seven days before it stops, and it has a hand-painted dial with a ship sailing the ocean. When the pendulum swings, the ship moves as if rocking on the ocean. It is really quite fitting for the Easlers, however I'm not sure where she would have hidden the pearls. Jake and I opened the case and ran our hands all along the inside, feeling for loose boards or another hidden shelf, but we didn't discover anything. We felt under it, around it, and over it. The face of the clock does open, but it's flat inside, and unless I want to start taking it apart, I have no idea where to look.

And then I see it.

The top of the grandfather clock, or the crown, has a split pediment design. Both sides curve up toward each other like a swan's neck, and in the middle it's adorned with a decorative brass ornament. This one is round, about the size of a tennis ball, and has a brass spire on the top.

That has to be it.

Dragging a chair in from the breakfast room, I place it in front of the clock and stand on it. The brass ornament is glued on, but after I wiggle it a few times, it comes loose. The sudden movement rattles whatever is inside it, and I start to sweat from the anxiety of this moment.

Climbing off the chair, I sit down on it and examine the ornament. It's two halves put together to make a whole. One side slides into the other, leaving a small lip overhang. I gently shake it, and the contents inside rattle again.

Oh man.

When I twist the two halves, they budge, and I realize it isn't glued but rather screwed together. Carefully, I twist and twist until they separate, pull the top half off, and stare down into the bottom half. My breath leaves my lungs.

I expected to find more conch pearls, which I have, but what I didn't expect to find was their wedding rings. Hers, three diamonds set into a yellow gold band, and his, a solid thick yellow gold.

They must have known.

Seek and you shall find a love that never dies. Like the ticking of my heart, it will stand the test of time. Where the light shines is where my soul resides.

He left it with her to keep it safe.

My eyes fill with tears for their tragic loss, and I now understand why she moved to the dock. The world thinks she's haunting that spot because she grieves for her husband and is waiting for his return, which she probably is, but it turns out she is also guiding them away from the house, the pearls, the treasure that was their marriage. Bauer said people have watched her light for years, but he never mentioned anyone trying to figure out why she stays there, why that spot.

Sifting through the pearls, I find the one I'm certain they are claiming to be the largest ever found. It's about the size of a nickel, just more oval in shape. It's the color of pink grapefruit, and it's beautiful.

I think about how many things could have gone wrong with the discovery of these pearls: the removal of the curtains or the clock, Willow's family moving, Willow getting rid of the photo albums or the quilt, Willow never finding the clues left behind, or the possibility of a storm coming through and just wiping it all out. So many variables and obstacles, but not one of them prevented things from happening the way they should.

And now, I have found the missing conch pearls.

All of them.

There's only one person I need to share this with.

Picking up my phone with shaky fingers, I send Jake a text.

I need you to get here as soon as you can.

35

The warmth of the sun's evening rays soaks into my skin as I watch them reflect off of the water and sparkle like tiny glints of crystals. It's therapeutic and calming, and as I push my sunglasses higher on my face and my hat down more securely on my head, I stretch my legs out across my new padded navy lounge chair and allow the salty air and the humid breeze to ease and erase the many points of stress I've felt over the last year.

This place ... it is my happy place.

I've been living in Chuluota Springs for six months, and last night, Jake, Garrett, and I celebrated the completion of the renovations with a bottle of champagne. The house is beautiful and everything I dreamed it would be.

I think anyone who knows me knows that several times over the last couple of months, I've asked myself if coming here was the right thing to do, and I know for certain that it was. People often talk about how things happen for a reason, and while I'd like to think destiny just isn't that cruel—I mean, after all, Carter had to die for me to end up here—I am grateful for having found my way to this house and to Jake.

"Hey, do you want something to drink?" Jake calls out. It might be November, but it's still hot outside—we do live in Florida.

He's decided we need an outdoor kitchen, so earlier today, to get started, he bought a grill and has been putting it together. And yes, that's right, I said we.

Since the night after the storm, we've pretty much been inseparable. Dash has moved in, Jake's met my family via Face-Time, and I've met his parents too. They arrived back in town earlier this week, just in time for the holidays.

"That sounds great, thank you," I tell him, looking over my shoulder and finding him shirtless and gorgeous walking up the back steps.

Coco says, "Hi, Jake," as he walks by her outdoor cage, and my heart flips as he smiles at her and says, "Hi, pretty girl."

I swear this man has no flaws. He's also so handsome inside and out that sometimes I find it hard to believe he's mine. But he is, and I'm going to hold on as tight as possible.

After I found the pearls, Jake and I decided it would be best to share the news with his family; they really weren't mine—they were theirs. Over dinner, here at the house with Bauer, Garrett, his parents and his brother Hayes dialed in remotely, they decided Bauer would find a jewelry broker, and they would go from there, including Willow in on the process. After all, none of this would have been possible without her, and she deserves part of the cut too. There was no need to keep the pearls—well, except for one. Out of the twenty-five total found, Jake picked one, had it circled in diamonds, and on a low-key Thursday night while sitting on the dock, overlooking the water as the sun had started to set and the moon had begun to rise, he asked me to marry him.

He said he knew without a doubt that I was his one, and I knew it too.

One of the things I learned from Carter is that life is a gift and we have to embrace all of the moments, because you never know what tomorrow may bring. What Jake learned from Rebecca is that if you have to constantly work for it, it's not meant to be. He's not saying relationships should be easy all the time, but it shouldn't feel one-sided, and no one should be made to feel less than they are. Relationships should feel like a team, a loving partnership, and really we do.

Through grateful, happy, and heartfelt tears, I said yes.

And Mrs. Easler's light glowed.

People toss around the word haunted to conjure something scary or unpleasant, but that's not how I feel about her or this house any longer. I find it mystical and romantic. Sure, some things can be explained, but others can't, and whereas before I was afraid of what that might mean, now I'm not.

The mysterious light at the end of the dock, the visions of her figure standing there staring out and waiting—I find them comforting, as if she's an old friend. She isn't here to hurt anyone; she's there waiting for him, her lost love, a love so great it tethers her to this world instead of the next.

That night, like many days and nights, I was able to share my tears of joy with the river, which has always openly accepted my tears of sorrow.

Feeling the pull, I get up from my chair and run down the dock. My feet pound hard across the warm old wood as I wildly kick off my flip-flops and drop my glasses and my hat. Then at the end, without a care in the world, I jump as high and as far as I can, feeling the wind whip through my hair just before the coolness of the water engulfs me. *Welcome home*, it says to me, and mentally I answer, *I'm glad I could make it.*

The tall seagrass brushes against the tops of my feet, and I laugh at the unfamiliar sensation. The water is so clear I can see through the blades to the smooth patches of white sand.

"What are you doing?" Jake calls out. He's returned with our drinks, and he sets them down on the little table next to the chair.

"What does it look like?" I answer, splashing the water with my hands.

I realize I look like a crazy person wearing all my clothes and floating around for no reason at all, but I can't help it. The river called, and I came. I wonder if I always will.

I tilt my head back, my ears dip under the water, and I close my eyes.

I came here searching for happiness, but the truth is, I don't think it can be found. It just is. I once looked at the dictionary definition of happiness, and of the words it used to describe the feeling, I realize I missed the most important one. Happy, cheerful, merry, jubilant, joyous, upbeat, glad, lively, delighted, and content. It's content that sticks with me more than the others.

Maybe I associated these two words, maybe I didn't, but I now realize this whole time, while I've been searching for happiness, what I've really been searching for is contentment.

Contentment is defined as a state of happiness and satisfaction.

Satisfaction.

Ivy was onto something when she spoke of the moments. Satisfaction does come from the sum of the little moments, like a smile from a friend, the completion of beautifully laid tile, the smell of fresh paint, a cup of coffee in a diner, spotting two floating nostrils in the water, gray feathers against my skin, the smell of coconut, sandalwood, and fabric softener as it wraps around me, and the coolness of the rain as it washes away the sorrows of yesterday.

These are things that can't be found. These are the things that just are.

The moments.

To the left of me, I feel the water dip, splash, and then wave over. Righting myself, I look to find Jake as he breaks the surface and shakes his head to clear his hair and the dripping water off his face. I'm momentarily awestruck by the lines and contours of his handsome features. This man is mine, and everything about that statement feels so right.

He breaks into a sexy grin as he swims closer to me. "Couldn't let you jump in alone. Where you go, I go, remember?"

"Yes," I say, and I know he means it. He pulls me to him, I wrap my legs around his waist, and he treads water for the both of us.

"Well, hey there, pretty lady," Jake says, and I turn in his arms to find Jessie swimming over to check us out. I can't help but gasp; I've never been this close to him, or should I say her! From the dock she looks large, but up close, she looks even larger.

Her head breaks the surface to look at us, then she dips back down, and she's gone.

"Jessie is a girl?"

"Yes," Jake draws out.

"I'm so happy to hear this. Natalie thought she was a he and I was disappointed."

"Why?" There's humor in his voice and I turn back to look at him.

"Because when I first saw her, all I thought was chubby mermaid. She was graceful and beautiful."

"Chubby mermaid." He doesn't even try to hide his amusement, as a smile stretches from one side to the other.

"Yes, and don't make fun." I shove him lightly in the shoulder, while at the same time moving a little closer. "Does it feel weird to you to be floating in the water knowing there are other animals and creatures down here too?"

"No, not really. Why would it?" he asks, water dripping down his face.

"We can't see them." I look past his shoulder and see nothing but the blue-green waters I adore so much.

He chuckles. "So? We can't see the animals in the woods either when we go for a hike, doesn't mean they aren't there."

"I guess you have a point," I tell him, and he grins.

His smile still takes my breath away, and he hears me exhale as I look at every perfect feature of his face.

I'm not sure when it happened, maybe at that very moment when I heard his voice behind me on the dock, but a fuse was lit, and with it tiny sparks rained down, settling on my soul. Right then and there, he changed me indefinitely, and neither one of us knew it. I'd like to think I changed him too.

Then again, there were all of the little things. His quiet strength that commands any place he's in, his thoughtfulness that shows he would give everything if he had to and take nothing in return, and then there's just him. Without him doing anything, just being, I'm drawn to the texture of his skin, the softness of his hair, the sharp edge defining his jaw, and his eyes. His beautiful intelligent blue eyes hold so much reverence for the people he loves, and it's impossible to not want to be reflected in them.

"I love you," he says calmly, his words forcing my gaze back to his. My heart squeezes with wonder and devotion. I'm not sure I'll ever be used to hearing this from him. Not being able to help myself, I lean in and take his wet mouth with mine. His lips are soft, delicious, and we lose ourselves in this moment.

Finding the hem of my shirt, he gently pulls it up and off along with my sports bra and tosses them up onto the dock.

"Should we be out here like this?" I ask, and his smile turns into one of mischief.

"Who's going to see us? There's no one here," he says, smoothing my hair back and out of the way.

"June," I state as if it's obvious, my arms draping over his tanned and freckled shoulders.

"Nah, we're too far away from her house. Besides, we'll be in the shadows soon, and I know you have towels in the boathouse." His hands run up the backs of my legs as I drop them from his waist, and he pulls down on my shorts.

"Well it's only fair then, yours for mine," I murmur, and he smirks. No need to ask him twice. He treads a few paces away, wiggles out of his shorts, and tosses the rest of our clothes up on the dock.

I've never skinny-dipped before, but I've got to say, as he pulls me back into him and the water heats between us, I am a fan. He moves us to the dock ladder, and with my back pressed against it, I hang on and lose myself in this moment and in him, from the warmth of his mouth as it contradicts the coolness on my skin, to the way he easily lifts me as we slide together. His hands are everywhere, my legs are wrapped around his, and although I loved the river before, I know I will never be able to look at it the same.

But then again, it's never the same. It changes with the tides, the seasons, and the years, just like we do. Although always present, it moves around us, carrying away bad memories and filling the empty places with good. It washes, cleanses, and heals. It provides comfort and a steadfastness to all who seek it out. It provides moments, moments that make up our story, our existence, because that's what rivers do. They do life.

A life I'm so excited to live.

I came to the river trapped inside my life with nothing left but a stack of fictional memories, a shattered heart, and regret. But now I'm free. I'm free to be me in a world I've chosen for myself, not one that was curated for me.

And it feels exhilarating.

With the crystal blue-green silky waters drifting through my fingers, the steady lapping sounds against the shoreline, and this man, my friend, I know I've found happiness, a contentment that's wrapped up in the sum of the moments, a life that's meant to be.

EPILOGUE

A cool January breeze drifts across my skin, leaving goose bumps in its wake. The leaves on the oak tree above me wave, the blue-green waters of the inlet ripple against the riverbank, and there are no clouds to hide the splendor of the late-afternoon sun. It's the perfect day, and the sky is so blue and so similar to the color of Jake's eyes that I know without a doubt winter in Florida will be my favorite time of the year.

"Why do they all look like professional athletes?" Ivy asks as Natalie, Corrie, and I all turn to look at Jake, Garrett, and Bauer where they're standing down on the dock and laughing with one another.

"Right? I thought the water in the Midwest made the guys taller and larger than average, but the salt water here wins hands down," I chime in while admiring the way Jake's clothes are molded to his body. He's wearing a white button-down with the sleeves rolled up and navy blue dress shorts. The clothes aren't loose or too tight, fitting him perfectly, and I could drool. He feels me looking at him, catches my eye, and winks. I swear this man loves to make me tingle from head to toe.

"Hayes is bigger than all of them," Corrie says as she grips her sun hat to prevent it from blowing away.

"Really?" I turn to look at her and smile as she looks so beautiful in her light blue sundress. Then again, everyone looks amazing today as Ivy has dressed us for the photoshoot with *Southern Living*.

"Yep. He's playing college football. He had his pick of schools too, but he chose the University of Colorado." I remember Jake saying he prefers the mountains to the beach.

Ivy laughs, and it is music to my ears. "I wonder what he thought about that first winter," she says, to no one in particular. She's been here for a little over a week now, since Christmas, to help us get ready for today, and I am soaking up every minute of our time together.

"Jake said he loved it. Spent every weekend snowboarding with his friends," I tell her.

"Snowboarding, huh? That's kind of hot. Maybe I should try to meet up with him so he can introduce me to some of his friends," she says matter-of-factly. She's wearing a long skirt with colors that remind me of a Draper James or Lilly Pulitzer ad with an off-the-shoulder white top.

"He's too young for you and you know it," I say, loving the feel of these linen pants she's put me in. We may be in Florida, but it's still January, and the temperature right now is cool. I'm grateful no one has complained.

"Five and a half years isn't too young. Aren't you five years younger than Jake?" she asks, smirking and proving her point.

"I am, but I'm wiser. I've had more life experience than he has." I grin, and she waves her hand back and forth in the air like I'm crazy.

"I'm still shocked that you are getting married again. That's twice before I've even had one." Her cheeks turn pink, and Natalie laughs. I also notice that Natalie looks Garrett's way, and she catches him looking at her. The two of them stare at each other for a moment, and then she breaks away. She always does. I asked her once what was up between them, and all she said was, "Nothing. Absolutely nothing." I think she's not telling me the truth, but I know I'll get it out of her one day.

"What if I let you design my wedding dress—will that make you happy?" I ask.

Her face lights up. I knew it would.

Jake and I decided we want to get married in May. While we're not in a hurry, we don't see any need to wait either. I'll have officially been living in Chuluota Springs for a year, Hayes will be done with his semester and free to come home, and although I owe Carter nothing, I do feel it's the right thing to at least get past the one-year anniversary of his death. There's just something about that day, and for now that month, and I need to leave it in remembrance of him. Will I always feel this way? Probably not, but for now I do, and Jake understands, just like I understand that there's no way I would ever leave him standing at the end of the altar by himself without me. We've picked the edge of the dock overlooking the water as the location. There will be a flower-covered wooden wedding trellis, and together we will make the journey from the house to the altar side by side.

"This is kind of like a precursor to what your wedding will look like," Natalie says as the four of us look around the decorated backyard, and she's right. We are keeping it very small, very intimate. For the honeymoon, on the other hand, we're going large—three weeks, in fact. The first on an African safari for my sweet animal-loving guy, the second to Australia because we both have it on our bucket list, and the third to Tuscany. I want to get lost with him in the vineyards drinking heavenly wines and eating delectable foods. I can picture it now and look forward to the many blog posts I'll be able to write.

Speaking of blogging, after the media broke the news of where I've been and what I've been up to, my website and social media accounts blew up with followers and people interested in the outcome of the house. I've since been hired on for two new renovation projects, one in New Orleans, Louisiana, and another in West Hamptons, New York. I'm so proud of myself and how things have turned out, and it also feels good to know Jake is proud of me as well.

Of course Mr. Williams also tipped off *The New York Times*, and a reporter showed up on our front door. The article was a then-and-now piece that made the front page of the Sunday paper, and the *Times* was thrilled with their small part in helping us uncover the hidden pearls. From what Bauer has told me, Jake has been contacted to have the brooch and my engagement ring photographed, and more ghost hunters have been in and out of town recently. Their focus, however, seems to be on the bell tower in the middle of town. The bell has been ringing by itself more frequently in an unexplained pattern, and it's stirring up some questions. It seems people are drawn to a good love story mixed with a mystery.

Which leads us back to today. There was no reason for me to turn down the feature in *Southern Living*, so here they are. My house went from Christmas to summer basically overnight. They shoot their magazine articles six months in advance, so down went the garland and poinsettias, we rang in the new year with gold champagne, and out came the royal blue, teal, and coral decorations. Seashells, fish, anchors, and floral arrangements filled with all kinds of white flowers have exploded throughout my home, and I have to admit, their stylist did an amazing job. The house looks beautiful.

From behind me, I hear a small bark, and one of the camera crew is scolding Chloe. That's right, Chloe after the couture designer. Can't have a Coco and not a Chloe, and Chloe is a way cuter name than Valentino. Jake and I both look over and see she is attempting to bite and pull at the poor guy's pant leg. I glance at Jake, he glances at me, and we smile at each other then go retrieve our fur baby. Butterflies still take flight when he looks at me like I'm his whole world, and I can't imagine a time when they won't.

For Christmas, I surprised Jake with the puppy. The house is big enough for Dash to have his own space, and I thought why not. I probably should have adopted one from the animal shelter, but I overheard a woman in Dockside Diner talking about how her goldendoodle just had puppies, and I couldn't resist. Chloe is shed-free, smart as a whip, and cuter than any dog you've ever seen. It was love at first sight.

"Sorry about that," Jake says as he reaches down and scoops her up, his deep voice nearly putting me in a trance. She licks his face, he beams, and my heart expands even further than it already has over the two of them.

"Jake Hawthorne, you better not get that shirt dirty," Ivy calls out as another lazy breeze sweeps across the backyard.

He looks down at it and replies, "Don't worry, I won't," and then he dips his head toward Chloe and whispers, "We just won't tell her, will we?"

He looks at me with those thick, dark eyelashes protecting my connection to his soul and leans in for a kiss. It means everything, and I feel it in each and every nerve ending over, under, and across my skin. Warm lips against mine. A small smile meant just for me. Coconut, sandalwood, and contentment. Forever.

"All right, folks, please make your way over to the table," calls out the shoot director. He's standing behind a laptop he's set up while two members of his team check the lighting. Most of his staff have already found the place they want to be, and there is all kinds of equipment from cameras and tripods to reflectors and flag kits.

"This is exciting," I whisper to Jake, and he grins as he cradles Chloe like a baby.

I catch Ivy's expression as she takes in Jake, Chloe, and me, and it's one of complete admiration. My eyes burn and my nose tingles as she places her hand over her heart, pats it twice, and then hooks her arm through Natalie's to head to the table. I'm so happy she's here. I didn't realize how much I needed to see her until I threw open the front door, and there she was, looking like the blonde bombshell that she is.

"I'll take her, Mr. Jake," June says as she skips down the back steps and reaches for Chloe. I didn't see Willow and June arrive, but I'm so glad they have. Willow is carrying a large glass pitcher of her famous sun tea vodka, and I know this party is about to move to a whole new level of fun.

One by one, Jake and I, Ivy, Bauer, Corrie, Willow, Natalie, and Garrett, who keeps looking at Natalie, make our way to the table. Of course Jake couldn't stop with just the grill. Once Garrett found out about the idea, the two of them designed and built an elaborate outdoor kitchen under a large gazebo that holds an eight-person table. Today it's decorated to the nines, complete with hanging mason jars filled with fairy lights.

Jake sits at one head of the table, I sit next to him, and Garrett sits at the other. It seems only right as he is the one who brought this vision to life.

"You may pick up your drink, but please don't touch the food," the director says. "Our team will move around the table with our equipment to take the photos, and then once we're finished, you may eat."

Mumbling rises amongst our guests, and I can't say I blame them. Dockside catered the food, and it all looks so incredible.

Jake leans over and, with his lips to my ear, asks, "Are you happy?"

I glance at the porch where June has Chloe and is sitting next to Coco in her outdoor cage. I want to tell him I don't remember a time when I wasn't happy, because that's how I feel and have felt for some time now, but we both know that wouldn't be entirely true. Instead, I answer him with a simple "Yes" that says it all.

For months—well really for the better part of last year—I wondered about my life with Carter. What did I do that was so wrong for us to end the way we did? Was our life a lie? Was I truly happy? How did I not see that things were so bad? But Jake helped me see that the truth is, my life wasn't a lie to me. I was happy and living my best life. Should I have noticed that things had turned for us? Maybe, but all I had to go off of was what I saw and felt every day and the life we lived together.

I've thought about that last morning, at our condo, just hours before I found him with Veronica. He came up behind me in our kitchen, wrapped his arms around me, and told me he loved me. I know he did, just not the way I deserved to be loved by a husband. Instead, he fed me just enough of the sense of security a husband provides to keep me unsuspicious. He was having his cake and eating it too, for as long as he could. He was the liar, and what I've realized is, no matter the outcome, my life wasn't a lie. I was honest, true, and faithful to him.

I was happy then, just like I am now, and it's okay to admit that. It's definitely a different kind of happiness, one where I feel free and cherished in a way I never knew, but this is my one life, and although it may have changed directions, it's embracing the unknown that provides the most adventure.

I took a leap of faith. I took the risk. I did something for myself, and look how that turned out, unexpected and extraordinary.

"Good," he says softly, brushing his hair off his forehead.

"Are you happy?" I ask him, the low hum from the conversations of our friends and family floating around us.

And just like that day on the dock, months ago, he reaches for my hand and entwines our fingers. His thumb rubs over the top of my hand and across my engagement ring as he leans in a little to look at me, to really look at me. With his other hand, he tucks a loose piece of hair behind my ear, and I feel the intimacy of his fingertips as they trace down the side of my face and his gaze locks on mine, his true emotions burning in it, just for me. It's with a simple nod of his head and a wordless answer that my heart hears him, accepts his word as the truth, and feels him say, "Always."

I am the luckiest girl in the world.

Somewhere behind me, the director is talking. I miss most of what he says, until the guests at our table laugh and his words connect.

He says, "Let's do this!"

I couldn't agree more.

The end.

ACKNOWLEDGMENTS

In 2019, author Kandi Steiner posted a picture of her and her friends kayaking on Weeki Wachee river with the manatees. Many times, we've taken our boys tubing down the rivers in this part of the state, but it wasn't until I saw these pictures that I went, "Ohhh." From there, my wheels started turning. Just down the road, Homasassa Springs State Park has an inlet so beautiful, of course in my mind it needed a house, an old rundown house. And while the town is completely fictional, I did use elements of the area to help create this new world: the river, the scalloping, the Seminole Indians, and the sugar mill. Is there a haunted town, not that I'm aware of, but wouldn't it be amazing if there was?

In April of 2020, I released Lessons in Lemonade. I don't need to mention how strange the world was, but during that summer, while quarantining with my neighbors, the bits and pieces of this story started to plant roots. It had to be told, it needed to be told, and so went my next eighteen months.

Up until this point, I'd never really given thought to writing women's fiction. I've always loved romance novels, and after many many long conversations with author Karla Sorensen and editor Kelli Collins, we decided that's what this story is. Could I have rewritten it to follow the formula for romance? Absolutely. But deep down I didn't want to. This story is all about Ryla's journey, and her unexpected chance at love with Jake came in second.

Here's what Kelli said that gave me the push to keep the story as is.

"I consider it firmly women's fiction, with a strong romantic subplot, and a slightly less strong (but still super compelling) mystery subplot. The main plot, however, is squarely about Ryla's journey, from escape to healing to learning to love again. It's narrative heavy, like we'd expect in women's fiction. It starts just a little slow, but the deep narrative and the slow start -- for me, as a reader -- actually felt appropriate for a Florida summer. Does that make sense? The whole story has a very deep south, lazy-ish, hot-and-humid feel. Maybe that's just my personal experience talking, since I spent so many of my own summers in Florida, as well as half my life in small towns, where the pace is so much slower than in a city. But for me, it just fits. You seem to have written the story you wanted to write, and it's pretty wonderful. You've done the women's fiction genre justice."

So, if you've made it this far, then I can't say thank you enough for hanging in there and seeing this new genre through. We're taught to stick to brand and to stay in our lane, but the older I get and the longer I write stories, I've realized what I want to be known for has less to do with genre and more to do with being an author who tells a great story. I'm hoping you'll agree.

First and foremost, I always have to say thank you to my amazing husband and our beautiful boys. Day in and day out you continue to be my support team, my biggest cheerleaders, and my strongest believers even though time spent working on these stories is time away from you. I am grateful that each of you understand me enough to know I have an immense passion for writing stories and you give me the space and love to follow my dreams. Thank you. You three mean the world to me.

Kelli B, outside of my three guys, I spend more time with you than anyone else. I am beyond grateful for how much you allow me to lean on you, plot with you, laugh with you, and ramble on about fictional places and characters. Daily you wait until it's time for us to go to work and then ask how the writing went. Usually the answer is, "terrible," but I love that I know you're always going to ask. I also love how deep down you fully believe it when you say, "This is going to be your year." One year it will be, I know it too.

Karla Sorensen, thank you for being my friend, my sounding board, and my industry guru. I am a better author and business woman because of you. I appreciate your honest feedback, the long rambling voice texts about life, and our continued journey to lose weight. One day we'll reach those goals...

Megan C, thank you for always being willing to alpha read my stories when they are in their worst shape, and for providing feedback that makes them better. I appreciate your honesty and love for my words, and I hope you know how much I adore you.

Taylor R, thank you for being my friend. I genuinely love how the book world brought us together, all our times we get to talk, and watching you grow from being an amazing mother to an author. I also have to give you a shout out for all of the social media posts and reels. My feeds wouldn't look nearly as pretty without you. xo

Julie, thank you for your continued patience and tolerance of my crazy when it comes to designing my covers. This cover is hands down my favorite. You brought my vision to life on a story that means so much to me and I just love it. Thank you for sticking by me.

Kelli C, thank you for your honest feedback on this story in a time when I needed it most. Your words have given me the courage to finally send this book out into the world. I did write the story that I wanted to write and it feels so good.

Caitlyn and Julia, thank you for your eyes and your editing expertise. I've always said grammar is not my friend, and you understand that about me. This story is crisp and polished and I can't thank you enough.

Kathryn's Krewe, to my favorite readers who have stuck by me for years, thank you. I've talked about Where the Light Shines for so long, I'm just so appreciate how you've patiently waited and supported me in this journey. I know this story is a little different from my others, but it's still me, and I hope in the end you love it as much as I do.

To the readers, thank you for taking a chance on Where the Light Shines. For those who have been with me for a while, I am forever grateful for your loyalty. For those of you who are new, I can't wait to give you more. More words, more meet cutes and inspired moments, and more stories. Happy reading . . . much love, Kathryn.

ABOUT THE AUTHOR

Kathryn Andrews loves stories that end with a happily ever after. She started writing at age seven and never stopped. Kathryn is an Amazon Bestseller for her much loved Starving for Southern series, Chasing Clouds and is a contemporary romance, women's fiction, and Southern fiction writer.

Kathryn graduated from the University of South Florida with degrees in biology and chemistry, and she currently lives in Tampa, Florida. She spends her days as a sales director for a medical device company and her nights lost in her love of fictional characters.

When Kathryn is not crafting beautiful worlds that incorporate some of her most favorite real-life places, she can be found with her husband and two boys while drinking iced coffee and enjoying the sun.

Website: www.kandrewsauthor.com
Facebook: Author Kathryn Andrews
Instagram: @kandrewsauthor